SHRAPNEL

ISSUE #13 THE OFFICIAL BATTLETECH MAGAZINE

SHRAPNEL

THE OFFICIAL BATTLETECH MAGAZINE

Loren L. Coleman, Publisher
John Helfers, Executive Editor
Philip A. Lee, Managing Editor
David A. Kerber, Layout and Graphic Design

Cover art by Germán Varona Galindo
Interior art by Jared Blando, Doug Chaffee, Dale Eadeh, Earl Geier, David A. Kerber, John Paul Lona, Natán Meléndez, Benjamin Parker, Marco Pennacchietti, Matt Plog, Steve Prescott

Published by Pulse Publishing, under licensing by Catalyst Game Labs
5003 Main St. #110 • Tacoma, WA 98407

Shrapnel: The Official BattleTech Magazine is published four times a year, in Spring, Summer, Fall, and Winter.

All material is copyright ©2023 The Topps Company, Inc. All Rights Reserved. BattleTech & MechWarrior are registered trademarks and/or trademarks of The Topps Company, Inc., in the United States and/or other countries. No part of this work may be reproduced, stored in a retrieval system, or transmitted in any form or by any means, without the prior permission in writing of the Copyright Owner, nor be otherwise circulated in any form other than that in which it is published.

This magazine (or any portion of it) may not be copied or reproduced, in whole or in part, by any means, electronic, mechanical or otherwise, without written permission from the publisher, except by a reviewer who may quote brief passages in a review.

Available through your favorite online store (Amazon.com, BN.com, Kobo, iBooks, GooglePlay, etc.).

ISBN: 978-1-6386113-7-0

TABLE OF CONTENTS

COMMANDER'S CALL: FROM THE EDITOR'S DESK 4
  Philip A. Lee

SHORT STORIES

THE SWAMP FOX 7
  Ben Klinefelter
ACCEPTABLE LOSSES 25
  Adam Neff
DRAWING THE SHORT STRAW 52
  David G. Martin
REVERSAL OF FORTUNES 77
  Giles Gammage
RUN, LOCUST, RUN 103
  Westin Riverside
TALES FROM THE CRACKED CANOPY:
  NO REST FOR THE ACCURSED 146
  Matthew Cross
STARVING VULTURES 164
  Joseph A. Cosgrove
THE WRECKONING 190
  Russell Zimmerman

SERIAL NOVEL

LONE WOLF AND FOX, PART 1 OF 4 115
  Bryan Young

ARTICLES

VOICES OF THE SPHERE: CUSHIONING THE CULTURE SHOCK 20
  Wunji Lau
THE CURIOUS CASE OF COLIN COOLIDGE'S CURSED COOLING SUIT . 73
  Joshua C. Perian
BAINBRIDGE'S GUIDE TO IMPACTFUL GEOGRAPHY 92
  Ken' Horner
A SHIP OUT OF TIME 111
  Eric Salzman
ASCENDING THE PECKING ORDER:
  A GUIDE TO POLITICAL WARFARE IN THE RAVEN ALLIANCE 157
  Eric Salzman

GAME FEATURES

TECHNICAL READOUT: ALB-6U ALBATROSS 44
  Stephen Toropov
UNIT DIGEST: WILSON'S HUSSARS 99
  Zac Schwartz
RPG ADVENTURE: TINKER, TAILOR, SEAMSTRESS, SPY 140
  Joshua C. Perian
PLANET DIGEST: GANDY'S LUCK 179
  Zac Schwartz
ALPHA STRIKE SCENARIO: STRIKE AND FADE 184
  Ed Stephens

SHRAPNEL

COMMANDER'S CALL
FROM THE EDITOR'S DESK

Goodness, has the past three months been a whirlwind! Between the last issue and now, the Mercenaries Kickstarter crowdfunding campaign dropped like a daisy cutter in the middle of a forest, blasting through every single expectation and stretch goal! By the time the smoke cleared, the campaign had surpassed $7.5 million, and we couldn't have gotten there without the help of our readership and the *BattleTech* community as a whole. Because of the success of the Kickstarter campaign, I am excited to announce that #15, our December issue, will be a double-size all-mercenaries blowout, featuring even more merc tales than you can shake the biggest wad of C-bills at.

But now that we have that out of the way, let's talk about our current issue, lucky #13. Luck, both good and bad, has always played a strong role in *BattleTech*, especially on the tabletop, but the bad-luck stories always stick with you and are often wildly entertaining. For example, the most unlucky turn I ever saw in a game of *BattleTech* was when a pristine *Jenner* ran full throttle on a paved road, failed their Piloting Skill check, so they skidded, fell, had enough momentum left slide through one side of a building, out the other side, and right into a level 2 lake nearby. Then, when it took damage from the fall into the lake, the head was damaged enough to breach the armor and drown the pilot. Untouched to *drowned*, all in a single turn. Even the player running that 'Mech was so impressed by the result of that string of bad rolls that he wasn't even mad, and we *still* talk about it nearly ten years later. Stories like that are what inspired me toward the theme of this issue.

This was a really fun issue to put together; for the game-content side of things, I challenged our authors to come up with articles and game features that highlighted bad luck in the *BattleTech* universe, and they delivered in spades. And when it came to finding stories for this volume, I kept noticing a theme among some of them—and bear in mind that these stories were all written and submitted long before I had the concept for this issue—which resulted in some kismet I honestly couldn't have planned. For example, Stephen Toropov wrote a Technical Readout entry for the ALB-6U *Abatross*, which highlights how the 'Mech has, much like its namesake bird, garnered a reputation for misfortune over the years. Then, as I'm reviewing a story by veteran author David G. Martin, "Drawing the Short Straw" (which, you'll note, is a phrase that means having some bad luck), and lo and behold, the main character in the story is piloting an *Albatross*. Cue the spooky music! Then I get to Giles Gammage's "Reversal of Fortunes," which is *also* a reference to bad luck!

Speaking of fiction, this issue features stories from four new authors. Ben Klinefelter has written *BattleTech* game content before, but his first foray into short fiction is "The Swamp Fox," which follows the rebellion on Verthandi in the Third Succession War. (If you're a fan of William H. Keith's Gray Death Legion novel *Mercenary's Star*, then you'll definitely love this story!) In "Acceptable Losses," Adam Neff shows us the hard choices mercenaries often have to make in the heat of battle. If you like *Locust*s—and let's be honest, who *doesn't?*—then you're sure to love "Run, Locust, Run" by Westin Riverside. And Joseph A. Cosgrove's "Starving Vultures" takes us to a true hard-luck world in the Davion Outback, where desperate people trying to leave a dying planet leads to explosive consequences.

From our veteran authors, we have the aforementioned "Drawing the Short Straw" by David G. Martin, which gives us a look at the bitter war between the Duchy of Tamarind-Abbey and the Marian Hegemony. Giles Gammage's "Reversal of Fortunes" dives into the FedCom Civil War, as seen through the lens of two battling brothers. In "No Rest for the Accursed," Matthew Cross' addition to the Tales from the Cracked Canopy series, a tormented Dragon's Fury member seeks some peace for the sins of his past. And finally, "The Wreckoning," Russell Zimmerman's follow-up to "Seal the Deal" from #11, takes us to the dangerous arenas of Solaris VII, where a risky gladiatorial experiment could spell disaster for not only a struggling MechWarrior, but every person and organization supporting him.

Also, our brand-new serial novel from Bryan Young, *Lone Wolf and Fox*, debuts in this issue! This story sees the Katie Ferraro and the Fox Patrol embroiled in their biggest endeavor yet! (If you've missed the previous adventures of the Fox Patrol in earlier *Shrapnel* issues, then check out the *Fox Tales* anthology at your favorite fiction retailer, as it also contains a brand-new story unique to that collection!)

For game content, we have a Voices of the Sphere article about how the Clans' culture has affected the Inner Sphere; the aforementioned *Albatross* Technical Readout; a dubious tale about a Star League-era full-body cooling suit with a checkered history; a Bainbridge's Guide to unique geographical features that can help or hinder your battles; a Unit Digest for Wilson's Hussars, a merc unit with notoriously bad luck; a report on a JumpShip that misjumped on a Friday the 13th; an RPG adventure set in the literally cutthroat world of Solaris VII's fashion industry; a culture article about the social climate of the Raven Alliance, with a focus on the Snow Ravens' political machinations; a Planet Digest for Gandy's Luck, a high-oxygen world dominated by large insects; and an *Alpha Strike* scenario set in the Wolf Empire, which only requires the *Alpha Strike Box Set* to play.

Before you charge further into this issue, I have a couple of shout-outs. First, the awesome cover image comes from new artist Germán Varona Galindo, a.k.a. Wallok. I love how this piece turned out, and I can't wait to see more from him in the future! Second, I want to extend special thanks to Ramón Ostolaza Fernández and Agustín Sieiro for their invaluable input for Planet Digest: Gandy's Luck. We all greatly appreciate your help!

All right, MechWarriors, time to move out! Cross your fingers and throw some salt over your shoulder, because, trust me, you're gonna need all the good luck you can get!

—Philip A. Lee, Managing Editor

SHRAPNEL

THE SWAMP FOX

BEN KLINEFELTER

SILVAN BASIN
VERTHANDI
DRACONIS COMBINE
31 DECEMBER 3016

"READY!" a harsh, accented voice called out as the line of soldiers standing at attention raised their rifles as one.

She could see the dust drifting in the courtyard, swirling in eddies from the breeze. The sun beat down, drenching the pristine courtyard in sunlight, in stark contrast to the dark deed about to take place. The damp splotches that had appeared on the soldiers' orangish-brown uniforms told her how sweltering the heat was. The prisoners facing the soldiers were dirty, disheveled, and forlorn. One in particular stood out to her.

"AIM!" the harsh voice shouted again.

The line of faceless soldiers leveled their rifles at the bound prisoners, some sagging against their restraints, most sobbing in fear or relief. Her husband stood stoically, accepting his fate at the hands of these monsters who had invaded and ravaged her home.

She gasped for air, not realizing she had stopped breathing in response to the unfolding scene. Her hands, claw-like from the tension of the moment, reached out as if to physically stop the next word from being spoken, knowing what result it would have.

"FIRE!"

Frances Marrion awoke with a start in her bunk, her sheets soaked with sweat. The cold clamminess seeped through her chilled skin, despite the oppressive humidity in this southern area of the Silvan Basin. Her heart pounded as the remnants of the nightmare faded. She thought she heard the echoes of the rifles' report bouncing through the small space of the captain's cabin, but that was just the memory of that fateful day. The gentle rocking of the Monitor naval vessel soothed her gradually. The ship rolled slowly up and down with the ebb and flow of the tidal waters.

She swung her legs to the side of the bed and rested her face in cupped hands. Her sweat-soaked, shoulder-length, dark blond hair, hung lank and disheveled around her, obscuring her view, and she rubbed her face vigorously to get the blood moving to her brain.

Gotta get moving. Dracs aren't gonna leave Verthandi of their own accord.

She dressed quickly, her eyes adjusting to the predawn darkness as she located her clothing and strapped her gun belt around her waist.

A fist banged on her closed door. "Fran, you up?" a deep voice called out.

"I'm up, Darren. Coming out," she said as she finished dressing in the darkness. She pulled the door open to find her second standing there with a mug of fresh coffee, steaming the sleep away from the last recesses of her mind.

While she came in at a whopping 1.7 meters tall and 60 kilos, Darren towered over her and outmassed her twice over. He was a burly crane operator from Port Gaspin. Where her rage toward the occupiers of Verthandi was fire and blood, his was a quiet, simmering anger from the loss of his wife a few weeks ago. Back in the summer, he had alerted the resistance to the security arrangements of then-named *Vengeance* so the rebels could take control of the ship before she was used against them. Darren was part of the group that had helped the rebels sneak aboard the *Vengeance* the night they stole her from the Draconis Combine garrison. He was quick to figure out the main guns, and had claimed them for his own.

"Let's go," Frances said as she took the mug, sipping it as she followed Darren down the passageway toward the bridge. "Everything ready?"

"We're on station. Slipped in nice and easy overnight. Everyone got a little sleep, including Shaw's folks." The big man squeezed through the small hatch and onto the bridge.

She followed him, nodding to Jerry manning the helm as she headed to the ferroglass of the main viewing port, where she looked out across the bow of the Monitor at the turret-mounted guns and the dull gray of the superstructure.

There was a total of thirteen people aboard, all part of the Verthandi resistance movement. The Monitor only required five personnel to operate it: a helmsman or captain; one gunner for each of the three missile launchers, port, starboard, and aft; and one gunner for Big

Ben, the massive dual autocannons on the forward-mounted turret. Darren had named the bow guns after their first engagement. When he had fired them, he said it sounded like a giant bell being rung inside the little fire-control compartment. Frances assumed he was probably a little deaf from working with heavy machinery all his life, because to everyone else, Big Ben made a deep-seated thumping noise that reverberated in the chest cavity of every person nearby. Frances was okay with the moniker, since it also reminded her of her own son's name, and she liked to imagine him being able to reach out and destroy the monsters that scared him.

In addition to the five crew, a seven-person squad of jump infantry filled the forward cargo hold.

And then there was her: leader of the small rebel crew, captain of the traitor ship *Swamp Fox*, planner of Kuritan destruction.

The faint sunlight was starting to seep through the tall jungle trees and into the misty portholes of the bridge. Directly across the bow, the Santee ran lazily in a northerly direction towards the Azure Sea, about ten kilometers off the starboard side of the vessel. It was a relatively wide river, a little less than a hundred meters across. It stretched to the south into the Silvan Basin, and was the *Swamp Fox*'s main hunting ground. Frances couldn't make out the far shore of the Santee yet. But soon the mist would dissipate with the coming of dawn. And with that eastern sunlight at her back, and the *Swamp Fox* charging toward them out of that same sun, she hoped the Snakes would feel some terror as Darren let Big Ben ring. Frances smiled at the thought.

She placed her steaming coffee mug on the sill of the main porthole and pulled an elastic band from a trouser pocket. Pulling her hair back in a ponytail, she secured it with the band. *Can't have this mess obscuring my vision when the shooting starts.* She grabbed the electronic binoculars from their hook and switched them on, her thoughts cascading between the past and present.

Swamp Fox sat idle at anchor just inside the mouth of a tributary of the Santee, the smaller Mattaponi, 500 meters from their target. It had taken four days to work their way down this feeder river, but luckily, the *Swamp Fox* had a very shallow draft. It allowed her to get through parts of the river thought unpassable by larger waterborne vessels. Although the shallow draft made for a fairly rough ride, they had all gotten used to it over the last couple months. No more seasickness from Jerry, the helmsman.

She surveyed the Drac supply depot through her binoculars, switching between vislight and thermal. Even with the drifting mist limiting vislight somewhat, she was still able to make out some enhanced shapes. But thermal imaging blazed through the fog, locating the steady orange glow of the depot's power generator. From the intel she had received, the depot was a simple rectangular shape with two small supply buildings, an office that doubled as a guard headquarters, and three guard towers, one of which watched the gap in the chain-link fence at the entrance to the depot at the bottom of the rectangle. The other two towers were at the opposite corners at the top of the rectangle. She could see faint orangish-yellow blobs of two guards, one in the tower and one in the office. She couldn't fully make out the two towers in the back, just the square shape of the towers.

Frances had always loved shapes. They just made sense to her. The lines, the symmetry, all of it just talked to her brain the right way. She had been eager to learn as much as she could about the new art coming out of Tharkad, but that was nothing but ashes to her now. At just twenty-two years old, she had come to Verthandi to work on her master's degree in art history in the hopes of eventually moving to the Lyran Commonwealth's capital and working in one of the great art museums there. Now, though, she was admiring a rectangle she was about to destroy. In two short years, she had arrived as a student, fallen in love, become a mother, a widow, a vocal opponent of the Combine, and finally a leader in the fight against the invading Dracs. Once more, it was time to fight back against the oppression.

"Let's do it, Jerry. Take us surfing." Fran gazed at the vague shape of the far bank through the mist and raised her communicator to her lips. "All hands, general quarters, general quarters. Man your battle stations. Plan Viper. Execute."

She felt the thrum of the engines spooling up, and the bow rose slightly as the *Swamp Fox* eased slowly forward, picking up speed. She looked at the LED readout on the control station and quickly did the math in her head in relation to speed and distance. At just 29 knots, or 54 kph, the *Swamp Fox* was relatively slow compared to BattleMechs or smaller wet-naval vessels. "One minute out, Shaw," she spoke softly over the thrum of the engine as the ship picked up speed.

"Copy, Fran," came the tinny response from the infantry below deck. The jump infantry squad had given Fran a bit of surprise striking power. Whenever the cargo bay's hatch rolled back, out jumped an entire seven-person squad of infantry firing captured rifles and submachine guns at the enemy.

They had been hitting the Combine's supply depots and troop centers along the northern riverbanks that followed deeply into the heart of the Silvan Basin, the breadbasket of Verthandi. For three months, the Dracs had been trying to gain control of the Basin, running convoys and hunting for the rebel encampments. Every time the Snakes had put a depot or barracks anywhere along a river in the Silvan Basin, the *Swamp Fox* had preyed on their poor planning.

Frances raised her electronic binoculars again and scanned the shore as it came into view. *Swamp Fox* rocked slightly as Jerry kicked the throttle up to flank speed. According to intel, the hastily erected buildings along the shore were meant to house munitions and supplies for the Combine troops in the area. She was about to ruin their plans. She had been up and down the coast of the Azure Sea the past few months, learning the various rivers that fed into the massive sea. "Steaming" upriver to strike at the Kuritans gave her more satisfaction than she realized. More so than the outdated word of "steaming" regarding ancient Terran naval vessels.

"I got a bad feeling about this, Fran," Darren said nervously from his protected gunnery cubicle.

"We've had this discussion already. Keep your eyes on your threat monitors and bring those guns online. This should be a pretty easy hit. The Dracs have slipped up on this one."

Without taking her eyes from the binocs, she said, "Shaw, thirty seconds." She could visualize the seven troops in the open bay, tightening the straps on their jump packs, hefting weapons, and looking up at the open cargo hatch with anticipation. Except Shaw, none of the infantry were formally trained. He was a veteran infantryman from the Lyran Commonwealth Armed Forces.

"I hear ya, but it still doesn't feel right," Darren muttered as he flipped switches and pressed buttons to bring Big Ben online.

Frances watched the turret-mounted autocannons swivel back and forth in their mount, testing the movement, like a wolf sniffing the air for prey. *Let them come*, she thought. *Let them try to stifle us.*

The revolution on Verthandi had stalled in the last few months. After the Revolutionaries had pushed most of the Snakes back into Regisport, the Draconis Combine troops had really cracked down in response. To Frances, none of the big-picture things the Council of Revolutionaries talked about really mattered to her. She just wanted to kill every single Kuritan soldier on the planet, and make the Draconis Combine pay in blood for her loss. After what they had done to her love, she had no more sympathy to give. At least her son was off-planet and with family—although she didn't know what would happen to him if she was lost. The only thing Fran *did* know anymore was to fight for vengeance. She was just an art student. She had thought about leaving Verthandi when the revolution broke out, but that wasn't an option. Jacim Feldhausen, the love of her life and the father of her child, had been a history professor at the University of Regis, and they had been romantically involved for almost two years.

Then the rumblings of revolution had started over a year ago. Jacim had gotten involved in the peaceful protesting, but protests alone could not close the camps of citizens the Kurita occupiers were using as slave labor to mine precious elements to ship off-world.

The blatant brutality of the Kuritans had reached full bloom in the spring. Jacim had been targeted by Governor-General Nagumo's secret police, and was part of a sweep that rounded up dissenters to the Kuritan government's handling of the planetary affairs. That's when she lost him. The governor-general had broadcast the summary executions to quell further dissent. She watched on the holovid as Jacim was murdered by a firing squad of Kurita troops while Nagumo watched, praising the Kuritan troops for their bravery at stomping out the dissension among the populace. But the rage she felt at the brutality and callousness of the Kuritan overlords didn't override her concern for their son. She knew the troubles would continue and get worse, so she'd scraped together all the money she had left, enough to smuggle one person off-planet, and sent her son to "vacation" with his grandfather on the Lyran Commonwealth world of Twycross. Frances had a feeling she would never see her baby's beautiful blue eyes again. No matter what happened, she had to keep Ben safe from the monsters. If she didn't do her part to uphold Jacim's vision of the future, what kind of example would she set for her own son?

At the last Revolutionary Council meeting, she had been appalled by their unwillingness to take the fight to the governor head on. They thought protests and little jabs in the side of the Dragon would eventually make them leave. Fran had advocated for hiring a mercenary unit to come and help them, but the Council had voted her down. She knew, from the history she had learned from Jacim, only direct action would get the Council's attention. Fran remembered railing at them for their lack of conviction and foresight, in just doing "enough" when overwhelming force was needed. She smiled at the memory of storming out of the meeting room. If the Council wouldn't act, she would.

The LED display flashed to ten seconds. Fran watched the numbers drift to zero as the coast of the far bank grew wider in her field of view. When *Swamp Fox* reached a hundred meters from the easy sloping banks, she activated her comm unit. "Launch," she said. She listened for the telltale activation of the jump packs, and then watched the seven troopers rise out of the small opening on the forward deck, angling towards the shore.

"Hard to port, Jerry," she ordered. "Get us in close to shore and then bring us alongside. I wanna give the port missile battery a clear line, and have our bow lined up for a cruise to the Azure as soon as we're done."

Jerry didn't respond but started adjusting the yokes to bring the 75-ton vessel around on a proper angle to comply with Fran's directions.

She raised the communicator to her lips and said, "Port battery, target the main guard tower and fire."

The murky water of the slow-moving river lapped at the shore. The fog was starting to burn off with the arrival of the full sun, and she was able to see farther back around the supply depot. The whoosh of two short-range missiles leaving their tubes sounded just before the first guard tower exploded in fire and smoke. She heard the rattle of the submachine guns from the airborne infantry squad as they shot up the remains of the guard tower, and then Shaw and his troops landed inside the depot's chain-link fencing.

Better to be sure, but nonetheless, a perfect start to another attack by the Swamp Fox, Frances thought.

Renaming the Monitor from *Vengeance* to *Swamp Fox* had been her idea. The first time she met Jacim, he had been giving a history lecture at the University of Regis on something about Terran history, and she remembered his passion telling a story about some mythical animal from Terra that had terrorized some settlers. She couldn't remember most of it, and it was probably completely wrong, but she didn't care. *Swamp Fox* reminded her of Jacim. *Swamp Fox* would be Jacim's revenge on his killers. And just like their animal namesake, she and the *Swamp Fox*'s crew had been terrorizing the Kuritan troops along the rivers for the past four months.

"Fran," Shaw's voice broke through her musings. "There's nothing here."

Frances froze, thoughts cascading furiously. "What?! Nothing?" She trusted Shaw to scrounge whatever he could from any of the locations they had hit along the rivers and the coast over the last few months. If he couldn't find anything, it wasn't there.

She sighed. She was disappointed, but her thoughts continued to churn. *Why set this up and not stock it?* She knew there were troops in the area. Just a week ago, *Swamp Fox* had launched a daring attack on a small barracks and killed almost a whole platoon of Dracos in the middle of their morning aerobics. "Copy. RTB."

"Fran, they're on us!" Darren yelled, shaking her out of her thoughts. "Multiple MAD readings coming!"

Fran white-knuckle gripped the handhold underneath the large ferroglass window that encompassed most of the bridge and leaned forward to try to see everything at once. With her head against the glass, she saw the churning water erupt on the port side, and a BattleMech emerged from the depths of the Santee less than 100 meters away from the side of *Swamp Fox*.

"Weapons free!" she yelled in her comm unit. "Target and fire at will!"

She watched the brownish water sluice off a 45-ton *Phoenix Hawk* as it rose from its position on the bottom of the river. The brown and black mud partially obscured the red disc with the black dragon head on its left-side chest armor.

Without taking her eyes from the *'Hawk*, she yelled at Darren, "Hit that port sonovabitch with both barrels!"

Big Ben made a small adjustment toward the closest threat as she stared at the river monster rising and lifting its right arm to line up the rifle-style large laser that was its main offensive weapon. The machine guns in the 'Mech's left arm belched out flame and hot metal that tracked through the water and across the starboard side of *Swamp Fox*. Two missiles from the portside battery slammed into the *Phoenix Hawk*'s right leg and arm, a mild inconvenience to the 'Mech.

Then Big Ben opened up. The deep, rumbling buzzsaw of the stream of autocannon rounds obliterated the Kurita symbol as fragments of armor and internal structure spalled away from the explosive shells impacting deep inside the 'Mech.

She was dimly aware of the starboard and aft missile batteries firing, so transfixed as she was the *Phoenix Hawk*.

"We got a total of four on us, Fran!" Jerry yelled, the worry in his voice apparent. "Scratch one. Make that three."

Darren whooped from his armored cubicle.

She shook herself away from the scene of the *Phoenix Hawk* falling backward, great rents in its torso, smoke leaking from the gashes as it splashed backwards like a human falling back into a pool. *The water will probably flood those compartments. Can't be good for it.* She was not the one in the family with that type of knowledge. Her father was. Or had been. The notification of his death was still in her pocket, crumpled and flattened over and over again. She'd read it hundreds of times over the last few months. He was gone, and there was nothing she could do about it but fight back like he had taught her in their early years together.

She squinted as man-made lightning struck the bow of the *Swamp Fox*—two hard thumps followed by a series of water explosions from the autocannon mounted on the *Marauder* that had risen from the depths. Standing more than 200 meters away just off the bow, the 'Mech blocked their escape downriver. The *Swamp Fox* shuddered from the hits on the port side where another *Marauder* was rising and moving towards the rebel vessel.

We must have floated right over that bastard. Ballsy of them.

The Santee covered the approaching 'Mech from the waist down, slowing its movement to a crawl. But *Swamp Fox* was faster in the water than they were.

Frances made a quick calculation in her head. "Jerry, move her forward! Flank speed!" She gripped the handhold again as the *Swamp Fox* shuddered from the blows coming from three directions. "Darren! Starboard side, target and fire!" She felt Big Ben slew around from starboard to port, but she was sprinting across the bridge to look out the rear window and see what lay astern. Another 'Mech, a *Shadow Hawk*. She knew this one, one of her favorites when she was a little girl. The memory of curling up in her father's lap to watch holovids from Solaris VII when she was little surfaced amid the chaos surrounding her now. She also knew the two *Marauder*s were the deadliest threat.

They were *all* deadly threats if she didn't keep the Monitor moving.

"Fran, Shaw," her comm unit barked out. "I'm under fire. Snakes in the grass." A rattle of gunfire as background noise.

"Snakes in the grass" was code for ground troops at the landing point. She knew Shaw was a pro, but she couldn't help him; she had bigger problems. And her problems might be the end of *Swamp Fox*. The least she could do was get Shaw's folks out so they could fight another day.

From all the Council codes she had memorized, she recalled the one she knew would get Shaw in contact with somebody who would hopefully be able to help them, someone who could do more damage to the Snakes than the current rebel leadership was willing to do.

Frances took a deep breath, dreading the words she was saying. "Shaw, break contact. Evac to X-Ray Kilo Seven-Seven-Two. Squawk Four-Four Lima on arrival."

The rattle of gunfire from Shaw's transmission was louder this time. "Four-Four Lima ain't ours. Who is it?" He neglected to release the transmit button, and Frances could hear his submachine gun barking as he yelled, "EVAC, EVAC, ON ME!" Then the comms went silent.

Swamp Fox shook from the combined fire of the three surrounding 'Mechs. Frances knew deep down how this was going to end. She heard Big Ben belch out stream after stream of autocannon shells as the ship picked up speed. She watched with horror as the *Shadow Hawk*'s laser and autocannon raked the aft decking, probing for the engines and finding the short-range-missile launcher that had been nipping at the big 'Mech.

"Shaw," she said, "that's a local emergency freq. Find 'em and they'll hide you until the Revolutionary Council is ready to fight. *Swamp Fox* is done. Good luck, my friend. Happy hunting. Marrion out."

She turned away from the destruction of the aft launcher only to see Big Ben ripping a third volley at the starboard-side *Marauder*, which was stumbling from the onslaught of the massive cannons. Armor peeled and shattered, and myomer bundles hung in tatters. The portside missile launchers followed up the strike, with one missile spiraling in through the massive hole Big Ben had made, sparking an explosion deep inside the crab-like 'Mech.

The missile touched off the ammunition stored in the menacing 'Mech's torso. The magnificent secondary explosions blasted the arms free, spiraling them away from the truncated body. When the fire and smoke dissipated, only the *Marauder*'s legs remained, folding on themselves and disappearing under the Santee.

The *Swamp Fox* shuddered again, her bow dropping ever so slightly, enough to bleed off speed. Frances turned to yell at Jerry to increase the throttle just as the ferroglass blew inward on the bridge. She felt a tingling sensation, and then crashed hard against the aft bulkhead. She felt rather than heard a *crack* and instant pain from her left leg.

The bridge was thick with smoke and scattered fire. A large blaze had broken out at the helm station. She realized it was Jerry, sitting slack in the half-melted chair, flames dancing across his body. The scent of charred, roasting meat prevailed over the smell of smoke.

She cried out at the loss of her longtime friend and steady companion in the movement. She turned her face away from the scene of carnage only to have her cry of anguish ring louder as she spied the limp form of Darren lying half in and half out of the gunner's cubicle. Her second-in-command. The ice to her fiery rage. He had a long bloody gash on the side of his head, a piece of ferroglass sticking out from the wound, the top of his skull misshapen from the blow. So much blood all over his face and chest.

She attempted to stand, but the pain overwhelmed her. Stabbing pain from her leg shot up her spine and made her gasp as she fell again. She dragged herself across the decking toward Darren, and checked for a pulse with sweat-slicked fingers. Through the tears, she watched his chest rise slowly and fall once. Not to rise again.

Boiling rage came from deep within her. She could feel herself screaming, but could not hear it, only a steady hum. *Probably deaf from the blast. I don't care. I'm taking them with me.*

Frances dragged herself toward Big Ben's seat. She could feel the *Swamp Fox* slowing, but the deck still vibrated with the running engine. *At least there's power.* She groaned from the agony as she pulled herself into the gunnery seat, blurry eyes finding the screens for targets and bloody, sweaty hands groping for the control sticks.

She saw on the main screen that the *Swamp Fox* was down to just 20 kph, creeping toward that damned *Marauder* blocking their escape into the Azure Sea. She centered the holographic reticle on the nose of the 'Mech as best she could and squeezed the triggers on both controls, launching a storm of explosive metal at the giant menace less than fifty meters away. The throbbing in her chest told her Big Ben was working. She watched the sparks dance across the screen as the dual autocannons smashed armor and tore myomer fibers.

Closer.

She felt the cassettes reload her cannons as the ready light blinked from amber to green, and she squeezed the triggers again. The *Marauder* shuddered from the hits just as the particle projection cannons in both its arms blasted their charged-particle beams into *Swamp Fox* one final time. The *Marauder* stutter-stepped and fell, and a tidal wave of the Santee River splashed over the *Swamp Fox*'s bow.

The Monitor slowed to a stop, drifting under momentum only. It shuddered and listed to port, the bow starting to rise. She knew there was another 'Mech out there, that damned *Shadow Hawk*.

She swiped a hand across her eyes to clear the moisture away, a mix of tears, sweat, and blood as the *Swamp Fox*'s bow started to come around, bringing the vessel broadside to the remaining 'Mech. Frances found it on the edge of the screen, growing as the Monitor foundered and drifted. She centered the reticle on the slab-chested 'Mech and jerked the triggers. Big Ben belched out its stream of shells, but the impacts fell short of the 'Mech.

Frances screamed in rage as the *Shadow Hawk* laid another volley into *Swamp Fox*. She felt cold and wet. At first she thought it was just shock from her injuries, but she tore her gaze from the gunner's screen long enough to see the water of the Santee filling the bridge, rising past her waist. She could try to swim out, but between her injured leg and the *Shadow Hawk* still out there, where could she go?

She tested her leg for movement, and searing pain shot through her body like the lightning from the *Marauder*'s PPCs. *Not gonna make it out of here. Time to make it count.* With the decision made, she doubled down on her vow to take the attackers with her as best she could. *I can do this. For Jacim. For Ben. For me. Come and get me you big Snake bastard.*

Frances centered the reticle over the big, coiled serpent emblem on the chest of the *Shadow Hawk* and squeezed Big Ben's triggers.

The thumping in her chest was indistinguishable between her heart and the pounding of the giant autocannons firing their 'Mech-killing shells. The volley smashed into the *Shadow Hawk*, tearing its left arm off and staggering the giant machine just as a volley from the *Hawk*'s own autocannon shattered the bridge's remaining support structures. The armored cubicle collapsed around her, and a piece of the superstructure fell across her abdomen, pinning her to the seat.

She was beyond shock as the gunner's station went dark. She smiled a bloody grin and coughed from the thick smoke that consumed the bridge as the water rushed into the compartment, rising to her chin.

Better to die on your feet, sword in hand, teeth bared, screaming at the storm.

She tried to think of where she had heard that as the darkness enveloped her.

**FOX ISLAND REBEL BASE
SILVAN BASIN
VERTHANDI
3 JANUARY 3017**

"FIRE!"

Frances awoke again to the echoes of the same dream she'd had the last several months. She opened her eyes to get her bearings, turning her head from side to side. The room was dimly lit and small, the smell of antiseptic and cleaning products assaulting her nostrils. The only other occupant was Shaw, slumped in a chair beside her bed, sleeping in tattered and dirty combat fatigues.

"Wha...where...?" Her voice cracked from dryness.

Shaw started awake and stood quickly, hand dropping to the sidearm at his hip. When he realized she was speaking, he relaxed and took a quick step to her bedside.

"Fran!" he said, his voice gravelly from sleep. "Easy now. You're safe. Don't move. You've got a broken leg and a couple of busted ribs." He reached for a small cup of water from the side table and held it to her lips, allowing her a small sip before returning it.

She remembered the fight on the *Swamp Fox*, the heat from the fires on the bridge, the cold of the Santee as the Monitor sank.

"How...?" Her words trailed off with exhaustion and pain.

"We saw what was happening. Once I broke contact with the ground troops, we looped around and came in on the other side of the Santee. The one 'Mech left was damaged to hell and back, and it had slipped into the jungle, probably looking for the rest of us. We found you on the shore. I don't know how you made it out of there, but we patched you up as best we could, and I brought us to the coordinates you gave me."

A storm of thoughts raced through her as the pain in her leg and abdomen intruded into her consciousness. "The others...? The *Swamp Fox*...?"

Shaw looked away and shook his head. "You were the only survivor we found, Fran."

She could see the tracks of tears in the dirt and dust on his weathered face as he looked back at her, his voice quiet in the silence.

"The *Swamp Fox* is gone, Fran. She took down three of Nagumo's 'Mechs before she sank. He won't be using those anytime soon." There was a trace of pride in his voice, and he grinned down at her to deliver the last bit of news. "We also just got word about a fresh vehicle-repair depot being set up around Hunter's Cape. Soon as you're ready, we'll go steal a tank and get back at it. This fight ain't over by a long shot."

It never will be for me, Frances thought as blackness overtook her.

VOICES OF THE SPHERE: CUSHIONING THE CULTURE SHOCK

WUNJI LAU

After a century of intermixing cultures, populations, and economies, the Clans and the Inner Sphere aren't quite a melting pot, but neither are they alien to each other anymore. This Voices of the Sphere article asks various individuals about their thoughts on the past and future of these merging, yet often conflicting cultures.

Ji-Min Huang, University of Robinson School of Business (Federated Suns): Cultural-sensitivity training for people who will interact with Clanfolk isn't a new thing, of course, but over time, the price of a faux pas has lessened significantly. Back in my grandmother's day, mistakenly asking a Trueborn about their birth parents would get you a stab wound or broken nose, but these days, a lot of Clanfolk respond to such errors with a shrug or maybe a low growl. Even so, we try to minimize the occurrence of any missteps.

The Sea Foxes are by far the easiest to get along with. They actually send people from every caste to attend our courses to share and learn, and quite a few of their representatives will even switch to non-Clan speaking styles for social interactions. Members of other Clans are less accommodating, but with proper preparation, interactions with merchants and even warriors eventually become routine. Unfortunately, little of our training makes it to outlying regions and worlds, where in many communities the Clans continue to be monster-under-the-bed topics of irrational fear and ignorance.

Laborer Obine, Skandia (Rasalhague Dominion): There have always been those unsuited to life in the Clans, but in the past, the stigma and hardships of relegation to the Free Guilds or the Dark Caste served as adequate deterrents to all but the most intractable of nonconformists. In the Inner Sphere, however, a skilled Clan laborer or technician who flees Clan-governed space can find not only acceptance in neighboring nations, but even wealth and prestige. Thus, with each passing generation, the number of dissatisfied Clan-born individuals has increased.

Propaganda, information control, iron-fisted policing, and even indiscriminate bombardment are effective countermeasures for some Clans, but as every Great House has discovered over the centuries, totalitarian force is no long-term substitute for giving a populace a reason to serve of their own accord. If we wish to maintain at least some semblance of our way of life, certain compromises are necessary. Often, simply the faint promise of potential advancement is enough to quell discord, as both the Capellan Confederation and Federated Suns have demonstrated. But certainly, the best proven outcome is to build a shared home for all, such that those who are born into that family have no desire to leave it, or turn resolvable differences into rash actions.

Bibili Imbrumio, Graceland (Tamar Pact): My grandda built a planetwide chain of groceries, and I got to watch the Jade Falcons turn them all into communal feeding troughs. Now that the turkeys are out, I've managed to claw back at least some ownership of the local branches and can start rebuilding the business. But if the Falcons come back, our assets will all get swiped again. So no, I'm not using a bank. Most business owners here won't. We store our money and valuables in safe places, 'nuff said. We got some deeds and financial holdings back, and those are going off-world soon as the papers are signed. It takes months to move funds these days, so everything is a long-term investment by default, but I'd rather my kids find an old account safe on Tharkad in thirty years than see all my hard work wiped out again.

Technician Martine, Csesztreg (Clan Hell's Horses): We get plenty of locally produced holovid shows, but let us face it: the Spheroids make much better shows. Not only do we have the strict oversight of censors like some Inner Sphere nations, but we also have an extremely limited scope of cultural references and a lack of funding and resources. No Clan administrator would approve the frivolous expense of gathering 3,000 extras to film a battle scene in a mountain range redressed to look like 15th-century New York

City as a Federated Suns production did in the recent *Wyatt Earp, Panzer Rider* historical drama. That kind of realism cannot be faked. Acquiring bootlegs of this entertainment is worth the effort, so long as the Watch does not take too stern a hand.

Hamish Samaroff, Dalton (Free Worlds League): Clan culture's been crossing over into the Inner Sphere for decades. Once they stopped being alien invaders and became just another group of weird and annoying neighbors, they lost a bit of their mystique. Likewise, as Clan warriors increasingly fought alongside Inner Sphere troops, their grudging respect percolated down-caste.

In places far from Clan territory, the impact is mostly casual and lighthearted. We have Talk Like a Clanner Days at workplaces, overpriced Clan-diet programs, and the always-popular Circle of Equals Dance Mat party game. Clan totem costumes show up a lot on kids as well as adults (but for very different uses). *The Remembrance* gets regular surges on bestseller lists for poetry, history, and business strategy, probably helped along by the fancy special editions produced by every Clan's merchant caste. I hear that Great Works by Dominion citizens are seen, heard, and tasted all the way out in the Periphery.

Closer to the borders, though, the imitation has an undertone of deadly seriousness. If a world changes hands, the folks there are very aware that being able to win a fistfight or quote the Great Father may make the difference in a caste assignment or work-credit allocation. That attitude is pretty one-sided, though; Clan laborers, merchants, and technicians are usually confident of their ability to survive and thrive should the Clan system be replaced by any of our governments.

Lacny Kaur, Koulen (Draconis Combine): There are many points on which we disagree, but there are also matters on which we're perfectly in line with Clan Watch and enforcement entities. Arms and chem smuggling, violent serial crimes, and violations of laws on artificial intelligence and genetics are just some of the cases where we've learned to cooperate closely on border worlds, regardless of broader political concerns. On the other hand, when they notify us of defecting "ungrateful lower-caste scum," weird data-loss glitches seem to happen on our end, and when we send the Watch requests for help with Chatterweb media piracy and cross-border tax evasion, they usually reply with a couple of words most people would be surprised to hear from a Clanner.

Helga Yingqing, Diboll (Raven Alliance): The Watch relies heavily on non-Clan monitoring and enforcement agencies to handle crimes outside the Clan enclaves. This policy fosters harmony between the cultures that make up our Alliance, but it has also resulted in some longstanding challenges. While ultimate oversight rests with experienced Clan administrators, in non-Clan civilian areas, things work much as they did in the days of the Outworlds Alliance. This means, for example, that if a Clan individual commits what they consider a minor indiscretion outside the Clan enclaves, they may be subject to unfamiliar local systems of adjudication and punishment. Likewise, criminal syndicates take advantage of administrative disconnects between the enclaves and non-Clan areas to smuggle contraband or conceal fraud (with the added consideration that even after decades of coexistence, we still have differing standards of what constitutes "contraband" and "fraud").

One area where we have less trouble than one might expect is in migration. In earlier years, both cultures struggled to handle disaffected individuals who perhaps sought structure with a caste or fortune outside the Clan. Today, a limited number of citizens each season may seek authorized sponsorship and legal reassignment, without fear of missing-persons reports, angry supervisors, or other repercussions. It is not precisely the Clan way or the Outworlder way, but it demonstrates that at the intersections of our neighboring cultures, we are able to find a path forward.

Technician Dirgwynne, Sudeten (Clan Jade Falcon): What, you ask, prevents the Clans from simply stealing each other's genetic legacies? Honor and respect. These virtues are absent from the Inner Sphere, which is why I should not be surprised to read disgusting rumors of black-market trading in viable, pure Bloodhouse reproductive material. Apparently, wealthy and depraved Inner Sphere degenerates, unable to produce worthy offspring with their genetrash mates, seek to improve the quality and potential of their legacies by leeching off our centuries of validated and refined work to circumvent the manifold difficulties of genetic engineering using non-Clan techniques.

This unearned conferring of superior human traits is bad enough, but additional Sea Fox news on the Chatterweb informs me that these vile miscreants also seek to bind their lineages, however tenuously, to renowned heritages. Am I alone in shuddering at the nightmare vision of hordes of Sphere-spawned mutated Prydes and Kerenskys sullying everything we stand for? They would have no standing in the Clans, of course, but who knows what political folly the coming decades might bring?

The true question: Who is responsible for allowing this desecration to occur? Not us, I know. The Ravens are tricky but respectful of tradition. Even the money-grubbing Sea Foxes would not sink to such insanity.

Anonymous, Location Unknown (Chatterweb): Oh, yes, they would.

ACCEPTABLE LOSSES

ADAM NEFF

**CIDE UNIDAS
DALCOUR
FREE WORLDS LEAGUE
7 OCTOBER 2865**

Zarek Hanlon jerked awake to the deep, booming thud of a fist pounding on the solid polyboard door of Marnie's tiny apartment.

"Hanlon!" came a sharp voice during a brief pause in the thumping. "Kid, get your ass out here!"

The hammering continued as the young MechWarrior threw back the covers and leaped out of bed to pull on his dusty red duty coveralls. Dim early-morning light sneaking in through the thin openings in the window blinds shone just bright enough to make out the unit patch on the left shoulder: a trio of white stallions at a full gallop.

He could sense Marnie pulling herself up on the bed behind him. She said something, but whatever it was got lost in the ceaseless pounding.

"Hanlon! *Now!*" the voice shouted again, certainly loud enough to wake everyone on this floor.

"Coming, Corporal!" he replied as he shoved his feet into his boots and strode forward.

He threw the lock and jerked the door open, then cranked his neck down to see the diminutive form of Corporal Amata Singh before him. Zarek's halfhearted attempt at a smile withered away at the look on her face, and his shoulders slumped.

"I know this is your first pump with a freelance merc company, and you may think you're something special, but you're a member of Red Stable now, kid, and Captain Dvorak, informal as he is, doesn't take kindly to his MechWarriors disobeying orders. More importantly—"

Her voice dropped into a hard growl. "—*I* don't take kindly to having to track you down in the early hours to keep your ass out of trouble. Let's go." She turned on her heel and started walking down the hall. "Now."

Zarek managed a quick glance back to where Marnie sat in bed, half naked and mortified, and offered a weak wave goodbye before shutting the door behind him and jogging after Amata's rapidly disappearing figure. His long legs ate up the distance between them and he caught up to her as she stepped into the stairwell. They made it down two floors in strained silence, with only the sound of their footsteps echoing off the ferrocrete walls, then he opened his mouth to try and explain himself. "Corporal, I—"

"Do *not* talk to me right now, Hanlon, I swear to God."

Zarek nervously chewed on his lip for a moment as he trailed just behind the shorter woman, but his restraint finally broke and he blurted, "Corporal, I saw the captain out last night, too! He was still drinking at the bar when I left!"

"But he didn't end up shacking up with his girlfriend across town, did he?" Amata barked back at him so sharply he recoiled. "Cap stumbled back to the barracks after last call like he always does, and just like *you* should've done. And what he does doesn't make a difference anyway. There are different rules for officers. Even someone as green as you should know that."

Corporal Singh hit the bottom landing and pushed open the side entrance so hard the door slammed into the wall and rebounded to knock Zarek sideways as he stepped through it after her. By the time he caught his balance, she was already halfway down the street, and he had to jog to catch up with her again.

Silence fell over the pair again, and Amata kept a pace so brisk Zarek had to work to keep up despite being almost a half meter taller than her.

Ten minutes later, they cleared the last of the mixed-use buildings, cheap apartments, and warehouses lining the edge of the city and strode across the wide boulevard separating the city proper from the spaceport. The main entrance, surrounded on four sides by a two-story-tall ferrocrete wall, buzzed with activity. As they approached the gate, the security officers waved the MechWarriors through without bothering to check their ID cards. Other guards, techs, port officials, and merchants walked past them in the other direction, streaming out of the port at a rapid pace.

"Whoa, wait a minute," Zarek said. "What's going on, Corporal?"

"You'd know if you were sleeping in your bunk last night like you should have been," Amata snapped, and the young MechWarrior again fell silent.

They continued on for another few dozen meters before the corporal glanced over her shoulder at him and let out a long, exasperated sigh. "The spaceport tower picked up an unregistered DropShip during one of their scans this morning. No response to hails other than increasing their burn, so it has to be pirates. They must've been able to hide their approach among the end-of-season traffic, because they managed to get close before the port authorities spotted them. ETA is only about two hours now."

"Oh, God. The depot..." Zarek's eyes widened and reflexively flicked in the direction of the hardened octagonal building ringed by landing pads in the center of spaceport. "They're gonna hit the DropShip service depot!"

"They're sure as hell not here to steal grain," Amata replied, a wisp of a smirk pulling at the corners of her mouth. "And even though there are plenty of folks who consider Dalcour Fujis a delicacy, I highly doubt we're getting raided for a few crates of apples. But the service depot—the spaceport keeps it overstocked with parts this time of year, since DropShip traffic is so heavy and they can make a mint on repairs." The corporal threw her hands up as she walked, casting her eyes to the sky. "Not that it matters much to us. They're coming here regardless, and we're the ones who have to deal with 'em. Now hurry it up, we're already late for the briefing. You're just lucky Cap is moving slow this morning, otherwise you'd really be in for it."

They headed toward the small, squat building that served as Red Stable's barracks and operations center, directly adjacent to the towering 'Mech bay making up the southeast corner of the port.

Amata stopped abruptly in front of the entrance and spun on her heel, turning to face the younger MechWarrior. He drew up short and yelped in surprise as she thumped him hard on his sternum with the palm of her outstretched hand. She took a deep breath and let it out with a long sigh, her shoulders dropping as she forced the tension from her body.

"Look, kid," she said, a softer, out-of-character note creeping into her tone. "You're a pretty hot sim pilot, no lie, and by just watching you in field exercises, I can tell you can back that up when you're behind the sticks of your *Cicada*. But you're also young and dumb, so I'm going to share some hard-earned life wisdom with you: know who your family is, and don't let us down. No one takes priority over the Red Stable crew. No. One," she reiterated, her palm pounding his chest for emphasis.

"These locals want us on-planet because they think we're here for them, but we're not. We work for DuraPaq Solutions. Their name is on our contract. They pay for our billet. They pay for our parts. They pay us the big fat M-bills you throw away on what's-her-name. They pay us, they own us. We were hired to do spaceport security here for this exact situation and nothing else. Barring an extension because they can't find anyone to do it cheaper, our contract is done in two months. Then we pull up stakes and move on to the next job, the next planet, the next system. I honestly doubt you'll ever set foot on this rock again. That means the only family you have, the only friends you have, the only people who matter, are Red Stable. You get me? The sooner you know this, really know it, the better for all of us."

Amata took another deep breath and then reached up to squeeze Zarek's shoulders.

"Remember, you signed up for this life. You signed up with us. Red Stable may not be the oldest or most storied merc unit out there—we're certainly not the best or most professional—but between Cap, Sarge, and myself, we've got more than a half century of fighting experience under our belts. Even on our worst day, the three of us are better than a lot of full lances out there. You can be a part of that. I know you want to, and we want you to be, too, but it starts with you following orders. Especially the simple ones. Listen, learn, and do as you're told, and you'll make a home and name for yourself with Red Stable. You may even make enough cash to get yourself an upgrade from that oversized metal chicken you like to sprint around in."

Zarek smiled weakly and nodded. "I read you, Corporal, but I like my *Cicada*. It was my dad's. Plus, it's too much fun to run circles around Sergeant Turner and the Captain in that rinky-dink little bird."

A broad, genuine grin split Amata's face, and her teeth flashed white in the morning sun as she threw her head back and laughed. "That's more like it. You keep up that attitude after Cap chews your ass today, and I'm sure you'll earn your home here." She turned back to the door, tapped a passcode into the keypad built into the frame, and yanked the handle.

The door to the makeshift operations center opened with a flood of noise. Red Stable was too small an outfit to employ many support personnel, but the handful of techs and admins made up for their lack in numbers with work effort and volume. One deep, gravelly voice rose above all the others, however.

"Patrick! Patrick, more coffee!" Captain Josef Dvorak yelled, far too loudly for such a small space, and one of the admins bolted from their station and slid past Zarek to grab a coffee pot from the back of the ops center. The CO's voice was sharp and clear, but the dark bags under his bloodshot eyes and the slight unsteadiness in his stance as he leaned on the edge of the low-res holomap table indicated he was still working off the effects of last night's revelries.

Captain Dvorak accepted the proffered cup from Patrick with a slightly delayed nod, then took a long pull of the steaming black liquid. "Keep it coming," he grunted, before turning to the tall, gaunt man standing before him. "Give me the situation, Sergeant."

"Aye, sir," Atticus Turner said with a crisp nod. His eyes narrowed as Zarek and Amata joined them in the center of the room, but he continued with the briefing and held up a single sheet of hard copy in his long-fingered hand. "Flash warning from our DuraPaq rep in the tower. Long-range sensors picked up an unregistered *Leopard*-class DropShip coming in on a hard burn. They have no active IFF and have refused to answer hails, so this has to be a raid. Their trajectory puts them landing somewhere in DeLond Forest, to the east of the port. ETA ninety minutes."

Captain Dvorak took another long sip of coffee. "Any force-size estimates?"

"The *Leopard* limits them to a lance of 'Mechs, and based on the DropShip's entry trajectory and speed, we can estimate a total force of roughly two hundred and fifty tons, roughly equivalent to our own, sir."

"Slightly *above* our own," Dvorak corrected, grunting into his mug. He set his coffee down on the edge of the holoprojector and powered it on before pressing the palms of his large hands into his eyes. He let out a deep sigh and sucked in a breath through clenched teeth, then straightened.

"All right, listen up," he said as he typed a series of commands into a keypad attached to the monitor. A two-dimensional satellite map showing the spaceport and surrounding area flickered to life above the holoprojector. More tapping outlined the port in bright blue and the vast, sprawling expanse of DeLond Forest to the east in red. The city proper, which lay spread out south of the port, was highlighted in light green.

Captain Dvorak cleared his throat and swept his hand over the mass of red-lined forest. "Wherever the DropShip comes down, these pirates will use the trees to mask their approach. DeLond is massive, but they will have to come at us from the east or northeast. So we'll form up in the grasslands here—" His hand shifted back to the broad area between the cool blue of the port and the ragged red outline of the woodlands. "—and let them come to us. These plains are open, and will give us the best fields of fire."

He extended a finger and pointed at a low rise positioned roughly in the middle of the largely flat fields separating the forest from the spaceport. "I'll anchor the north end of our line from this point. I want my *Thug* to be the first thing they see. If we're lucky, just seeing an assault 'Mech will be enough to scare them off. If not, I can take the brunt of their weapons fire and keep them focused on me while you all tear them to shreds."

"Turner, Singh, you're our long-range fire support. You'll take up positions south of me, here and here." The captain's thick index finger stabbed through the map twice in a line below where his 'Mech would be. "Your *Crusader* and *Trebuchet* will both mass-fire on targets I call out. Between your LRMs and the twin PPCs on my *Thug*, we should be able to chew deep into anyone who steps clear of the tree line."

Captain Dvorak leaned back to look at his noncommissioned officers and crossed his arms. "We need to keep them at distance. That's key. We don't yet know the strength or makeup of the enemy force, but we can deal the most damage by keeping them at arm's length. As they move out of the forest, we will fire and fall back, fire and fall back, all the way to the spaceport. If we can soften them up, maybe take down one or even two of their lance before they can close with us, I very much like our odds. If they try to bum rush us and close, though…" He drew a deep breath and blew it out in a rush of air. "Those odds I like a hell of a lot less."

Shifting his head, the captain's eyes flicked to the youngest MechWarrior present, and Zarek felt himself stand a little straighter. "Hanlon, that's where you come in. You will be here—" Dvorak uncoiled his thick arms and stabbed a finger into the map again. "—on the southernmost point of the line. Your position will also be the most mobile. As we shift the formation, you'll be swinging wide and watching our flank. You see anything out there, I expect you to harass them and keep them off us until we can adjust our position. Not much can match the speed of your *Cicada*, so if you get in over your head, disengage and get back to the line. Always stay under the umbrella of Turner and Singh's LRM fire. That way they can cover you if you get into a tight spot."

Dvorak paused to let his words sink in, then continued. "This next part is important, Hanlon, so listen up. If we get rushed, your job is to slow or disrupt their advance. Flank 'em, get in close, backstab, and get the hell out. If even one of 'em turns and chases you, it will give us the breathing room we need to fall back to our optimal range, stay in the fight, and stay alive."

The captain paused again and looked the young MechWarrior directly in the eye. "Can you handle that?"

Zarek rocked up onto the balls of his feet, pulled his shoulders back, and thrust out his chin, a smile splitting his youthful face. "Yes, sir. I can handle it."

"Good man." Dvorak gave a single sharp nod. "I know we can count on you." Then his mouth tightened into a thin white line. "But rest assured, you and I are going to have a long chat after this fight us over."

His composure wilting under the captain's hard gaze, Zarek swallowed past the lump in his suddenly dry throat and uttered a quiet "Aye, sir."

"That's it, then," Captain Dvorak said, once again addressing the whole of Red Stable, "Questions?" None of the other three MechWarriors replied, so he shut off the holoprojector, then stood and stretched with a groan and a series of audible pops cascading down his spine. He yawned wide and deep and shook his head. "I really wish they would've picked the afternoon for a raid."

With a quick glance at his watch, he snapped, "All right, get your 'Mechs fired up. I want us out there and in position in forty-five minutes."

Less than three quarters of an hour later, the BattleMechs of Red Stable, all painted deep crimson with a trio of intricately detailed white horses galloping across the left breast, stood like a quartet of giant metal monoliths rising from a sea of waving grass.

Of the four 'Mechs, only two displayed any movement. The stubby wings of Zarek's small, birdlike *Cicada* twitched, and the toes of its armored feet cut furrows in the soil, betraying his anxiousness as he shifted his weight back and forth. On the opposite end of Red Stable's position, Captain Dvorak's *Thug* stood atop a low rise in the plains, its massive frame, hunched shoulders, and overly long arms slowly turning as the commander surveyed the distant tree line. The pair of 'Mechs standing between the small, nervous bird and the hulking metal ape were more humanoid in configuration, and both Sergeant Turner's *Crusader* and Corporal Singh's *Trebuchet* remained completely still while awaiting orders.

Minute after minute stretched on with no sign of the pirate lance. The Red Stable comm channel remained silent as well, save Captain Dvorak's intermittent statements of "Steady."

Zarek obsessively cycled through his visual scan modes, looking for any indication the bandit force had moved within striking distance of the plains. He suddenly leaned forward against the restraining straps in his seat as his eyes caught the briefest flash of color between distant, dark tree trunks before it was gone again. Boosting his radar gain and maxing out his magnification, he focused on that patch of land deep in the forest. Staring hard, he waited. Then the color flashed again.

"Contact! Contact, Captain!" Zarek's voice cracked as adrenaline surged through him and embarrassment flushed his cheeks. He prayed the radio static hid how nervous he was. "I've got a magscan hit in the trees, bearing zero-six-five degrees and moving fast, about a klick and a half out."

"Good copy, Hanlon," the captain's deep voice came back in his headset, "You've got sharp eyes, son."

Relief flooded through the young MechWarrior, and he let out the breath he'd been holding.

"Look alive, Red Stable," Dvorak said. "We've got contact from the lead pirate element at zero-six-five. Go ahead and pivot north twenty-five degrees off my position. Hanlon, keep watching that tree line to our east."

Zarek drifted his *Cicada* forward in line with Turner and Singh, but kept his eyes glued to the blob of color coming toward them through the forest. It was moving fast, very fast, and as it closed on the thinning tree line, Zarek could pick out details of its small, bobbing outline.

"Captain, I can ID the bandit as a *Locust*. It looks alone, no other contacts I can see. Fifteen seconds till it's in range, if it holds course."

"Copy that, Hanlon," came the reply. "Stick to the plan, people. Prepare to engage."

The *Locust* hooked a sharp left as it reached the very edge of the woodland and sprinted across the front of Red Stable's position, dodging in and out of the sparse evergreens lining the edge of the plains. Hanlon's crosshairs flashed red as he tracked the path of the small, speeding BattleMech running well outside his maximum range. Static cracked his neurohelmet headset a half second before Captain Dvorak's voice broke through the Red Stable's comm channel.

"Turner. Singh. Burn that scout."

Sergeant Turner's *Crusader* responded immediately, but the slight pause in Amata's reply told Zarek she had the same thought he did: this was a waste of ammo, with the *Locust* moving at that speed. But the corporal's "Aye, sir" came regardless.

From Zarek's left, the *Crusader* and *Trebuchet* took a few strides forward before letting loose with a double volley of long-range missiles each, the upper torsos and arms of both 'Mechs vanishing momentarily in a haze of missile exhaust. The quadruple flights arced up and away from the Red Stable lance, and even with both Singh and Turner leading the fast-moving *Locust*, Zarek could tell the barrage would have little, if any, effect.

As if sensing their approach, the light 'Mech's pilot put on a burst of speed just before the missiles impacted, launching the *Locust* forward as the ground behind it erupted. Sixty missiles arrowed down, littering the edge of the forest with a wave of explosions, balls of fire leveling trees and scooping great divots out of the earth just on the *Locust*'s heels. Only three missiles scored hits, but none slowed the sprinting machine as it continued along the curved edge of the woods, never venturing fully out into the open grassland.

"Dammit. Cease fire," came Dvorak's order. He paused as the small 'Mech sped toward the southeast, farther and farther away from the spaceport. "Let 'em go. Hold your positions and wait for the rest of the lance. Hanlon, watch our flank and make sure they don't try to slip in behind us."

A chorus of affirmatives filled the commline, and both the *Crusader* and the *Trebuchet* backpedaled until they returned to their original positions.

Zarek watched his radar as the red arrow representing the bandit *Locust* continued its long arcing run away from the Red Stable line. He was about to turn his attention back to the forest when he noticed sudden movement on his secondary screen.

The *Locust* abruptly cut to the right, and in the moment Zarek thought the 'Mech would turn again to swing into the rear of their formation, he almost keyed his mic to call Captain Dvorak. But the bandit made no second turn northward and instead continued sprinting due west. Zarek watched in silence as the red arrow moved closer and closer to the green-highlighted area denoting the city.

"Wait," Zarek said to no one but himself as the red blade pierced the green line and plunged deep into the heart of the residential district. "Wait wait wait, no." His hands clamped down on the controls, and he spun his *Cicada* on the spot to face the city. Even without bumping up the magnification, he could see fireballs from explosions rise above the low rooftops.

"Captain Dvorak! The *Locust* has breached the city!"

"Understood," came the immediate reply, "Maintain surveillance on our flank, and let me know if it tries to sneak in behind us."

"Sir, I don't know if I was clear," Zarek stammered, taken aback. "The city is under attack. I—I can see the fires, sir."

"I said 'understood,' Hanlon. Now face your 'Mech forward and keep watching our ass. We don't know where the remainder of the pirate lance is."

Moving his controls unconsciously to the order, Zarek slowly turned his *Cicada* in place until he was once again looking at the forest. Sitting frozen in his seat, mouth working wordlessly as he tried to make sense of the captain's orders, a full thirty seconds passed before he could form a coherent thought.

"Sir, I—we have to do something. People are dying."

"And that's not our concern, Hanlon. We're contracted for port protection, nothing more. The city has its own security force. They'll sort it out."

Exasperation flowed into Zarek's voice. "Captain, sir, all they have are rifles and a pair of ancient armored cars. Even if they could do any real damage, that *Locust* will run rings around them. We have to—"

"Can it, Hanlon!" Dvorak shot back, irritation rising in his tone. "There's still most of a lance out there and we're not getting paid to protect the city. This discussion is over."

Zarek started to object, but then Amata's voice came through the comm. "Listen to Cap, kid. You know that's not our job. Just take a deep breath and stick to the task at hand."

"I can't just let them *die*!" Zarek yelled back, "Somebody has to help them, and we're in a position to do it!" He wheeled his 'Mech around again, pointing the *Cicada*'s blunt nose back toward the fires in the city.

Anger flooded the commline as the captain's patience broke like a dam. "Enough! Resume your station, MechWarrior! *Now*, goddammit! That is an order!"

"No!" Zarek shouted back into the mic. "They need our help!"

"Don't you dare, you little sh—"

"Captain!" Sergeant Turner's voice suddenly cut in and over-rode the rest.

Zarek gritted his teeth and jammed the throttle forward, sending his 'Mech bounding southward away from the Red Stable's line.

"Hanlon! Hanlon, you get the hell back here!"

"Wait, kid!" Amata called out after him. "Stop! What are you doing?"

"Captain!" Sergeant Turner's voice cut in again, more urgent this time. "I read th—"

The babble of voices abruptly cut off and silence filled Zarek's headset as he stabbed his hand down and switched off his comm. Maxing out his speed, he drove the *Cicada*'s long legs into a full, loping sprint toward the city's outskirts.

The point where the *Locust* had entered the city streets was obvious: the back half of a bulk hauler was ripped apart, its contents spilled wildly over the street, and a four-story apartment building was engulfed in flames. Terror tore through the crowd of emergency workers and Good Samaritans at Zarek's approach, but the screams turned to cheers as they recognized his 'Mech's coloring and the galloping horses emblazoned on the left side of his *Cicada*'s torso.

He dove into the tunnel of destruction left by the smaller bandit 'Mech and followed a long passage marked by shattered glass, gutted vehicles, and burning shops and apartments scarred by careless sprays of bullets and laser fire.

Zarek was so focused on closing the distance between him and the pirate that he was caught completely by surprise when the *Locust* stepped out of a narrow alley and unloaded on him just as the *Cicada* was sprinting past.

Heavy-caliber machine-gun bullets tore parallel lines of deep divots in the hardened ferroglass of the *Cicada*'s cockpit, rattling and almost deafening Zarek, but the armored viewport withstood the onslaught. The *Locust*'s medium laser slashed across the *Cicada*'s belly, leaving a molten scar. Zarek wrestled with the controls as his 'Mech stumbled backward, off balance from the viciousness of the surprise attack and loss of armor, and the *Cicada* smashed against the green-glass and red-brick facade of the office building across the street.

In the seconds it took him to fully recover, the pirate spun their light 'Mech around and sprinted away, disappearing down an empty side street.

"You're mine!" Zarek snarled as he levered his *Cicada* back to its feet and took off in pursuit.

The two birdlike 'Mechs tore through the tight streets of the residential quarter in a high-speed game of cat and mouse. While they were matched for speed, the *Locust*'s smaller profile allowed the bandit to cut tighter corners and work their 'Mech down narrower alleyways, repeatedly forcing Zarek to sprint to the next block to find a wider cross street.

Building after building flashed by his cockpit with barely enough time for their reflection to show in his viewport before they were behind him. Small gaps marking streets and alleys showed him tantalizing glimpses of the smaller 'Mech, but never with enough time to line up a shot. Gritting his teeth, the young MechWarrior urged every last meter of speed from the *Cicada* and focused on trying to close the gap between the two machines.

Suddenly, the walls of high apartment buildings lining the streets ended as the tangled web of side streets opened onto a broad, multilane thoroughfare. Zarek and the bandit emerged into the urban clearing simultaneously, only thirty meters apart and much to the surprise of both MechWarriors.

Zarek reacted first, snap-firing all three of his lasers at the smaller 'Mech. One of his medium lasers slashed an angry scar down the *Locust*'s jutting torso, but the other two beams shot wide as the pirate recovered and danced their small machine to the side. Then, clearly aware they were outgunned in a straight-up fight, the bandit 'Mech spun on its heel and leaped forward into a full sprint, eager to put as much space between it and its larger cousin as possible.

"Oh, no you don't," Zarek muttered, baring his teeth in a feral snarl as he jammed his throttle bar all the way forward to send his 'Mech off pounding afterward.

The pirate dodged off the thoroughfare and back into the side streets, the *Locust*'s birdlike legs pumping in frenzied circles as the bandit took the turn at more than 120 kph. The 'Mech's clawed feet sparked as they skidded and tore across the ferrocrete. Zarek's *Cicada* followed immediately behind, cutting the corner so close he flattened a hoverbus stop and a nearby streetlamp.

Zarek hammered his thumb down on the trigger just as the smaller 'Mech came into view, but again the bandit showed their skill, juking the sprinting machine hard to the left at the last second.

"Dammit!" Zarek snarled as heat flooded his cockpit and he watched his lasers burn a trio of deep furrows into the ferrocrete where the *Locust* had been.

The green and red beams continued on, slicing through the curb and across the sidewalk before drilling through the front wall of a deli. Glass and debris exploded out of the store front as the lasers touched off something inside the building, leaving behind the flicker of flames. Sprinting his 'Mech at full speed down the street, Zarek only had a half second to think about the damage before it flashed behind him, and his attention fixed once more on the small 'Mech trying to escape.

Looking ahead down the long street the two 'Mechs traveled, Zarek saw they were approaching a series of alleys, and he knew his window was rapidly closing. He took careful aim at the fleeing *Locust*'s back, and as soon as his weapons cycled, he depressed his right thumb stud, and the *Cicada*'s small laser flared to life. The thin ruby beam flashed just wide of the light 'Mech's stubby right wing as the bandit pilot once again lurched the sprinting *Locust* sideways to avoid the shot. This time, however, Zarek was ready.

Having already shifted his remaining weapons to the middle of the street, the young MechWarrior shouted "Yes!" as the *Locust*'s momentum carried itself left across the avenue and directly into his targeting reticle. The crosshairs flashed gold, and he jerked his triggers, goosing the smaller 'Mech with his pair of medium lasers. Intense green light from both beams speared the back of the *Locust*'s right leg. The first beam sliced deep through the armor from the hip down over the thigh before winking out, but the second struck lower, scything through the entire ankle assembly of the sprinting machine.

Moving at well over 100 kph, the *Locust* met its demise quickly. The 'Mech's birdlike foot flew free, propelled like a cannonball a block and a half down the street, where it caved in the back of a hoverbus. Even the skill of the bandit pilot could not save the machine this time as it stepped down onto the glowing stump of its right leg. The *Locust* lurched hard to the right and careened into the side of the apartment building it was sprinting past. The 'Mech's small right wing tore a deep furrow into the brick facade, ripping the stubby appendage and its machine gun free in a hail of sparks and staccato pops. The impact spun the *Locust* off its remaining foot and violently rolled the 'Mech's spindly body across the face of the building, crushing armor panels all over its angled torso. Still airborne, the *Locust* twirled with sickening speed back into the middle of the avenue. A ring of light encircled the cockpit, and small, controlled explosions blasted the cockpit roof free a split second before the pilot's ejection seat rocketed into the sky.

Zarek's eyes traced the path of the chair—both pilot and ejection seat spun madly as they arced up and back toward the grasslands and

the forest beyond—then his attention snapped back down in front of him with a curse as he had to dance his *Cicada* around the *Locust*'s limp, flailing legs. The now-dead machine continued on its path across the street and smashed through the windowed front of a salon before finally coming to rest. Chunks of wood, plaster, and ferrocrete cascaded into the street, partially burying the ravaged upper torso of the light 'Mech as burst pipes sprayed water out in long streams.

Pulling sharply back on the throttle, Zarek slowed his 'Mech to a walk before stopping alongside the sparking, smoking remnants of the *Locust* and taking a deep, shuddering breath to slow his racing heart. The air in the cockpit tasted of ozone and still radiated heat from his last laser barrage.

From somewhere at the farthest reaches of his hearing, rising in the background over the faint mechanical whir of moving actuators and the low, deep thrum of the *Cicada*'s fusion engine, Zarek picked up a faint staccato sound, irregular and muffled by the armored walls of his cockpit. He listened. Whatever it was, it was getting louder.

Reaching down, he toggled the external mic pickup, and a roar of applause filled his headset. His eyes flicked away from the corpse of the *Locust*, and he saw townspeople filling nearly every doorway and window of the nearby buildings, all of them clapping and whistling, the bravest souls spilling out into the street to crowd around the downed 'Mech, celebrating with their crimson savior like the kill was their own.

A wide smile broke across his face, and tension released across his shoulders. Collapsing back in his seat, Zarek cleared his throat, keyed his mic, and said, "Captain, this is Hanlon. Scratch one *Locust*."

Silence.

"Captain Dvorak, this is Hanlon. The *Locust* is down, sir."

More silence.

"Captain?" Zarek's face scrunched up in a quizzical mask. Then, realization hit home and he felt his stomach drop. "Oh, no. Oh, God," he whispered. His comm system. He had shut it off.

In a panic, Zarek searched for the switch to toggle his comm back on. He stabbed his index finger down when he found the button and snapped it into the *ON* position. An explosion of sound buffeted his ears as desperate terror suddenly replaced dead air.

Shouts. Orders. Curses. The voices of Red Stable fighting for their lives. All punctuated by the muffled roar of missiles leaving their launch tubes and bursts of static from PPC fire.

"—place! Displace! Get the hell back to the wall—"

"—trying to turn us! Watch your right, Si—"

"—ey're pushing! They're pushing!"

Zarek instinctively jerked his controls to spin his 'Mech around before slamming his throttle full open, sending the mass of cheering townspeople diving back to cover as the *Cicada* darted forward into a flat-out sprint.

"Captain, this is Hanlon! I'm inbound! Three minutes out!"

But Zarek's call was lost in the mix of frantic voices and crosstalk.

"—is down! Focus fire on the—"

"—take much more! I need help he—"

"—too fast! I can't get them off me!"

The raw, desperate terror of the Red Stable commline taunted Zarek as he drove his *Cicada* hard back through the maze of crisscrossing city streets toward the spaceport. Distant plumes of dark smoke were visible between the buildings, rising ominously into the afternoon sky. Zarek pushed his machine to a point he had never known, trying to eke every last bit of speed from the 'Mech.

"—ammit! Just hold on! We—"

"—move it! Get out of there—"

"—ap! Help! Please!"

At almost 130 kph, the dark-red *Cicada* burst from between the last of the residential buildings and out onto the flat, grassy plain surrounding the edge of the city. Zarek's 'Mech ate up a dozen meters with every bounding stride as he steered it on the fastest path back to the port. Making the last turn around the southeastern corner of the spaceport wall, he toggled his viewport magnification and zoomed in on the source of the thickest smoke.

"Oh, God," he moaned.

Countless craters and small fires littered a broad swath of blackened plain, the soil torn up in long, looping circles from the wide feet of multiple heavy 'Mechs, marking the site where Red Stable had made their last stand.

Tight tendrils of smoke rose from three smoldering, dull gray-brown mounds spread out at intervals across a 300-meter arc before the spaceport wall, all that was left of the raiding force. The closest pirate 'Mech was smashed almost flat, as if danced on by raging giants, and next to it stood the two largest Red Stable 'Mechs: Captain Dvorak's *Thug*, its entire right side shredded and missing an arm, and Sergeant Turner's *Crusader*, charred black from its knees to the tops of its broad shoulders. Both 'Mechs were locked rigid, and Zarek could tell even from a distance their cockpit hatches were open.

Zarek's eyes panned toward the wall, and his unconscious flinch almost sent his sprinting 'Mech tripping headlong over itself.

"Oh, God" was again all he could say.

Propped up in a sitting position against the thick ferrocrete of the spaceport's defensive wall lay what remained of Corporal Singh's *Trebuchet*. The missile boat's right arm was severed and lay at the 'Mech's feet, and the left arm was melted clean away above the wrist.

Craters from a large-caliber autocannon had stitched a jagged line across the armor of the medium 'Mech's upper chest, ending at the lower edge of the cockpit, where the last round had penetrated and blown a hole clear out the back of the machine's head. The polarized cockpit viewport was dark and still, but a swarm of white-suited medtechs and emergency personnel moved over and around it like a frenzied army of red-crossed ants. Mixed in with the white were the dusty red overalls of Red Stable's support personnel, already rallied to offer any aid they could.

Zarek slowed his *Cicada* to a stop 100 meters from the downed 'Mech, and locked it in a standing position before switching the engine into standby. After unclipping his harness and dumping his neurohelmet into the seat, he opened the cockpit hatch, and the sharp smell of ozone and carbon filled his nose. He did not even make it halfway down the retractable chain-link ladder before the shouting started.

"Where the goddamn hell were you?!" Captain Dvorak roared, stalking through the blackened hellscape in nothing but his cooling vest, shorts, and armored boots. The right side of his head and neck were covered in blood, matting his dark hair and beard into jagged crimson-black spikes. "You left us! I gave you *a direct order*, and you left us to die!"

Zarek dropped the last meter down to the ground and turned, sputtering to answer, but the captain did not wait or pause his advance. Striding right up to Zarek, Dvorak pistoned his palms into the young man's chest, dumping him hard on his back beneath the legs of his 'Mech. Even with the heavy ballistic cloth of his cooling vest to cushion the fall, the breath was driven out of Zarek's lungs and he croaked and gasped as he rolled into a ball on the ground, looking up at his hulking commander looming over him.

Dvorak's eyes blazed with rage, and Zarek was sure in that moment the captain would have throttled him if given the chance, but the tall, gaunt form of Sergeant Turner materialized as if from nowhere and held him back. Turner's long-fingered hands seized Dvorak by the shoulders, and the words exchanged were too soft for Zarek to hear.

Captain Dvorak locked eyes with his second-in-command for a long second then broke away, jerking free of his grip and casting his head to the heavens as he struggled to master himself. He took a deep, ragged breath, then ran his tongue over his teeth and spat on the ground. Spearing Zarek with a gaze of utter contempt, he shook his head.

"You're out. You're done. Get your shit and get out of the barracks. I never want to see you again." He spat again and threw his arms wide as he backed away. "I hope it was worth it." Then he turned and strode off without another glance, leaving Zarek slumped in the burnt dirt and broken grass under the shadow of his 'Mech.

Zarek watched him go and then slowly stood, brushing charred earth off his damp skin in mottled streaks of black and brown. His gaze flicked to Sergeant Turner, who stood silent and ramrod straight as always only a few meters away. His hard, dark eyes pierced Zarek's, ice cold to the captain's fire, and Zarek knew there was no mercy there.

"You've forfeited any salvage, but we will cash out the end of your contract," Turner said, his voice curt and honed like a razor. "You'll have a marker waiting for you at the DuraPaq office in the port within the hour. Turn in your uniforms before you leave and—" He stabbed a long finger at the blunt shoulder of the *Cicada* looming over Zarek's head. "—strip those stallions off your 'Mech. You don't deserve 'em."

He started to turn away, but Zarek held out a hand. "Wait," he said. "Where am I supposed to go?"

Turner paused, his face remaining chiseled and impassive. His granite facade finally cracking, he scoffed and tossed a small shrug back in Zarek's face. "We don't care," he replied, and then the sergeant, too, turned his back on the young MechWarrior, and walked away to help the captain direct the emergency and salvage crews.

Zarek didn't dare approach the broken form of Amata's 'Mech, or the mix of bright-white and dusky-red forms swarming over it, and he lingered in the blackened grass near the feet of his *Cicada* for only a few minutes before the dagger-eyed stares of Red Stable's support staff grew too much to bear.

He walked his 'Mech back inside the spaceport walls mechanically, with little thought and no clear idea where to go, finally finding a space just large enough to park between two stacks of shipping containers near the far corner of the port facilities center, though still uncomfortably close to the barracks housing the remnants of Red Stable.

After snapping switches through the shutdown sequence, Zarek popped his five-point safety harness as soon as the deep, soft rumbling of the fusion engine at the heart of his *Cicada* quieted. Then he lifted the heavy weight of his neurohelmet off his head and shoulders, and gently placed it in the storage space above his seat before pulling on coveralls emblazoned with three racing horses for the last time. Soft noise flooded the cockpit as he cracked open the back hatch and crawled out, the purr of combustion engines as the port's IndustrialMechs loaded freight and the blaring of faint sirens in the distance, all punctuated by intermittent *ping*s of hot metal from his cooling 'Mech.

He climbed wearily down the side of his *Cicada*, avoiding the charred, still-warm scars left by the *Locust*, and then warily looked out across the tarmac for any Red Stable personnel. Seeing no one, he jogged off to collect what few possessions he had.

Less than twenty minutes later, Zarek, now in an old, wrinkled pair of khaki cargo pants and an undershirt, stood in front of his 'Mech and stared up at a dripping smear of black paint someone had dumped over the insignia on the *Cicada*'s left breast. From the spray of dark blobs splashed over the blunt, forward-jutting head of the machine, it was clear whoever had done this had also tried to hastily throw the rest of the paint over the cockpit canopy. Fortunately, though, most of the paint had missed the ferroglass panels and the sensor arrays around the canopy. He didn't bother to see if the vandal had stuck around to watch him discover the mess; instead, he just shouldered his small bag and walked toward the massive building that dominated the southwestern portion of the spaceport complex.

Forty minutes later, he was sitting alone in the lobby of DuraPaq Solutions' spaceport office, watching a steady stream of better-dressed people check in at reception and be swiftly shown through the opaque sliding doors behind a pair of bored-looking contract security guards.

Finally, a stern-faced woman in a very expensive suit emerged from the inner offices and walked up to the man at the reception desk. She leaned in to whisper to him and tossed something onto the desk. Then, shooting Zarek a single look of disdain, she strode back through the double doors without another word.

Zarek was already starting to stand when the receptionist cleared his throat and said, "Mr. Hanlon?"

As Zarek reached the desk, the man was holding out a small black fob with DURAPAQ emblazoned on the side in bold, gold letters. "Here is an electronic payment marker for the remainder of your contract. Take it to the banking establishment of your choice, and they will transfer the funds to any account you wish. Would you like to confirm the balance while you're here?"

"No, that's fine," Zarek replied as he pocketed the device. He paused a moment and said, "Is…is there anyone here I could talk to about, maybe, getting a new contract? Nothing big, I mean, it's just me, but…I dunno. Maybe something like a security contract for the offseason?"

The receptionist visibly cringed and cast a look back over his shoulder at the dark double doors. "I am sorry, Mr. Hanlon," he said, again looking over his shoulder, "Ms. Johansson wanted me to tell you, explicitly, that you have no future here at DuraPaq or any of our subsidiaries on Dalcour. Captain Dvorak made sure of that in his communications with the company." The receptionist chewed his lip, and Zarek saw genuine pity in his eyes. "You have been blacklisted."

Bracing his hands wide on the polished composite top of the desk, Zarek sagged forward, his head bowed. As he stood there unmoving, he heard the rapid scribble of pen on paper and a soft rip. Suddenly, an off-white square of DuraPaq stationery slid into view. The receptionist cleared his throat again, and Zarek looked up with red-rimmed eyes.

"This is my cousin's number," he whispered, quiet and fast. "She and her kids live only a block and a half from where you killed that bandit. It's all everybody in town is talking about. Give her a call. She owns a warehouse just outside the port, and I promise she'll let you store your 'Mech there for next to nothing. If you wait, just till the freight prices drop after the end of the season, I think you have enough on that marker to get you and your 'Mech off-world. Maxwell is close, and the Planetary Defense Consortium is always hiring factory security or test pilots to pit their tanks against."

"I—" Zarek's voice choked off as his throat closed up. He broke eye contact and gingerly picked up the square of paper, folding it once and placing it reverently into his pocket. "Thank you," he said softly, and then turned away from the desk, slung his bag over his shoulder, and started to walk out of the lobby.

He stopped short, though, just before the door, and turned on his heel back toward the reception desk.

"Hey," he said. "Can I use your phone?"

SHRAPNEL

ALB-6U ALBATROSS

Mass: 95 tons
Chassis: Albat-75 Composite
Power Plant: GM 380 XL
Cruising Speed: 43 kph
Maximum Speed: 64 kph
Jump Jets: None
    Jump Capacity: None
Armor: Jolassa 328 Ferro-Fibrous with CASE II
Armament:
    1 Zeus Slingshot Gauss Rifle
    1 Fusigon Shorttooth Light PPC
    1 Irian Weapons Works V7 LRM-15 Rack
    1 Irian Weapons Works 60mm SRM-6 Rack
    1 Diverse Optics Type 57 Large Variable-Speed Pulse Laser
    2 Diverse Optics Sunbeam Extended-Range Medium Lasers
Manufacturer: Irian BattleMechs Unlimited
    Primary Factory: Washburn
Communications System: Irian Technologies HMR-35s
Targeting & Tracking System: Omicron TrackerKeeper

For a shining moment, the *Albatross* pointed the way to a bright new future as the signature BattleMech of the noble Knights of the Inner Sphere. The 'Mech's glorious reputation died with the Knights and their idealism early in the Jihad, and the *Albatross* came to represent the shame of the shattered Free Worlds League more than the dream of renewal. It remained a potent-enough battlefield presence to avoid total obscurity, with a series of variants walking off the factory floor of Irian BattleMechs' Washburn plant and into the inventory of the Army of the Marik-Stewart Commonwealth, though demand for export sales proved limited. Mobile and powerful, if temperamental, the *Albatross*' solid performance during the AMSC's doomed campaign to hold off Operation Hammerfall rehabilitated the 'Mech's reputation just as the re-formed Free Worlds League was forced to cede the factory to the nascent Wolf Empire.

Capabilities

The modern ALB-6U *Albatross* combines solid all-range firepower with impressive speed for its size, a feat accomplished by relying on a fragile composite structure and an extra-light gyro. It often serves as a bodyguard in Marik heavy fire-support lances, where the grand bird's hollow bones are less of a liability. In this role, the 'Mech can ably contribute to ranged bombardments while the lasers and SRMs suffice to discourage raiders or cover the lance's retreat. MechWarriors must be mindful to withdraw from any brawl once the thick outer armor is breached.

Battle History

During the Commonwealth Secession Crisis of 3119, *Albatross*es fought on both sides of the clashes on Midkiff. Pro-independence insurgents seized several older models from a Militie National armory, while the Atrean Hussars deployed their newly issued ALB-6U's to suppress the disorder. An infamous photograph of an AMSC *Albatross* standing over a downed rebel counterpart amid the ruins of a playground in a municipal park helped turn public opinion in the Marik-Stewart Commonwealth against further military occupation of the secessionist worlds. More pragmatic Commonwealth operational analysts studied the vulnerabilities of the ALB-6U during the street clashes to learn how to deploy this variant for maximum effectiveness in later, more symmetrical conflicts.

Operation Hammerfall landed squarely on the Thirteenth Atrean Dragoons during the Battle of Uhuru. Facing off against the Fourth Lyran Regulars, the Dragoons' *Albatross*es initially acquitted themselves well, weathering repeated raids by lighter forces and racking up several kills. As attrition mounted, *Albatross*es were rotated into the regiment's depleted heavy-cavalry formations. Though able to keep pace with the *Juliano*s leading these formations, the *Albatross*es eventually crumpled under concentrated fire, and left their more resilient lancemates exposed. Only one company of the Thirteenth survived the disastrous final charge on Uhuru.

Variants

The ALB-5W was built at the behest of the Word of Blake during the Jihad, serving most infamously as the basis for Precentor Dantalion's custom command 'Mech. The ALB-5U sought to maintain the 5W's robustness while appealing to the new AMSC. The high-survivability internal components left the ALB-5U with underwhelming firepower, prompting IrTech to fall back on the revised ALB-4Ur model while development progressed on the fragile but heavily armed ALB-6U.

Clan Wolf's migration to the Wolf Empire abandoned the only manufacturing site for the capable *Night Wolf* in their former occupation zone. A crash retooling of the Washburn factory produced the *Albatross C* as a replacement, but it proved a pale imitation of the rapidly dwindling original. Plans to mass-produce the derisively dubbed "Sooty Albatross" were shelved until Star Colonel Othar's desperate rearmament of the Wolf Empire, and even then, assignment to this "failed" model was thought to be an ill omen.

Notable 'Mechs and MechWarriors

Baron Zeruul: One of the many pirate lords scouring the independent worlds in former Marik territory in the early 32nd century, Zeruul cultivates a mystical, supernatural reputation to strike fear in the hearts of his victims. His *Albatross*, *Ferryman*, is in such an advanced state of disrepair that establishing its exact provenance is difficult. Zeruul's raids grew less frequent as the number of independent worlds dwindled after the Free Worlds League reunified, but no credible accounts of his death or capture have surfaced. The Baron's current whereabouts remain a mystery.

Knight Daniel Schulz: More renowned as a diplomat than a warrior, Knight Schulz served as Alys Rousset-Marik's personal envoy to her cousin Corrine Marik on several occasions, including the signing of the peace treaty that ended Operation Golden Dawn. To mark the sour occasion, Corrine gifted Schulz the first production model ALB-5U in mocking reference to the code name he used during his first mission to Atreus. To refuse the gift would have been impolitic, but Schulz then embarrassed the Captain-General by pointedly using the 'Mech during several Knightly pursuits of fugitives over the border into former Free Worlds League territory.

Type: **ALB-6U Albatross**
Technology Base: Inner Sphere
Tonnage: 95
Role: Brawler
Battle Value: 2,159

Equipment		Mass
Internal Structure:	Composite	5
Engine:	380 XL	20.5
Walking MP:	4	
Running MP:	6	
Jumping MP:	0	
Heat Sinks:	13 [26]	3
Gyro (XL):		2
Cockpit:		3
Armor Factor (Ferro):	293	16.5

	Internal Structure	Armor Value
Head	3	9
Center Torso	30	48
Center Torso (rear)		12
R/L Torso	20	28
R/L Torso (rear)		12
R/L Arm	16	32
R/L Leg	20	40

Weapons and Ammo	Location	Critical	Tonnage
Large VSP Laser	RA	4	9
2 ER Medium Lasers	RA	2	2
LRM 15	RT	3	7
SRM 6	RT	2	3
Light PPC	LT	2	3
Ammo (SRM) 15	LT	1	1
Ammo (LRM) 16	LT	2	2
Ammo (Gauss) 16	LT	2	2
CASE II	LT	1	1
Gauss Rifle	LA	7	15

Notes: Features the following Design Quirks: Bad Reputation, Easy To Maintain, Improved Targeting (Long).

Download the free record sheets for these 'Mechs at:
bg.battletech.com/shrapnel/

Type: **Albatross C "Sooty Albatross"**
Technology Base: Mixed Inner Sphere
Tonnage: 95
Role: Sniper
Battle Value: 2,885

Equipment		Mass
Internal Structure:	Composite	5
Engine:	380 XL	20.5
Walking MP:	4	
Running MP:	6	
Jumping MP:	4	
Heat Sinks:	15 [30]	5
Gyro (XL):		2
Cockpit:		3
Armor Factor (Ferro):	293	16.5

	Internal Structure	Armor Value
Head	3	9
Center Torso	30	48
Center Torso (rear)		12
R/L Torso	20	28
R/L Torso (rear)		12
R/L Arm	16	32
R/L Leg	20	40

Weapons and Ammo	Location	Critical	Tonnage
ER Large Pulse Laser (C)	RA	3	6
2 ER Medium Lasers (C)	RA	2	2
ATM 9 (C)	RT	4	5
Ammo (ATM) 21 (C)	LT	3	3
Plasma Cannon (C)	LT	1	3
Ammo (Plasma) 10 (C)	LT	1	1
Ammo (Gauss) 16 (C)	LT	2	2
CASE II	LT	1	1
Gauss Rifle (C)	LA	5	12
2 Jump Jets	RL	2	4
2 Jump Jets	LL	2	4

Notes: Features the following Design Quirks: Easy to Maintain, Improved Targeting (Long), Bad Reputation.

Download the free record sheets for these 'Mechs at:
bg.battletech.com/shrapnel/

Type: ALB-4Ur Albatross
Technology Base: Inner Sphere
Tonnage: 95
Role: Brawler
Battle Value: 1,893

Equipment		Mass
Internal Structure:		9.5
Engine:	380 XL	20.5
Walking MP:	4	
Running MP:	6	
Jumping MP:	0	
Heat Sinks:	13 [26]	3
Gyro:		4
Cockpit:		3
Armor Factor (Ferro):	293	16.5
	Internal Structure	Armor Value
Head	3	9
Center Torso	30	48
Center Torso (rear)		12
R/L Torso	20	28
R/L Torso (rear)		12
R/L Arm	16	32
R/L Leg	20	40

Weapons and Ammo	Location	Critical	Tonnage
Large Pulse Laser	RA	2	7
2 ER Medium Lasers	RA	2	2
LRM 15	RT	3	7
SRM 6	RT	2	3
Ammo (SRM) 15	LT	1	1
Ammo (LRM) 16	LT	2	2
Light PPC	LT	2	3
Ammo (LB-X) 20	LT	2	2
CASE	LT	1	.5
LB 10-X AC	LA	6	11

Notes: Features the following Design Quirks: Easy to Maintain, Improved Targeting (Long).

Download the free
record sheets for these 'Mechs at:
bg.battletech.com/shrapnel/

Type: **ALB-5U Albatross**
Technology Base: Inner Sphere
Tonnage: 95
Role: Brawler
Battle Value: 1,885

Equipment		Mass
Internal Structure:		9.5
Engine:	380 Light	31
Walking MP:	4	
Running MP:	6	
Jumping MP:	0	
Heat Sinks:	13 [26]	3
Gyro (Heavy-Duty):		8
Cockpit:		3
Armor Factor (Heavy Ferro): 293		15

	Internal Structure	Armor Value
Head	3	9
Center Torso	30	45
Center Torso (rear)		15
R/L Torso	20	30
R/L Torso (rear)		10
R/L Arm	16	32
R/L Leg	20	40

Weapons and Ammo	Location	Critical	Tonnage
Large X-Pulse Laser	RA	2	7
2 ER Medium Lasers	RA	2	2
MML 7	RT	4	4.5
Ammo (MML) 34/28	LT	2	2
ER Small Laser	LT	1	.5
Ammo (RAC) 45	LT	1	1
CASE	LT	1	.5
Rotary AC/2	LA	3	8

Notes: Features the following Design Quirks: Easy to Maintain, Improved Targeting (Long), Bad Reputation.

Download the free record sheets for these 'Mechs at:
bg.battletech.com/shrapnel/

Type: **ALB-5W Albatross**
Technology Base: Inner Sphere
Tonnage: 95
Role: Juggernaut
Battle Value: 2,370

Equipment		Mass
Internal Structure:		9.5
Engine:	380 Light	31
Walking MP:	4 (5)	
Running MP:	6 (8)	
Jumping MP:	0	
Heat Sinks:	13 [26]	3
Gyro (Heavy-Duty):		8
Cockpit:		3
Armor Factor (Heavy Ferro):	293	15

	Internal Structure	Armor Value
Head	3	9
Center Torso	30	45
Center Torso (rear)		15
R/L Torso	20	30
R/L Torso (rear)		10
R/L Arm	16	32
R/L Leg	20	40

Weapons and Ammo	Location	Critical	Tonnage
Large VSP Laser	RA	4	9
Medium Pulse Laser	RT	1	2
ER Medium Laser	RT	1	1
ER Small Laser	RT	1	.5
Medium Pulse Laser	LT	1	2
ER Medium Laser	LT	1	1
ER Small Laser	LT	1	.5
Guardian ECM Suite	LT	2	1.5
ER PPC	LA	3	7
PPC Capacitor	LA	1	1
TSM	CT/RL/LL	2/2/2	—

Notes: Features the following Design Quirks: Easy to Maintain, Improved Targeting (Long), Bad Reputation.

Download the free record sheets for these 'Mechs at:
bg.battletech.com/shrapnel/

SHRAPNEL

DRAWING THE SHORT STRAW

DAVID G. MARTIN

FOREST GRID 98-2 ALPHA
CADMUS CONTINENT
ILLYRIA
ILLYRIAN PROVINCE
MARIAN HEGEMONY
19 NOVEMBER 3150

From the cockpit of his *Albatross*, Lieutenant Senior Grade Gallan Ranton watched the *Neanderthal* raise its six ton hatchet and bring it down onto another massive tree branch. The branch splintered with a satisfying crunch as it crashed to the ground, and the BattleMech paused for a moment as its pilot admired his handiwork.

"I still don't get it," said Karral, the *Neanderthal*'s pilot. "Why did they send *us* on a scouting mission?" He moved his 'Mech forward and chopped at the next collection of low-hanging branches blocking their path. The trees in the forests of Illyria were enormous, towering beasts that dwarfed even BattleMechs, and clearing a path through them had proven a challenge. But Karral's BattleMech was uniquely up to the task.

"Because, Karral," Niesselee answered from the cockpit of her *Sirocco*, "they knew you were getting antsy to swing your hatchet at something, and they didn't want it to be them."

The rest of the lance chuckled at the comment, but Gallan refrained from participating in his soldiers' mirth. Instead, his attention was fixed on a screen that tracked their progress through the thick Cadmus megaforest via a sensor uplink provided by a DropShip in low orbit. In the six hours since they had left the main body of the Seventh Tamarind Regulars, his Bravo Lance had made painfully little progress toward their objective. This forest was just too thick for them to quickly make any real headway, but that did not mean they were behind schedule.

"How about it, Lieutenant?" Karral asked, pulling Gallan's attention away from the screen, "Why *did* they send us? Don't they know we're an assault formation?"

Gallan understood Karral's confusion. Bravo Lance was part of an assault battalion, so the decision to send a full lance of assault BattleMechs out on its own did seem strange, but Gallan had a hunch as to why the higher-ups had made the decision. Ever since the Tamarind forces had landed and started their march toward the capital, the Marians had been harassing them with medium-to-heavy maniples. A single lance of four 'Mechs venturing off on its own was a compelling target for a ten-'Mech maniple looking to deplete the invading force's fighting strength.

And more than that, it was clear that the Two Legio forces on Illyria were moving much more efficiently around the main continent's megaforests than the Tamarind forces. That meant there had to be hidden paths, passes through the forests the Marians were using to keep ahead of the invaders.

Still, that did not mean Gallan's people were in a good position. Bravo Lance sported a significant amount of firepower and armor, but trying to draw out what could be a full maniple of Marian Hegemony BattleMechs was a huge risk. Gallan had not taken the orders lying down: he had voiced many concerns to his company captain *and* battalion commander when they gave him the mission. But what was done was done. Their hands were tied, they'd said. They were all soldiers, they all had jobs, and sometimes that job included courting extreme danger.

Well, at least we're also bringing some extreme danger with us.

"Karral," Gallan ordered, "turn left up ahead and head for the nav point I just set. Looks like the woods thin out there for a short stretch, and I'd like to push your 'Mech as little as possible before we get where we're going."

Karral grumbled a complaint about Gallan not answering his question and muttered something about what the brass was likely to do with a goat behind a barn, then he turned his *Neanderthal* toward the indicated grid location and chopped more tree branches. The constant physical work would keep the hot-headed Karral in line for now, but Gallan knew the man was bothered by their orders.

"We're all on edge today," Toman said on their private channel as his *Awesome* fell into step beside Gallan's *Albatross*. "These orders stink all the way back to Tamarind."

Gallan did not admonish Toman, because he was right. Sending them out on their own was nothing but setting a hook with bait. Expensive, experienced bait, but bait nonetheless. And it was up to Gallan to get them all out of this alive, or as many as he could.

"Yes, Tom," Gallan replied, "but you and I both know what we're doing out here. Somewhere, out in these woods, there's probably a whole maniple watching, waiting until we get far enough from the main force that there's no hope we'll survive whatever they can do to us. That's when they will strike. There's only four of us. They will have the upper hand, no matter how it happens."

Toman was silent. There was nothing left to add.

"Okay, Lieutenant," Karral interrupted their side conversation. "Where to now?"

Gallan looked up to see Karral's *Neanderthal* approaching the nav point, a wake of downed branches and smaller trees behind him. Gallan set more nav points, forming a defensive semicircle near the clearing where all four BattleMechs could stand relatively close to one another, and sent the coordinates out to the rest of the lance.

"We break here for an hour. Eat. Drink. Stretch a bit, but stay in your cockpits and don't fully power down. There's no telling how long we'll be out here, so don't overdo it." Gallan said the last part for Karral's benefit.

"It's okay, Gallan," Toman said later, as they called back and forth to one another, their cockpit hatches popped to let in some fresh air.

"What's okay?" Gallan called back.

"It's not your fault we're out here. It's just what we got for drawing the short straw."

Gallan chuckled, but the attempt at humor did not lighten his mood. The foreboding sense that command had sent them out here to die was building, and he had to somehow hide it from the rest of his lance if any of them were to have a prayer of surviving what he knew was coming.

Short straw or not, before we're done on Illyria, some of us are going stay here. Permanently.

Gallan leaned back and closed his eyes, hoping his thought would not be prophetic.

Principes Rillius Krause studied the live data feed on the cockpit screen of his *Hercules*. The Free Worlds League forces had made steady progress through the megaforests of Cadmus in the week since their landings, and as yet the *legatus* had done little to delay the invaders' progress. While the Marians were outnumbered, Illyria was their planet, and as such belonged to *Caesar*.

Rillius had fought these Tamarind Regulars before, and he remembered being unimpressed by both their skill and grit. Had he not been wearing a neurohelmet, he would have spit in disgust that the Leaguers had succeeded in pushing the Legios back into the Hegemony so decisively and with speed. That would change, starting today.

"*Principes*, that lance is moving out on its own, away from the main body of the Tamarind advance," *Centurion* Cira reported the obvious interpretation of what Rillius witnessed on his screen.

Remote sensor stations still operated in that section of the forest, and what they currently showed Rillius confused him. The lance was moving slowly, heading southeast, while the main body of the Tamarind advance continued its drive toward Dalmatia, through the thick forest and the guerrilla ambushes of Tertia Cohors. The governor and the bulk of Two Legio was in Dalmatia now, save for a few heavier maniples from Secunda Cohors, Rillius' included, positioned near important choke points in the forest. If discovered, these paths would make the Tamarind Regulars' progress through the continent that much easier, and Rillius' job was to delay the advance.

"*Principes*—" Cira's voice sounded in Rillius' ear again.

"I heard you, *Centurion*," Rillius cut her off before she could say any more.

He said nothing further as he contemplated the errant lance striking out on its own. It had to be a scout lance looking for the kind of path his maniple was charged to protect and conceal. The Leaguers had likely heard about the hidden passes, like the Prima V pass Secunda Maniple currently defended, from locals disloyal to *Caesar* who erroneously thought the League was here to liberate them. No such fate would be granted those who betrayed the Hegemony. Rillius' mission was clear: hold the enemy's advance until help could arrive. The whole of Two Legio would sell their lives to that end. *And the lives of everyone on this planet, if we need to.*

"Secunda Maniple, prepare to move out," Rillius said into the comm.

Lights on a secondary screen turned from green standby mode to yellow ready mode as each BattleMech in his maniple acknowledged the order. All except for one.

"Cira, are you not ready to move out?" Rillius suspected she would fight him on this one. Their orders were to protect the Prima V pass through the forest, and while Rillius saw give in the spirit of those orders, Cira tended to go by the letter. Too often, however, she bordered on insubordination when it came to Rillius' interpretation of his orders.

"*Principes*," Cira began, her voice stolid, "I recommend leaving my century on station at Prima V."

"No, *Centurion*," Rillius responded in a firm tone. "You will follow my orders. These Tamarind Regulars need to be taught their place, and I will have them crushed without losing any of my maniple. The best way to ensure this is to overwhelm them. I don't know why I must continue to explain myself to you, but you *will* follow my orders and lead your century. Am I clear, Cira?"

"Yes, *Principes*," Cira replied, stiff but crisp.

While Rillius valued her skills as a *centurion* and a MechWarrior, he was growing tired of her insubordinate attitude, and doubted she would ever achieve higher rank.

"Secunda Maniple," Rillius called out, "set navs and proceed to target destinations. Attack order to follow."

Rillius watched from the cockpit of his *Hercules* as Secunda Maniple moved out, beaming with delight at his plan. His initiative would not go unnoticed among Two Legio's commanders, and soon, perhaps even before the Free Worlders were ejected from Illyria, Rillius Krause would be recognized for his worth.

Gallan stared out his cockpit at the empty buildings of a long-forgotten supply base. From the look of it, it had not seen use since before the Marians took over Illyria nearly a century ago. It was a strangely serene sight. The buildings, showing signs of wear, had begun to give way to the forest once more. The original perimeter line, where Bravo Lance stood to survey the 2,000-meter circle of relatively open area, was overgrown, and only identifiable by a marked thickness and density disparity between the previous forest edge and the trees that now dotted the depot. One of the buildings a few hundred meters away had lost its roof entirely to the branches of a tree that had somehow grown up from under the building.

"There's nothing here, Lieutenant," Karral said after the lance conducted their scans. And he was right.

"Are we sure this is the right place?" Niesselee asked.

"Affirmative," Gallan answered. "It was possible we might find something else here, and if there was a presence of some kind, command believed we could handle it. Let's take a closer look before we go, just to make sure, and we'll be on the way back in two hours."

Green indicator lights from Bravo Lance confirmed his orders as they picked their way through the abandoned depot. Gallan chose a spot on the grid to check out for himself and set his 'Mech toward it. The depot was all he had hoped for and less than he expected. Being sent on a wild goose chase for a secret path through the megaforest was not the worst thing that could have happened.

As his *Albatross* stomped through the depot's underbrush, the sense of total stillness stayed with him. The state of the trees and grass indicated the depot had not been visited by any vehicles or 'Mechs in many decades. As the lance moved farther into the ruins, Gallan noticed they were disturbing no animals. No game trailed away, speeding in fear from the behemoths stalking through their territory. No birds flew from hidden nests in the trees or from perches in the abandoned buildings.

We're not the first to have been here recently.

Gallan did not know how, but he felt it was the truth. That explained the stillness, the complete lack of any living thing here save the four pilots of Bravo Lance. Gallan was about to key in a silent order to withdraw via the way they came when Toman's cool, steady voice sounded over their channel.

"Gallan, we're not alone."

Gallan stopped his *Albatross* in its tracks as Toman's *Awesome* did the same. Toman faced the far side of the clearing, so Gallan could not see into the cockpit to get a sense of what the other pilot was doing.

"Spotters," Toman said, "two of them. A hundred meters past the woods. Caught a glint of something over there. Might be nothing, but..."

Gallan's sense of growing unease now had a target, which made it easier to grasp and force it into the background as he finished keying in his orders. The lance would finish its survey and leave via the route they had arrived, making no overt indication they had discovered any spotters. Several minutes passed as Karral and Niesselee both finished their sensor sweeps and Gallan continued through his course. Only Toman changed his planned route, keeping his *Awesome*'s heavy particle projection cannons ready to fire in the direction of the spotters, should the need arise.

Ten minutes later, Bravo Lance was back together at the abandoned depot's perimeter.

"Do you think they know we spotted them?" Gallan asked Toman as they withdrew deeper into the woods.

"Maybe, but I can't be sure. I know they didn't move. At least, if they *did* move, they're really good at not being seen."

"So it's a good bet the Marians know where we are."

"What was that all about anyway?" Karral asked, butting into the conversation on the lance's channel.

"We might have a tail," Gallan replied. "And if we do, it's time to figure out how far ahead of us the Marians are, and plan accordingly."

He looked to his right to see Karral's *Neanderthal* raise its hatchet into a defensive position and twist its torso slowly to the left and right. Karral was on the hunt now.

"I like that idea, Lieutenant," he said, and Gallan could hear the other man's toothy, grinned expression over the comm. "I like that idea a lot."

"Update," Rillius grumbled into the comm. His mood was souring with every passing moment. A ten-man infantry contubernium had spotted the Tamarind Regulars lance near the old supply depot by, and the report was not as favorable as he had hoped.

A bloody assault lance is traipsing around the forest! What are these madmen thinking?!

"They are continuing along the reverse course that took them to the depot," Cira reported. "It appears their mission was to scout the facility as a possible active base, and having found it empty, they are marching back to rejoin their unit."

Her lighter century of five 'Mechs currently occupied a forward position ahead of Rillius' heavier command century, and had been able to get eyes on the Tamarind lance to confirm its size. It was only a mild surprise that the entire lance was assault 'Mechs. The Seventh Tamarind Regulars were known for their assault 'Mechs, but still, Rillius *had* been expecting this lance to be from the battalion of mostly medium chassis. The presence of four such assault machines, combined with the advantageous circumstances, presented Rillius a unique opportunity, and he intended to make the most of it.

All of that still did little to temper his rising mood, however. The only assault 'Mech in his maniple was *Legionnaire* Herra's *Cyclops*. There was no conceivable way to engage the enemy lance without some losses to his maniple, and that stung his pride. He did not care so much for the risk to his soldiers. They were his to wager in battle as he saw fit. But he still hated the thought of losing combat resources. Still, a ten-versus-four situation was great odds, and Rillius was committed to his course. Backing down now would validate Cira's belief that this whole venture had been a bad idea, and Rillius was not about to lose face to the rest of his maniple and prove her right. Victory for the Hegemony was the only way forward. Victory, and glory.

"Prepare to engage," Rillius said on the Secunda Maniple comm channel. "Century Prima will form up with me and approach the enemy from the south, with Century Secunda moving ahead of their route. We will catch them in an engagement between the two sides, one from the front, and one from the flank. Century Secunda will engage first, and Century Prima will join once battle is engaged."

"*Principes*," Cira predictably began her objection, "this risk is higher than we originally thought. It would be irresponsible to—"

"It would be irresponsible to allow such a potent enemy fighting force to continue operating in our territory unchecked," Rillius interrupted her.

"But *Principes*—"

"*Enough!*" he chided, openly rebuking Cira over the channel. If she would challenge him in the open, he would openly put her in her place in return. Rillius was done with her questions. "Century Secunda *will* follow my commands," he ordered. "Is that clear?"

"Yes, *Principes*." Cira's answer was short and cold.

Rillius did not care to know her thoughts on the matter any further, and if...*if*...she managed to follow his orders and survive the coming battle, he *might* consider not formally reprimanding her.

"Now," he continued in a more measured tone, "take your century ahead and cut them off here." He created a nav point on the grid screen that was visible to the whole maniple. "Engage the enemy when they come into view and hold them at this position until Prima flanks them from the south. Then we will move in and crush them with numbers. Should they retreat, we will drive them toward the depot, and away from any of their friendly support."

Cira and the rest of the maniple indicated their understanding of the plan with green-light indicator lights on their respective positions on Rillius' map display.

He nodded. "Good."

"Glory to *Caesar* and the Hegemony!" Rillius yelled into his comm.

"Gloria Caesar!" the maniple yelled back in response.

And, once this battle is won, Gloria Rillius Krause.

"How would you do it?" Gallan asked.

"Two groups, in front and to the south," Toman answered without hesitation. "They want us to fall back toward the depot, away from the rest of our battalion. Isolate and destroy. Simple. Easy. We're never heard from again."

Toman was not wrong. That was how Gallan would've done it.

Intermittent sensor blips over the past hour had given away that Bravo Lance was being shadowed by a force of BattleMechs. They estimated it as large as a maniple, but that was mostly conjecture.

"A stand-up fight would be risky, for us and for them," Niesselee added. "But that's assuming they are a lighter force than us, 'Mech to 'Mech."

Gallan nodded, his dislike of the truth of Niesselee's contribution already a factor in the planning. The Marians had to be a faster force, that was for sure. Gallan suspected that was the reason some of the Marians had managed to get ahead of them, and were even now undoubtedly waiting not far ahead to ambush and delay Bravo Lance until the rest of the maniple could arrive. That left little time to come up with a plan.

"You're sure you would attack us from the south?" Gallan asked.

"Without a doubt," Toman replied. "The ground slopes slightly up in that direction, and they'd have a high-ground advantage, even though the trees. No question, that's where I would be if I was waiting for us."

Both options were full of risk. Numerically, they were outclassed, but if Gallan could manage to dictate the time and place of the engagement, perhaps they would have a chance. Were the Two Legio forces ready to die to the last to defend Illyria? Unfortunately, that was something Bravo Lance was about to find out.

"Okay, let's strike south, then," Gallan said.

A mighty roar of approval from Karral told Gallan the burly man in the even burlier BattleMech had been waiting for such an order.

"South," Gallan said, "and try to engage the secondary force before the Marians waiting up ahead know what we've done. Perhaps we will catch them all by surprise."

His lance began moving to newly set nav points on the grid. Karral thrashed his 'Mech's hatchet as he cut a new path through the forest. The enemy was in that direction, and Gallan hoped the Marian commander would anticipate none of what he had surmised about the enemy's plans.

The alternative, of course, was that *this* course of action would be the trap—and Gallan had just decided to walk Bravo Lance directly into it.

"How slow are these guys anyway?" *Legionnaire* Gus complained as Cira and the rest of her century waited for the Tamarind Regulars to round a bend in the path ahead.

The ambush point was precisely chosen to give Cira's unit prime line of sight on the approaching assault 'Mechs, providing for difficult return shots and easy repositioning opportunities. Not a clearing by any stretch, the forest thinned here just enough for lighter BattleMechs to have an easier time navigating through the patchy trees. Cira hoped it would be enough to mitigate the massive weight advantage the Leaguers had over her century before Rillius' century could flank them.

If they can manage it, that is.

She'd had her doubts about Rillius' leadership, and not for the first time during her service in Secunda Maniple. The *principes'* lust for greater glory sometimes clouded his judgment, but so far this had not caught up with him in any negative way. That bothered Cira most of all. Consequences never stuck to him. They slid off him like swamp slime on the side of a power-washed hovertruck.

Cira shifted nervously in her cockpit. The *Icarus II* was still fairly new to her, and this would be her first engagement using it. The 'Mech was a recent addition to Two Legio, part of an initiative by *Caesar* to update the Legios with better technology, and Cira had been assigned one specifically to lead her unit. It was a little on the slow side for what she wanted to use it for, but it had served her well in exercises and war games. Out here in the megaforests of Cadmus, however, it felt like a brick.

Cira paused as her 'Mech's exterior microphones picked up what sounded like a tree splintering. It was not close. It was in the distance, off to the south.

The south!

The splintering sound was quickly followed by an unmistakable *crack-crack-crack* sound that could only have come from an autocannon being fired. The Leaguers were not coming in Cira's direction after all, and had somehow found Rillius' century. The enemy was engaging *them* instead of the other way around.

"Secunda!" Cira yelled, "To me! The *principes* is engaged, and needs our help!"

Even as Cira throttled up and headed toward the distant sounds, she could not help but admire the Tamarind Regulars, just a little bit, for seeing through Rillius' plan of attack. This Leaguer lance commander, whoever they were, was no slouch, and Cira wondered who was actually the bait here, and who was the hunter.

"Yeah, I suppose I'm a *little* disappointed they were this predictable," Toman said as his *Awesome* unleashed another barrage of PPC fire into a Marian *Thunderbolt*. The enemy 'Mech reeled from heavy particle impacts to its torso and left leg, and looked for a moment as if it might topple. But it recovered, and unleashed a return barrage of laser fire. Toman's BattleMech easily shrugged off the hits, and took another step forward to punctuate that it was not backing down anytime soon.

"Good shots!" Gallan replied as he planted his *Albatross*' feet and felt a slight rush of heat as he unleashed an alpha strike into a Marian *Hercules*. Many of the lasers caught errant tree branches instead of hitting the enemy 'Mech, but both his pulse laser and light Gauss rifle round found their marks. The *Hercules* took the impacts on its legs with what seemed like contempt, and it stepped forward and returned fire in kind. Gallan's BattleMech rumbled at the impacts across its arms and torso, and he marked the *Hercules* as a potentially tough opponent. The pilot showed no signs of backing down, even in the face of a huge tonnage deficit.

Niesselee and Karral were both engaged on the other side of Toman, Niesselee's *Sirocco* exchanging fire with both a *Cronus* and an *Apollo* that had taken up a support position behind the rest of their century. Gallan had no idea if the other Marian force out there was already on its way to the engagement, but the tide needed to shift in his lance's favor before they found out, or the fight would get incredibly interesting with lightning speed.

"Gahhhh!" Karral yelled out over the comms, and Gallan risked a look at the *Neanderthal*'s status panel. The arm not carrying the hatchet showed signs of extreme damage as Karral rushed forward to engage a *Cyclops*, the only assault 'Mech among the Marian force.

"Bravo Four, are you okay?" Gallan said, keeping a wary eye on the *Hercules*, which had not let up slashing his *Albatross* with laser fire. Gallan continued the duel with his opponent while Karral worked out his own problems. He moved into a better position and let loose with another barrage of Gauss rifle, pulse laser, and missiles. This time the hits were more true to the target, and the *Hercules* reeled from the impact, stumbling to keep its footing amid the underbrush.

A sudden explosion on the far side of the fight ripped Gallan's attention away from the *Hercules* as the *Cyclops* erupted into a gaseous ball of shrapnel. Karral's *Neanderthal* stood in the smoke cloud the destroyed Marian assault 'Mech had left behind, and Gallan smiled as the hatchet raised in a salute. Karral was an odd and unpredictable man, but Gallan was always glad to have him on his side.

Gallan's attention returned to the *Hercules* in time to see the smaller BattleMech move toward him. His eyes narrowed as he wondered what the Marian pilot must be thinking by closing range with his *Albatross*, but such moves on a battlefield made him extra cautious.

"Lieutenant!" Karral yelled, again drawing Gallan's attention away from his fight. "The other group is here, on our flank! Moving to engage!"

Gallan looked at his screen briefly. "Toman, move to support Karral. Leave the *Thunderbolt* to me, or it will follow you. And try to give Niesselee enough time to join you."

Toman's comm clicked twice in affirmative response, and the *Awesome* disengaged from its fight with the badly mauled *Thunderbolt*. The Marian 'Mech probably still had some fight left in it, but Gallan did not want just Karral to take the brunt of those newly joining in the fray.

Gallan looked back in the direction of the *Hercules*, and his eyes widened in terror as it was somehow just in front of his *Albatross* and charging to close what little distance remained between them. He pulled the trigger on his stick, but even all his weapons impacting across different armored locations on the 70-ton BattleMech rushing toward him were not enough to stop what was coming.

Well, that was stupid, taking my eye off—

He couldn't finish the thought before a bone-shattering crash accompanied the impact of a massive force against his BattleMech. He felt instantly dizzy as his world began to tumble over. His sense of balance was temporarily confused, which meant so was his BattleMech's.

As the *Albatross* hit the ground, Gallan's head snapped back and hit the seat rest harder than he thought possible. Stars exploded in his vision, and he blinked several times to try getting a sense for what had just happened.

He regained his vision moments later, and stared out of his cockpit into the eyes of a dangerous looking man. From the *Hercules'* cockpit, the Marian pilot's gaze bored into Gallan, expressing a hatred he had rarely seen on the battlefield, even between bitter enemies. This man, whoever he was, was hell-bent on Gallan's destruction—and Gallan just might have delivered him his wish.

Cira reflexively turned her head away from the exploding *Cyclops* until the flash subsided. The scene in front of her was depressing. The Tamarind lance had somehow found Rillius' century before they were in position to strike, and had started a pitched battle. Perhaps the Leaguers thought to rely on their superior size and firepower to down the heavier Marian force before Cira's century could reach them, but Rillius' 'Mechs had proven more of a fight than even she would have guessed under the circumstances.

"Centurion!" Gud yelled as his *Storm Raider* surged forward in a burst of speed. "The *principes* is in trouble! We must reach him!"

Cira turned her 'Mech to look across at the far side of the engagement. It was tough to see through all the intervening BattleMechs and weapons fire, but it looked like Rillius' *Hercules* had just collided with the Tamarind *Albatross* and taken it to the ground. Cira cringed at the sight and wondered what had gone through Rillius' mind to attempt such a maneuver.

"Secunda," she replied, getting her head back in the game, "down that *Neanderthal* first. It's already damaged and needs to be dealt with before we can move in to help Prima."

Legionnaire Gus' *Storm Raider* was the first Century Secunda BattleMech to reach the battle line, and he approached the *Neanderthal* from the flank, peppering the larger 'Mech with autocannon fire as he closed in to deliver a swift strike with his mace. Cira heard the dull *thud* of the mace strike the *Neanderthal*'s massive left leg. The blow crunched a couple of armor plates but did little to stop the assault 'Mech from standing directly in their way.

"Ha!" Gus screamed. "Take that!"

Battle fervor had overtaken the young pilot, and he did not notice as the *Neanderthal* slowly lifted its own massive melee weapon above its head and brought it down directly onto the *Storm Raider*'s cockpit, obliterating the smaller 'Mech's head and cutting into the torso beneath. Gus never had time to scream in pain as his life abruptly ended, and Cira's own battle fervor ignited at the sight.

Her 'Mech roared to life as its autocannon belched out round after round of ammunition. Alternating between solid slugs and cluster rounds, Cira was beyond any sort of plan. The *Neanderthal* had to die, or it would kill them all.

The hulking BattleMech turned toward Cira's approaching *Icarus II* and fired its weapons. Twin streams of charged particles struck her 'Mech like lightning bolts, the PPC shots sloughing off tons of armor and rocking her back in her command couch.

The *Neanderthal* stepped forward to meet Cira's advance just as laser and PPC fire from three more angles cut into the assault 'Mech. It stopped and twisted its torso to return fire in a direction away from Cira, and she breathed a momentary sigh.

The reprieve was short lived as two solid autocannon slugs slammed into her BattleMech's legs. Her 'Mech nearly fell over at the impact, but she managed to keep her footing. For some reason, the *Sirocco* had turned away from its two current opponents to deliver a downrange barrage at her, with several shots impacting on her 'Mech, and Cira witnessed the quadrupedal 'Mech pay a heavy price for ignoring the Marian *Cronus* and *Apollo* in front of it. The *Cronus* sent a PPC and laser barrage into the assault 'Mech, followed by a rain of long-range missiles from the *Apollo*. The impacts of the incoming attacks rocked the *Sirocco*'s legs and lower torso, causing the pilot to widen the 'Mech's stance on the uneven ground. This temporarily halted the heavier 'Mech's own weapons fire, but it did not attempt to reposition or use any nearby trees for cover. This confused Cira: the *Sirocco* was surrounded but showed no signs of seeking a better position.

The Tamarinds' tactical situation became a little clearer when the *Awesome*, which was fast approaching Cira's position, performed a run-by PPC barrage aimed at the *Apollo*. The shots were true, and they must have touched off an ammo bin, because seconds later the *Apollo*'s pilot ejected from her BattleMech only moments before it exploded in a similar fashion as the *Cyclops* before it.

But Cira had little time to worry about it. The Tamarind 'Mechs were once more handing off targets between them, as the *Sirocco* turned back to reengage with the *Cronus*, and the *Awesome* was now swiftly advancing in her direction. The brickhouse of a 'Mech had suffered minimal damage so far, but Cira was confused as to why it had left the *Albatross* to fend for itself. The Tamarind tactics made little sense, and she was beginning to wonder if that was the point. If they could keep her forces off-balance by varying targets and using unpredictable engagement protocols, they would have a chance to cause some real damage in this fight. But Cira would not give them that chance.

"All right then!" Cira yelled out over an open comm channel. "Let's do this!"

She throttled up her 'Mech and sent autocannon rounds in the direction of the approaching *Awesome*. If her century was all going to die, at least she would take something with her.

Rillius stared across the distance between him and the *Albatross*' pilot. The man in the other 'Mech looked shocked to find himself in this position. As both 'Mechs lay entangled on the ground, Rillius screamed and triggered his autocannon. A low thudding of fire and impact echoed throughout his cockpit as the slugs exiting the barrel detonated against the *Albatross*' torso. Rillius' screens flashed red in warning as he realized the autocannon had suffered damage after only a couple of rounds, the explosive shells critically affecting his own fire-control system.

"Gah! Curse you and your damnable League!" he spat.

The other pilot had regained his senses, his hands furiously flying across control panels and manipulating his sticks. Rillius felt the effects of this effort moments later as the *Albatross* moved under his *Hercules* and twisted its body on the ground. Using a hand to brace the maneuver, the *Albatross* shoved Rillius' 'Mech off it, pulling his body against his seat restraints in a way that jerked his back and caused a twinge of pain that ran from his neck down to his toes. The *Albatross* made one more quick movement, and it was suddenly free of Rillius' 'Mech and attempting to stand.

Not to be outmaneuvered, Rillius also stood his 'Mech up. The process took only a handful of seconds, but the *Albatross* beat him to it. When Rillius' 'Mech rose once more, he breathed a quick sigh of relief to find Legionnaire Indrewe's *Thunderbolt* firing at the *Albatross*. The Tamarind pilot was quick to react, much quicker than Rillius would have expected from an assault 'Mech pilot, and snapped off a point-blank shot with its light Gauss rifle. The impact shattered what was left of Indrewe's cockpit protection, and Rillius was close enough to the action to see the *legionnaire*'s body explode from the force of the hit.

The *Thunderbolt*'s momentum carried it a few steps toward Rillius before it teetered and crashed down, landing on its chest in a cacophony of mangled metal, shredded undergrowth, and burning tree foliage. The freshly downed 'Mech landed between Rillius' *Hercules* and the *Albatross*. Both pilots looked down at the *Thunderbolt*'s remains, and then up at one another. In an insolent, vile act of nonchalant dismissal, the *Albatross* pilot made an exaggerated shrugging motion and lowered his hands back to his controls.

"Oh, yes," Rillius said over his BattleMech's external speaker, "you are correct. It is on now, you Marik lackey. Now we will find out which one of us will see glory this day. For the *imperator*!"

Both 'Mechs fired everything they had, one more time.

A flood of heat rushed into Gallan's cockpit as every operational weapon his *Albatross* had sent dangerous projectiles toward the *Hercules*. Based on how the *Thunderbolt* had attempted to intervene and the markings on his target, now observed up close and personal enough to confirm, the pilot of the *Hercules* was undoubtedly this maniple's commander, a *principes*. The *Hercules* bucked and bowed even as Gallan's heavily damaged 'Mech swayed under the barrage of weapons the Marian commander sent toward him.

Both 'Mechs swayed, but neither broke. Gallan smiled. This Marian commander, whoever he was, was proving quite the handful. He had not been in a battle like this in some time, and he knew he should have felt embarrassed about enjoying it as people died around him. But this fight had turned personal. Being stalked through the Cadmus megaforest, predicting this commander's moves and intentions, and then the ensuing fight, had all awakened a need for Gallan to prove himself better than the man before him.

"I'm losing it!" Niesselee screamed, and Gallan snapped out of his tunnel vision on the *Hercules* to see the *Sirocco* topple onto its left side. The Marian *Cronus* charged the remaining distance between them and kicked in the *Sirocco*'s cockpit, killing Niesselee instantly.

Gallan's face went slack, and his eyes flickered back to the *Hercules*, the cloud of tunnel vision returning. He and Niesselee had served together since their first days with the Seventh, and she had always had his back. Today, though, nobody had hers, and Gallan put all the blame for that on the 'Mech directly in front of him and the man inside its cockpit.

"Oh, what a shame, to see a brave MechWarrior killed so suddenly like that," the Marian commander blasted over his external speakers.

"Taunting *me* now, huh?" Gallan said under his breath, unwilling to engage this monster in his petty games. "You'll regret that."

"Gal," Toman's voice broke in. "Are you okay? That was brutal."

Gallan wondered at Toman checking up on him. His friend was much more perceptive than he gave him credit for, and judging by how the battered *Awesome* was now dueling both the *Cronus* and the *Icarus II*, Gallan hoped Toman would keep his cool as well.

"Ye…yeah, Toman," he choked out after a moment.

The *Hercules* continued to taunt him with laser fire as they stalked in a circle around the fallen *Thunderbolt*, each looking for a weakness to exploit.

"You don't sound it," Toman said, and Gallan heard a massive rumble as the *Cronus* hit the ground, steaming, PPC-beam-sized holes cored into its chest.

"I'll be…I'll be fine," Gallan said, regaining his voice and hoping he sounded the part. "Help Karral."

"Roger that. I'll try to pull this *Icarus* toward Karral and set up a defensive stance with him for when your fight is done," Toman said as he pushed his *Awesome* forward in the direction of the beleaguered *Neanderthal* in the distance.

Now, Gallan thought, centering his gaze once more on the *Hercules*, *now you and I shall end this!*

"*Gah!*" he shouted as he slammed the throttle forward toward the *Hercules*. "Your charge was okay, but I can do better!"

The *Hercules* paused and began taking steps backward, firing its laser and PPC as rapidly as possible to stall the *Albatross*' implacable advance. Warning light and klaxons sounded in Gallan's cockpit. Something important had been hit, but he did not care. This man had to pay for what had been done to Niesselee.

The *Hercules* continued to fire, and Gallan answered in kind. His *Albatross* crunched through the remains of the *Thunderbolt*, tore over fallen branches and through roots. Twice Gallan had to fight hard to keep his balance as his 'Mech's foot struck a root it could not sweep aside, and then, he was there.

Back in face-to-face range with the *Hercules*, Gallan drove his 'Mech's shoulder into the torso of the enemy machine. The result was like before, but this time the *Albatross* stayed on its feet. And despite the armor-shattering impact of a 95-ton BattleMech barreling into it, so too did the *Hercules*.

Are these things indestructible?

As if it heard him, the *Hercules* raised a balled fist and punched Gallan's BattleMech just below its chin. The high pitched squeal of metal scraping metal filled his ears as more warning lights flashed. Gallan was thrown hard to the side of his command couch, and he felt something *snap*. The hit was solid, and had torn away some of the armor protecting his cockpit.

Gallan moved his sticks to retaliate as the giant war machines bashed at one another in a futile struggle to gain an upper hand. The *Albatross* failed to move when Gallan tried to throttle up. He looked to his throttle bar to find his arm limp and numb at his side. He could not feel it, and his hand refused to respond to his commands. It was broken, the result of the snap he had felt moments before. In desperation, he looked down to his feet and saw the right pedal might still function enough for one last maneuver.

Gallan cried out in pain as he stomped on the pedal, suddenly felt the injury his arm had sustained from the earlier punch. The *Albatross*' right leg swept out, severing the *Hercules*' left leg at the knee. Gallan let out a short cry of triumph as the Marian commander's BattleMech began to fall, a look of surprised disbelief written on the pilot's face.

Gallan's stomach lurched as he realized too late that he would be unable to rebalance his 'Mech due to his injured arm, and his *Albatross* fell once more. But this time, he was able to affect the way he would hit the ground, and was rewarded with the *crunch* of a destroyed cockpit as his assault 'Mech's elbow landed directly on the *Hercules*' cockpit, crashing through the viewport and wiping the smug Marian commander from existence.

Unable to brace himself, Gallan hit his head on the console and blacked out.

With a chill, Cira witnessed the mash of metal created by the *Albatross* falling on Rillius' downed *Hercules*. But she had no time to ponder the fate of her fallen *principes*, as two of the Tamarind Regulars BattleMechs still stood to oppose what was left of Secunda Maniple.

And there is not much left of it.

Rillius' century was now completely gone, and the *Awesome* was the only Tamarind 'Mech that still looked fully combat capable. Once she had regrouped with the rest of her century, it was obvious they should concentrate fire on the more damaged *Neanderthal*. It was a risk, as the *Awesome* would not tolerate being ignored for long, but Cira had to force a victory somehow.

Cira pivoted her *Icarus II* toward the overwhelmed *Neanderthal* and added two of her precious few remaining autocannon rounds to the bevy of shots still pouring into it. By all rights it should not still be standing, and Cira imagined the stubborn will of its pilot alone kept that machine running well past when it should have laid down and died.

The *Neanderthal* turned toward Cira in response and shot both its torso-mounted PPCs. The pilot had to be burning up at this point, with the 'Mech running well over the red line. It had fired those PPCs almost nonstop for the last few minutes without much accuracy beyond a few hits and grazes. The lighter 'Mechs in Cira's century easily managed to evade the haphazard firing and return more accurate fire of their own. But this time the *Neanderthal* had better aim.

The impact of one PPC shot whipped Cira's *Icarus II* around, shearing off its right arm. She tasted blood in her mouth, and realized she had bitten the inside of her cheek. The pain that followed a moment later was just enough to drain her battle vision away and bring her back into the role of a *centurion*. Her century was in trouble, whether they wanted to admit it or not.

In defiance of that judgment, *Legionnaire* Xina's *Hermes II* stepped around a tree on the far side of the *Neanderthal* and let loose with its heavy PPC. The bolt flew as true as any shot Cira had ever seen, and it struck the badly mauled side of the assault 'Mech. Cira watched as the *Neanderthal*'s arm dropped to its side, slumped over, and stopped moving. It did not look like it would fall, but it did not move for several seconds.

"Did we get it?" *Legionnaire* Toppa asked.

"It appears we did," Cira replied.

"I'll go check!" Toppa engaged his *Stinger*'s jump jets, taking the light BattleMech into the air.

"No, Toppa, wait!"

But Cira's order was too late.

Two massive PPC beams sizzled through the air, striking the *Stinger* at the apex of its jump. Both sides of the 'Mech's torso were torn apart, destroying the fusion engine. The *Stinger*, now a fiery ball of free-falling ferro-fibrous armor and endo-steel frame, missed the mark Toppa had intended, and impacted the ground just in front of the still-quiet and unmoving *Neanderthal*.

The *Awesome*'s smoking PPC barrels greeted Cira as she turned toward the remaining enemy, her eyes burning with tears and rage. *How dare they kill Toppa like that, like he was in a shooting gallery! Like it was a game!*

Cira triggered her autocannon and was met with a beep and a light warning that her ammo bins were now dry. She had nothing left now but a small laser and a badly damaged 'Mech. She braced herself for what was to come, closing her eyes and waiting for the Leaguer to end her. She had been right. Rillius had killed them all, and at least she could die knowing he had paid for his arrogance and ineptitude.

"You can go if you want," a voice came over the comm on an open channel.

"Wha...what?" Cira's voice sounded nothing like her own as she stammered the simple question.

"You can go," the man repeated, the voice of the *Awesome*'s pilot. "There's no reason to continue here. We've both lost so much. Just go. I don't want to kill the rest of you if I can help it."

"It's a trick, *Centurion*!" Xina said in Cira's ear. "That one 'Mech can't take all three of us! We can avenge Toppa and Gus and the *principes*!"

Cira badly wanted to give in to Xina's request. They had the numerical advantage. But did they really? Xina's *Hermes II* had taken some damage, and Ullor's *Ostscout* was missing both of its arms. None of her 'Mechs were fresh enough to continue the fight. While the *Awesome* had taken some damage, it still functioned well enough to have blasted poor Toppa out of the sky. Its pilot was no one to be trifled with, and he was offering to let them go.

"Secunda," Cira said, a heavy sigh overtaking her between breaths, "withdraw. We're done here."

"But Cira—" Xina began.

"*No*, Xina," Cira said. "We're going. This...Leaguer...is right. This fight is over."

Cira turned her BattleMech and walked back into the forest toward the pass, the location they were supposed to have been guarding, and never should have left.

"Farewell, *Principes* Rillius Krause," Cira said as she and the remainder of Century Secunda followed suit. "I hope you burn in a special hell for this one."

Lieutenant Gallan Ranton sat on the chest of his fallen *Albatross* and gave one last tug on the makeshift sling his left arm was now confined to, wincing in pain as it settled to his side.

Looking up, he stared out into the forest. The Marian 'Mechs that had retreated were now out of earshot, and the quiet of the forest was all that remained. He stared out into Cadmus for several minutes, not wishing to ruin the stillness with any of the battlefield that existed behind him. This was a moment he needed, a moment he had earned. And then it was over.

"Karral didn't make it," Toman said as he walked up from behind and took a seat next to his lieutenant.

"So that's two I lost today," Gallan said. The sting of losing Niesselee and Karral had already overpowered the pain in his arm.

"Yeah, that's true," Toman said. He withdrew a flask from under his cooling vest and took a long draft before offering it to Gallan, who refused, but Toman insisted. "It'll make the arm hurt less. It looks pretty bad. Think it will heal?"

Gallan grudgingly accepted the flask and drained the rest of it. He knew the burning liquid would do little to calm him, but Toman was difficult to deny when he insisted.

"I hope so," he replied, but he wasn't sure. His command of this mission was questionable at best, and getting two of his subordinates killed would not sit well with him, short-straw mission or not.

"Well..." Toman said, drawing out his pause. "Good mission is a done mission."

Gallan could not remember when the two of them had started using that saying. On the surface it made no sense at all, but the phrase had taken on a meaning for them over the years as an acknowledgment that no matter how, if they lived long enough to say it to one another, then they would live to see another day.

Gallan shook his head and lay back on his 'Mech. The first of the evening stars were visible overhead, and he wanted nothing more than to be among them and off the rock called Illyria.

"Yeah," he said with a weary sigh, "good mission is done."

SHRAPNEL

THE CURIOUS CASE OF COLIN COOLIDGE'S CURSED COOLING SUIT

JOSHUA C. PERIAN

Dr. Bixby,

Over the weekend, while cleaning out a dusty storage closet in Subbasement Three, I found a box of old personal items belonging to a Dr. Stevens. Most of the stuff was junk, scooped up when the box was placed in storage in the 3080s, but a few items were more than just cheap trinkets. This holo-tape could be a promising lead. Give it a listen. I have fast-forwarded to an interesting entry and transcribed the text for you to read. I left some notes of my own at the end.

> *Claxisto's Traveling Curiosities thanks you again for purchasing a self-guided tour for our Sphere-famous* Hall of Dangerous Doohickies. *You are listening to Exhibit Seventeen: The Curious Case of Colin Coolidge's Cursed Cooling Suit.*
>
> *Perhaps the most famous MechWarrior you've never heard of, Colin Coolidge was once a serious contender to win the Solaris Grand Tournament in 3029. He was also an enigma whose rise to prominence and untimely death were the subject of great interest and intense speculation.*
>
> *Colin's story starts with his arrival on Solaris VII. No one knows when he arrived at the Game World with his customized* Warhammer, *which by itself might be considered odd, but with the Fourth Succession War raging, it's possible his record was lost. Newcomers fleeing the war or simply seeking their fortune arrived daily. Colin's first known duels at Hartford Gardens and*

THE CURIOUS CASE OF COLIN COOLIDGE'S CURSED COOLING SUIT

the King of the Mountain arena in mid-3028 immediately put the young man on the gaming map. Not only did he win both fights against veteran gladiators, but the unknown warrior was apparently already under contract with Starlight Stables.

As the gladiatorial season moved into 3029, Colin blazed through the circuit rankings, advancing into Class Five and Class Six matches, but what made headlines and kept Colin in the public eye was the rare lostech cooling suit he wore in combat.

Fiercely protective of the incredibly rare suit, Colin refused any inspection of the valuable technology and carried it with him in a special backpack wherever he went, regardless of what other clothing he wore. He even appeared at the ultra-glamorous black-tie Grand Tournament Gala wearing the backpack over his tuxedo. When questioned about the suit's origin, Colin spoke about the suit in third person and insisted it was merely a family heirloom passed down from a relative

who once served in the Star League Defense Force, even though images of the suit of showed it in almost pristine condition. Colin claimed the suit would only work when a Coolidge wore it, and it would kill any other wearer. In the press, Colin Coolidge was the mysterious newcomer, a capable warrior, and just the kind of strange character the media and public ate up.

With the cooling suit, Colin pushed his worn Warhammer into the Top 20 and the 3029 Grand Tournament finals, where he died dueling Anya Terrel in the final round. When rescue crews opened his 'Mech's cockpit, to their surprise they found Colin wearing a used cooling vest—not the famed suit, which had mysteriously disappeared sometime before his final match.

After Colin's death, everyone assumed one of his competitors had stolen the suit, but a Gaming Commission investigation turned up nothing. Interested parties, collectors, and even ComStar were rumored to be searching for Coolidge's suit, but it was never found. Within a few years, Colin Coolidge and his cooling suit were largely forgotten. Only a handful of diehard lostech prospectors and down-on-their luck types continued to search. Eventually the suit became another gaming myth, a unique piece of lost Solaris history.

But the suit resurfaced a decade later in the hands of Richard McAllister, who possessed it just long enough to die during a raid on Bordon. Then it disappeared again, only to resurface with a new owner, Helena Stanakov of Narhal's Raiders, who possessed the suit long enough to die in a training accident. In each case, the new owner died the first time they wore the suit in a 'Mech. After 3040, the cooling suit wasn't seen again until 3051, in the hands of Abi Gundarson. Before his death fighting the Jade Falcons on La Grave, Gundarson was recorded talking about the cooling suit, saying it just "showed up."

After La Grave, Coolidge's curse followed a succession of new owners, all to their deaths. The suit traveled across the Inner Sphere and beyond, into the hands of a member of the Brotherhood of Randis who died during a pirate raid, and eventually returning home to Solaris VII just in time for the Word of Blake's Jihad. The war against the Word gave Coolidge's suit the opportunity to reap dozens of new victims as it passed from one desperate warrior to the next in the Solaris Home Defense League. While each MechWarrior died differently, surviving battleROMs all showed the same thing: a pristine-looking cooling suit.

> Then the suit landed with Sharon Henning, who wore it in the final battles against the Word, and later in some of the open Class Three arenas before retiring in 3086, when she sold the suit to Claxisto's capable stewardship. How did Henning survive when so many others hadn't? Our capable sleuths learned the truth: Sharon Henning was a direct descendant of Colin Coolidge! The result of a one-night liaison between Coolidge and her grandmother, Henning could wear the suit when no one else could.
>
> Today, Colin Coolidge's suit is safely ensconced behind our warded ferroglass, where it can no longer claim new victims.
>
> If you're enjoying this tour, remember that tour tapes, along with all manner of fantastic baubles, trinkets, and toys, are available for purchase in our gift shop.
>
> Up next, Exhibit Eighteen: the Damocles Dagger of Robert Marsden...

Out of morbid curiosity, I searched the archives for any vids of Coolidge's suit. There are some great close-ups from Henning's run in the '80s. Look at the enhanced images from before her last Anchorage Arena match. You can clearly see the suit's mint condition, but what caught my eye is the manufacturer's number on the outside collar: PTS:001XM. I cross-referenced the number with old Star League records, and that number belongs to the Terran Hegemony's first cooling suit prototype.

I know this suit can't possibly be real, but it turns out Claxisto's Traveling Curiosities is still around. They peddle the Solaris-Bolan circuit, and may still possess it.

So, am I booking us two tickets on the next outbound transport or what?

—J

SHRAPNEL

REVERSAL OF FORTUNES

GILES GAMMAGE

THE BEGINNING (THE END)

MARGRAM BASE
FORT LOUDON
LYRAN ALLIANCE
7 DECEMBER 3062
0345 LOCAL TIME

The *Victor* lay on its back.

Inside its cockpit, Neven stared up at the sky. There was nothing to see there—only faint stars fading with the dawn into nothing—but that was all right. That was better. He didn't want to see anything, didn't want to think about anything, didn't want to be anything. He didn't want to *be*, period, full stop, end of sentence, end of thought, end of life.

My fault. It was all my fault.

No, another part of him said. *It was my brother's fault.*

The thoughts chased each other around and around his head. Who was right, who was wrong, who had done what to whom and why (or who hadn't—who *hadn't* done what, for so very, very long); it was a Möbius strip without sides or ending, an automatic hourglass, continuously upending itself whenever one side got too heavy, forever reversing its own fortunes.

Long before that. Years and years ago.

Both brothers followed in their father's footsteps, of course, even the younger son. Despite everything. There was no question of doing anything as dishonest as commerce or industry. Or medicine. God forbid, never medicine.

They were a military family with two military sons. Neven joined the Guards, a regiment with a long, proud, and honorable tradition. Reinier was assigned to a Federated Commonwealth Regimental Combat Team, a unit barely ten years old, half-filled with foreign Lyrans.

Their father attended only one of their graduation ceremonies. He was, an assistant informed them, unfortunately too busy to attend the other. The assistant claimed he sent his regrets, but they all knew better.

No, that was just one of many bitter fruits born from the same seed. That wasn't the start of it, of course, not by a long shot. You had to go back, back, retracing the path of time's arrow to see where it all began.

0335 LOCAL TIME

"Get out of there!" Neven screamed into his mic. He hammered his own controls in futile despair. "Reinier, get out of there! *Get out of there!*"

He didn't need the sensors to see the heat blazing from his brother's *Zeus*. The air around the 'Mech shimmered; taloned fingers of flame clawed from the joints and rents in the amor as internal components slagged in the hellish heat, burning first red, then brightening to orange. Yellow. White.

"If it blows in here, everybody dies," Neven's brother Reiner said. His voice was raw, gasping, robbed of all moisture. The inside of the cockpit had to be a furnace. His *Zeus* reeled and lurched toward the 'Mech bay doors, dragging one leg behind it, shedding great feathers of fire-retardant foam like angel wings. The 80-ton machine staggered against the wall, sparks flying, pushed off, half threw itself onto the ferrocrete outside. Dense, black, ember-flecked fumes erupted from the 'Mech's joints—myomer muscles melting, burning, smoke boiling out with volcanic ferocity.

Neven followed a few steps behind, as close as he dared. The other 'Mechs in Neven's command lance took one look at the burning, boiling *Zeus* and hastily backed away.

"You're clear!" Neven shouted. "Eject, dammit, eject!"

"Too close…" his brother gasped. "Still too close."

Reinier's 'Mech found its feet. It had gone only about two steps when the missile ammunition detonated. At first, it didn't seem so bad. The *Zeus* was equipped with CASE—Cellular Ammunition Storage Equipment designed specifically to limit this type of catastrophic damage. There was a series of pops and crackles, tiny blisters of fire erupting from the 'Mech's rear armor. The *Zeus* lurched sideways, thrown off-balance. It went down on one knee again.

"Eject, Reinier, *eject*!"

"Just a few more—"

The force of the blast was contained and redirected, but it had exposed the 'Mech's already-damaged reactor shielding directly to the air. It was not much, but it was enough. Safety systems that should have shut the reactor down had been destroyed. Neven heard an metallic *thud* as the reactor's tungsten-carbide shell cracked. Warm air rushed in and met multimillion-degree plasma.

The entire top half of his brother's *Zeus* disappeared in a blinding, brilliant fireball.

Farther back.

Reinier had attended the Nagelring, Neven, the New Avalon Institute of Science. Despite his "foreign" origins, Reinier was accepted on the strength of his excellent academic scores, athleticism, and charismatic personality. Neven was the eldest son of a count. There were...channels. Unspoken arrangements. A certain trading of favors for a thumb placed on the admission scales. Officially, such things never happened, but they did. Of course they did.

They both tried to score small victories off the other for that, as part of their interminable war. Neven, for the clear mark of their father's favor, Reinier for not needing it. Neither let the other forget, but that still wasn't it.

0320 LOCAL TIME

Neven roared in wordless rage and fired everything in his *Victor*'s arsenal. His fingers clenched about primary, secondary, and tertiary triggers. At this range, he couldn't miss.

Pulse lasers hissed and spat green fire, missiles screamed from their launch racks, and his Gauss rifle split the air as its solid slug tore from the barrel at hypersonic speeds, slamming into the other 'Mech's shoulder, cracking and tearing off the armored pauldron.

"Treason!" Reinier cried as his *Zeus* staggered under the weight of fire and was blown backward against the opposite wall. "Traitor!"

Reinier pushed off from the wall and charged straight at Neven. Reinier's PPC and long-range missiles were almost useless in close-quarters combat like this, but lasers in the *Zeus*'s torso scored black carbon lines across the *Victor*'s chest and thighs. Then the two 80-ton war machines collided in a thundering scream of metal on metal.

The impact drove the *Victor* back, sent it sliding along the ground until its back heel crunched into the wall. The two 'Mechs wrestled awkwardly, the *Zeus* with no humanoid hands, the *Victor* with only one. The *Victor*'s right arm ended in the barrel of a Gauss rifle, forcing Neven to swing it like a club, hammering against the *Zeus*' already-damaged shoulder. The first blow left a dent, the second deepened it into a valley, then the third caused the entire armor plate to shatter and flake away.

Neven tried to bring his left-arm lasers around to hit the *Zeus*' exposed shoulder joint, but Reinier jammed the stubby barrel of his right-arm missile launcher against the elbow joint, and the laser beams missed, stitching hits across the skeleton of a 'Mech gantry behind Reinier, slagging the metal spars into red-hot ruin.

Reinier fired and fired and fired his lasers, clawing at the *Victor*'s belly. The armor schematic in Neven's cockpit quickly warmed from static green to warning yellow, then dangerous red.

There wasn't room enough to bring the *Victor*'s jump jets into play—unless... Neven tapped the jump pedals, a microburst, producing a sudden blast of superheated air against the bay wall and floor, throwing the *Victor* forward and up, unbalancing the *Zeus* and sending it tottering backward.

The *Victor*'s right arm came free.

The *Zeus* collided with the weakened gantry behind it. Spars bent and snapped with firecracker *pops*. Individual detonations rose into a crescendo as the gantry's top level collapsed onto the next, then both fell onto the next and then the next in a cascade, a metal landslide, a rain of metal spears crashing down on the *Zeus*' head. The BattleMech stirred slowly, drunkenly.

Giving Neven plenty of time to line up a shot and fire.

The Gauss slug took the *Zeus* through the heart. It blasted straight through the reactor shielding controls before exiting out the 'Mech's back and impacting like a meteorite against the bay wall.

The *Zeus* wobbled, but did not fall.

A warning on Neven's head-up display began to flash: PROXIMITY ALERT, HIGH HEAT SOURCE DETECTED.

With the reactor controls shot away, the *Zeus* was beginning to burn up, even without firing, just standing there.

"Give up, Reinier," Neven crowed. "Either my next shot takes you down or you blow yourself up on your own. I win, you lose. Give up. Surrender."

"You'd like that wouldn't you?"

The *Zeus* stabbed a laser at the *Victor*. The heat-sensor alarm in Neven's cockpit chimed more insistently, but he was beyond hearing them.

Damn him, damn my brother, it's all his fault, damn the stupid little damn him damn him his fault damn him—because of his—if he hadn't been—fine, then I'll show him.

Neven's next shot pulverized the *Zeus'* right knee. Titanium bones snapped and splintered.

Reinier fired again.

Damn that little damn him it's all his fault! A Gauss shot gouged a line along the side of the *Zeus* and tore the Cyclops XII laser from its housing on the left side of the torso.

Reinier fired back with his one remaining pulse laser.

It's all his fault!

The bay's own heat alarms were screaming with ear-shattering wails so loud Neven could even feel them as micro vibrations through the *Victor*'s feet. Warning lights drenched the area in scarlet. The fire-suppression system's vents in the ceiling ripped open, each one wide enough to swallow a 'Mech, and began dumping massive waterfalls of foam on the two BattleMechs. A solid Niagara thundered down in seconds, an Iguazu of seething white, enough to cause even an 80-ton battle machine to rock under the hammering pressure.

The cockpit's forward view bleached out under the deluge, breaking Neven's view of his brother. Neven blinked and shook his head. He finally looked down at the angrily buzzing heat alarm on his control panel. He blinked for a moment, not quite understanding the numbers flashing before him, then his eyes widened.

He looked back up at the foam-drenched figure of the *Zeus*, now looking like some kind of battered Olympian bather.

His brother. Despite the long ache, the hollow hurt, the, the, well, the *everything*, it was still his brother. *What was I thinking?*

"Reinier, stop."

Reinier's lone laser stuttered in answer, scorching a line of soot along the far wall, nowhere near Neven's position. The *Zeus'* battle computer and fire-control systems were probably fried by the heat.

"Reinier listen to me. You're burning up."

"I know."

"This isn't worth dying for."

"Listen to yourself."

"Reinier, you've got to get out of there."

The *Victor*'s warning system pinged again, more urgently now: EXTREME HEAT WARNING. EVACUATE AREA. EXTREME HEAT WARNING. EVACUATE AREA. EXTREME...

What was I thinking?
"Get out of there!"

They argued about anything, everything. The less it mattered, the more heated they got.

During a family dinner, they came to blows over the assassination of Archon Melissa Steiner. Reinier blamed her eldest son, Neven defended him heatedly. "Came to blows," ah, what a bloodless expression. They brawled like dive-bar drunkards in their ancestral home. Reinier threw the first punch. And the second. Neven sat on the floor, wiping blood from a split lip, more in surprise than pain, while servants restrained his brother. Then Neven leaped up and socked his brother in the jaw while he was helpless.

In that instant, Neven had been ashamed. He had not meant for things to go this far. That shame built into anger and wormed its way into the old wound, the ancient wound between the two.

"This is your fault," Neven said, an accusatory finger held in his brother's face. "I wish you had never— All your fault."

Their father was a statue through it all. A raised finger, a twitch of an eyebrow. The servants understood. Reinier was packed off back to the spaceport and the Nagelring (a footman who suggested sending for a doctor was immediately fired). Neven remained at home.

That was the ragged end of their relationship, when brotherly love finally petered out and allowed itself to be replaced by more abstract things, but it was just an excuse, not the inciting incident. The death of an Archon, the rise of a Prince, ironically these events were too important to really matter. Not on the smaller scales, where humans actually lived their lives. A break between brothers, or say, between brother and sister (even when one is an Archon, the other a Prince) rarely happens because of something so dramatic.

No, it had been something both greater and yet smaller. Tiny, even.

0315 LOCAL TIME

"In the name of Katrina Steiner-Davion, Archon-Princess of the Lyran Alliance and Federated Commonwealth, I order you to surrender," Reinier told his brother. "Power down your BattleMechs, exit your cockpits, and turn yourselves over to the military police. I will vouch for you, Brother, but I need you to stand down."

The *Zeus* faced the *Victor*, which entirely blocked the 'Mech bay's main doors. Behind the *Zeus*, the rest of Reinier's company was still scrambling into their BattleMechs, tech crews racing to uncouple coolant feeds and power relays, close and stow ammo bins, and disengage the restraints holding the BattleMechs in place.

"Can't do that."

"Yes, you can, Neven," Reinier urged. "Stop being blind and stupid. Think about what you are doing for a moment."

"I have. And I have my orders."

"Illegal orders, Neven! Orders you are duty-bound to disobey. Orders issued by a rogue general out of misguided loyalty to some arrogant, absentee Prince who can't even be bothered to rule!"

"The laws of inheritance are quite clear, Reinier. Unless he abdicates, Victor Steiner-Davion is the only rightful ruler of the Federated Commonwealth, and the only one who commands my allegiance. Anything else is treason and mutiny."

"This world belongs to the Lyran Alliance. Your unit has been allowed to stay here as guests, only on our sufferance. You stand there and threaten the men and women under my command and talk to me of treason? Look at yourself! Listen to yourself! How am *I* the one committing treason here?"

"We are only defending ourselves."

"Defending yourselves against *what*?" Reinier yelled. "This installation belongs to the Fifth Alliance Guards. This is *my* company's base, how is your trespass—no, your *invasion*—any kind of defense?"

"Don't play schoolyard games, throwing sand in our face and then crying foul when we react," Neven replied evenly. "We know you tried to separate us from our base, our dependents and supporters."

"As a precautionary measure, yes," Reinier cried. "Precautions clearly justified by your presence here now. We have done everything we could to avoid conflict and keep the peace, in spite of your provocations. If you truly cared about your dependents, you would never have come here. If there is any violence here today, they will be the first to suffer for it."

"What do you mean?" Neven's voice was suddenly cold. "What have you done?"

"What do you think?"

"They are civilians."

"They are extremists like you, devotees of Victor's bizarre cult of personality, potential insurgents, subversives, terrorists, and saboteurs. A danger to the stability and security of the planet, and our society as a whole."

"I'll ask you one more time: What have you done?"

"We have acted in the defense of the realm and its people, instead of the private ambitions of a megalomaniac. Can you say the same?"

"*What have you done?*" The *Victor* took a step forward and raised both of its arms. The covers over the chest-mounted missile launcher slid open.

Reinier brought his own weapons up. He would not be intimidated. "Put them in camps where they belong—like we should have done a long time ago!"

It was not all arguments and fights, not at first. As children, they had a hard time staying angry at each other, and it took them years to learn how to hate. Neven would remember those times, later, before the end. But by then it would be too late.

The father's coldness, his refusal to even look at his younger son's face, cast a long shadow, but increasingly he locked himself in his office when he was home, and left them to amuse themselves. So the brothers played at Davions and Kuritas in the long, hollow halls and empty, echoing rooms of the house. And if Neven was always Davion and Reinier always Kurita, well, wasn't that always the way with siblings. The pair made expeditions to the woods that ringed the family's many properties, armed with net and bucket and spade, and if Neven always got the newer and better net or spade, Reinier the broken castoffs, well wasn't that the way with families.

There were still fights, of course. Over the things that mattered when you were young: toys and games and who got to choose what to watch on holovid. Squabbles and tiffs and pushing and crying. Words said in anger that would be remembered long after the fight itself was less than memory. And if Reinier got more than his share of the blame for them, well. That too was the way with some families, even the greatest and most powerful.

That was close, but not quite it. A symptom of the hole torn in their hearts.

0245 LOCAL TIME

"All right, Guards, listen up," Neven said to his company. "Katrina's kids have crossed the line. First, they declared martial law, then they ordered us halfway across the planet, now they've tried to oust General Orsina as our commander. If they want to play rough, we'll play rough."

A reckoning, no more than his brother deserved.

An assault company on the move was a fearsome sight. A dozen war machines spread out across the plain, the smallest twelve meters tall, the lightest weighing seventy-five tons, their collective footfalls shaking the ground with nonstop micro earthquakes, their collective firepower enough to raze a city block in seconds. In the predawn air of Fort Loudon, the BattleMechs were black monoliths moving against a granite and gold sky.

"Our plan is simple: we are going to take control of the Fifth Alliance Guards barracks at Margram Base and intern all personnel for the duration, until someone either shuts Katrina Steiner-Davion up or puts her down. All military hardware is to be seized to prevent its use against the one, true, rightful ruler of the Federated Commonwealth."

With martial law in place, the early-morning roads were almost deserted. One or two ground cars pulled over. The occupants got out to gawk and take holos of the BattleMechs thundering by, looked around and asked one another what was happening, shrugged and gawked some more.

"If they resist?" asked a leftenant.

"I hope they do." Neven grinned. "Let me be clear: the Fifth Alliance Guards is considered a hostile enemy force. Treat them the way you would the Clans or the Dracs. If they shoot, shoot back. Don't wait for my okay. We aren't coming to play."

Neven would show him. Time to repay him for all the hurt.

"Margram Base? Isn't that your brother's unit?"

"Not a factor," Neven snapped quickly. "If we move fast, we can be all over them before they know what is happening. Maybe catch them in their beds. Nobody's going to challenge an *Atlas* when they're in nothing but their pajamas."

All his fault anyway.

A highway toll booth had been converted into a militia checkpoint, a simple affair with a couple of flimsy guardhouses under an awning to protect against sun and rain, barriers to block the lanes, a clutch of light armored vehicles and a slightly more solid command building to one side. The militia, mostly bored recruits barely out of college who had been on duty since local midnight, looked up and rubbed their bleary eyes as the BattleMechs approached.

Without slowing or stopping his 'Mech, Neven aimed and put a Gauss rifle round straight through the command building's front door. The building exploded, blasting the checkpoint with concrete and glass and steel debris. Militiamen staggered and tumbled from their guard posts, dazed and shell-shocked. One or two groped for their weapons. Neven swept them with laser fire as he bore down on them, through them, crashing straight through the awning, snapping metal posts and plastic sheeting to splinters about his 'Mech's knees, then continuing past them.

"Sir, those were just militiamen."

Damn my brother! All his fault anyway.

"I told you, they are the enemy. Wrap your minds around this, folks: as of this day, this hour, we are at war."

Beyond the toll booth-turned-checkpoint there was a low and gentle hill, either side tangled in palm, balsa, and kapok trees, with the arrow-straight slash of a six-lane, gravel-shouldered highway cutting through the center, garlanded at intervals with signposts and speed-limit signs. The BattleMechs paused at the top, a line of Easter Island Moai gazing impassively over a rippling grass sea.

Margram Base spread out below them, a roughly hexagonal plate of flattened earth double-ringed by a low fence and razor wire, then a trench line with firing pits and gun emplacements. In the center stood a cluster of unlovely bunkers, housing the command center, the barracks, and the 'Mech bay.

There was little movement at this hour. A handful of black-on-gray shadows clustered by the gates, sentries at their posts. A sleepless jogger ran laps about the barracks. Scattered lights striped the side of the command center. It was quiet. Peaceful.

Wouldn't take them long to notice twelve BattleMechs bearing down on them. Neven signaled his company to move forward.

He didn't bother trying to open the gates to the base; he simply crushed them underfoot. "Recon Lance, secure the barracks, Fire Lance, the headquarters and communications tower. Command Lance with me, we're heading for the 'Mech bay."

His BattleMechs fanned out quickly. There was no gunfire, he noted with pride, the base personnel cowed, shocked into awe by the massive weight of arms that had come crashing down on them without warning. He turned his *Victor* toward the bulk of the ferrocrete-and-steel 'Mech bay.

His smile slipped as the bay doors groaned and began to slide open with the gritty, grinding rumble of metal moving on metal. A spear of bright interior light carved a line across the gray-dawn ferrocrete. A shadow moved.

"Sir, I have at least one contact, BattleMech powered up on the other side."

"Damn, knew it was too good to last." Neven exhaled a long breath. "Let's hope nobody tries anything foolish. Form up on me."

The light from inside the bay dimmed. A black shadow filled the gap between the gates. Neven groaned inwardly when he recognized the silhouette. A *Zeus*. Of course, it would be a *Zeus*.

His HUD lit up as the battle computer identified the 'Mech, boxed it, and tagged it with sensor data on its tonnage, weaponry, armor. And temperature. A warning flashed to let him know the 'Mech had pinged him with an IFF query and fire-control sensors.

"Neven, what the—" Reinier's voice crackled over an open channel. "What are you doing here?"

Beyond the *Zeus*, Neven could see the 'Mech bay had been transformed into an angry wasp nest of activity. The rest of the BattleMechs in Reinier's company still stood immobile as statues in their steel-girder cradles, but they swarmed with techs and astechs rushing to prep them. Ammunition and coolant trucks raced recklessly through confused crowds of staff, nearly running them over or ramming into one another in their haste to get to safety.

"Power down, Reinier, and nobody gets hurt."

"What are you talking about?"

"Power down. Won't ask you again."

"You're in no position to ask me anything."

"I don't want to hurt anyone."

"*That's* why you've invaded our firebase with an entire company of 'Mechs? To *avoid* violence? This is insane. You're insane."

"It's the only way. Power down."

Neven heard Reinier take a deep breath.

He was closing in now, tracing back through memory, burrowing down to the black kernel of cancer that had eaten away at them. Their story had no grand, operatic beginning, only a small and malignant lump. Ache and loss and blame slowly metastasizing about a hole and looking for an outlet, a home, a target, and finding the closest and most convenient one.

"It's your fault."

There. That's where it started. Three little words. A small thing. Tiny.

"It's all your fault."

A child's blunt weapon, used to win a children's argument, yet nonetheless one that would slowly be honed through years and repetition to a cutting, cruel edge.

One of them looked like their father. The other didn't. Oh no, not that. It was nothing so dramatic. Not infidelity or adoption. No, all their friends and family all knew the real reason for the father's coldness and the brother's antagonism. They knew who the second son looked like: his face was the same shape as the hole at the heart of this family.

0015 LOCAL TIME

"Think she'll do it?"

"What do you think?"

"I think the colonel doesn't hold an all-hands briefing in the middle of the night for funsies."

Neven stood on the periphery of the knot of officers, listening to them talk. They sounded nervous, scared even. There had already been fighting on Kathil and Kentares. It was just been a matter of time before it was their turn, and that was fine with him. Just fine.

"What even is it between those two?"

"Who, the S-Ds?"

"That's families for you, man. You know how they get all tangled up and whatnot. Politics is all well and good, but it takes a family to *really* get the hate going."

The briefing took place in the middle of the 'Mech bay. The great metal doors at the end stood open, allowing the cool night air to whistle the length of the bay and sing among the metal latticework holding each BattleMech upright, a mournful sighing sound that made Neven's skin prickle. He glanced around at the colossal war machines looming over them, silent and faceless and oppressive, and struck by a sudden premonition, hugged his arms close to his sides and hoped the others didn't notice.

"Jealousy, envy, a change in fortunes, that's all it takes. He's the Inner Sphere's golden child, she isn't. That's enough to get the resentment simmering. The blood boiling. Know what I mean?"

"Shh, the colonel."

The officers fell silent as Colonel Dempsey strode into the center of their circle, pacing about like a tiger in an arena, eyes flashing in the blue-white dagger light that stabbed down from lamps set high into the walls above them.

"Sorry to trouble your beauty sleep, ladies and gents, but we have a situation," she began.

"Only one?" one of the majors joked. Nobody laughed.

"Ito has given General Orsina an ultimatum." Dempsey continued to prowl the floor. "He's given her a week to resign. In the meantime, he's moving troops and materiel into position, stockpiling munitions, canceling leave. We can expect the Fifth Guards to move against us once the deadline runs out, if not before."

"Reinier," Neven spoke without thinking.

Dempsey froze, her tiger eyes scanning the crowd until they locked on Neven's face. "Captain?" she asked, voice colder than the night and sharper than the light.

The officers standing around him shifted slightly aside, as though to avoid being caught in any potential blast area.

"I..." He swallowed hard. "Nothing, sir."

"I am about to give all of you one of the hardest orders of my career. I think you know what is coming. What is about to start. This is going to be ugly, folks, no two ways about it. We've been one realm, one people, one family for so long, there's no way this isn't going to hurt. Family fights always do."

The colonel's eyes swept the crowd, then focused back on Neven. "You up for this, Captain?"

Neven stiffened. Every eye was on him now, their gazes silent and heavy with judgment. He was aware of standing on a precipice, at a point where his next words would determine the course of his life, his brother's life, the lives of those serving under them. The future.

He took a deep, steadying breath before replying. "Have I ever given you cause to doubt my loyalty to the regiment, the realm, or the First Prince, sir?"

"No, but I've never had to order you to fight against your own brother."

The question was directed at him, but Neven knew it was meant for everyone: Did they have the will to fight against their own family, their old comrades-in-arms? Turned out to be an easy question for him to answer.

There was no snap decision on his part. No sudden change of heart. His answer was almost foreordained, the long slow and inevitable result of very nearly a lifetime's worth of loss.

"It's his own fault, sir," Neven spat. "If anything happens, he is to blame. Sir."

The colonel did not immediately react, but with her silence she held Neven pinned in place, a prisoner of the moment. Sweat coursed down the insides of his arms. Finally, she nodded, curtly, just once, neither approval nor dismissal, a gesture of guarded acceptance.

"Glad to hear you say that, Captain," she said, "because your company's target is Margram Base."

You had to go back, right back, all the way to the beginning. Only place to start, really. Obvious once you think about it.

There had been a house. A grand one, as befitted a count. Columns and dazzling white paint. An island of solid stone and tile amid a sea of brilliant green. Summer sunlight trapped in time like amber toffee, cicadas singing in the trees.

A family of three: a boy; a serious, somber yet caring father; a mother, thin and frail at the best of times, now wincing under the weight of her second child. A difficult pregnancy at the mother's age, her frail health, but doctors were so good these days, technology and medicines rediscovered, nothing to worry about. Another son would be a blessing, the family's future was bright.

Until their fortunes changed. Until the mother left in a white car with flashing red lights and only a baby brother came back.

A crying baby brother, with his mother's eyes. He was such a small thing.

Tiny, really.

THE END (THE BEGINNING)

SHRAPNEL

BAINBRIDGE'S GUIDE TO IMPACTFUL GEOGRAPHY

KEN' HORNER

Terra is a unique planet, but as humanity spread throughout the stars, they often sought worlds as similar to Terra as possible, even engineering some to become more similar. A few worlds have unique locations that will play a role in active combat. This serial is a practical guide to non-Terran geography that will affect the battlefield. Many entries have analogs that, while different to experts in their fields, are not noticeably different on the battlefield.

(*Note:* Alpha Strike *rules are in parentheses.*)

The Deadly Sands of New Samarkand

New Samarkand is home to the headquarters of the Draconis Combine's Internal Security Force. There are many layers of security to this installation but perhaps the most unique is the synthetic sand surrounding the facility. This material is known to be erosive to a myriad of materials, including human tissues, most polymers, and even BattleMech armor. Little is known about this material, rumored to be principally constructed of diacetylsilicate, but between its destructive nature and the security of the New Samarkand facility, there is minimal opportunity to properly study it. Despite the New Avalon Institute of Science offering a reward of 2 million D-bills per gram of this synthetic sand, no one has ever been known to collect.

Any BattleMech, vehicle, or battle armor ending its turn in a hex containing synthetic sand takes 1D6 damage (AS: 0* damage; see Minimal Damage, p. 48, Alpha Strike: Commander's Edition*). BattleMechs split the damage across their leg locations evenly, rounding up, while combat vehicles, including hovercraft, take this damage to the front.*

Conventional infantry also takes 1D6 damage per turn (AS: 1 damage). BattleMechs that fall take 1 point of damage to each hit location on either the front or back, depending on the fall direction. MechWarriors in BattleMechs that lack operational, sealed life support take 1D3 points of damage per turn they are on a hex containing synthetic sand. Crews of combat vehicles that lack operational, sealed life support suffer the effect of a Crew Stunned critical hit (see p. 194, Total Warfare; p, 50, AS:CE) at the end of every turn the unit is on a hex containing synthetic sand; a third consecutive turn on synthetic sand results in a Crew Killed critical hit (see p. 194, TW; p, 50, AS:CE).

The Rock Monsters of Styx

Early settlers on the Yolo Badlands of Styx encountered unusual formations of boulders, but didn't have the inclination to deal with strange geology. That quickly changed when the colonists would wake up to find entire formations of boulders surrounding their small settlements. A nonsignificant portion of the settlers immediately returned to the main city of Sunder Falls, while the shorthanded group that remained tried to push on. Cameras showed the rocks moved of their own volition at seemingly random times, yet always toward man-made facilities. The conspiracy theories dwindled from sentient aliens or hoaxsters to some sort of new silicoid lifeform or automated weapon. After finally hiring a geological team from New Earth, the Rock Monsters were discovered to be strange geodes with high amounts of silicon surrounding them. After enough electrical activity, the boulders would be charged enough to interact with the magnetic minerals in the ground. Prior to human arrival, the rocks would move randomly, but the electrical activity of settlements acted as a sort of antenna for these odd Rock Monsters, causing them to roll toward settlements when they discharged their stored energy.

Each Rock Monster patch is a rubble hex (AS: 2" template). During the end phase, roll 2D6 for each Rock Monster patch. Add 1 to the roll for every 2 PPCs fired during the Weapon Attack Phase (AS: Add 1 to the roll for every unit with the Energy (ENE) Special Ability that attacked during the Combat Phase). On a result of 10+, the Rock Monster patch moves one hex (AS: 2") toward the nearest BattleMech or combat vehicle. If two or more units are the nearest, randomly determine which unit the patch moves toward. Any infantry in a hex that a Rock Monster patch moves into take 1D6–3 damage (AS: 0* damage).

The Quicksilver River of Alhena

During the heyday of the Star League, immense amounts of military and consumer devices were manufactured, from WarShips down to music players that could fit in an earring. One thing they all had in common is that their manufacture often created hazardous waste. To prevent future explorers from stumbling on hazardous waste dumps on uninhabited planets or moons, the Star League maintained a large bureaucracy for keeping track of what waste went where. This cost money, and some individuals chose to skirt or even ignore these regulations. One such industry was Cinaver Metals, which chose to store waste mercury in an underground dome near their smelting facility on Alhena. Millions of liters a year accumulated until Cinaver collapsed during the Amaris Civil War. After centuries of the mercury being trapped underground, new geological activity pushed the element out through a fissure, where it flowed down an empty gorge on its way to the Beaumont Badlands. This river of mercury, dubbed the Quicksilver River, wasn't near any populated areas, so the populace of Alhena cordoned off the area. While this has limited the environmental impact, treasure seekers in search of hidden warehouses from Cinaver Metals can be found occasionally fighting in the area.

The Quicksilver River functions as a normal river on the battlefield but due to the increased density of the river, the increased buoyancy means all wheeled and tracked vehicles will float on it; hover and WiGE units are unaffected. BattleMechs will automatically fall, though they take half of the normal fall damage due to the cushioning effect of the mercury. Units with aquatic movement (AS: Naval or Submersible Movement types) are reduced to half movement in the Quicksilver River. Units without aquatic or hover movement are unable to move on their own, though BattleMechs can use crawling movement to escape with a +4 Piloting Skill penalty (AS: Use the Bogging Down rules, p. 60, AS:CE. 'Mechs whose roll succeeds may move 2" that turn).

Kavar Valley

Asta II is littered with crystal rock formations in the desert canyons that populate the supercontinent of Balerdo. The most famous of those is Kavar Valley, which contains the most efficient naturally occurring conductors of light ever found. These crystals were sought out only by scientists or occasionally used for knickknacks to sell to visitors. However, when the Twelfth Star Guards attacked during the Fourth Succession War, they discovered a unique aspect of the valley when a company of their 'Mechs engaged a lance of Draconis Combine defenders. Errant laser shots were reflected and could hit unintended targets. While the effect caused considerable damage to both sides, it didn't tip the scales of the battle in favor of either side, and the Combine forces soon surrendered.

Any laser attack that misses its intended target is reflected (AS: If a unit with the Energy (ENE) Special Ability misses its attack, the attack reflects in a different direction). After all attacks against a target are complete, roll 1D6 for the direction the lasers reflect, with a roll of 1 being the same facing as the unit attacked (AS: Roll 1D6 and use an AoE template to determine the direction the attack reflects). Randomly determine a unit in the direction of the reflected attack to be the target of the crystals. Treat the crystals as a stationary attacker with Gunnery of 5 (AS: Skill of 5). Any hits against the target of the crystal do half damage, rounded up.

The Quicksand of Odell

Quicksand occurs on Terra and many other planets when fine granular material is suspended in water that cannot escape. Modern machines of war have little concern with the relatively shallow patches of quicksand that occur, but the strange geology of Odell allows for much deeper quicksand pits. While the cinematic terror of Major Quintin Carver's *Caesar* vanishing into quicksand in *Fox Squad Five* left lasting nightmares to those who fell in love with the character, the quicksand on Odell will just impede movement and leave a unit stranded until they can extricate themselves from the messy morass.

For each hex traversed by a BattleMech or a vehicle with wheeled or tracked movement, roll 2D6: on 11+ the unit has stumbled across a quicksand hex (AS: For every 2" moved by a BattleMech or vehicle with Wheeled or Tracked movements modes, roll 2D6: on 11+, the unit has stumbled into a 2" quicksand template). Use the Bog Down rules—see p. 60, Tactical Operations: Advanced Rules—but apply a +1 modifier to the Piloting/Driving Skill Roll to break free of the quicksand instead of the standard -1 modifier (AS: Use the Bogging Down rules, p. 60, AS:CE, but apply a +1 modifier to the roll to break free).

The Yamity Lava Field

Tourists willing to brave the dangers of an active volcano can see some amazing sights on Pompey's Cumae continent. The Yamity Lava Field isn't one of the top destinations, but the exceptionally brave can take unlicensed hovertours that fly by geysers of erupting lava, some shooting up to thirty meters in the air. Hovercraft is the preferred ground transportation due to the patches of hardened lava that are not very thick, and can collapse under the weight of heavy vehicles. The hardened lava is more uniform than typical magma crust, but it can be stronger or weaker from place to place. The Lava Field acts as a spot for adrenaline junkies and as a natural highway between the Pozzuoli Salt Flats and mining warehouses that contracted with the

Hadrian Mechanized Industries smelting facilities on Pompey, a route that avoids the dense jungle occupying much of the region. Raiders will often land in the salt flats and hurry across the lava fields to quickly raid the smelted ores.

    The Yamity Lava Field has two dangers. The first are the lavacrusts, different from typical magma crusts. When any unit enters a magma crust hex for the first time (AS: When entering a magma crust, and for every 2" moved on this terrain), roll 2D6. On 10+, they are on a lavacrust (AS: a 2" lavacrust template). Roll another 2D6, multiply by 10 and add 20; this is the CF of the lavacrust (AS: Roll 1D6; this is the Terrain Factor of the lavacrust). Any unit whose tonnage exceeds the current CF of the lavacrust breaks through the surface and falls into a lava pit 1D3 levels deep (AS: Any unit whose Size exceeds the Terrain Factor of the lavacrust falls into a lava pit 1D6 inches deep). Treat the fall as if the unit were on top of building that collapsed, per p. 176, Total Warfare (AS: Treat the fall as if the unit were atop a collapsing Medium Building).

    The second danger is the lava geysers. Randomly determine and place approximately 5 geyser holes (AS: 2" geyser templates) per mapsheet. Each turn during the Heat Phase, roll 2D6 for each geyser and add the number of turns since the geyser last erupted; assume the last eruption was before the game began. On a result of 12, the geyser erupts. Any unit in the hex takes 1D6 damage to a random location on the

front facing and 5 additional heat (AS: Any unit within the 2"template of the erupting geyser takes 1 damage and increases its heat level by 1, if applicable). Units in adjacent hexes add 3 more heat from the turn, this amount can exceed the maximum from external sources from combat as with normal magma heat effects (AS: Units within 2" from an erupting geyser increase their heat level by 1, if applicable).

Specter Island

Specter, a medium-sized island on the planet Saffel, is uninhabited due to the high levels of electromagnetic and radioactive interference generated by the various ores beneath its surface. Mining operations are performed in campaigns of three to five months, with the miners using a combination of low-tech and hardened electronic equipment to extract as much of the mineral deposits as possible before they rotate back to the healthier areas of Saffel. The mining hauls can make an inviting target, and the brave—or stupid—pirate can make a considerable haul if they can survive combat on Specter Island. In addition to the general health risks, the interference hampers communications and targeting, with the most notorious effect of creating multiple ghost targets on active scanners.

All units on the island act as though they are in the area effect of an enemy Guardian ECM suite; Beagle Probes can counteract this effect in lieu of their normal features (AS: All units are affected by the ECM

Special Ability; see p. 77, AS:CE; units with probes—the LPRB, PRB, or BH Special Abilities—can counteract this effect).

After declaring a target in the Weapon Attack Phase, roll 2D6 - 6 for each mapsheet (or area of equivalent size); the result is the number of ghost targets that exist on the battlefield that turn. Randomly determine the locations and facing of each ghost target. Attack fire that crosses through a hex containing a ghost target receives a +1 to-hit modifier for each ghost target it crosses (AS: An attack whose line of sight to its target crosses within a 6" radius of at least one ghost target receives a +1 to-hit modifier for each such ghost target within 6" of the line of the attack). If an attack is made against a target in the same hex as a ghost target (AS: within 2" of a ghost target), roll 1D6. On a result of 1–3, the attack targets the ghost target; on 4–6, the declared target is attacked. Attacks against ghost targets use the same modifiers as the original target, such as to determine whether Streak missiles fire, but they do not cause any damage to the original target or terrain. Attacks against a hex, such as artillery fire, ignore the ghost target effects. In a double-blind game, if the opposition is not in visible range, ghost targets should be mistaken by either side as the opposition.

In addition, all Gauss weapons suffer a +1 to-hit modifier due to the highly varying magnetic fields.

UNIT DIGEST: WILSON'S HUSSARS

ZAC SCHWARTZ

Nickname: Wilson's Wimps (2996–3067); Wilson's Winners (3067–3076)
Affiliation: Mercenary
CO: Major Donna Wilson
Average Experience: Veteran/Questionable
Force Composition: 1 medium 'Mech battalion, 3 armor lances (Drillsons), 2 infantry platoons
Unit Abilities: The Hussars receive a −1 to-hit modifier for all attacks made at a range of 0–2 hexes. Any Hussars BattleMech can spend 2 MPs at the end of its movement to prevent any enemy 'Mech from entering the first three hexes in the unit's forward arc this turn; this cannot stop an enemy 'Mech from exiting these hexes. If the opposing 'Mech has jump jets, the Hussars 'Mech may not deny these three hexes unless it also has functioning jump jets.
Parade Scheme: Purple and white

UNIT HISTORY

The quintessential hard-luck mercenaries of the 31st century, Wilson's Hussars were, for most of their existence, a literal textbook example of how the merc life could go wrong. Beginning as Lafarge's Hussars, a battalion of the Capellan Confederation Armed Forces' Seventh Andurien Hussars, they had an exemplary record in the 2980s, led to glory in the Siege of Fletcher in 2985 and the Third Battle of Tsingtao in 2988 by the renowned Major Alexander Floyd. However, the Hussars were shattered in their 2996 defense of Buchlau. A combat drop by the assault 'Mechs of the Sixth Syrtis Fusiliers crushed Major

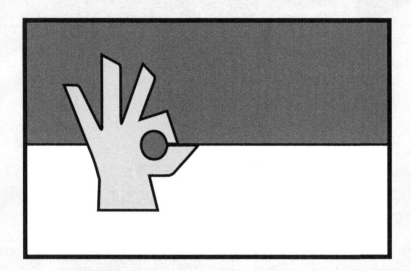

Floyd's *Warhammer* with a drop pod and killed a third of the battalion's MechWarriors in the short, savage fight that followed. Ranking officer Captain Jennifer Langstrom surrendered, and the remaining Hussars were allowed to retain their equipment in exchange for swearing fealty to House Davion.

Subpar treatment led to grumbling within the Hussars in the years that followed, and after three months without pay, the Hussars abandoned the Davions for the alluring freedom of mercenary service. In 3007, a successful contract defending New Samarkand, which netted the Hussars a lance of 'Mechs and a *Leopard* DropShip, seemed to vindicate the decision. However, when House Kurita used them in a disastrous assault on Suk II, the Hussars left the Combine for Capellan employ. While Maximillian Liao was not thrilled to employ CCAF deserters, he couldn't afford to be picky, and successful defenses of Highspire and Redfield confirmed the pragmatism of his choice. However, the Hussars' luck ran out once again when Jennifer Langstrom died at the controls of her *BattleMaster* in 3014, overrun by a Davion assault on St. Ives. Her brother Michael assumed command, and the true downward spiral began.

In the landmark 3076 textbook *Studies in Military Incompetence*, Michael Langstrom is infamously described as a "fascinating case study in how nepotism can elevate those with no discernible positive qualities and nearly every known character flaw." Despite a tenure of just two years, Langstrom's foolishness cost the Hussars dearly. While the Hussars defended a Free Worlds League raid on Ingersoll in 3016, clumsy strategic maneuvering left them surrounded by a Marik regiment. Langstrom ignored the loss of their air support and called in one of their DropShips for rescue—only for League fighters to shoot it down, whereupon it crashed into the Hussars' position, wiping out half the unit. Unable to stomach Major Langstrom's idiocy any longer, Captain David Wilson pivoted his *Marauder* and obliterated Langstrom in the confusion, then led the survivors on a successful breakout from the Marik encirclement. The newly minted Wilson's Hussars came full circle, once again fleeing the Capellan Confederation's service.

Forced to sell their remaining DropShip to stay afloat, the Hussars subsisted on low-paying contracts to survive. Two years later, after a corrupt Draconis Combine liaison ripped off the mercenaries, an ill-advised reprisal raid on Kobe ended with the unit escaping into the Periphery. From there, they found themselves working for bandit kingdoms, first Redjack Ryan and then Helmar Valasek. Valasek used the Hussars as sacrificial decoys in the notorious assault on the Longbow Mountain fortress on Sterope in 3024, then marooned them on Lushann during the return trip. Psychologically broken, the unit spent the next three decades recuperating in the Deep Periphery as David focused on raising his daughter Donna to one day take command.

In 3056, when Wilson's Hussars returned to Outreach with barely two BattleMech lances and the (possibly stolen) decrepit *Union*-class DropShip *Raconteur*, most observers believed the beleaguered mercenaries would not last through the year. Major Donna Wilson proved them wrong, first by arranging a canny merger with a small security force that bolstered their numbers, and then winning a lucrative retainer contract with the Federated Suns. Garrison duty in the Capellan March paid the bills for the next five years. Freeing up Allied forces as the FedCom Civil War raged, the Hussars eventually found themselves playing a minor but notable role in the conflict's conclusion. Placed in command of a two-battalion collection of mercenaries from around the Chaos March, the Hussars were dispatched to Small World. There they led the decisive actions of the campaign, first thoroughly flogging the Seventeenth Arcturan Guards over two weeks, and then breaking their morale with a massive combat drop on the Lyran landing zone. Further mergers with other mercenaries from the task force left Wilson's Hussars the strongest they would ever be.

Another long-term Davion contract saw the Hussars on the breadbasket world of Nopah when the Word of Blake Jihad broke out. A Blakist assault came in 3068, and the Hussars went to ground. After a lucky shot by a Hussars sniper killed the Blakist commander, the mercenaries took advantage of the Word's paralysis to overrun the spaceport, liberate their DropShip, and escape to Valexa to repair and refit. But their streak of good fortune was finally coming to an end. Operating in support of the Second Federated Suns Armored Cavalry on Schedar in 3076, Wilson's Hussars were wiped out while valiantly holding off a counterattack by the Protectorate Militia, with Donna Wilson's *Catapult* the last to fall. The Hussars' heroic sacrifice was not in vain, however, as it allowed the Second to flank and rout the Blakists.

COMPOSITION

Wilson's Hussars fluctuated in size over the years. At their lowest point, they were reduced to just five functioning BattleMechs. At their height during the Jihad, they possessed a full 'Mech battalion and an oversized support company of Drillson hovertanks and conventional infantry.

SHRAPNEL

RUN, LOCUST, RUN

WESTIN RIVERSIDE

**NEUER WIESBADEN
NEW HESSEN
CAPELLAN CONFEDERATION
20 JUNE 3007**

They say Locust *pilots are a little bit crazy,* Abby thought as she looked up at her ride. Some attributed the craziness to the nature of the 'Mech, some called it a nuance in the neural feed, and others simply dismissed *Locust* pilots as having a penchant for self-destruction.

However, MechWarriors who drove the LCT-1M *Locust* often enough differed: they swore the machine had a spirit of its own. Abby wasn't one of those, but she felt there *was* something about the 'Mech itself, something that got into your head, something she liked. She anticipated that feeling as she climbed up the ladder to the cockpit. Every time she donned her neurohelmet and activated the interface, it was like her *Locust* was humming some sort of vibration directly into her brain.

On her climb to the cockpit, she took a moment to admire the stylized cartoon cricket in running shoes, smoking a cigar and dual wielding six-shooters, the bold red stylized script spelling out the 'Mech's name, *Corredor*. None of the techs could remember who originally painted the mascot or how long ago, but Abby always took time to touch it up whenever she could.

Techs were removing the lines that secured the 'Mech to the DropShip's cocoons, and the chief tech merely gave Abby a thumbs-up when she made eye contact. *Corredor* was ready to go, as there had been plenty of time in transit to address routine maintenance.

Swinging into the cockpit, Abby scanned the boards: wireframe green, reactor on scram, sensors online and returning pings from the immediacy of the 'Mech bay, long-range-missile bin half full. After donning her neurohelmet and connecting the leads, she tightened the straps to the command couch and took a deep breath before determinedly reaching over and switching the reactor off scram. When the engine thrummed to life, the myomers tensed with initial charge, and she felt that bond to the machine. Immediately, she wanted to charge out at full throttle, sprinting around like a madwoman who had mistakenly been given 20 tons of war machine. But not right now: there was a lot of rubble to navigate to the first waypoint on her recon route.

After easing *Corredor* out the bay and down the DropShip's ramp, the next hour consisted of minimal throttle and constant course correction through rough terrain, the burnt remnants of an older conflict. To Abby, *Corredor* seemed almost annoyed, the slow pace incompatible with its nature as a fast mover. *Easy there, boy! Almost clear.*

Her company was holed up in the ruins of Neuer Wiesbaden, on a scavenging hunt for their next big score. Coming off a Free Worlds league garrison contract, her unit, Garret's Freebooters, was scavenging a city that had been destroyed during the First Succession War. Or the Second? She thought the Third was still officially going on, but was slowing down as all sides were running out of resources. The Freebooters, like many small mercenary units, often supplemented their income through scavenging opportunities, and their CO, Captain Garret Ross, had both a predilection for history and a knack for picking good sites.

From the boss's briefing, she gathered they were looking for a high-value something, supply-cache something used by the Caps way long ago, and which got bombarded from orbit by the Fed Rats, maybe? Abby tended to daydream through briefings, but the boss knew when a site is destroyed from orbit, scavengers generally pick from the top and outskirts of the rubble pile. He also reasoned that the site warranted orbital bombardment because it was protecting something, often deep underground, the theory being that if an opposing force couldn't destroy what was underground, you could just bury it and deny the enemy those assets. Locals generally don't appreciate strangers showing up with IndustrialMechs and digging through their graveyards while BattleMechs run patrols around the site, but fortunately, these particular locals were occupied elsewhere. ComStar News Bureau vids showed the garrisoning Ariana Grenadiers currently duking it out with a Deneb Light Cavalry detachment over more intact cities 200 klicks to the north.

The ruins of Neuer Wiesbaden were open for what Garret Ross referred to as an "appraisal-in-force." Records from a civil-engineering test case, obtained from Garret's frequent library trips on their last assignment, depicted a reinforced bunker with military characteristics in the eastern portion of the city. The opportunity was too good to pass up, so the Freebooters had burned in under an obscure cargo company's transponder and plopped their *Union* right down in the rubble close to the suspected bunker. The faux transponder probably didn't fool anyone, but as long as they made no moves to look like they were reinforcing the Grenadiers or the DLC, they would probably be left alone.

It had been six weeks since Abby felt *Corredor* sway beneath her, and she was excited for the first patrol outside the city. Down into and out of the last crater, a flat expanse lay before her. If she were more superstitious, she would swear *Corredor* was braying to run. As the internal gyro spun up to balance the 'Mech, she throttled *Corredor* forward at half speed.

The *Locust*'s frame settled into a rhythm. Unlike most 'Mechs, the back-canted knee and proportionally longer lower legs caused a lot of movement in the torso, even at a walking pace. It significantly jostled the pilot in the command couch, enough that more than one new *Locust* driver had regurgitated lunch over the command console when throttling up for the first time. No simulator had ever been able to accurately reproduce the motion. Most *Locust* drivers left the safety-harness straps a little loose so they could rock their hips and shoulders to counter the chassis's sway, like an experienced equestrian moving with the horse. Abby had a quick tightener on her five-point harness, so if she felt *Corredor* about to go over, she could yank the tightener and lock her firmly into the command couch while she awaited impact with the ground. Her techs had claimed she wouldn't have time to do so, but being able to sway with the machine's gait seemed to further bond her with the 'Mech. *Maybe we are crazy?*

A quick glance at her screens showed no magnetic-resonance traces, no heat blooms on thermal, and no radio traffic outside Freebooter channels. She brought the throttle up to two-thirds and nosed down the torso a bit to lean into the run. She cut to the right quickly, leaning deep into the turn and springing out of it. She cut left, twisting the torso into it and opening the stride. Full throttle now, she leaned *Corredor* left and right, serpentining the 'Mech between the few remaining obstacles on the open plain.

To the left she spied a canal, deep but narrow, about five meters across. She shouldered the 'Mech toward it, lining up the timing. Lacking jump jets, *Locust*s were often considered a substandard recon 'Mech, so consequently—*or because we* are *crazy*—*Locust* drivers seemed inclined to hurdle obstacles whenever possible. The canal proved too tempting an obstacle for Abby to ignore.

Approaching at near top speed, she timed the left foot to land just at the paved edge of the canal, then shoved the throttle forward. A quick throttle tweak planted the right foot on the opposite side, and the 'Mech resumed the fast, rocking gait of full throttle. She let out a *whoop* only she and *Corredor* could hear.

It seemed like utter freedom, tearing up the plain in one of the fastest 'Mechs ever made. Perfect concentration, eyes forward, looking for other obstacles to snake around or stride over. Rigorously putting the *Locust* through its paces, right up to the design limit. Which was probably why she didn't notice the pips dropping one by one down on the mag-res screen, heat blooms blossoming on the thermal. At least, not until the sound no MechWarrior wants to hear chimed through the earbuds inside the neurohelmet.

Target lock! I'm being painted!

Without thinking, she fell back on instinct and juked *Corredor* to the left, both legs extended to the right under the 'Mech's torso. Laser burn flashed across the targeting screen, and tracer rounds from an autocannon sailed past the right side of her cockpit. She twisted the *Locust* farther to the left and throttled back up to full before sparing a moment for her screens.

Damn, where'd they come from? Wasn't paying attention.

The first salvo came from a *Shadow Hawk* behind her, tagged by the battle computer as a standard -2H. To her left, the computer tagged an STG-3R *Stinger* that was still spinning up its reactor to full. On the right was another *Stinger* raising its Omicron 3000 laser to line up a shot on her. Dead ahead at long range was a JR7-D *Jenner*.

Damn, looks like I ran right past a powered-down recon lance, some patrol preventing a wide flank, or maybe looking to exploit one. No time to think, just run, run, run, run!

A quick glance at her three-sixty viewstrip did not give her much confidence. Both *Stinger*s were in her ten o'clock, an excellent flanking position. The *Jenner* was ahead, to her one o'clock, throttling up to flank the right side. All three light 'Mechs were moving to box her in so the *Shadow Hawk* on her six could line up the kill.

Double damn!

Abby keyed on her comm. "Freeboot Home, Freeboot Home, this is One-Four. Contact, contact, one medium and three light 'Mechs, vector two-eight-zero from Home. One-Four is escape and evade."

The warning out, she spun 120 degrees to the right and toggled her weapons to hot. *Gotta get past the* Shadow Hawk *before they box me.* She fired a quick salvo at the *Jenner*, both the Martel laser and the Holly LRM 5. The intent wasn't to hit so much as to slow the enemy 'Mech down, opening a gap between it and the *Shadow Hawk*.

Both *Stinger*s fired their lasers; one shot passed behind, not compensating for the speed, but the other tagged her right arm, turning her armor wireframe yellow in an instant. She had figured one of the *Stinger*s would land a shot, but their mistake was not making it on the run. She was throttled up full while they were at barely a walk, so with any luck, she would significantly extend the distance by the time their lasers recycled.

But the *Jenner* had recovered from its scare, and was now lining up a shot on her left side, which held one of her Holly 5s. Also, the *Shadow Hawk* had planted its feet and was carefully tracking her, its torso twisting.

Damn. Crossfire!

She wrenched *Corredor* to the left, closing slightly with the *Jenner*, but extending the range to the *Shadow Hawk* although exposing her rear. Any shot from the *Shadow Hawk*'s main weapons to her back, and it would be over.

The moment her Martel and Holly 5s showed green on her board, she cracked off a shot at the top of *Corredor*'s stride, where her 'Mech was least affected by movement. The laser went wide and only one missile hit the *Shadow Hawk*, which still felt like a victory. Two steps later, she wrestled *Corredor* another 120 degrees to the right, leaning her 'Mech into the turn at an incredible angle that seemed impossible to hold, only the gyro and momentum carrying *Corredor* out of the turn.

Then the *Shadow Hawk* fired. The autocannon passed high, and the LRM salvo dug up the ground in front of *Corredor* as the enemy pilot attempted to lead their target. Abby knew why though: they were gauging speed and distance for the follow-up shot with the laser, which required no lead. The laser hit and took the right-side Holly 5 clean off. *Corredor* weathered the rest of the blast, but off-balance, it stumbled for two steps before resuming its run.

Abby's comm clicked on. "One-Four, One-Four, this is One-One. Sitrep?"

"This is One-Four," she replied. "Survival mode, returning to base ASAP."

"Copy, One-Four. Rolling out welcome wagon. Good luck."

All just down to moving now, but where to?

Abby estimated the recharge time for the *Shadow Hawk*'s weapons while gauging the *Jenner*'s speed. Luckily the *Stinger*s were now at an extremely long range; they may have already fired again and missed for all she knew, but she couldn't keep up with all the threats. The *Jenner* was paralleling her track to keep her herded inside the *Shadow Hawk*, which was still at an optimum firing distance, the medium 'Mech casually walking backward while its torso lazily swiveled to track her.

It's gonna go for an alpha strike, probably aimed at my legs. Then let's see how fast you can really track...

Abby leaned the *Locust* farther to the right, to cross the *Shadow Hawk* while the *Jenner* fired another shot that went wide.

The maneuver seemed to catch the *Shadow Hawk* pilot off guard as it throttled in reverse and increased its torso twist. It seemed to stutter a little over some large rocks, causing it to momentarily lose its track. She roared past the 'Mech's twelve o'clock, hoping the pilot hadn't thought to use their jets to quickly hop and rotate. Fortunately, the *Shadow Hawk* stayed on the ground, but it was able to get around enough to line up its autocannon, laser, and LRMs.

Even knowing her throttle was at full, Abby pushed it again in a vain effort to squeeze few more kph out of *Corredor*. Assuming the *Shadow Hawk*'s weapons were reloaded and ready, she figured she had one chance, and only the truly crazy would even think of trying it.

Risking a glance at the three-sixty, she saw the *Jenner* back off, yielding the kill to its commander, the *Shadow Hawk* settling in for the shot. *Corredor* rocked hard at full throttle, the canal approaching rapidly, while she assumed the *Shadow Hawk* pilot was making their last-second adjustments.

Just short of the canal, she slammed the throttle down. The gyro whined in complaint at the sudden shift in momentum, shock absorbers in the upper and lower legs shrieked as they exceeded their design limits, and the cockpit pitched violently forward, looking almost straight down. She twisted *Corredor* to the left and pulled its nose up just short of the canal. The forward unspent momentum was converted into lateral momentum as she placed the 'Mech directly over the middle of the canal in midstep and throttled hard back to stop, pulling the harness tight as she did.

Corredor dropped right into the canal bed on both feet. She lowered the 'Mech until the legs, from ankle to back-canted knee, lay flat on the ground in the middle of the canal, as far hull down as she could go. Explosions and light above her threw debris down on the cockpit. She was correct on the alpha strike, but the canal edge took most of the hits, no effective damage to *Corredor*.

Not waiting for the dust to settle, she lurched the 'Mech up and sped down the depression in the canal. *Corredor*'s cockpit just clearing the top of the canal, Abby spared a look back at the *Shadow Hawk*. It seemed confused, if a 'Mech could look confused: *Corredor* had been painted and locked on, then had simply just dropped out of view.

Abby gave the opposing pilot a wink and let out a solid "Whoop!" of victory.

In a half klick, the side of the canal closest to the city banked less steeply, and using her 'Mech's momentum and long legs, she raced up the side. The three-sixty now showed all the enemy 'Mechs at the edge of their weapon ranges. They could've tossed a few LRM salvos at her, but their most effective weapons couldn't have hit her.

The annoying rubble of Neuer Wiesbaden now looked more welcoming than when she had left an hour ago. In the distance she saw her company mates sortieing out to cover her. In her rear, the enemy 'Mechs looked to be regrouping in a more formal battle line.

Garret's MAD-3R *Marauder* pivoted its torso to get a better read on her and the enemy. "One-Four, this is One-One. Sitrep?"

"Whoop, whoop, whoop!" Abby let out with joy, clear of danger, and *Corredor* sprinted forward, spirited by the sheer abandon of its pilot.

"You *Locust* drivers are a strange lot." The *Marauder*'s torso straightened in line with its legs. "All 'Booters, looks like we've been made. Let's grab what we can, then bail. We're not in this for a slugfest."

The Freebooters 'Mechs began forming a battle line while IndustrialMechs picked up the pace inside the rubble. The clock was now ticking.

That was irrelevant to Abby, though. Minus one arm and some armor, she jolted the throttle up and down, jerking her 'Mech left to right in an odd dance. For a moment she thought she could feel *Corredor*'s mood, if a machine could have one: content with a small victory and disproportionately showing it off.

We Locust *drivers certainly* are *a bit mad*, she mused to herself.

SHRAPNEL

A SHIP OUT OF TIME

ERIC SALZMAN

Decrypt 13066L454E
EYES ONLY: ovKhan Fergus Sennet
From: Sea Fox Watch, Field Delta, Team Zeta
Date: 1 July 3152

OvKhan,

    Our team preparing to restore HPG services on Callison had the fortune to be in position at the nadir jump point to witness the arrival of a rare *Liberty*-class JumpShip on 13 June 3152. The Wolf Empire garrison scrambled interceptors, expecting the vanguard of an invasion.
    Adrift and powerless, the vessel offered no resistance when a Wolf boarding party cut its way in and seized the crew. Our agents in the Wolf Watch obtained access to interrogation records, alerting our HPG tech team to the crew's unusual claims. Sensing opportunity, they issued and won a Trial of Possession. Our technicians subsequently recovered the ship's logs.
    The most recent entries were made by Micaela Corte, currently a guest of the Wolf Empire:

[BEGIN LOG ENTRIES]

13 FEBRUARY 3046
Testing. Testing. Yeah, Jerry—whatever you did to the computer worked! Still can't access the corrupted logs, but at least we can run diagnostics. <ahem> This is Dr. Micaela Corte, heading the Interstellar Expeditions survey mission to Aquileia. We detected a derelict *Liberty*-class JumpShip drifting at the edge of sensor range following our arrival. Initial flyby

showed no apparent structural damage, but all bays were opened to space. Putting a survey team aboard, we've found no sign of the crew, though one shuttle is missing.

17 FEBRUARY 3046
We've managed to get access to the four attached DropShips. Every hold is full of strange crystals that give off unusual EM readings. The Kearny-Fuchida drive's initiator was burned out—probably a misjump. With the spares we have on our vessel, Jerry thinks we can fix the drive, but it'll take weeks. We managed to activate the transponder—it reads as the *Mogami*. I think we've stumbled across the Cult of the Saints Cameron's lost treasure ship!

13 MARCH 3046
Diagnostics show the *Mogami*'s K-F drive fully operational and all systems within acceptable parameters. I am leading a skeleton crew to bring the ship back to IE's regional offices on Denebola, via Callison. The rest will jump simultaneously in our expedition ship in case something on this hulk blows in transit. Next stop, fame and fortune!

[END LOG ENTRIES]

Our technicians were able to recover the original ship's logs recorded by Captain Walter Wilfred:

[BEGIN LOG ENTRIES]

13 JUNE 2758
As of 1227 hours, ship time, Cargo Chief Han-sik reports successful docking of all four *Mule*s, each carrying capacity loads of shuksam and mirst crystals. Ever since the Believers started using these rocks to commune with dead Camerons, they've become more valuable than germanium. Lucky I was in position to cut a bulk deal before the rubes on Shiloh saw the market projections. I had Han-sik schedule extra runs to bring back another 500 tons for our internal cargo bay. With my cut of the profits, I can finally scrap this old bucket and upgrade to a *Star Lord*. Shiloh customs has cleared us for jump to Aquileia at 1300 hours.

15 JUNE 2758
The *Mogami* suffered a misjump on 13 June when transiting from the Shiloh system to Aquileia. The jump was accompanied by a massive electromagnetic surge that disabled key systems. Maintenance teams have restored power, but are still running down malfunctions in the drive core. Navigator Selak speculates that we may have displaced from our arrival

coordinates, since crews performing external repairs report no other vessels or stations in visual range. Now that sensors are online, Selak will attempt to ascertain our location.

16 JUNE 2758
It...it seems impossible. Selak confirms we are exactly where we should be—Aquileia's nadir jump point. But the customs station, normally servicing dozens of JumpShips, is missing. We haven't monitored any other traffic within range, and all communications channels are silent. I've dispatched a shuttle under XO Lott to the planet, to investigate further. Where *is* everyone?

23 JUNE 2758
Chief Hayworth has secured Han-sik in his quarters, under guard. Yesterday, he reported to medbay, complaining of headaches and vision problems, and was given a sedative. At 0633 this morning, he overrode the safeties and opened the main cargo bay door to space, jettisoning three crewmen. When security reached his control station, he was raving that "they" were out there, calling to us, and that we "had to join them."

25 JUNE 2758
I've placed the *Mogami* under shipwide lockdown after several more instances of the crew exhibiting self-destructive behavior. Tried to beam a status update to the shuttle. Got back only static. Or...was it...screaming?

27 JUNE 2758
I...I can hear them now. God help me, they're...calling me...so loud...so many. Richard...Richard says it wasn't his fault!

[END LOG ENTRIES]

The following logs aboard the remaining shuttle are from Executive Officer Nada Lott:

[BEGIN LOG ENTRIES]

25 JUNE 2758?
Aquileia has suffered an unimaginable calamity. Orbital imaging shows deep blast craters where major population centers and atmospheric processing plants once stood. The climate has become unlivable. But it would take *decades* for the atmosphere to de-terraform, and we were here just last month! The only sign of civilization was an orbital beacon that activated as our shuttle approached. It warned that Aquileia had been placed under quarantine by order of something called "ComStar."

2 JULY 2758?
Returned to the *Mogami* after losing communication with them on the 25 June. Found the ship had drifted, its station-keeping drives disengaged. External ports were open, and the entire ship had been vented. No crew remained aboard. Repairs to the DropShips appear to have been abandoned—none are flight-capable. We have gathered what remains of the food and water, plus tools and EVA suits, and are returning to Aquileia in the second, fully fueled shuttle, hoping to scavenge sufficient supplies to effect repairs.

[END LOG ENTRIES]

I strongly recommend a full scientist team evaluate the derelict before attempting to activate the K-F drive. Like Walter and Micaela, I see the potential for immense profits from the *Mogami*, but we must proceed carefully or risk following them into misfortune and madness.

Field Delta Commander Luminita

SHRAPNEL

LONE WOLF AND FOX

BRYAN YOUNG

PART 1 (OF 4)

PROLOGUE

ALYINA MERCANTILE LEAGUE HEADQUARTERS
EXCHANGE PLACE TOWER
NEW DELHI
ALYINA
ALYINA MERCANTILE LEAGUE
9 AUGUST 3151

Syndic Marena heard they'd begun calling her the "Merchant Queen of Alyina," and didn't hate it as much as she thought she would. Surveying the whole of New Delhi from the top floor of her office tower, she knew she could create a new way of doing things. The city lay before her in every direction, covered in clouds threatening another impressive storm. Fortunately, it was not yet typhoon season.

On the eastern side of the Exchange Place Tower were more high-rises like the one she'd taken for her headquarters for the Alyina Mercantile League. Beyond that was a vibrant downtown and the more residential districts, as well as the vertical hydroponic farms. Originally the buildings had been covered in ornate tilework, but the trappings of beauty in New Delhi had fallen into disrepair since Clan Jade Falcon had taken possession of the planet.

To the north was the entertainment district. A multipurpose stadium was the centerpiece of that part of town. In the earliest days of Alyina, it had been used for cricket and other games, but nowadays it was as likely to be used for cricket as it was for 'Mech combat, like they had on Solaris VII. But those sporting events were few and far between, as the stadium had fallen into disrepair over the last hundred years. There were long-abandoned theaters she'd finally allowed to open again after a generations-long ban by the Jade Falcons. It also housed the New Delhi planetary library, a hub for all the knowledge accumulated on the planet since its founding—all the knowledge the Jade Falcons hadn't declared seditious or detrimental, at least. To the south, where the elevator and walls obscured her view, was the river and the spaceport. And to the west?

To the west lay the jewel of her holdings: Factory Zone 4. The massive industrial area had been built over the old jungle, and over the decades it had pushed farther and farther into the tree line on the edge of the city. It produced so much of the wealth and components that made Alyina the perfect place for Marina to form her new empire. And BattleMechs. It produced the BattleMechs that were the currency of the Inner Sphere.

Because of its importance, Factory Zone 4 had been the most well-maintained sector of the city. In fact, most of the capital beyond the all-important Factory Zone had crumbled into disrepair after a century of Clan rule. That was the problem with a society that valued warriors above all else: warriors saw war as the solution to everything. And when those warriors piloted BattleMechs, the solution to every problem became one they could simply shoot at. To shoot those problems, the warriors always needed more 'Mechs, so the means to produce their 'Mechs trumped any care for the citizenry. The Inner Sphere and those Kerensky swore to eventually defend needed something better, and that was what the Alyina Mercantile League would be.

Marena was used to being underestimated. She was a Black woman and a merchant in a world dominated by barbarous Clan warriors like the lily-white Malvina Hazen. Yes, she was a Trueborn Jade Falcon, but that did not matter, since she was a member of a caste considered "inferior" to the warriors.

Her new order was going to take some work to accomplish, but she would succeed or die trying.

"Ma'am," a voice said over her desktop comm unit.

"Yes?" Marena replied.

"Star Captain Margolian is here to report on the raid."

Just hearing the name brought tension to Marena's chest, a hot blossom of anger blooming there. "Send him up."

"Aff."

After a few moments, the elevator doors opened, and Star Captain Margolian exited. He clenched his jaw and held his head high, but she knew he felt the double sting in his pride. First, because he was reporting to a merchant instead of a warrior. Second, because no warrior liked reporting bad news, especially when they might be viewed as partially responsible.

"Star Captain Margolian," Syndic Marena said as she walked back from the windows to her massive desk in the center of the room. The office was designed to be more opulent than functional, a place to have meetings that would impress and confound the other party in negotiations. For a MechWarrior explaining his failure, it must have seemed beyond absurd.

Margolian stood at military attention in green Jade Falcon coveralls. As much as she'd been raised as a Jade Falcon, she'd grown to despise the color and everything it represented. Since she'd been doing her best to manage the merchant caste in the wake of Malvina Hazen's folly, she'd come to see exactly how sick Clan culture had become.

"Syndic Marena," he said deferentially. His coveralls were wrinkled and dirty, a smear of oil across one side—clearly something he'd just thrown on over his piloting gear after losing the battle, to get the information and bring her the report as quickly as possible.

"I hear you have a report for me," she said.

"Aff." He placed a memory cartridge into the desk's holoprojector, and the device whirred to life. The windows around the room turned opaque in an instant, and the blue light of the projector filled the room. It showed a detailed layout of the southern landing port inside Factory Zone 4. Resting in the blast pit was a standard *Mule*-class DropShip with the telltale markings of a Jade Falcon merchant vessel. It looked more haggard than other ships in Marena's mercantile fleet, but otherwise not out of the ordinary. "This is the DropShip in question."

"It looks like one of ours."

"*Neg.* That is where the trouble began. Using Alyina-based transponder codes, this ship landed *with* authorization."

That thought troubled Marena, but she could ask about it later.

Margolian gestured with his hands, pointing to spots on the security holo as he spoke. "They unloaded several 'Mechs and salvage vehicles—again, nothing out of the ordinary. They all bore the correct parade colors, which averted enough suspicion to let them march right into the 'Mech facility in the Eden Quadrant without being accosted."

Marena watched the holographic 'Mechs marching, furious at what she knew she was about to see. "At what point did we determine that this was a pirate incursion?"

"Here." Margolian sped up the recording. One of the incredibly precious 45-ton *Hierofalcon*s stepped out of the factory and up the loading ramp of the pirate DropShip. As a second 'Mech exited the factory, something happened to the salvage loader, and the driver got out to fiddle with something in the inner workings of the vehicle.

Another figure came out from the factory and offered to assist, and then the image froze at Margolian's gesture. "One of the pirate salvage loaders seemed to have some issue, so one of our people went out to help. We do not have audio of the altercation, but the astech seemed to realize what was actually going on."

Margolian advanced the holo, and the pirate pulled out a needler pistol and shot the loyal astech, the flechette rounds ripping holes through him.

Feeling each wound deep in her gut, Marena couldn't help but regret the waste. This was their old ways coming back to roost. Everything solved by the muzzle of a gun.

Margolian allowed her a moment before proceeding with the report. "It was at this point the alarm bells went off. Why the pirates made such a mistake in the middle of a sophisticated heist like this is anyone's guess."

"Where were you and your warriors?"

"I received notice approximately four minutes later." The view on the holo switched to a building some distance away from the blast pit, in a another quadrant of Factory Zone 4. A *Jade Phoenix*, two *Night Gyr*s, and two *Ion Sparrow*s marched from the garrison. "I activated my Trinary immediately, but we were stationed across the city, and are its only defense. It was to my great fortune that my command Star happened to be closest to the engagement zone, but by the time I arrived, the pirates had loaded two more *Hierofalcon*s into their DropShip's hold."

The holo switched from the security cams to the battleROM footage of Margolian's *Jade Phoenix*. Audio of him coordinating his Trinary against the DropShip bled into the room and filled the space.

Margolian lowered the volume of the battle and narrated it personally. "I had my Trinary engage from three directions to expedite contact. My intent, given my limited information, was to scare them away. They were doing something more brazen than we would have expected. They knew their window of opportunity was limited, they were so deep behind enemy lines, and they knew they would be overwhelmed."

The first Star of the Trinary engaged. To his credit, Margolian scored the first kill, obliterating the cockpit of one of the pirate *Locust*s, an old 'Mech outmatched by everything the Mercantile League fielded. The second Star arrived, but not before the pirates had loaded two more *Hierofalcon*s onto their DropShip. They were fighting brutally over a sixth *Hierofalcon* when the Trinary's third Star arrived from the opposite direction. The DropShip opened fire, much more dangerous than the pirate 'Mechs that rapidly pulled back inside the DropShip itself.

"They made off with six *Hierofalcon*s. We fought to subdue the DropShip as long as we could. I lost three warriors in my Trinary, and the third is in the infirmary. We sacrificed much to defend the city. I accept full responsibility for this failure, Syndic, but I must also state my defense."

Marena calmed herself with a deep breath. "And what defense do you have for this?"

"My Trinary is the only meaningful defense for a city that stretches for kilometers, houses millions of civilians and workers, and is a major industrial complex and military target. We are spread too thin. The

only bona fide warriors we have came from service on the VaultShips. The Jade Falc—"

"The Mercantile Militia," Marena corrected him.

"*Aff*. The Mercantile Militia simply does not have the resources or trained warriors to defend against these attacks. Doubly so if they become more frequent."

"Do you know where these pirates were stationed?"

"*Neg*. We are working on it."

"Do you know *who* these pirates were?"

Margolian's jaw clenched tighter. "*Neg*."

"Find out."

"*Aff*, Syndic." Margolian bowed and retrieved his data chip from the console on the desk. The holoprojector's light faded, and the windows returned to their prior transparency.

Marena felt the embarrassment radiate from him. As much as she despised the way warriors ran things, she was sympathetic to their training. They had been inculcated by their Clan to be the best at everything they did. To have lost so thoroughly in the safety of their own nest felt just as shameful for Marena. She felt that vulnerability as well, and knew she had to either fledge or fall.

"Have faith, Star Captain. The Mercantile League will survive where the Jade Falcons have not."

He nodded, unable to bring himself to speak.

"And, for what it is worth, I am deeply sorry for the loss of your warriors."

"Thank you, Syndic."

The elevator doors opened automatically as he approached. Marena watched him step into the elevator, looking so small in the distance. He turned to her once he stepped inside, and she saw the defeat on his face. The elevator doors closed and took him away.

Marena sighed.

Morale was low.

And if the Mercantile League could not defend its people, there would be no Mercantile League for long.

She had to come up with some answer to their problems. Some way to defend themselves against all the vultures coming to pick their bones clean.

There were plenty of options, but none were good.

The language she understood was money. But how could money give her an answer?

She only knew the solution was out there. Somewhere.

CHAPTER ONE

**CONFEDERATE-CLASS DROPSHIP *FOX DEN*
GALAPORT
GALATEA
31 AUGUST 3151**

Her name was Katie Ferraro, and she seemed to be having an even more difficult time than usual convincing her five-'Mech mercenary unit, the Fox Patrol, to take on the job she'd already accepted.

"Why do I get the feeling we've just been sold some magic beans?" Rhiannon Ramirez said at the conference table aboard the *Fox Den*, and Katie couldn't help but feel stung by her words.

Katie straightened her back and raised her head. "I think it's a great opportunity. They said they made their name fighting for Hanse Davion."

Dexter Nicks, the grizzled veteran of the Fox Patrol, rested his chin on his artificial palm. "Wrong Hanse Davion."

"Huh?" Katie said.

"It was the double."

Katie blinked. She had no idea what he was talking about, and maybe it was for the best. She made a mental note to look up "Hanse Davion double" as soon as she could. She loved rabbit holes of history, especially when they involved 'Mechs and merc units.

"Anyway," she said, "it was really fortuitous. We made it just in time, that Federated Suns command circuit we happened into was really a stroke of luck. But the leader of the Committee in charge of this co-op outfit—Heidegger—said we'd land a contract for credits, sure, but the real prize would be the chance to get our hands on some Clan-made 'Mechs. I don't know about you all, but I'd kill to get my hands on a Clan 'Mech for one of us."

Standing at the back of the conference room, Frankie, the Fox Patrol's lead technician alongside Katie, cleared their throat. "Your *Kit Fox* is a Clan 'Mech, Captain."

"I mean *another* Clan 'Mech. For the outfit. That would be great for all of us."

"I like my *Quickdraw*, though," Arkee Colorado said from the back of the room. He sat next to his husband and fellow Fox, Evan Huxley. They occupied their usual spot, trying their best to discreetly hold hands under the table, even though everyone knew exactly what they were doing.

Aside from Katie, Arkee and Evan were the other founding members of the Fox Patrol. They'd gotten married the last time they were on Galatea and, for as different as they were, Katie saw them as a perfect pair. Where Arkee was a big guy with dark skin and a darker beard, Evan was thin and wiry, with a fair complexion. Where Arkee felt at home driving a 60-ton 'Mech like a *Quickdraw*, Evan piloted a tiny 20-ton wisp of a *Locust*.

They both liked to bicker, though. With each other. With Katie. With the rest of the crew. Random passersby. It was all done with love and a hint of sarcasm, though, so everyone found it charming.

Katie decided *witty repartee* was a better way to think about it than *bickering*.

At least it *sounded* nicer.

"No one said you'd have to give up your *Quickdraw*," Katie said. She knew where his consternation came from. When Arkee and Evan had joined the Fox Patrol, the only things they had to their names besides debt were their 'Mechs. It was how they'd been able to form a unit in the first place.

Arkee nodded curtly. "Good. I love that thing. I'd just as soon give up Evan."

Evan tugged at Arkee. "Hey."

Arkee raised his hands in offended surrender. "I said I *wouldn't* give you up."

"You give me up in a dream, you better wake up and come crawling back."

"Obviously."

Evan pulled Arkee in close and gave him a quick peck on the cheek, then Arkee sort of shrugged there, feigning sadness before turning to see Evan smoldering at him. Katie tried her hardest not to roll her eyes at them. They were too adorable for their own good. It was kind of sickening sometimes, but she wouldn't trade them for the world.

Nicks raised a cybernetic finger for a chance to speak.

"What is it, Dexter?"

"Fine. We're taking this job. What's next?"

"I have one last meeting with our... He's not our employer, per se, but he runs the outfit. He's going to get us provisions and get our ammo all topped off, which should be music to your ears. Then we'll see if we need to take on any of the other units, in case they don't have DropShips of their own, and then we'll be on our way."

Dexter folded his arms in front of himself. "Where are we going, then?"

Katie smiled. "We're heading to Clan space."

"Clan space?" Dexter shook his head. "Clanners don't hire mercs."

"Well, Heidegger seems to think they'll hire us this time. They haven't asked for help, but he seems to have a sixth sense about things."

Evan and Arkee glanced at each other, then looked to Katie, but Arkee was the one to speak. "People don't have sixth senses about things, Cap'n."

"Heidegger was very convincing."

Rhiannon sighed loudly, but Evan rolled his eyes at her. "Are you sure this is what you want to do, Cap'n?"

Katie nodded again. "It is. I really feel like this is the right place for us right now."

Evan gave a reassuring smile. "Then we're with you. All the way, even if we ride to ruin and the world is ending."

CHAPTER TWO

**SAFDARJUNG SPACEPORT
NEW DELHI
ALYINA
ALYINA MERCANTILE LEAGUE
15 SEPTEMBER 3151**

Marena preferred to conduct business at the spaceport, close to the VaultShips and other members of the merchant caste. She understood why she needed the grandeur of the Exchange Place Tower, but it felt like the real work was done here with her merchants. She could be less formal, too. Her corkscrew coils of hair spiraled neatly over her shoulders, and she wore the blue-and-silver uniform that had become synonymous with the Alyina Mercantile League's merchants—anything to get away from Jade Falcon green.

Surrounding her at the conference table, her chief merchants were similarly outfitted in blue and silver. Merchant Helen sat immediately to Marena's right. Helen's skin was a much lighter brown than Marena's, and she kept her own hair in curled twists and pinned to the back of her head, showing off her ears and neck. Merchant Helen oversaw VaultShip Beta.

To Helena's immediate left was Merchant Claudio, who commanded VaultShip Delta. He was the fairest in the group, with a sharp smile and a sharper jaw line. His close-cropped hair made it easy to confuse him for a MechWarrior, but in her dealings with him, Marena had found him as prone to violence as a member of the scientist caste—which was to say not really.

Scattered around the rest of the table were various other merchants and former Jade Falcons she had worked with during her time as the Merchant Factor of the Clan. They had all seen fit to join her, understanding what she was trying to do, and knowing they could make a better life for themselves and the people who followed them.

The meeting had been heated. Not everyone liked the options on the table, but they had to defend themselves and keep reality in mind.

"We are not warriors," Merchant Claudio said, his voice smooth and firm. "Nor should we be."

"That does not mean we cannot use warriors to our benefit," Merchant Helen countered. "Just because we are working to remove warriors from the ruling council does not mean they should hold no place in our power structure."

Another merchant from the far end of the table coughed to let everyone know they had something to say. "Why can we not simply fold the Jade Falcons of Sudeten into our defense? Bring them here?"

All eyes looked to Marena. The conversations about Sudeten had already been heated. "I have made my offer to them, but I assume they will refuse. If they do not, then we can worry about how to combine Alyina and Sudeten, but frankly that does not help our current situation. It would triple our territory, yes, but without giving us sufficient means to defend it. This self-styled Khan, Jiyi Chistu, is having the same problems we are when it comes to defense. Especially with the Hell's Horses champing at the bit to absorb us, and the pirates are bad enough on their own. I do *not* want to be folded back into a Clan, Jade Falcon or otherwise, and I feel we have all made that clear. So, give me other options."

"What of bringing the surrounding systems into our fold as allies?" another merchant asked, as though they didn't know the answer already.

"We have sent emissaries with negotiating power to make alliances to half a dozen worlds. Butler. Denizli. Parakoila. Blackjack." Marena said that last one with hope in her voice: that was the home of the Jade Falcon School of Conflict, and if she could undo the cadets' Clan-based brainwashing, she would have a steady source of troops for her militia.

"I wonder what we *can* do." Merchant Claudio leaned back in his chair. "We seek alliances, surely. And more than anything, we have brought every resource we have to bear on the defense front. We have worked to bring the city's stationary defenses online. We have pressed every *solahma* warrior we can find back into service. The few *sibkos* in our control are not ready to graduate any time soon, and warriors, like money, do not simply grow on trees."

"They do not," Marena agreed.

Merchant Helen stood from her chair, letting her voice cut into the proceedings. "But the one resource we do have in abundance is money, comparatively speaking." She paced along the back of the room, apparently struggling with her words, clearly uneasy with what she hoped to say. "With the regrettable exception of VaultShip Gamma, we have the lucre left behind by the fallen Jade Falcon empire. For all intents and purposes, we have all the money in the Inner Sphere to do with what we want. We are now *of* the Inner Sphere. We are not chained to the Clan way."

Marena arched an eyebrow, fully anticipating where Helen's little speech was heading, and frankly, she did not completely disagree.

Helen took in a deep breath, steeling her resolve, before she could finally say what she had tried so hard to. "Mercenaries."

"*Dezgra,*" muttered Merchant Julio from the back of the room, loud enough for the word to catch in Marena's ears.

"You are seriously proposing the Alyina Mercantile League get in the business of hiring mercenaries?" Claudio frowned. "We just stroll up to Galatea or Kandersteg or wherever else and say we are ready to hire lucrewarriors? Just like that? Throw what little Clan tradition we have left out of the airlock?"

Helen nodded. "That is exactly what I am saying."

Marena raised a finger and gathered her thoughts. Then she looked over to Claudio, her mind practically made up. "What use is the Clan way to us? Clan Sea Fox and their roaming aimags have been dabbling in the mercenary trade themselves. They see profit and prosperity in it, yet they remain a Clan. And make no mistake, they are our chief competitor for the commerce and trade in the Inner Sphere. If the merc trade is something they can do, why not us?"

Merchant Julio cleared his throat and tried hiding his sneer. "With all due respect, Syndic, they are working as intermediaries. Are they actually hiring MechWarriors directly? Or has Clan Sea Fox renounced all of their 'Mechs and stopped fighting on their own behalf?"

Marena had to concede the point, and cocked her head in Julio's direction. "We are merchants. Our laws are not of the Clans, but of supply and demand. Of being in the right place at the right time with the right goods, whether foodstuffs or BattleMechs. Right now, because of our tenuous position and the vultures circling our heads, our greatest demand is safety. And the marketplace is full of things that will supply us that. So, instead of debating morality and the Clan traditions that no longer matter to us, let us go through a cost-benefit analysis. Does it cost us more to remain vulnerable and undefended while pirates continue stealing our 'Mechs with inside information—another problematic issue we need to discuss—or does it cost us more to swallow our pride and contract mercenary companies to defend us?"

She was careful to include the accusation in her speech—the accusation that someone had sold them out to the pirates, and had likely profited handsomely from it. How the pirates' heists had been so successful was something Marena still had not gotten to the bottom of, and she wanted answers. And blood.

Merchant Claudio spoke first. "With your permission, Syndic, I will head to Galatea and see how many mercenaries I can bring to our defense."

Helen stood practically at attention as though she were still in some sort of military. "I will head to Kandersteg and bring back what commands I can from there."

They stood there, waiting for Marena's blessing.

Being honest with herself meant admitting she was still not convinced. This entire enterprise could all go south. Mercenaries had less honor than Clan warriors, and she already had a low enough opinion of them. Would this open her up to more pirate attacks? What if the mercenaries decided to void their contracts and simply claim control of Alyina and the rest of the Mercantile League's worlds for themselves? She had had few dealings with mercenaries, and this meant gambling with a variable she had not researched and explored fully on her own.

But she knew she had no other choice.

Nodding curtly, she gave the order. "Do it. Leave today. Now, if you can. Bring back a defense worthy of the Alyina Mercantile League."

"Aff, *Syndic*," they all said as though she were some sort of Khan.

Perhaps that was something else she could get used to.

ALYINA MERCANTILE LEAGUE HEADQUARTERS
EXCHANGE PLACE TOWER
NEW DELHI
ALYINA
ALYINA MERCANTILE LEAGUE
17 SEPTEMBER 3151

"Ma'am," a voice said on the intercom, rousing Syndic Marena from her slumber.

Exhausted, she rubbed the sleep from her eyes. She knew better than to think she would get a good night's sleep on this or any night. There was always a question to answer, a decision to be made. That was the thing she had found since becoming the Jade Falcons' Merchant Factor, and it had carried on as she became the so-called Merchant Queen. No one could make a decision but her. Not that her subordinates were incapable of making decisions, but they always wanted her approval first.

It was practically a trauma response. The Jade Falcons had so abused their merchant caste that the merchants could barely think for themselves without express, written permission.

Marena had to change that.

Rolling over in her bed, she pressed the button on the intercom atop her nightstand. "Go for Syndic Marena."

"Ma'am, we have a situation in orbit we thought you should be apprised of case it turns out to be another attack." The comms officer's voice wavered on those last words.

"Pirates?"

"*Neg*, ma'am. An assortment of DropShips arrived via JumpShip and are heading toward orbit. Their transponders claim they belong to a variety of mercenary outfits."

Marena's brow furrowed. She had only sent her merchant envoys to Galatea and Kandersteg two days prior. There was no way they'd returned so quickly without a command circuit to Galatea and a lot of luck. "What do they want?"

"They want to speak to you, actually. It feels thin for a cover story, but they claim to be looking for work from the AML."

"When do they make planetfall?"

"Tomorrow."

"Monitor them. Scramble whatever fighters we have to escort them planetside. If they make one aggressive move, blast them out of the sky."

"*Aff.*"

All Marena could do was think about what would happen if these mercenaries had already been contracted by someone else. There were a dozen factions fighting for scraps in the old Jade Falcon Occupation Zone, so it stood to reason that one of them could have hired mercenaries to disrupt the AML and bury it once and for all.

There was no honor left in the Inner Sphere. Why should she have expected any left for her burgeoning empire?

CHAPTER THREE

SAFDARJUNG SPACEPORT
NEW DELHI
ALYINA
ALYINA MERCANTILE LEAGUE
18 SEPTEMBER 3151

Albert Heidegger—though everyone called him Bugsy—loved the feeling of gravity after spending so much time without it. He didn't like the way weightlessness made his ample stomach feel, floating there loose all the time. His insides couldn't take it, but such was the life he had chosen.

Standing on the landing platform, enjoying the use of his legs, and looking around for his escort or welcoming party, Bugsy took a long sniff of the air, and choked into a coughing fit. The atmosphere on Alyina was not the best he'd ever breathed. It had a rusty taint to it he couldn't quite say he liked. The air was thick and humid, and it felt like every breath was going to draw more poison in his lungs.

From the vantage of the spaceport, the cityscape looked evenly divided between the industrial center on one side and the city proper on the other. From the industrial center, the tall warehouses and ten-story factory complexes belched acrid smoke that met with the clouds and hung like a pall over the city.

"Nice place," he said to no one in particular.

He'd only gotten clearance for the one DropShip to land. The others were still waiting in orbit. Whether any of them made planetfall depended entirely on his negotiations with the locals. From what he could gather, he would likely be dealing with Syndic Marena, the self-styled Merchant Queen of Alyina. A lofty title, but one worthy of a woman who had completely turned her back on the Jade Falcons. Bold and probably smart, given the stories of how badly the Falcons had allegedly got their asses beat at Terra.

And really, it had made the most sense to go offer services in the biggest power vacuum in the Inner Sphere. All of his studying of history had shown that the mercenaries who made the most money were those in the right place at the right time—and there was *always* a power struggle somewhere in the Inner Sphere.

The steady thrum of helicopter rotors filled his ears, and Bugsy turned around to see it low and close, coming right for him.

For the sparest moment, he thought the VTOL had its guns trained on him and was going to turn him into a dark spot on the landing pad, but it was coming for him in an altogether different manner.

It landed on the pad, and a merchant in a blue-and-silver uniform emerged. She wore nothing like anything Bugsy had seen before. New for the new Mercantile League? It seemed likely. The whirr of the blades didn't allow much for conversation, but the merchant let him know exactly what she wanted of him: to follow her.

Bugsy Heidegger wasn't in the habit of getting on strange helicopters and being whisked away to parts unknown, but the merchant was actually wearing a sidearm, and he did want the work, so he decided it best to not protest.

"Take me to your leader," he said with a smirk, though the blades of the helicopter drowned the joke into a secret only Bugsy knew.

The merchants aboard the VTOL offered him no headphones or microphone, so they passed the time sans conversation. It afforded Bugsy a better aerial view of the city than from his DropShip, and he found it quite illuminating. The city was impressive in its way, but clearly falling apart. The industrial center looked like the only part of town that had been well maintained, but it was old, too. The Alyina Mercantile League was at the end of their rope, whether Syndic Marena would admit it or not. That would give him some leverage in the negotiations.

The AML was hungrier than he'd realized.

Bugsy clapped his hands together and rubbed them as though just sitting down to a feast.

ALYINA MERCANTILE LEAGUE HEADQUARTERS
EXCHANGE PLACE TOWER

The helicopter landed on the tallest building in the city. Bugsy was led to an elevator and taken down a single floor that opened out into a massive, windowed office overlooking the city.

"Mr. Heidegger," the woman behind the desk said. Her skin glowed a deep, dark brown, and her face, framed in tight, curly locks, meant business.

"Major, actually."

"Major Heidegger, my apologies," she corrected herself. "I am Syndic Marena, of the Alyina Mercantile League."

Heidegger approached her desk and offered a slight bow. "I'm familiar with you, Syndic. They call you the Merchant Queen. Has a nice ring to it, don't you think?"

"I am grateful the people I represent put that much trust in me. Now, tell me what brings you all the way out here to Alyina."

Bugsy smiled. "Cutting right to the gills, I like that. As you're probably aware, I am the senior chair and officially designated spokesperson of the Committee for the Lone Wolves."

"So I'm told." She waved at the chair for him. "Please, sit."

Hoping his knees didn't creak, Bugsy took the chair and found it plush and comfortable on his backside. Not at all like he'd expected. "As I'm sure you're also aware, we're a mercenary co-op looking for work."

"A co-op?" she asked.

"Essentially, we're a *lot* of small mercenary units and individual freelancers, and we band together to take on bigger jobs. I've got folks in my command you might have heard of, ranging from Julian Ellison of the Foul Tempered to Katie Ferraro of the Fox Patrol, and all points in between."

She nodded as though maybe those names meant something to her.

Normally, he could read people, but Marena shrewdly kept her emotions in check, giving nothing away. He wouldn't want to play cards with her, but that was exactly what he was doing. A lot of money was on the table here, and he didn't want to walk away without winning at least one hand.

Silence permeated the room, and he knew it was like a game of chicken. The first one to ask for what they wanted would be at a disadvantage, but he was already disadvantaged. Marena had the home turf, and the crowd was rooting for her. And, frankly, she held everything Bugsy wanted. There was no sense in making her beg him for help. She was a proud Clan merchant and wouldn't just ask for help. He would have to coax it out of her.

"The Lone Wolves are hoping you might be interested in contracting our services. I know it's a bit unorthodox thinking on our part, you all being Clan folk who don't normally throw in with lucrewarriors, but the way we figure it, you're in a bad spot. You're out here, you're exposed, and you need all the help you can get."

"You are only half right, Major Heidegger. We are no longer Clan folk. We are but humble merchants trying to make our own, better way in the universe."

"And as merchants, you must see the value in how we can help you make a better way in the universe."

"I see potential."

Bugsy grinned. She had chosen her words carefully, but she had finally said enough to make it seem she was open to negotiate. Though the invitation to her penthouse office and the helicopter ride were also solid clues. He'd guessed right. They were caught between a rock and the deep blue sea.

"In that potential, do you see your defense centered on Alyina? Or spread out among your holdings?"

"The influence of the Alyina Mercantile League covers many planets."

"And I imagine you want that influence to spread, eh?"

"*Aff.*"

"*Aff*, indeed," Bugsy said. *Not Clan, my ass.*

"What size of force do you have?"

"In our current configuration, the Lone Wolves are currently just over battalion strength. I have about forty 'Mechs spread across our DropShips and ready to deploy or jump where we might decide is the greatest need."

"And what would you ask in return?"

Bugsy withdrew a small, tablet-style noteputer from his pocket and loaded up the appropriate screen. There were definitely a lot of zeroes on it, but at the bottom was the real ask: Clan 'Mechs. He wanted to secure at least one for every outfit currently under the Lone Wolves. That would put many of them on much better footing, and the Lone Wolves would be more fearsome as a whole for it.

It was a higher price than necessary, but he knew negotiation would bring the price down.

He slid the noteputer across the table.

Syndic Marena lifted the noteputer, and her eyes scanned back and forth, weighing the offer.

"This is a nonstarter," she said.

Bugsy knew it was his turn to keep his mouth shut.

She manipulated the screen back and forth, reviewing the offer once more.

Then she protested again. "There is no way your services are worth that many of our 'Mechs. And what's to stop you from turning around and using our 'Mechs against us after you learn our defenses?"

Bugsy smiled and noted carefully that she didn't balk at the cash price at all. Only the 'Mechs. That was where the negotiation would happen. "For one, we're licensed and bonded with the Galatean outfit Mercenarius Illimitata Fiduciary. Then, point B is that when you buy us, you buy our loyalty. I know the Clans feel differently about mercenaries and the ethics of fighting for money, but we'd likely never work again at this level if word got out that we turned on a client. I am not in the business of turning sides. We're the Lone Wolves, not Stefan Amaris. We're going to do the job you ask hire us for, and we'll fulfill our contract to the letter. We'll take salvage where we can, and we'll leave the Alyina Mercantile League stronger and better defended than it was when we arrived."

"It sounds nice, but who is to say that you would not fulfill the terms of your contract and then gain employment with our competitors?" She set the noteputer down and slid it back across the desk. Her body language was controlled enough to suggest he was getting a definitive no from her, but he knew better. She wouldn't still be negotiating if she wasn't at least half-interested.

And he hoped to convince her to be more than half-interested. The cost to get the Lone Wolves all the way out to Alyina had not been insubstantial.

But it was a risk he thought worth taking.

He took the noteputer back and tapped on the screen to change the terms of the agreement. "What if we included a clause that precluded us from taking any work against the AML or its designated personnel for at least one year after the completion of our contract?"

With that clause in place, he slid the noteputer back toward Marena.

She didn't even bother to pick it up. "As I said before, a Trinary of 'Mechs is not worth what you can provide."

"Ten 'Mechs then, just a Binary. You've got my solemn word we'll earn every one of them."

Marena's face didn't change. She tented her fingers in front of her, deep in thought.

What would she come back with for the counteroffer? Would it be five 'Mechs? An extension on the noncompete clause? Her face was a steel trap, revealing none of her motives.

She was *good*.

Marena inhaled sharply. "I just do not see how this can make sense for the AML. We will not offer 'Mechs as part of any sort of payment. If that is what you have come here for, then I am afraid you have wasted your time."

"Be that as it may..." Bugsy stroked his dark beard, doing his best to look aggrieved. Prospective employers always liked to think they were getting the best of the Lone Wolves. "How many 'Mechs will it cost you if you *don't* hire us to fight for you, eh? So, what if we do this? What if we sign up for a six-month contract. Just six months. You can terminate the contract at any point of your choosing, and for every month we do a job to your satisfaction, we get a 'Mech. At the end of the six months, we end up with six 'Mechs. When that six months is up, we can either renegotiate, or we're free to leave. But I look at your situation and can't help but thinking six months with an extra battalion around would make things a lot easier, give you some room to breathe. More than that, we can pull training duty. We'll be able to show your local militia how to make the best use of their tanks, and how to take 'Mechs down with infantry. You can't have your warriors on every world in every situation. Teach a person to fish, you know? But if not, I understand. Completely. We can leave you to your devices, and we'll just go our merry way."

Syndic Marena lowered her hands and cocked an eyebrow. "Perhaps we can find a way to make this amenable to both of us."

Bugsy grinned.

CHAPTER FOUR

GARRISON WAREHOUSE
FACTORY ZONE 4
NEW DELHI
ALYINA
ALYINA MERCANTILE LEAGUE
25 SEPTEMBER 3151

Katie Ferraro hated taking so much money from Evan Huxley, but he just never seemed to get the hint. She laid her cards down. "There you go, Evan. Read 'em and weep."

She fanned out a straight Great House, all Suns, from seven to MechWarrior, all in a row.

"Damn it," Evan said, slapping his cards facedown the table while Katie raked the credits from the pot toward herself with both arms. "When are you gonna give the rest of us a chance, Katie?"

Katie stuffed credits into the front pouch of her mechanic coveralls. "I mean, learn to play cards better if you don't want to lose."

"Arkee's gonna kill me."

With her pockets full, Katie began to arrange her remaining chits into neat stacks on she'd left on the table in front of her into neat stacks. "I thought love meant never having to say you're sorry."

"No, it means having to say you're sorry a lot." Evan buried his face in the crook of his elbow.

Dexter Nicks sighed from the other side of the table, collecting cards for the next deal. "You are really bad at this, Huxley. I thought for sure you would have learned your lesson by now."

Nicks was a real hard-ass, but Katie found him to be lovable. At one point he'd been Dispossessed due to losing his 'Mech, but he was a grizzled veteran, and had joined the Fox Patrol when they really needed a seasoned hand. And his hand was artificial—he'd lost the genuine article fighting in a 'Mech for another outfit. At least that's what Katie assumed. He never spoke about how he lost it. He just kept on keepin' on.

At about forty, he was easily the oldest member of the unit. Katie frequently let him know his hair had begun to gray. It looked distinguished on him, but the life of a 'Mech commander was one of hard laughs and teasing.

Evan offered Nicks a wry smile. "Thank you, Dex. I thought I had her, I really did. Why would I think she was sitting on a Great House straight? Nobody gets cards that good. I thought she was bluffing."

Nicks laughed. "Katie's never bluffing."

"What do you mean?"

"She doesn't bluff." Nicks shuffled the cards in front of him. "It's why I folded. I was holding a three of a kind, but I knew she was going to come up with that Suns MechWarrior. When she's got something in the pocket, it's always the nuts."

Hearing this, Katie suddenly got nervous and her cheeks got hot. And self-conscious. She hadn't thought about it, but Nicks was probably right. She didn't like bluffing. She had on occasion, but she was much more interested in sure things. Was she really that conservative of a player?

She didn't like the sound of that.

She also didn't like the idea of being so predictable.

"I'll have to see for myself," Evan said.

"See what for yourself, lover boy?" came Arkee's voice, booming from the next room. He carried in two steaming plates of food, one in each hand, as though a server in a restaurant.

"Oh, just Katie's ridiculous luck at poker."

Arkee looked down at the few remaining chits in front of Evan. "Evan Huxley, we have talked about this."

"I know, I know." Evan's shoulders hunched, as though trying to shuffle off responsibility.

"Well, you don't deserve this then." Arkee slid the sandwich and fries across the chips in front of Evan. "But I love you anyway."

"Oh, my God. I love you so much. I am so hungry." Evan gripped the sandwich with both hands, not even caring what it was.

But Arkee clearly did. "That's a local catch. A fish indigenous to Alyina, a local thali. Sort of like tuna. They're terrific and I wanted you to have one." He pulled a chair up to sit between his husband and Nicks, then set his own plate down.

Suddenly the card table looked more like a dinner table, and Katie realized she was hungry, too.

Just as she thought about getting her own heaping plate of thali sandwiches and fries, the alarm bells blared. Red lights circled around them.

Katie pushed back from her spot at the table, leaving the chits there. A few more spilled from her pockets as she stood. "Red alert then, fellas."

Evan looked back and forth suspiciously, snatched his sandwich up to take a giant bite, and put it back down on the plate. Then, he left it behind, chewing in his overstuffed mouth.

Arkee took his sandwich as they raced to get to their 'Mechs.

It was a call to battle stations.

"I'm not letting this one get away," Arkee said.

Evan patted his husband on the ass, racing by him and calling out with his mouth half-full. "I'll finish when we get back."

"Let's hurry it up, folks," Katie said. "There's a battle to win."

It wasn't more than five minutes and Katie had her *Kit Fox*—the one she had so lovingly named *Kagekitsune* all those years ago—ready to go and in front of the formation.

Major Heidegger—he kept telling her she could call him Bugsy, but it felt weird—buzzed over the comm. "We've got a situation on the outskirts, Fox Patrol, and it's in your defensive zone."

He had divided the Lone Wolves into defensive zones to protect the factories until they had a more cohesive battle plan and distribution across Alyina and the worlds of the Alyina Mercantile League itself. She didn't know what went into deciding what they'd be doing on the job. And, for the most part, Katie was happy with the contract. She could leave anytime she liked, but if she didn't stick around, she wouldn't get paid. She just hoped the Fox Patrol stuck around long enough to get their hands on one of the Clan 'Mechs they'd been promised.

"What's the scoop, Major?"

"I'm beaming you some coordinates. There's a contingent of pirate 'Mechs heading for the Factory Zone, on a trajectory that puts them in your area. I need you to scare 'em off."

"What sort of 'Mechs are we talking about?" The Fox Patrol boasted a *Kit Fox,* Arkee's *Quickdraw,* Evan's *Locust,* Nicks' *Griffin,* and Ramirez's *Marauder.* It wasn't the most balanced unit, but they had enough firepower and spunk to balance out whatever got thrown at them. And since they'd joined up with the Lone Wolves, they'd been outfitted with enough ammo to actually fill their 'Mechs' magazines for once. Despite all that, the Fox Patrol worked best as a recon lance. If they were up against something bigger than a medium lance, they were at a distinct disadvantage.

This was part of why she wanted to get Dexter out of his *Griffin* and into an assault 'Mech.

"I'm sending you the telemetry of what we've identified so far," Heidegger said. "Keep an eye out. Scare 'em away as best you can. Make sure they don't get to the factory."

"Understood, sir." For Katie's part, she didn't mind Heidegger at all. She just couldn't tell if she liked taking orders. In all the years she'd been running the Fox Patrol, everything had revolved around their little family unit with her as its too-young mother. Now it felt like they had some weird uncle calling the shots. On one hand, it took the pressure off her for big command decisions. On the other hand, it made her feel a little like she needed to be rebellious—but who to rebel against or why, she couldn't tell.

The info on the enemy 'Mechs came through and started displaying on her head-up display: two 75-ton *Night Gyr*s and a trio of 20-ton *Ion Sparrows.* Seemed like they were all 'Mechs stolen from the Factory Zone, and only sported gray primer. The *Night Gyr*s were deadly to any of Katie's 'Mechs. Dual PPCs mounted in their left arm and an LB 20-X autocannon in their right meant they could crack open any of the lighter Foxes like a nut.

She switched over to her own command line that let her talk to the rest of the Foxes. "Here's the deal. We're simply to harass and keep them from coming back into the factory. There are five 'Mechs out there, and they're coming from the jungle. Our job is to interdict. Evan and I will use our speed to hit and run. The rest of you, find positions. We'll focus fire on the heavies first. That might be enough to scare them away."

"Cap'n," Arkee said, "is there any other resistance coming for the factory?"

"Unknown." She'd wondered the same thing and figured it worth asking. "I'll find out, but let's get started."

As Katie pushed her *Kit Fox* toward the jungle and the incoming pirate 'Mechs, she switched back to the frequency for the Lone Wolves Committee, of which she was nominally a part because she commanded one of the larger units in the co-op. "Major Heidegger, this is Fox Leader. Happy to report that we are in the field and engaging."

"That's just bully."

"I did have one question."

"I don't have a lot of time to play twenty questions, Fox Leader."

"Are there other engagement zones?"

"Indeed. This is an attack-in-force. Repel those pirates and keep this channel clear."

"Got it."

Katie switched back to the Foxes. "Looks like there *is* a bigger battle, but this is our part. Stick to doing what you're best at, and we'll have a grand ol' time."

"Got it, Cap'n," Arkee said.

The gap between the factories and the jungle was likely the engagement zone. It ran about a kilometer between the two, maybe less. A road passed through the swampy area, allowing hovercars and supply trucks to roll through. Tanks, too, if the need arose.

"Form up, Foxes," Katie said. "Evan, you ready for this?"

"As I'll ever be. Which *Night Gyr* have you got your sights on?"

"This one." Katie tagged the one just coming out of the jungle, and shared that data with Evan. "Let's do it."

"Let's go, Cap'n."

The tree line reminded her of home. The jungles of Jerangle. That's where she'd found her *Kit Fox* all those years ago. And she was going to make damn sure her 'Mech didn't get lost in the jungle again.

Evan outpaced her. His *Locust* was a lot faster than her *Kit Fox*, but they were the fastest two 'Mechs in the Fox Patrol, and they were a lot nimbler than the others. It made sense for them to keep moving fast to make a hard target for the enemy. They could pick away at and harass the pirates, making them think twice about the overall attack.

"On your nine, Captain," Evan said as his *Locust* pulled beyond her from her left. Their strafing run would come at the *Night Gyr* from the side, hit it, and then they would keep on going.

If the pirates were attacking in force, they likely didn't know about the Lone Wolves hanging around. Or maybe they'd been fed false information. Because with so many Lone Wolves stationed in New Delhi, the pirates would have a hell of a time getting whatever they were coming for.

The *Night Gyr*s opened fire, their PPCs picking at Evan and Katie, coloring the battlefield in sizzling blue-white light. Rhiannon's *Marauder* fired back at them from the road with her own PPCs, her longest-range weapons. Nicks fired his, too, with his *Griffin*'s single PPC. The engagement zone was nothing short of dangerous. Arkee launched a volley of long-range missiles across the road, and they crackled against the *Night Gyr*'s armor. Of all the Fox Patrol 'Mechs, he was the only one to score a hit, the PPC beams missing on both sides of the fight.

"Watch your fire, Foxes." Katie knew they could do their jobs without her chiding them, but it felt better to remind them she was there for them.

Evan sprinted his *Locust* ahead of her, planted his legs, and let loose with his machine guns and medium laser. Then Katie came in right behind him with her mix of lasers and autocannon. Their combined fire scattered across the front of the humanoid *Night Gyr* from head to toe. Lasers carved off armor, and the autocannon shells hit solidly in the torso.

"Keep moving, Evan," Katie said. "Let the others take a shot, and we'll come back around for another pass."

"Way ahead of you, Cap'n."

The *Locust* burst ahead and turned around on the road to line up another attack. The rest of the Fox Patrol opened up on the damaged *Night Gyr*, blistering more armor from its front side, the melted panels dripping steaming slag onto the ground.

Both *Night Gyr*s shot at Evan, but he was too quick for them. The *Ion Sparrow*s came for Rhiannon in her *Marauder*, jumping across the battlefield on their fixed wings. They landed in a cluster and fired everything they had at the biggest 'Mech opposing them. Their antipersonnel Gauss rifles were more effective against infantry than 'Mechs, but their heavy medium lasers were extra deadly, packing more than enough punch to flatten a lighter 'Mech. Katie was grateful they'd picked the larger target. She had no plans to die here on Alyina, nor did she plan for anyone in her command to die either. Living was mandatory.

The combined fire of Gauss flechettes and lasers took nasty chunks out of Rhiannon's *Marauder*, one across an arm and the other in a knee joint.

Katie looked down at her console to see how Rhiannon was faring. "You doing okay, Ramirez?"

"It's not as bad as it looks," Ramirez's voice crackled through the comm. "All systems are still go."

"Should we switch to those nasty *Ion Sparrow*s, Captain?" Nicks asked.

"Nasty is right, but no. We're almost through with this *Night Gyr*. We take it down and its buddy, then we'll outmatch them with everything."

"Yes, ma'am," Nicks said. His PPC cracked into the *Night Gyr*, and all of his missiles corkscrewed across the engagement zone to pepper more holes in the pirate 'Mech's armor.

Then Rhiannon's PPCs hit the *Night Gyr* right in its gut. And then Arkee's missiles arrowed in, each of them exploding across the cockpit and torso.

The damn thing didn't have a chance.

The impact of the final cluster of missiles cascading across its front knocked it backward.

"These pirates'll think twice before coming back here again." Evan shifted his aim to the second *Night Gyr* and singed it with his medium laser.

Katie really needed to get him a better 'Mech. That *Locust* was fast, sure. And he was pretty on target with his laser, but those *Ion Sparrows*—those 'Mechs could serve the same purpose but better, and put Evan in less-risky situations. The harder he could hit, the better defended he was.

"Careful there, Evan."

"I'm always careful, Cap'n."

Katie steered her *Kit Fox* toward the second *Night Gyr*, ignoring the *Ion Sparrow*s threatening Ramirez. She moved at top speed, zooming across the battlefield to make herself difficult to hit. Ramirez also shifted forward at top speed, making her a harder target despite being slower than Katie. And the *Ion Sparrow*s, moving as fast as they were, weren't taking the time to stop and aim anyway.

Still too far away for her missiles or small pulse laser to make a difference, Katie fired everything else she had. Her large laser and autocannon were enough to damage even a heavy 'Mech, and she was determined to do everything she could to take this bastard down. She wanted to earn one of those *Ion Sparrow*s, get Evan something better to pilot.

The *Night Gyr* walked backward, taking potshots. The *Ion Sparrow*s jumped into the air, but they got smaller instead of larger. And that meant—

A smile crept across Katie's face. "They're retreating!"

Heidegger's voice came in over the comm, confirming her suspicions. "Fox Patrol, this is Bugsy. The pirates met resistance in all quarters and are pulling back in force. Continue pursuit and take out what you can."

Katie made sure she was keyed into her entire unit and gleefully gave them the orders. "Fox Patrol, the pirates are leaving. We are to pursue and destroy."

"Got it, Cap'n," Evan said, and the rest followed suit.

Katie willed her *Kit Fox* forward, pushing the pirates back farther into the jungle.

She watched Evan's *Locust* speed in front of her and take another shot at the *Night Gyr*. The laser bored into the pirate 'Mech's leg, but even though some armor had been ablated, the damage wasn't enough to slow the damn thing, let alone take it down.

The *Night Gyr* took another step back and lined up a shot on the *Locust*.

The white-sapphire light of the PPCs brightened the *Night Gyr* and flashed across the battlefield. Then the massive red-orange report of the autocannon firing cut into the brilliant particle beams.

A confused breath caught in Katie's throat.

Evan's 'Mech crashed into the ground, one of its legs splintering off from the torso.

"Evan!"

Through the comm, she heard Arkee scream.

She looked down to her console, and the indicator for Evan's 'Mech was black.

"Evan," Arkee said through his tears, "you come in *right now* and tell me you're okay!"

The *Quickdraw* fired on the *Night Gyr*, but the *Night Gyr* had already faded into the jungle, escaping with the other pirates.

"Evan," Katie said, also through her tears, "answer your husband. That's an order."

The wreckage of the *Locust* smoked and smoldered in the berm between the road and the jungle, and Evan did not respond.

TO BE CONTINUED IN SHRAPNEL #14!

SHRAPNEL

RPG ADVENTURE: TINKER, TAILOR, SEAMSTRESS, SPY

JOSHUA C. PERIAN

The following three-part role-playing adventure can be used with either *A Time of War* or *MechWarrior: Destiny* rules. Each part features a background section and an adventure section a gamemaster can use as the framework for a short campaign.

Solaris VII's fashion scene has always been at the forefront of high fashion. Even within the highly regarded Lyran fashion industry, Solaris VII holds a special place as a trend-setting incubator where the latest ideas and talent congregate year after year. The Game World serves as a nexus for up-and-comers and veteran garment creators alike, and its densely packed mix of design competition is the kind of creative crucible found nowhere else in the Inner Sphere or beyond. Driven by money, prestige, glamour, and patriotism, Solaris fashion is cut-throat—literally—and rife with violence, sabotage, and theft. Like the Games, fashion designers must remain relevant and destroy their competition to stay on top. And in this industry, you are either on top or nothing at all. The high-profile gala events of the Grand Tournament to the lowest *yakuza* parlors in Kobe and everywhere in between are the arenas where Solaris' fashion battles are fought. On the Game World, what you wear says as much about who you are as where you are going. Whether you are an upper-class Tumor, a crime-syndicate Gremlin, or an undercover Ghost, to move through Solaris VII's social circles, you must dress the part, and the House of Perducci has been dressing Solaris VII for over two centuries.

A family of skilled garment makers from the Milan metroplex on Terra, the Perducci Fashion House rose to prominence when Marcello Perducci dressed a handful of influential civilians and nobles at the 2677 and 2678 royal courts. Consistent business with the Star League's Terran natives and visiting elite kept the fashion house busy, and Marcello's family business built on his legacy. The Perduccis were early investors in the Something Wonderful fashion chain, which ensured steady income in their often-volatile industry and created new material and client contacts across the Inner Sphere. Later, while violent gangs ravaged the Italian peninsula during the Amaris Coup, the Perduccis survived by dressing high-ranking Amaris officials and by clothing gang capos in exchange for any garment assets pilfered from their competition.

After the liberation, the Perducci family fled Terra with their accrued wealth and built a new home on Tharkad, where their bold designs and Terran pedigree made them popular with the Steiner Royal Court. Having ingratiated themselves on Tharkad, in 2812 Marcello's young granddaughter, Paola Perducci, set her eyes on Solaris VII, as the growing popularity of the Games and the planet's unique legal position made it an attractive investment opportunity. She set up shop on Herd Street in Silesia's Upper East Side, and Solaris' finest were soon garbed in Perducci originals, thanks to Paola's business acumen and ruthlessness.

Over the centuries to follow, the Perducci family fortune continued to rise. They used fashion to connect with every level of Solaris society, using their skills and deniable assets to tap those connections for secrets. In doing, they amassed influence and considerable favors from Solaris' powerful elite, which the Perduccis have used sparingly to stay one step ahead of their many enemies. Through the FedCom Civil War, the Word of Blake's Jihad, Black Monday, and the recent Clan Wolf conquest of Terra, the House of Perducci's information gathering, broker network, and cultural influence remain a discreet yet powerful force to be reckoned with.

PART 1: TEST PATTERN

Adventure Overview
Recommended Group Size: 3–6 players
Recommended Group Type: Black Ops
Recommended Skill Levels: Regular–Veteran

Description
Your team is new to Solaris VII's complex criminal underground, and your local contact set up a "professional interview" for a client in

the form of a courier job that is no doubt being used to see what your team can do. The players are not known, and the details are light, but your contact has you delivering a box from a Silesian garment shop to a high-rise in Kobe. How you pursue this objective is up to you.

COMPLICATIONS

The Competition: Other groups in Solaris City were originally contracted for the job. You do not know why they were dropped off the courier gig, but they are not happy about losing the business to outsiders. When the spurned competition learns who is making the delivery, what steps will they take to sabotage the team—or worse, ensure they finish the job instead?

Tickets, please: Transporting cargo on a tight schedule between Solaris City zones can be tricky, especially for inexperienced couriers and doubly so when the Grand Tournament is in full swing. Between the accidents, delays, and congestion, the streets of Solaris City are packed, and public transportation is falling further behind schedule.

Is this a setup?: As soon as the package is delivered, the Solaris police show up to raid the drop. The team must escape the trap and figure out why their contact sold them out, or perhaps their unknown employer was duplicitous. The team needs to learn the truth quickly and discreetly if they hope to stay alive long enough to get paid.

TIPS

This is a courier job with a twist.

PART 2: HOT COUTURE

Adventure Overview
Recommended Group Size: 3–6 players
Recommended Group Type: Black Ops
Recommended Skill Levels: Regular–Veteran

Description
Among certain Solaris circles, the team is particularly well known for their discreetness in handling difficult tasks with precision, and the House of Perducci stays on top by ruthlessly destroying their competition by hiring professionals to handle their difficult tasks with precision. The Perduccis expect perfection and pay a premium for the expected results.

COMPLICATIONS

Showtime: A hot new fashion designer from the Federated Suns is making waves among the visiting nobility, and the House of Perducci thinks they are gaining too much positive attention. The team must discreetly ruin a flash show with only a few hours' notice before the runway starts at Freedom Gate. Security at the event will be heavy, and there will be media present, but the Perduccis want it done cleanly and without bloodshed.

It's not who you know: The team is posing as contract staff for a private Perducci fitting for a member of the Bertoli family at the Glass Tower in Cathay. Besides maintaining the appearance of garment assistants while surrounded by mafia muscle (a.k.a. Gremlins), the team is tasked with planting listening devices to spy on the Bertoli family. The job gets complicated with the arrival of a hit squad from the Red Cobras Triad, leaving the team and their employer to survive a bloody firefight.

Message received: The Perduccis do not take betrayal lightly. The team is hired to stop a former apprentice garment maker from selling sensitive documents she stole when she quit. Rumor has it she is meeting with potential buyers at the Solaris Hilton and the Stargazer Lounge at the end of the week. Her exact location is unknown—only her present city sector is known—but she has reportedly hired elite protection until the deals are done.

Date night: The Perduccis made a one-of-a-kind dress for a prominent member of the Solaris City Civic Council, but rumors claim the dress is not in his wife's size. The team is hired to confirm the council member is having an affair and collect evidence of it for the Perducci's use. Things go sideways for the team when the other woman turns out to be a House Marik noble with deep connections to SAFE.

TIPS

These are repeatable jobs for every era; simply swap the target and location to take the team through various levels of Solaris society.

PART 3: FAR AND RUNWAY

Adventure Overview
Recommended Group Size: 3–6 players
Recommended Group Type: Black Ops
Recommended Skill Levels: Regular–Veteran

Description

While conducting business in their own backyard on Solaris VII, the Perduccis often refrain from killing. After all, bodies garner exactly the type of attention the Perduccis like to avoid. Off-world, however, is a different story entirely. The team is hired by the Perduccis to deal with problems away from Solaris VII.

COMPLICATIONS

Interception: What cannot be bought is procured by other means. The Perduccis want a rival's designs, and the team must abscond with the original outfits, materials, and all digital design copies, then destroy everything else. The job is complicated by the rival's use of a mercenary-protected *Princess* Luxury Liner DropShip to host their traveling show.

Big Game Hunting: Unique outfits call for utterly unique materials. The team is hired to capture a particularly dangerous specimen from Hunter's Paradise. The Perduccis want a live, undamaged animal so they can harvest the best sections for themselves. Unfortunately for the team, some of the planet's wildlife can take on even BattleMechs, and the local game trackers have a violent distaste for poachers.

Message received: A businesswoman thought she could buy a Perducci wardrobe and not pay for it. She thought the Perduccis could not reach her beyond Solaris VII, but she was wrong. The team is hired to track down and eliminate her, with a bonus if the stolen clothing is recovered intact. The team's Perducci contact will furnish the details, but beware: the target has personal military connections.

Secret Shame: The team is hired to recover passenger baggage from the remains of a recently rediscovered Star League-era civilian transport found near the Taireed Valley on Crellacor. Passengers of the lost ship were rumored to be fleeing Amaris officials who may have possessed some incriminating evidence of collusion the Perduccis would like to see destroyed. Besides local scrappers and collectors who might reach the cargo hold first, a New Oberon Confederation raider group is also en route.

TIPS

These are repeatable jobs for every era; simply swap the target and location to take the team across the Inner Sphere and beyond.

SHRAPNEL

TALES FROM THE CRACKED CANOPY: NO REST FOR THE ACCURSED

MATTHEW CROSS

At the Cracked Canopy, a MechWarrior bar on the gaming world of Solaris VII, a Memory Wall displays mementos of glorious victories and bitter defeats, of honorable loyalties and venomous betrayals, of lifelong friendships and lost loves. Each enshrined object ensures that the past will not be forgotten, and the future is something worth fighting for.

INTERNATIONAL ZONE
SOLARIS CITY
SOLARIS VII
LYRAN COMMONWEALTH
23 MAY 3136

Yuri Agamato had to be rid of his curse. It wasn't a real curse; at least, he didn't think so. After his encounter with the Banshee of Sadachbia, he really wasn't sure of anything in the months following the battle.

Well, not quite a battle, more like a slaughter, he thought, nervously checking his surroundings. Yuri had become increasingly paranoid with each passing day since the incident. His journeys had led him halfway across the Inner Sphere, until he ended up in the same place countless MechWarriors had found themselves over the centuries: Solaris VII.

As he bounced from location to location on the Game World, he had finally found a worthy resting place for his curse. It was a rainy evening, as so many were in Solaris City, with the sky already dimming, despite the relatively early hour. As he turned the corner, he could see the damaged *Catapult* canopy hanging above the door, and he knew this was the place.

A nondescript man of Asian ancestry, Yuri could have been anyone in the crowds. He was only afraid he was trying too hard to look like no one. And even then, he wasn't sure why: no one was hunting him, no one wanted him dead. He was a washed-out failure haunted by nothing more than the horrors of war, a war he had invited on himself.

He carried his curse with him, both metaphorically and literally in his jacket pocket. The trinket had traveled with him ever since the day of the incident, and only one other person in the Inner Sphere even knew it existed. Despite it being just a "thing," he couldn't shake this foreboding feeling, so he held onto the capsule as a mark of his sins. Or something like that. Yuri had never been religious, or so he thought.

Inside the Cracked Canopy, the dim lighting was surprisingly warm and smelled just like one would expect such an establishment to smell. The scent of beer and liquor and fried foods wafted in from the kitchen, and it was almost enough for Yuri to forget the burden he carried. He spotted the Memory Wall, but knew he couldn't just walk in and claim a spot on it. Others had spoken of the cost of adding something to the wall. A story.

Only a half-dozen patrons were inside, fewer than Yuri had expected, but that was probably for the best. After just a moment of standing too long at the entrance, he stepped to the bar and signaled for the bartender's attention. The man behind the bar looked elderly, but spry for his age; his nametag read JONATHAN.

"What can I get for you?" he asked in a curious tone, seeming to ask more than the simple question laid before them.

"Something strong. And…maybe an opportunity to add to your Memory Wall over there," Yuri said, trying to sound both resolved and brave—emotions he did not currently feel.

In the top center of the wall was a photo of two men standing in front of the bar with a label that said SEDGE AND LEO: NEVER FORGET THE LEGENDS. Below that was a plethora of memorabilia, armor scraps, unit patches—anything and everything. It was clear the wall had been rearranged a few times over the years, but each piece that had earned a spot remained.

Jonathan poured two fingers of whisky from an expensive-looking bottle and set the tumbler on the bar. Yuri had never been much of a drinker, but today he gladly accepted the drink, knowing he'd probably regret the bill when it came. But it would be worth it.

"Leo and Sedge were always better at this," Jonathan said, "but I'm all ears. What's your story, good sir?"

YURI'S STORY

***LEOPARD*-CLASS DROPSHIP *FURY OF THE BROTHERHOOD*
EN ROUTE TO SADACHBIA
PREFECTURE III
REPUBLIC OF THE SPHERE
29 JULY 3134
1400 HOURS**

The briefing had told *Sho-ko* Yuri Agamato that this hit-and-run mission was a milk run, a lightly defended world with an abundance of supplies for the taking. In this case, the supplies were IndustrialMech parts and light ammunition, conveniently located at neighboring industrial centers on the edge of a larger city complex. The Brotherhood, an ad hoc command under Duchess Katana Tormark, would fly in with two small DropShips, raid the factories of whatever parts and ammunition were on hand at the facilities, and leave. And while Duchess Tormark didn't specify that they should keep the casualties low, it seemed this would be a relatively bloodless battle, something Yuri preferred.

He and his lance commander, *Chu-i* Amir Hadi, were piloting proper BattleMechs, but the other two lance members piloted converted IndustrialMechs, which made Shoto Lance more vulnerable to attackers. Yuri didn't even know much about the lance's two newest 'Mech jocks, added after a reorganization resulted in forming a new company. All of this combined gave him a bad feeling. They were quite possibly woefully unprepared for this raid. Or it could just be a milk run.

Although inexperienced, the IndustrialMech pilots were dedicated, if not clumsy in their awkward machines, which were barely fit for a warrior. Yuri would have taken a suit of Kanazuchi battle armor over the converted IndustrialMechs, but in the decades after the Republic of the Sphere's demilitarization, good military equipment was hard to come by. Until the Dragon's Fury captured more mothballed manufacturing facilities here in Prefecture III, these converted pieces of junk would have to do.

Yuri himself was more experienced. His Draconis Combine-loyal family was one of the few to turn down the Republic's offer for relocation, instead choosing to secretly harbor their dedication to the Dragon. Yuri was technically a lieutenant in the Republic Armed Forces, but he had only joined up so he could get behind the controls of a BattleMech. When the Blackout hit and Katana Tormark put out the call for all loyal sons and daughters of the Draconis Combine to join her, he jumped at the opportunity to join the Brotherhood. The only thing the Republic had ever done for him was put him in the seat of a 'Mech, and he'd had to jump through a lot of hoops to make that happen. On the day the Combine accepted Duchess Tormark's gift of Prefecture III, he knew he would be welcomed with open arms and made a proper member of the Draconis Combine Mustered Soldiery. Or so he hoped. Each raid, each battle, was one step closer to officially returning to House Kurita's fold.

Sadachbia didn't have much of a garrison listed from pre-Blackout records, and in the chaos of the past two years, Yuri doubted it would be anything larger than listed, as most militia would either get relocated to defend other worlds, or they would pledge their allegiance to one of the many coalitions that had popped up in the wake of the Blackout.

"All right everyone," said the DropShip's pilot, "we are preparing for final descent."

Yuri prepared to experience some extra g-forces and focused his thoughts on the mission ahead.

NEW WORKS
SADACHBIA
PREFECTURE III
REPUBLIC OF THE SPHERE
29 JULY 3134
2100 HOURS

The fog was exhausting on the eyes. While the short-range scanners of Yuri's *Wight* showed where the buildings were, he couldn't see much else.

"Keep moving, Shoto Lance," said *Chu-i* Amir Hadi, a middle-aged man with a temper Yuri failed to appreciate or possess. "We need to get these transports to the industrial complex, load them up, and get them out of here. Hell, we may even have time to get two trips in before these incompetent defenders even know we're here."

"On it, sir," responded Shoto Three. The young woman, Mariko Kamato, was likely a former IndustrialMech operator, as most of the new recruits were. She was mostly unremarkable except for the shaved portions of her temples for completely unnecessary neurohelmet connection points, since she wasn't piloting a BattleMech. She probably didn't have the patience to join the Republic Standing Guard, and saw joining the Dragon's Fury as a way to get some action in an otherwise uninteresting life.

It seemed strange that they had encountered no resistance thus far, but this wasn't the first time Yuri had conducted a bloodless raid. These rare instances only improved the reputation of the Brotherhood, and by extension, the Dragon's Fury. Maybe a milk run was what he needed to lift his spirits a bit. It was always hard walking as an invader in his own country. Maybe the Republic of the Sphere meant more to him than he thought.

After a short pause, Kamato spoke up with what Yuri assumed would be good news from the DropShip. "Sir, we are being jammed. All I'm getting is static on all channels."

"What!?" Hadi responded. "No one knows we are here. You probably just have the wrong frequency." But Yuri could tell the *chu-i* was clearly disturbed, and was trying to project an air of grit and patience.

As Shoto Lance neared the brightly lit intersection on the edge of the industrial district, the city's power cut out without warning. All lights from the block and the surrounding kilometer-plus radius of city light vanished, leaving only the soft glow of the other three cockpits visible through the wisps of fog floating throughout the urban jungle.

"Spotlights on, *now*!" shouted the *chu-i*.

Yuri immediately complied, switching his *Wight*'s small running lights on at maximum brightness. Unfortunately, all that did was create a bright white wall of fog in front of him, rather than cut through the impenetrable fog that had previously filled his viewport.

After another three tense minutes in the dark, one of the transports exploded.

"Why the hell aren't we using magres?" shouted the *chu-i* over the insistent comms static. "Thermals? *How could this happen?!*"

"Sir," Yuri spoke up, hoping to spare his lancemates another tongue lashing, "the urban environment drastically interferes with our magnetic-resonance sensors, and the city's unique thermal-vent rerouting system throws hotspots everywhere. I believe that is the source of our fog. This whole city is built on a network of geysers."

New Works had been created when the old city of Works was destroyed in a volcanic eruption some eighty years ago. Thankfully, the city's leadership had known the eruption was coming, and they had properly abandoned the doomed city before any life or material could be lost. New Works was created on a similar spot of volcanically active land, but in a theoretically more stable location than the old city. That way, most of the infrastructure that relied on the planet's geothermal anomalies could still operate. Word was that New Works had plans to relocate the city yet again in case of a future volcanic event.

"Keep trying the DropShip," the *chu-i* said, clearly trying to rein in his anger.

"Sir, I'm getting something through the static. It sounds like..." Shoto Three paused.

"What the hell is it, *Sho-ko*?"

"Sir, it sounds like bagpipes."

Before the *chu-i* could respond, his *Quickdraw*'s cockpit caved in just before the distinct *pop-thud* of a Gauss rifle shot rang out between the buildings. The massive machine seemed to just stop mid-stride, but with no living pilot there to give it balance, it toppled sideways, almost falling on Shoto Three's *Crosscut MOD*.

Yuri blinked at the sudden carnage, and with a sick feeling in his gut, realized he was in charge of Shoto Lance now.

"Where did that come from?!" shouted Shoto Four, a young man whose name Yuri couldn't remember for the life of him.

"Keep it calm, Shoto Four," Yuri said. "It looks like they have a Gauss rifle on the field. Probably just a hotheaded *Hollander* pilot with an ego. Lucky shot, the bastard."

Suddenly, a feminine voice with a Scottish brogue called out over the bagpipes and fiddles on the open channel. "Nah, wee lad, this ain't no *Hollander*. The Banshee of Sadachbia wouldn't lower herself ta such an unworthy machine."

A flight of long-range missiles burst through the fog, tracking for Shoto Four's *StrongArm MOD*.

"Take cover, Shoto Four!" Yuri shouted. "Shoto Three, track where that missile flight came from." It was impossible to figure out what was going on, or even how large of an opposing force they were facing.

Fifteen of the twenty missiles landed on the ungainly IndustrialMech, chipping away at its already-thin armor.

"I can't take this, Shoto Two!" screamed Shoto Four in a panic. "This is not what I signed up for!"

"Aye, lad," said the mysterious voice once more. "Did Tormark promise ya fame and fortune? Well, 'tis time tae pay th' piper."

Trying to remain calm, Yuri replied in a cool voice that did not at all reflect how he was feeling. "Keep your head on, Shoto Four. Get yourself behind a building and stay put. I'll deal with this threat." His particle projection cannon was charged and ready for whenever he had a bead on this so-called Banshee.

As soon as Shoto Four had himself in a hiding position, laser fire raked across the *StrongArm*'s cockpit, and his one usable weapon was sheared off at the elbow.

"I can't do this!" Shoto Four shouted.

The next thing Yuri knew, the young pilot had bent his IndustrialMech at the waist and jumped down from the cockpit, then ran off into the foggy night.

Yuri shook his head. *Fool.*

As soon as Shoto Four was clear of the *StrongArm*, a Gauss slug hit it square in the cockpit, destroying the already worthless machine. Yuri fired his heavy PPC in the direction the lasers had come from, but the terrible visibility almost ensured the shot would miss. The fog was so thick he didn't even know what he was shooting at.

The Banshee spoke again in a delighted and ghoulish tone. "Two down. Two ta go."

"Shoto Three, are you still there?" Yuri was now struggling to keep the calm in his voice. "We need to get an eye on whatever this *akuma* is, and clear our path for the convoy."

Kamato's *Crosscut MOD* was pinging strong and clear only 200 meters away, but the fog and magres noise made it impossible to see here. Over the din of the bagpipes and fiddles, he could barely hear Kamato chime in an affirmative. Audio sensors were picking up the whir of her enormous chainsaw as she prepared for a fight.

Yuri took a deep breath to calm the fear in his voice. "It's time to smoke this bandit out."

"Sir, aren't *we* the bandits?" He could almost hear a little smirk in her voice through the static, and didn't know what to think of that.

"Never mind that," Yuri said, readying another PPC strike. "Form up on the main street. Whatever this force is, we can take it."

Just as Yuri was about to reach Kamato's position, he watched a nightmare happen. One second she was there in her *Crosscut MOD*, and the next, a different 'Mech was somehow standing in its place. A 90-ton *Highlander IIC* painted in the tan, green, and tartan scheme of the Northwind Highlanders, except its head was painted a jet black. Under its feet were the remains of Kamato's *Crosscut*.

Yuri had just witnessed a genuine Highlander Burial. And, somehow, he had also managed to avoid wetting himself.

Panic took root as he tried to find some way out, but he couldn't concentrate on his map or anything but the towering *Highlander* now consuming his viewport. Before he could even turn his 'Mech or get a shot off with his heavy PPC, the Banshee of Sadachbia grasped one of his *Wight*'s arms and ripped it from its socket. The force of the blow threw Yuri and his 'Mech to the ground, sliding nearly thirty meters away from where he had just been standing.

The *Highlander IIC* plodded over to where Yuri's 'Mech lay on the ground as he tried pointlessly to stand the machine, or even get it into a sitting position. As he struggled, the imposing form of the Banshee leaned over and pointed its arm-mounted Gauss rifle in his direction.

Yuri resigned himself to the honor of being killed by a superior foe, and closed his eyes to brace for death.

But death did not come. Instead of aiming for the cockpit, the Gauss rifle rang out with a deafening *thud* and shot right into and through the barrel of his PPC. Then, placing one of the *Highlander*'s feet on the *Wight*'s chest, the Banshee spoke over the now static-less channel.

"Dead lads tell no tales, my love. Why don't ye head back to yer DropShip and tell Ms. Tormark she is unwelcome here on Sadachbia. Now, pop yer hatch."

"I...I am not afraid of you," Yuri responded in unsure tones.

"Aye, ye are. Pop yer hatch," replied the Banshee. It almost sounded like she was smiling.

After a moment of deliberation, Yuri finally complied. He opened the top hatch on the machine opened and started to clamber out.

"No need ta get all th' way out, love."

And then he could see the hatch on the *Highlander* had also opened, and the silhouette of a slight woman appeared at the top of the 'Mech. She dropped something, and with surprising precision, a small capsule landed in Yuri's hands.

Inside the capsule was a thistle, with a note tied to it and labeled KATANA TORMARK. For a moment he just stared up at the *Highlander* pilot. As he watched her drop back into her cockpit, he buttoned up his own hatch and set the thistle aside. When he finally brought his 'Mech to a sitting position, he saw that the Banshee of Sadachbia had turned her 'Mech and began to walk away.

Overcome with a strange sense of curiosity and knowing he was going to live today, Yuri keyed the comm. With a nervous quiver in his voice, he said, "One last thing."

She paused, turning her 'Mech to look at the sad little *Wight* sitting in the middle of the intersection where she had maimed it.

"Aren't Banshees Irish, not Scottish?"

"Aye, lad, but no one can pronounce *caoineag*."

And with that, she was gone, lost in the fog, and Yuri was alone, holding the perfectly preserved thistle in his hands. The remains of the convoy had scattered in the battle, and there was nothing left to do except return to the DropShips in defeat.

**INTERNATIONAL ZONE
SOLARIS CITY
SOLARIS VII
LYRAN COMMONWEALTH
23 MAY 3135**

"That was nearly two years ago," Yuri said after he had finished his tale. "The Banshee got me Dispossessed, kicked out of the Dragon's Fury, and left for dead in the chaos of this damned Blackout."

All of that was true. After returning with his failure, Yuri obediently forwarded the note to Katana. Two days later he was informed that his 'Mech, if it could even be repaired, would be reassigned to another MechWarrior who could "actually hit an assault 'Mech standing five meters away."

They didn't understand. No one could.

"I don't expect you to understand," Yuri said to the bartender, "but I need to put this behind me."

With that, he pulled out the capsule with the single thistle and the empty envelope labeled KATANA TORMARK still attached.

"That encounter ruined my life," he said with a saddened expression, "and this is my chance to start again. I am honestly hoping to find my way back into a cockpit soon, for better or worse."

"I think we can find a place for this. This Memory Wall is many things to many people. One more memory can only make it more complete."

With that, Yuri reluctantly gave the capsule to the bartender. Jonathan took some hanger wire from under the bar and gently crafted a mount for the capsule and found a small section with a few blank spots for it to hang. Yuri watched with anticipation during this act of reconciliation, for the pains he had caused his fellow Republic citizens, and for leading those kids into battle. For following that traitor, Katana Tormark.

Just before hanging the capsule, Jonathan placed it under the UV disinfector, a practice started because of some rotten-smelling tributes in past years. While under the disinfector, Jonathan paused, examining the capsule, looking closely at one corner of the ferroglass. "Yuri, did you know there's an inscription on this capsule?"

Just as he was going to relax, just as the capsule had found its final resting place, Yuri felt a twinge of doubt, a feeling that something could ruin this moment.

"What inscription?" he said with a note of nervous curiosity.

Jonathan squinted at the tube in his hand. "My eyes are old, and the UV is bright, but it looks like there's an inscription here."

"Let me see that."

Yuri examined the capsule with shaking hands. He had never really examined the tube closely before. It was an omen, a curse, and he had actively avoided looking at it despite never being able to let go of it.

The inscription read:

> I'LL ALWAYS BE WITH YOU, YURI.
> ——THE BANSHEE

The script was utterly tiny, but completely readable in the bright bluish ultraviolet light.

Yuri muttered something so quiet he barely heard himself speak: "I never told her my name."

"What was that?" Jonathan said.

"I never told her my name," Yuri said a bit louder this time. "Our operational guidelines had us only refer to each other by call signs or ranks, never names. There was no possible way she could know my name."

"Maybe you'd been to Sadachbia before that mission?" Jonathan suggested after a short pause. Or maybe someone else handled the capsule?"

Yuri had already thought these things. "No, that was my first time there. And I didn't show it to my superiors when I returned to the Fury, only the note to Tormark. No one knows the capsule exists except you, me, and the Banshee."

Jonathan nodded, though his expression said he wasn't entirely convinced. "I can still hang it if you'd like."

Yuri was trembling. He would never be rid of this curse.

"Yes, p-please do," he finally said. "I think I might be skipping those merc trials I have scheduled for tomorrow. It may be time for me to look into other work. Thank you for your time. And the drink."

He downed the rest of the whisky in a single swig, stood up, and gave a low bow, then dropped a fifty-stone note on the counter.

And with that, Yuri got up and walked out the bar, not fifteen minutes after he had entered. He stood for a moment with his head hung low, disappointed and broken, and contemplated the list of sins that had led him to this moment.

Then he disappeared into the night.

SHRAPNEL

ASCENDING THE PECKING ORDER: POLITICAL WARFARE IN THE RAVEN ALLIANCE

ERIC SALZMAN

To: Loremaster Acton Howe
From: Warder Regis, Sukhanov Sibko 476-Theta, Columbia Academy
14 May 3152

    Loremaster Howe, supplementary to my *sibcadet* evaluation ratings for your next List update, I am forwarding a journal entry from one of my *ristars*, Fleur. She has been annotating exercise transcripts, officially for review and self-improvement, though I suspect her true intent is to find weaknesses in other *sibcadets* she can exploit in the future. She is unaware I have access. This entry, in particular, demonstrates the efficacy of the political training I have imparted on my Fledglings, in line with Sukhanov family traditions. Based on her combat skills and grasp of political theory, I expect Fleur to contest for Sukhanov family leadership within a decade.

**CSR *ROOKERY*
HIGH ORBIT
RAMORA II
RAVEN ALLIANCE
13 MAY 3152**

    Crushing g-forces pressed my body into the acceleration couch as the electromagnetic catapult expelled my *Wusun* OmniFighter from its

Titan-class mothership. Maneuvering into formation with the other nine *sibcadets*, I took in the cloudless dun-and-ochre orb of the planet below, as well as its four moonlets. Another day, another exercise, another chance to climb the List.

The familiar hoarse wheeze of Warder Regis crackled over our Star's secure channel. "Good morning, Fledglings. Following yesterday's exercise, Malcolm now ranks highest on the List, followed by Fleur. As such, Malcom is acting Star Commander." I joined the chorus of *"Aff!"* responses, inwardly cursing Malcom's ascent.

Regis continued. "In our new Star League, expect to regularly face superior numbers. Today, we separate the *ristars* from the *surats*. Your sensors should detect the *Almirante*, a *Vengeance*-class carrier, emerging from behind the largest moon. Aboard are Outworlder freebirth cadets from the Columbia Academy. Their goal is to destroy the *Rookery*. Stop them. Weapons are in simulator mode. The Rangemaster will disable systems remotely."

I dialed up magnification, picking out the lethal dart of the carrier deploying its fighters. My WarBook identified the twenty specks, a full Alliance air regiment, as *Corax*-class light OmniFighters. Though lacking Clan technology, they held a slight edge in speed over our *Wusun*s.

"As a special treat, Fledglings, your family head, Star Admiral Jezebel Sukhanov, is personally overseeing this exercise. Star Admiral?"

A new voice cut in over the frequency, stern and demanding. "Fledglings of the Sukhanov bloodline! The coming age offers great opportunity to win battle honors. But forging a new Star League will require more: quick thinking, analysis, insight, and skill in subtle manipulation. The Sukhanov family wins renown by applying the teachings of ancient philosopher Niccolò Machiavelli. During today's exercise, I require your analysis of our Raven Alliance through the framework of Machiavellian theory. Failure will bring consequences."

I groaned inwardly. A philosophy debate in the middle of a firefight!

Malcom's command channel opened. "Fleur, lead your Point to the left flank and engage at extreme range. Disable them before they reach effective Spheroid weapon range. Sweep through, then harry them from behind."

"*Aff*, Star Commander." I gritted my teeth at the honorific. "Good hunting." *Just not* too *good...*

Jezebel commenced. "First question! Nuha: Why do we permit the freebirth Alliance Military Corps to exist?"

A strained silence lasted nearly a minute before Nuha responded. "Star Admiral, disbanding the AMC would have shown that we distrusted the Outworlders, considering them either cowardly or disloyal, and this would have bred hatred against us. By arming them, our faith was returned, and those arms became ours."

"A textbook answer, Fledgling, but a slow one. Rangemaster, disable her targeting computer."

I winced, hoping Nuha's unassisted aim had improved over prior exercises.

"Ferris: What mistakes did the Outworlds Alliance make in managing its relationship with the Federated Suns and Draconis Combine prior to the Raven Alliance's formation?"

Ferris' response came swiftly. "They maintained neutrality, supplying tribute to each. Machiavellian theory demands that when two powerful neighbors come to blows, one should declare oneself and make war, earning the friendship of the victor."

"Excellent, Fledgling. But incomplete. Fleur: Additional mistakes?"

My mind raced. Ferris had already plucked the low-hanging fruit. I would have to approach from another angle.

"Star Admiral, the Outworlds Alliance erred by offering us sanctuary. Machiavelli warns against bringing soldiers of a stronger foreign power into your borders for protection, as they may not willingly depart."

I thought I heard a hint of a smile creeping into the Star Admiral's voice. "*Aff*, Fledgling. It was opportune for us that House Avellar failed to study Machiavelli. And Snow Ravens never waste an opportunity."

As our fighters hurtled through space towards the Outworlders, Jezebel continued. "Vanara: Our fleet is an unmatched strategic asset. What would justify its use in orbital bombardment against planetary targets?"

I did not envy Vanara. The ethics of mass destruction was a tricky topic, and Warder Regis had made us well-aware that the Smoke Jaguars' unrestrained use of planetary bombardment was a key factor in the Inner Sphere alliance's decision to target them for Annihilation.

"'It is only through violence and the willingness to destroy enemies that a ruler survives and keeps his grip on power. Foes must be crushed, leaving no potential for survivors to exact revenge.' I cite the case of Dante, which Blakist pirates had turned into a planetwide base of operations. In 3069, our fleet obliterated all Blakist assets and installations on the planet and drove the cultists from Alliance space, never to return. Per Machiavelli, a rapid, massive strike may be justified by the need to instill fear in potential rivals, and thereby to guide their future actions."

"Acceptable. Fledgling Wolfram: Would you use the same justification for Galedon V?"

"Star Admiral, Galedon was the result of the Draconis Combine ignoring Machiavelli's axiom. Their *dezgra* booby trap's destruction of the CSR *White Cloud* failed to degrade our military capabilities, and obligated us to retaliate. The civilian population was given a week's notice to evacuate all cities, avoiding the casualties that made the

Smoke Jaguar action on Turtle Bay *dezgra*. The catastrophic release of the Combine's secret bioweapon vaults during the bombardment was not our intent, but we took responsibility for enforcing a quarantine to keep the Curse of Galedon from spreading. Our overwhelming force dissuaded the Combine from further covert operations against us."

"Well said. Brennan: In the Diamond Shark affair, what would Machiavelli regard as Khan Liam Howell's failure?"

I almost snorted in laughter over the channel. This one was easy.

"Star Admiral, Khan Howell's directive to breed a super-predator species to exterminate the Sea Foxes' totem animal was retaliation for the Foxes' use of *dezgra* espionage, which was not an accepted part of Clan trials of the era. His failing was in admitting before the Grand Council that the extermination was his doing, resulting in his immediate execution through a Trial of Grievance declared by our *sibko*'s genefather, Niamh Sukhanov. 'Take care never to let anything slip from your lips that is not replete with qualities that make you appear merciful, faithful, humane, and upright.' His own words branded him a villain."

"Well argued."

Proximity alarms shrilled as the freebirth fighter formation entered weapons range. I locked my targeting computer onto the leftmost *Corax* and triggered my extended-range lasers, spearing neatly through the cockpit. The "killed" ship began an uncontrolled tumble.

"Malcolm: Why did the Raven Council elevate Christián Avellar as Alliance President over his elder brother Eustace?"

I could hear the strain of the combat-maneuver g-forces in Malcolm's voice. "Apologies, Star Admiral. I am attempting to execute my battle plan!"

"Nonsense, boy! A Snow Raven commander must be able to think about the big picture during combat, not just react to the local tactical situation. Answer, or see how your battle plan does without you."

I saw Malcolm's *Wusun* flash through the Alliance skirmish line, leaving two *Corax*es "killed" in his wake. "Star Admiral, once our Clan positioned itself as the Outworlders' defender, Machiavellian theory called for us to weaken the powerful among them. House Avellar represented the logical locus for opposition to Raven rule, and Eustace had associated with anti-Raven extremists. Christián, however, focuses almost exclusively on gorging himself and writing satirical plays. Machiavelli warns that when leaders think more of ease than arms, they have lost their states. Even if President Avellar sought to reclaim the authority ceded by his predecessors, 'a prince who does not understand the art of war cannot be respected by his soldiers, nor can he rely on them.'"

"Acceptable answer. Unacceptable delay. Say farewell to your missile launchers."

Punching through the Outworlder line, our *Wusun*s emerged intact, leaving half of the enemy *Corax*es dark and adrift. As the survivors scattered and broke for the moon's cover, I redirected my thrusters on a pursuit course. Out of the corner of my eye, I noted the needle shape of the *Almirante*, closer to the battle than I had expected.

"Jarod: Why have we established enclaves on every world in the Alliance?"

"Star Admiral, the enclaves' presence is a reminder of our power, and keeps the populace cowed and submissive."

I rolled my eyes. Jarod's sneering disdain toward the Outworlder freebirths kept him at the bottom of the List.

Jezebel was similarly unimpressed. "Warder Regis, what drivel are you teaching your Fledglings? Rangemaster, Fledgling Jarod has been 'killed.' Leave his comms active so he can be enlightened. Jose?"

"Star Admiral, when acquired territories are accustomed to different laws and customs, the new rulers must reside in colonies among the people to make their position more secure and durable. Thereby, unrest may be spotted early and quickly remedied. We rely on the Outworlders' goodwill."

"Acceptable. Wendell—you are not forgotten. Hypothetical: Khan McKenna intentionally engineered the Davion defeat at Palmyra. Why?"

I was glad I had dodged that question. Second-guessing a Khan's motives could be hazardous, especially when the official story was that the flotilla promised to First Prince Caleb Davion for Operation Mandragora had encountered "technical difficulties," leaving his army at the mercy of the Draconis Combine.

"Hypothetically...the Khan has chosen to back the Draconis Combine to win against the Federated Suns. The three systems ceded to the Alliance demonstrated the Combine's gratitude. Informing the Combine of the First Prince's plans eliminated Davion leadership, and the Annihilation of Caleb's family line forestalled revenge against the Alliance."

"Inapplicable, Fledgling! The Federated Suns had other Davion cadet lines and secondary leadership. You are comparing the Khan's intent to Stefan Amaris, who exterminated House Cameron, *quineg*?"

I hastily interjected, hoping to prevent my Pointmate from becoming another "kill." "Hypothetical, Star Admiral: During the Pax Republica, Khan McKenna secured peace with the Suns by manipulating First Prince Harrison Davion, freeing us to fend off the Combine. Having assessed Harrison's successor, Caleb, the Khan saw him as a potential threat who could not be similarly neutralized. She leveraged his perception of our Clan as a subservient ally to draw him into a trap, gaining territory and security for the Alliance. 'Men will not look at things as they really are, but as they wish them to be, and are ruined.'"

As I spoke, I had a flash of insight. I opened a channel to the Star Commander. "Malcolm, we need to break off pursuit!"

"Why? We will shortly have won this battle."

"That is what they want us to think. The *Vengeance*-class carries *forty* fighters, not twenty. While we chase these *Corax*es, the other regiment will destroy our mothership!"

The channel remained silent for agonizing moments before Malcolm responded. "*Aff.* Your analysis is sound. All Points, disengage and burn hard for the *Almirante*. Disable it before it can launch a second wave!"

Star Admiral Jezebel's voice cut in. "Very good, Fledgling Fleur. You spotted the trap. A final question: Why do we allow Outworlder cadets to train for attacks against us?"

"Machiavelli tells us we must inspire fear while avoiding hatred. These cadets will remember that they lost, despite their numbers, and dread the prospect of ever facing us in real battle. Yet, presented as a training exercise, there is no malice attached. Thus, we manage perceptions and maintain control."

"You do the Sukhanov family proud, *ristar*. I look forward to your Trial of Position."

SHRAPNEL

STARVING VULTURES

JOSEPH A. COSGROVE

BAMBURGH
CRUCIS MARCH
FEDERATED SUNS
11 APRIL 2783

"Can a fella get somethin' to eat, Merrill?" Jim McCullough asked hopefully, one hand on the diner's porch railing, the other on his stomach.

The cook, in mid-swing with a rusty hammer, glanced over his shoulder at the hungry young man. "You're always welcome here, Jimmy." The nails clenched in Merrill's teeth appeared to dance through his gray mustache as he spoke. "Just not today." With a deep sigh, he gestured at the wooden board partially nailed to the doorframe. "Closin' early."

Jim nodded. "Can't blame a guy for asking. The farmer's market closed after that stupid brawl last week, and now the general store's already picked over. Figured Patty's would be my salvation. Where's she at, anyway?"

Merrill set down his tools and sat on the diner's front steps. "Patty got wise—staying at her summer cabin on Cherry Lake. Said she's gonna wait out all the nonsense, come 'round after everything blows over."

"What about you?" Jim groaned as he sat down heavily, the stairs creaking under him.

"I got the ol' scattergun. Plannin' to set up cot in the back and keep eyes on the place until things get back to normal." Merrill shook his head, "You think you know people. Grow up with 'em, go to church with 'em, but they're different inside. I say let any one of 'em try their luck."

"I don't fancy their chances against you and that boomstick. I'll be your first customer when you open back up." Jim slapped Merrill on his shoulder and stood up. "Say, if you see Wesley, tell him to come by my place, will you?"

"Sure thing," Merrill said. "Stay safe, now. Say 'hi' to your pa for me."

Jim loped down the few stairs and resumed his walk through town. He thrust his hands into his jacket pockets and was glad his mother had reminded him to bundle up, since the bright white sun was stingy with its warmth today. An unnatural chill had fallen over town, in both the weather and the people. Neighbors didn't wave anymore. Blinds were drawn shut and left that way. Doors were locked at night, with deadbolts that squeaked from lack of use. Jim didn't like it. He didn't like it one bit.

His ears perked up as the familiar puttering of a small, two-stroke engine approached from behind. Jim knew engines, a result of working at the family scrapyard his whole life, and he knew only one vehicle in town made that noise: the veterinary clinic's battered, three-wheeled rickshaw. His heart began to beat faster. Kate Mulligan, the girl he'd been sweet on since grammar school, worked at the veterinary clinic. She was gentle, good with animals, and the prettiest girl he'd ever seen.

He straightened up, walked a little taller, and resisted the urge to turn around and see who was driving. The rattling machine pulled up next to him and matched his pace.

"Hey there, Jim! Where you headed?"

It was her.

Jim allowed himself to look at the driver. "Oh, hey, Kate. Just takin' the slow way home. What about you?"

"Been trying to trade for saline bags. Even the municipal hospital's out now, and it's just insanity over in the city. Want a ride?"

Jim's body responded faster than his mind could keep up. He'd already climbed into the rickshaw before saying, "That'd be great, thanks." His mouth had gone dry, so he paused before speaking again. "You say the city's just as crazy as here?"

Kate's brows lifted, and she shook her head. "No, much, much worse. The metropolitan folk are up in arms, burning down buildings and stealing from each other. It's absolute anarchy. Even the militia got brought in, but they don't know what to do. Nobody does. This isn't another dust storm or quake. It's..." She struggled to find her next words. "It's the end of the world."

Jim wanted to put his hand on hers, to comfort her, but he held back. Instead, he said, "All this over trade ships in space? Seems like overkill. Life will go on." He grabbed the rickshaw frame as they went over a deep pothole.

"Not just 'trade ships,' Jim. This is the last *JumpShip* run to the Bamburgh system. We're no longer considered profitable. After next week, the mercantile guild is just gonna go around us. We'll be an island, cut off from the rest of humanity." Her eyes got watery. It occurred to Jim that the situation might be worse than he'd thought, because she seemed really upset about the whole thing. Kate had always been smart in school, so when she took a problem seriously, he knew there was something to it.

"Our world is *dying*, Jim," she said. "We've got no petrochemicals, we can't make plastic or medicine, or even fertilizer. We're mineral-poor, too. Can't build solar panels, can't form alloys. I just don't know how we're going to keep going without the trade route."

"We've still got the nickel mines," Jim said. He risked a playful elbow into Kate's ribs. "So it's not all bad. They still need nickel in the rest of the March. They'll be back when they run out."

Kate wiped the moisture from her eyes and spoke softly, "No, they won't. They found nickel on other planets in the Crucis March, closer to the trade lanes. It's just plain old economics."

Jim didn't know what to say after that; he'd never tested high enough to take an economics class. He was relieved when the rickshaw turned a corner and his family's timber-framed home came into view, the scrapyard not far behind it. He saw his father on the front porch, whittling a small piece of wood, stopping to wave at them.

"Howdy, Kate," Mr. McCullough said. "Thanks for finding my boy!"

Kate's face looked fresh again, but Jim knew of the roiling waters underneath as she pulled the rickshaw alongside the property. "No problem at all."

"Won't you stay for some ribs? Wesley's come over and started up the grill out back."

Jim couldn't hide his hopeful expression as Kate considered the offer. "I'd love to, thank you," she said. "It's been a long, exhausting day."

Jim smelled the barbecue before he saw Wesley, his best and oldest friend, tending the grill. He clapped a hand on the young man's shoulder and said, "My God, those look amazing."

"You know it," Wesley said. "Hey there, Kate."

Kate smiled and inhaled a deep breath of barbecue smoke. "You've outdone yourself again, Wes."

Mr. McCullough pushed open the screen door and walked into the backyard, carrying four bottles of beer. "I'll finish up there, Wes. Why don't you take a seat and tell 'em your master plan."

The three took their beers and found seats. Jim and Kate sat on a couple of lawn chairs, and Wesley perched on an old tractor tire.

Between them, a fire pit made from a broken washing machine issued sparks into a darkening sky.

"So," Wesley began, "everybody's trying to gather up enough supplies to outlast the end of days, or they're stealing and selling anything that can buy them passage off this rock, right?"

Jim and Kate nodded.

"What if I told you I found something that can get all of us, and all our families, off-world?"

Kate scoffed. "I'd say your boss needs to provide a better mask filter, 'cause you've been breathing too much mine gas."

"Yeah," Jim said, "I'm not sure there's anything you could steal from Bamburgh Mining Incorporated that'd be worth thirty berths on a DropShip, much less the connecting ride on a JumpShip."

"That's where you're wrong." Wesley said. "We're gonna steal a 'Mech—or at least part of it—and buy our way off this rock."

"Now I *know* you're high on that gas," Kate chuckled, and sipped her beer.

Wesley cracked a conspiratorial smile. "Well, bear with me, here. What do you know about the Mercenary?"

"He's some kind of terrorist, right?" Kate said.

Jim shrugged. He'd heard of the legend, but didn't know fact from fiction.

"About three years ago, a band of pirates tried to raid the city," Wesley said.

"Well, yeah," Jim said. "Everybody knows that. The militia sent 'em running with their tails between their legs."

Wesley shook his head. "No, not true. The militia doesn't have any BattleMechs. They didn't stand a chance. Something else got the pirates retreating. They left of their own accord, and to this day nobody knows why."

Kate pursed her lips in thought. "Something probably threatened their DropShip in orbit. Maybe pirate-hunters, or a different faction looking for an easy capture? No score from the city would be worth putting their DropShip at risk."

Wesley looked like the idea had never occurred to him. "Well, yeah, maybe. Actually, that's a pretty good theory. Regardless, they left someone behind. In their rush to get away, a single 'Mech, a *Marauder*, was abandoned, along with its pilot."

"Poor guy," Kate said.

"Ha!" Wesley snorted, "'Poor' my left foot! The Mercenary, as we've come to call him, has been making a fine living ever since. He hires himself out to Bamburgh Mining and our chief competitor, Advanced Planetary Resources. He takes part in all the corporate raids as the two companies try to disrupt each other's operations."

Just then the screen door burst open with a clatter, and Max, the McCullough family dog, barged out and rumbled down the steps. A retriever-mix and lifelong customer of Kate's clinic, Max gave each of the friends a sloppy greeting before racing over to the grill.

"Speaking of disruptions," Jim chuckled.

"You know I'm his favorite," Kate chided.

"*Pork ribs* are his favorite," Wesley said as he sipped his beer. "Now, where was I?"

"You said the Mercenary fights for both sides." Jim glanced at his now empty bottle, wishing for another one.

"He works for the highest bidder, and he's changed the name of the mining game. At first, he would wipe whole operations off the map, much more efficiently than my company's security forces ever could. It was just dumb luck that it always happened on my time off, or I might not be here today. Anyway, the Mercenary was too good at his job, and he was causing so much destruction on both sides that we all needed to calm down or go bankrupt. A sort of cold war developed. An unspoken truce." Wesley paused to take a swig of his beer.

Max returned to the fireside, dejected that the meat wasn't ready. He lay at Kate's feet and rolled onto his back, demanding a belly-rub. As Kate bent over to oblige him, she cast a haughty look at Jim that said, *See? I'm his favorite.*

Wesley continued. "Eventually, the Mercenary would stomp over to one camp or the other and just march around the operation. All of us miners knew the game. We'd put down our tools, walk away from our equipment, and end the shift early. We started to like these 'raids,' 'cause there was no more shooting or killing. Morale rose, attendance rose, turnover stopped. Once we quit work, the Mercenary would just wander off until someone hired him for another round of intimidation. It was hell on our logistics and supply chain, but it's cheaper for both sides when nobody's shooting."

"Wow," Kate said as she set her empty bottle down. "That's the smartest stupid solution to an entirely avoidable problem. I'll never understand why those mining companies can't just get along and share the wealth."

"You know those corporate types," Jim said. "They're not like family businesses. No sense of shared struggle. There's only so much cargo room on each DropShip, gotta make sure it's full of your product."

"That's the truth," Wesley said. He fixed them both with an unblinking stare. "The Mercenary is our key off this world. His *Marauder* is how we get out."

"Don't be ridiculous," Kate said.

"You really want to steal a *BattleMech*?" Jim asked.

"It's impossible," Kate said as she shifted to look at Jim. "It can't be done. Even if you got past the ignition code and voice identification, none of us could pilot it. Have either of you even seen a neurohelmet?"

"We're not going to *steal* it," Wesley said. "We're going to trap it. We're going to cut it apart and sell the juiciest bit to buy passage off this dying planet."

Pork fat popped and sizzled on the grill behind them. The smell, and the opportunity before them, were intoxicating.

"This is nuts," Kate said. "If that thing's even half as powerful as what we see in the vid releases, there's nothing in the world that can stop it. Except maybe another *Marauder*."

Mr. McCullough handed each of them a plate of hot, succulent ribs. Max, with a herculean effort, restrained himself as the meat was passed around, and his patience was rewarded with several pieces tossed at his feet.

"Thanks for bringing these over, Wesley," Mr. McCullough said.

"Don't mention it. We were out of gas, you were out of meat. Seemed like a match made in heaven."

Mr. McCullough swallowed a bite of meat and wiped his mouth with the back of his hand. "I think I better chime in here. I've got an old friend, more of an acquaintance, who's looking for a specific part of that 'Mech. He runs an import/export business—or he did until the last JumpShip leaves—and is willing to pay us handsomely if his final shipment has something truly valuable."

"Dad," Jim said, "are you talkin' about the black market?"

Jim's father nodded. "Yes. I'm not proud to say it, son. I never raised you to consort with criminals. But sometimes you gotta make a difficult choice to survive. A long time ago, before you were born, I needed to work with some shady men to make ends meet every so often."

Night had fallen. Their faces were illuminated by the campfire light. Even in only hues of orange and red, Jim could see Kate's concern writ large on her face. Wesley, however, seemed to glow from within.

"What part does your friend want?" Kate asked.

"A weapon," Mr. McCullough said. "Most *Marauder*s carry a pair of particle projection cannons, PPCs for short. They're huge, so we'll only be able to take one of them on the flatbed trailer. The specific type of PPC on the Mercenary's 'Mech is exceedingly rare. It's called a Kinslaughter."

He paused to pick a bit of gristle from his teeth before continuing. "I've seen pictures taken by Wesley's coworkers during the raids. This is the real deal. A Kinslaughter will shoot farther and hit harder than anything. They're rare as clouds in summer. Utterly priceless."

Max looked up from the bones he was gnawing, searching the assembled faces for a clue to their contemplative silence. Failing to find one, he returned to his happy task.

12 APRIL 2783

It was early when Jim sat up in bed and cracked his neck loudly. Blinking away the last vestiges of sleep, he pulled aside his bedroom curtains and looked out on the scrapyard behind the family plot.

His dad was already up, checking the tire pressure of *Goliath*, their largest wrecker. Each tire stood almost as tall as Jim himself. The massive truck looked like a blockhouse on wheels, complete with a flatbed trailer that could haul any ground vehicle on Bamburgh. It was the pride of the McCullough truck fleet.

Jim saw Wesley walk out from behind the cab, checking a diagnostic tablet and flexing the trailer's integrated crane. As the crane's grabber claw opened and closed, Jim got dressed and headed outside, ignoring his grumbling stomach.

"I think it can take the weight, no problem," Wesley said.

"It will be if the roads through the Blackbriar are still muddy," Mr. McCullough said.

Jim shaded his eyes as he stepped into the sunlight. He saw Kate pulling another large truck up alongside *Goliath*. It was an unnamed, obsolete fire engine. He scratched his chin, curious.

"Did y'all sleep here last night?" he asked.

Kate leaned out of the fire engine's window. "We had to. The roads were too dangerous after dark. You didn't hear the gunshots?"

"Huh," Jim said. "Must've slept through 'em."

Wesley patted *Goliath*'s hood. "It's getting worse the closer that JumpShip gets to our system. People are getting more desperate for a way out every day. Sooner we pull this off, the better."

"Remind me," Jim said. "What exactly do we need a fire engine and a wrecker for? That's an odd combination."

Mr. McCullough took the tablet from Wesley's hand as it alerted a new message. "I'll tell you on the way, son. We need to get these vehicles moving. Grab a sticky roll from the kitchen and put on some boots. If you're in, now's the time to say so."

"Of course I'm in," Jim said, defensively. He looked at Kate. "You're in, too, right?"

"I am," she said. "This is dangerous work. People could get hurt, and I've got medical experience."

She gave Jim a look he'd never seen before. Pleading? Fearful? Perhaps she'd felt guilty at the thought of staying behind when others would need her. Jim couldn't place her expression, but it made him uncomfortable, and he looked away.

Jim sat in the fire engine's cab with Kate as they trundled away from town along a straight, dusty road. Ahead, Mr. McCullough drove *Goliath* while Wesley rode shotgun. The bulky headphones and mics they all wore cut through the road noise and helped coordinate multi-crew salvage operations.

Jim keyed into the group's shared channel. "Okay, I get that we need the flatbed to haul off one of those particle cannons, but what's the fire engine for? Do we need to cool the particle cannon off before we touch it?"

Wesley's reply was tinny over the headset speakers. "The opposite, actually. Your rig is full of inferno gel, so drive carefully, Kate. We're gonna link up with the rest of the BMI boys for their last raid, the big one, and when the Mercenary shows up, we're going to hose him down."

"With inferno gel?" Jim asked.

"Yes. *Marauder*s can run hot. By now he'll be out of autocannon ammo—he'll have to rely on his energy weapons, and those generate a lot of waste heat. And I mean a *lot*. If we cover him in burning inferno gel, his 'Mech will automatically shut down to try to cool off."

Jim's dad activated his mic. "That's when we give him a gentle shove over and begin the disassembly. I've got a couple of the fellas from the garage meeting us en route. They'll handle the buzzsaws and plasma cutters, and I'll work the crane. Wesley will drive *Goliath* once it's loaded up, and Kate here is driving the fire rig."

"What do you want me to do?" Jim asked.

"You get to operate the squirt gun."

Kate gave Jim a look from across the cab.

"You signed me up to kill *the Mercenary*?" Jim was flabbergasted.

Wesley snorted. "If he knows what's good for him, he'll eject."

"And what if that doesn't work? What if his ejector seat is broken? It hasn't exactly been getting regular maintenance, right?"

Kate nodded, almost imperceptibly, but remained silent.

"Look, son," Mr. McCullough started, "it's the APR guys and the Mercenary, or it's us. We have to take some risks. This is the last chance for either mining company to steal the other side's stockpile and secure a ticket out of here. It's all or nothing, and pretty much every worker lookin' for a berth is taking part. The Mercenary will be there, and he knows the stakes as well. Whichever side he fights for doesn't matter. In the heat of the battle, we're gonna get our salvage no matter what."

"All right. I get it," Jim said quietly. He hoped the pilot would be safe. He didn't want to kill anyone, even if it helped him escape his dying homeworld. He glanced at Kate. *I would kill for you, though,* he thought. If it kept Kate safe, he'd burn an entire BattleMech regiment to ashes.

Two backcountry-capable utility vans pulled onto the dirt road at a rough intersection—Mr. McCullough's garage employees. The vehicles were loaded with crews and cutting equipment. This PPC thing must've be huge if it took an entire shop crew to remove. Jim wondered what it looked like, and wished he'd paid closer attention to the 'Mech cartoons he'd watched as a child. The machines had seemed big, but he had no relationship to them outside of the realm of fantasy. Gallant knights of the stars waging high-tech warfare were as fanciful as Bamburgh's old legends of forest spirits and sea monsters he'd grown up on.

The vans took a position between Jim's vehicle and *Goliath*. One of the workers waved at them, and Jim waved back. He didn't recognize the man. His father employed so many of the local townspeople, it was difficult to keep track.

Kate spoke for the first time since the journey had started. "Where does the Mercenary go when he's not scaring the wits out of hapless miners? Where does he live?"

"Nobody knows," Wesley said. "He probably has a camp in the Bleeding Hills, because he always seems to leave in that direction, but nobody has the guts to follow him. The tree cover is pretty dense up there, so drones can't get in either."

"Must be a lonely existence," she said.

The channel hissed and popped, but nobody spoke. They drove on in silence.

Jim jumped in his seat as he heard another explosion, this one not as distant as the others.

"Is it happening now?" Kate asked over her mic.

"Yeah, I think so," Mr. McCullough said.

Wesley swore. "It's too early. We were supposed to push in two days. I think APR beat us to the punch."

Jim could see the dark, foreboding woods of Blackbriar ahead. Many of the BMI company vehicles were parked along the tree line creeping toward an escarpment several hundred meters away.

"That's the ridge line we want to hold and jump off from," Wesley said. "We get on that crest, and we can see all the road approaches and can fire down on the rest of the woods. Kate, can you hear me?"

"Yes," she replied.

"I want you to pull off the road once you get thirty meters from the crest, okay? We're gonna wait up there, but we don't want to be on the firing line."

Both utility vans broke formation and pulled up alongside the mining vehicles. BMI workers regarded the garage employees with suspicion, but appeared relieved to have reinforcements.

As Jim scanned the approaching tree line, he saw a trio of Scorpion tanks pushing their way over rotten logs and knocking down creeper vines with their main cannons. "Whoa, Wesley," he said, "That's some serious hardware over there!"

"Yeah, we don't mess around," came the reply.

Jim noticed infantry now, troops in a variety of mismatched camouflage uniforms, some in mining coveralls, equipped with a wide variety of personal weapons. They ducked behind tree trunks and scattered boulders, trading snappy shots with unseen enemies.

Jim's hands began to sweat. "I think we should stay out of the woods, guys," he said.

"No," Mr. McCullough said. "Inferno gel is heavier than water, so our pump won't squirt it far. You need to be nestled in, ready to ambush that *Marauder* the second it stumbles on you. We're approaching the center of the battle line. That's where it'll show up, to have the most impact."

Kate brushed her hair back with one hand while steering with the other. "I don't know if I can do this," she said. "It seems pretty obvious the Mercenary isn't on our side. He'd be here by now, wouldn't he?"

"You stay the course, Kate," Mr. McCullough warned. "Think of your family and how proud of you they'll be. You're gonna save them all."

Kate gripped the wheel tightly, wrenching it from side to side. "Something's wrong."

"Oh, no," Wesley said. Jim could see his friend peering out of *Goliath*'s window. "The ground's gone soft. It must've rained recently."

Jim saw *Goliath* begin to sink into the muddy road, its giant, oversized tires flinging mud wildly. The three Scorpion tanks, now much closer than before, began firing at enemies Jim still couldn't see. Even through the headphones and the insulating cab of the fire engine, the tanks' weapons were thunderously loud. Mine workers flinched among the explosions, but the battle seemed inconclusive so far.

Nobody wants to be here, he realized. They'd all become accustomed to laying down their weapons, believing the age of corporate battles had ended. Now, forced back into their old habits, neither side was willing to stick its neck out. The Scorpions stayed away from the contested crestline. Any closer, and the enemy infantry could use cover to sneak up on them and wreak havoc with satchel charges or mining explosives.

Jim winced, and Kate screamed as a terrifyingly loud *bang* echoed through the forest. An unseen enemy vehicle had taken a shot at one of the Scorpions. The burst of autocannon fire had barely clipped the turret, but the crew were clearly shaken, and the tank reversed out of the woods, leaving its two fellow tanks behind.

Jim couldn't tell who was in charge. It seemed like Wesley's coworkers were engaged in their own small skirmishes, with no overriding strategy. Muzzle flashes appeared in the distance. Stone cover splintered and chipped away. Heavy ordnance felled trees. And everywhere, everywhere infantry hastily scrambled for protection.

The fire engine came to a stop.

"This is close enough," Kate said. "The mud won't let me go any farther."

"Yeah," Jim said, "we're in a good spot, I think."

Ahead, *Goliath* continued to struggle in the mud, swimming forward as slowly as a beached whale.

"Damn!" Mr. McCullough shouted over the radio. "We're stuck. Wesley, get out and find some of my workers. We need to dig this thing out and get closer."

If Jim heard Wesley's reply, it didn't register. Amid the racket of gunfire, snapping tree branches, and the pings of bullets skipping off stones, he heard a singularly dreadful sound. A deep, percussive rumble that settled in his gut. He knew instinctively that the *Marauder* was nearby. Its heavy footfalls trod closer, and in the distance of the dark forest, he could see old, gnarled trees being casually knocked aside like so many wildflowers. He grabbed Kate's hand and gave it a squeeze, then pulled her close and kissed her on the lips.

He knew what he had to do.

Jim leaped out of the cab and took up the nozzle controls built into the side of the rig. The small turret atop the truck swiveled at his command, and he primed the pumps, filled with dangerous flammable liquid. He hoped the brush Kate had parked in would conceal them long enough for him to get off a single good shot.

Suddenly, Jim saw the venerable BattleMech. Cresting the ridgeline, it silhouetted itself against the dark forest behind and drew the attention of every opposing weapon on the battlefield. Its thickly armored, bird-like legs were firmly planted in the soft, muddy ground. It stood as tall as the twelve-meter trees it knocked aside so carelessly, and its sleek hull swayed from side to side as its pilot evaluated a multitude of targets. Bullets pattered harmlessly off its weatherworn armor, chipping away at the marred pirate colors adorning the ancient machine.

The two remaining Scorpion tanks, clearly outmatched, reversed throttle as quickly as possible to abandon the field. They were large, noticeable targets. The wicked, weapon-laden arms of the *Marauder* followed its deadly gaze and settled on the two hapless tanks struggling in the dense undergrowth.

The Kinslaughters spoke a language of hateful violence. The PPCs, one in each arm pod, lanced forth bolts of azure lighting at the Scorpions. The accelerated particles cast errant wisps of lighting that burned leaves and illuminated foliage with ghastly electrical shadows. The first bolt struck the nearest Scorpion precisely on its turret ring, penetrating the crew compartment and atomizing the men inside. The turret, under immense pressure, blasted off with a gout of fire and landed nearby, igniting the undergrowth.

The second bolt of lightning slammed into the farther tank's tracks, scattering links across the forest floor and savaging the armor and running wheels. Jim saw the crew bail out of their hatches. The *Marauder* ignored them, instead turning its medium lasers on the infantry that harassed its cockpit with machine-gun fire. Jim was transfixed by the coherent green light repeatedly stabbing into the woods, causing troops and their cover alike to explode into scraps of flesh and splintered timber.

"Now! Do it now!" Jim heard his father screaming.

He depressed the firing stud on the controls. An arc of glistening liquid jetted from the fire engine's turret and landed on the flank of the *Marauder*, which was busily slaughtering Wesley's compatriots. Jim worked the turret, trying his best to coat the fearsome BattleMech as thoroughly as possible. Although it felt like an eternity, it was mere seconds before a wayward bullet ricocheted off the *Marauder*'s hull, igniting the inferno gel with a shower of sparks.

Jim held his forearms over his face as the BattleMech burst into incandescent flames. The 75-ton monster paused its merciless slaughter of the infantry, who turned from their pell-mell retreat to watch the *Marauder* burn. They were transfixed, like so many moths amid a glowing white flame. They cheered, but their voices were drowned out by the rush of oxygen funneling in to fuel the raging inferno. Jim risked a glimpse into the radiant glare, his eyes drying amid the backwash of ferocious heat.

"Oh, God!" Kate wailed.

The inferno gel burned bright and fast, turning the *Marauder* white-hot. Compressors mounted under the *Marauder*'s armor whined to life, sucking down as much air as possible while ramming it through the radiator fins of the beleaguered 'Mech's heat sinks. The whine of the compressors turned to a shriek as even the turbines themselves expanded under the immense heat load, and metal ground against metal in what was surely the machine's death-wail.

Before long, the compressors sucked in errant scraps of inferno gel. White flames began to vent through the 'Mech's exhausts and, as heat sinks burned out and burst, oily black smoke poured like rising blood from the stricken *Marauder*. Combat ceased as both sides stared in awe at the glowing 'Mech, waiting with bated breath for signs of life.

None were to be found. The overheated BattleMech stood still as a statue.

Jim heard Wesley shouting over the mic: "Go! Punch it!"

Goliath's trailer had been disconnected, and without that cumbersome burden, Jim watched the wrecker crawl out of the mud and fling itself at the *Marauder*'s leg. The truck impacted forcefully, crumpling the cab, and the great BattleMech listed, slack and out of control. It teetered as one foot left the ground, the other ankle rolling without bracing. The glowing 'Mech toppled over, crushing trees and underbrush as it went, settling on the ground with a thunderous roar. Smoke and ashes filled the air, and Jim could see the *Marauder*'s paint had peeled away, exposing sooty, bare armor.

The miners raised another cheer and began firing their guns wildly in the air. Jim watched as his father, Wesley, and the garage crew unlimbered their cutting tools and struggled to work on the hot metal as it shifted from blazing white to molten orange. They hacked and ground away at the elbow joint of the *Marauder*'s right arm, sawing slowly and with great difficulty through its ancient hull.

"The pilot!" Kate said.

Yes, Jim thought, *the pilot must be in agony.* Nobody deserved to be cooked alive. The taste of last night's barbecue returned to his mouth, and he forced down a gag.

"We have to get him out of there," Jim said.

Kate leaped out of the fire engine and grabbed Jim's sleeve, pulling him toward the nose of the *Marauder*. Jim resisted for a moment, just long enough to grab a prybar and sledgehammer.

Together they approached the spiderwebbed glass of the cockpit. Jim forced the prybar under the lip of the canopy. "I need you to hold it," he said to Kate as cutting torches and sawblades screeched in the background. She nodded, trusting him, and knelt to keep the tool in place. Jim swung the sledgehammer overhead and brought it down smoothly on the end of the prybar.

The heavily damaged canopy slid open willingly with a pneumatic hiss. Smoke billowed out of the cockpit, and a limp form was visible within, among the melted plastics of the control surfaces. Kate balled her sleeve over her hand and pressed the restraint releases, dropping the unconscious pilot out of his seat. Jim dragged him roughly out of his hellish coffin and laid him on the muddy ground.

The Mercenary gasped for air and clawed weakly at his dented neurohelmet.

"You'll live," Kate said. "Just breathe, breathe with me."

Jim was relieved he hadn't killed the pilot.

As the confused MechWarrior's eyes darted around the battlefield, machine guns resumed their chorus. Both sides flung themselves into a frenzy, sensing the battle was nearing its conclusion. Jim could hear enemy infantry on the other side of the BattleMech, whooping and taking prisoners. Gunshots rang out nearby, and he risked a glimpse around the flank of the machine, only to be chased back by bullets whanging off the metal.

"We have to get out of here!" Jim yelled.

The superheated 'Mech had started fires among the foliage it landed in. As the flames grew, the fighting around the wreckage became ever more confused. Crossfire and friendly fire led to screams of pain and surprise. Jim coughed in the thick white smoke given off by the water-fat plants as they ignited.

"Grab him!" Kate shouted above the din.

Together they gripped the shoulder straps of the Mercenary's scorched cooling vest and dragged him deeper into the woods, away from the flames.

The Mercenary coughed and grabbed Jim's arm. "I can get us out of here."

"How?" Kate asked.

The Mercenary coughed again, this time issuing blood. "A DropShip is inbound, any minute now. To the delta that feeds Cherry Lake. Passage for my 'Mech is half paid for. Get me there. It's plenty of money for just the three of us."

Kate looked at Jim. "What about your dad? What about Wesley?"

The sound of battle had died down, and the cutting blades were silent. The *Marauder* looked intact, and *Goliath* stood, divorced from its trailer, where his father had left it. The garage crew had scattered.

Jim returned Kate's look, and tears rolled from his eyes, making tracks through the soot and grime on his face. Single gunshots rang out as prisoners were dispatched. Kate held back tears and bit her lip.

"Let's go," Jim choked the words out. "I know the way."

Kate had located an abandoned, idling delivery truck that had been discarded at the edge of the forest. As the APR forces pushed on toward the BMI mine, the two friends loaded the Mercenary onto the truck's bench seat and struck out on the dusty road.

"Thank you," the Mercenary said. "Thank you for sparing my life."

"We couldn't leave you to burn," Jim said, from his seat next to the battered MechWarrior. "It wouldn't be right."

"The end of days turns us all into animals," the Mercenary said. "I'm glad I found the last two decent folks on this rock."

Jim and Kate exchanged guilty expressions as the Mercenary exhaled deeply and rested as comfortably as he could, wincing with the effort.

Over gently rolling pasture Jim saw the glittering profile of Cherry Lake. The sun was beginning to go down, and it set the clouds to glowing with warm light. A single speck of fire descended from the sky, gradually resolving itself into the shape of an aerodyne DropShip. A *Leopard*, by the looks of it. The boxy craft nestled itself at the confluence of Cherry Creek and its namesake lake.

As their delivery truck bounced and bobbed over uneven ground, Kate spoke. "Where do we go from here, Jim?"

He looked into her eyes when she glanced at him. "We start over. We start over, together."

Jim put his hand in hers as the setting sun cast long shadows before them.

SHRAPNEL

PLANET DIGEST: GANDY'S LUCK

ZAC SCHWARTZ

Star Type (Recharge Time): F5V (176 hours)
Position in System: 5 (of 8)
Time to Jump Point: 14.94 days
Number of Satellites: 2 (Coniraya, Cavillaca)
Surface Gravity: 1.1
Atm. Pressure: High (Breathable)
Equatorial Temperature: 35°C (Warm-Temperate)
Surface Water: 80%
Recharge Station: Nadir and Zenith
HPG Class: B
Highest Native Life: Insects
Population: 37,000,000
Socio-Industrial Levels: D-C-B-A-C
Landmasses (Capital City): Los Destrozados, La Selva (Vetamadre), Verdecito

Catalogued by Terran Alliance interferometers in 2145, the world that would come to be known as Gandy's Luck was not initially flagged as a colonial prospect. While clearly possessing a breathable (if thick) atmosphere and abundant surface water, it orbited a Delta Scuti variable star whose potentially unstable luminosity portended a slim possibility of future stellar disaster.

Nearly a century later, infamous interstellar prospector Emiliana Gandy was combing through a region that, according to old Alliance charts, held a globular cluster of young, high-metallicity stars, a promising sign of worlds with rich deposits. A jump in 2238 brought

Gandy to the muggy orb that would soon bear her name. Mining satellites detected a region on the largest continent with enough rare minerals and radioactives to last for centuries. In exchange for planetary naming rights and cold hard cash, she sold her claim to a consortium of oligarchs connected through the Peruvian Nikkei community.

While cooperating on paper, these hyperelite families quickly moved to establish individual claims on the planet's riches. The first waves of colonists were miners in search of life-changing wealth far from the slow-churn downward spiral of Terra. Instead of wealth, they found themselves living in clusters of hastily erected dome cities, each administered by a different family and serviced top-to-bottom by that family's portfolio of integrated subsidiaries in neo-*zaibatsu* style. Colorful names that promised future fortunes like Vetamadre, Diamante, and Lágrimas de Oro concealed a tendency toward exploitation and incompetent management. Unwilling to live in such conditions themselves, the oligarchs sent their most superfluous scions to this distant sinecure, where their inadequacies would not overly impede family affairs. Ruling as corporate *daimyo* (the equivalent of feudal marquises), they quickly turned the domes into virtual worker's camps, eventually resulting in militant unionizing and even uprisings. These conditions made Gandy's Luck an obvious target for the nascent Draconis Combine. Such was their fearsome reputation that when House Kurita troops landed in 2321, the *daimyo* surrendered immediately. Some of the more belligerent mining unions, however, fought back.

The Combine crushed the armed workers, then deposed the inept *daimyo* and replaced them with *tozama daimyo*, mere counts, from within their own ranks as further punishment. But as long as the spigot of raw materials kept flowing, House Kurita was happy to continue the status quo: *zaibatsu* continually luring impoverished workers from other worlds with promises of the next big payout. Over the centuries, a cycle arose. News of a "spectacular new find" would bring another wave of eager but misguided colonists, most of whom would find themselves trapped, unable to escape the combination of company-store economics and a corporate police state; attrition from the brutal conditions would cause population decline; then another "rich new vein" would entice a new wave of newcomers.

Life outside the domes was tantamount to suicide: pre-Cambrian levels of atmospheric oxygen left the two main continents covered in tenacious, kudzu-esque jungles filled with enormous insects, and fires tended to start quickly and ferociously. (Only the military spaceport dome of Haslet, its local environs thoroughly and continually defoliated for DCMS operations, was free of such encumbrances.) Leases on specialized MiningMechs with expensive, rust-prone waterjet cutters trapped miners in cycles of debt the *zaibatsu* were only too happy to leverage. The immense environmental damage wrought by hydraulic mining turned huge tracts of Gandy's Luck into strip-mined wastelands.

Though the Star League may have been a golden age for most of humanity, the technological advances that came from the Star League era only increased the efficiency with which the *tozama daimyo* kept the miners immiserated. Networks of state-of-the-art surveillance satellites encircled Gandy's Luck, monitoring communications and tracking large gatherings via dome-penetrating infrared. Ironically, this made the locals ripe for cultivation by House Davion intelligence; nearly every major worker uprising from the 26th century onward relied on weapons, intel, and training provided by MI4. This potential disruption to the planet's vital output forced the Combine to deploy a heavy Internal Security Force presence.

The planet also became a popular target for pirates looking for a quick score. The Draconis Combine Mustered Soldiery routinely began rotating lighter regiments from the Galedon Regulars, Arkab Legions, and even the Sun Zhang Cadres through the system to help compensate for the higher gravity. However, the Combine preferred to stop pirate raids with the Draconis Combine Admiralty squadrons posted at each recharge station, due to the incendiary risks posed by ground combat on Gandy's Luck.

In 2811, the Federated Suns established the New Aberdeen Salient, putting Gandy's Luck within a single jump of their border. In 2830, the Twenty-Seventh Galedon Regulars and Fifth Sun Zhang Cadre were on station when the AFFS attack came. A risky jump into a transient point at the biweekly syzygy of the planet and its moons gave the Thirty-Third Avalon Hussars a two-week window until the jump point recurred. Colonel Hieronimus "Harry" Zibler's by-the-book attack targeted ore refineries in the wastes near Salto de Tungsteno, but the Galedon Regulars responded far more rapidly than Zibler had anticipated while a Fifth Sun Zhang battalion moved to pincer the Hussars. Realizing the Thirty-Third was trapped, Zibler launched a fuel-air bomb strike against the Regulars' base in a last-ditch gambit. The high-oxygen environment guaranteed their utter annihilation, and ignited a massive firestorm that engulfed multiple nearby dome cities. Millions died. Follow-on nuclear attacks against Vetamadre and Diamante—the capital and largest city, respectively—killed tens of millions more, and the Fifth Sun Zhang Cadre was too busy aiding the firefighting and rescue efforts to mount an effective counterattack. By the time the Hussars jumped away, nearly half the population of Gandy's Luck was dead or displaced. Colonel Zibler's mission, to damage critical resource infrastructure and soften up the planet for possible capture, was arguably a success, the unspeakable atrocities just the price of doing business. It was a bitter irony that the salient which made the attack feasible would be lost shortly thereafter, rendering Zibler's monstrous actions pointless cruelty. His death in the fighting on Harrow's Sun would repay some small modicum of justice for his crimes.

Relief soon came from the *Minbushō* (Ministry of the Interior), as House Kurita had no intention of abandoning a world at the base of their industrial pyramid. However, the larger depredations of the Succession Wars had taken their toll, and reconstruction efforts would be a slow and arduous process. The population would not fully recover until just after the War of 3039. To speed recovery, the *daimyo* finally relented and allowed the miners to own their MiningMechs, relieving the debt peonage that had made life on Gandy's Luck so difficult. With the twin boosts of the Helm Renaissance and the increased demand for raw materials brought on by the Clan Invasion, the economy reached heights it had not seen in centuries. By the time of Coordinator Hohiro Kurita, Vetamadre and Diamante had both been decontaminated and repopulated, and a détente developed that saw the *tozama daimyo* fulfilling their *noblesse oblige* via basic healthcare and worker pensions. This progress began to backslide during the administration of Vincent Kurita, but rebounded under Yori, for which Gandians are profoundly thankful.

Under the rule of Count Hifume Ruiz, modern Gandy's Luck, while not exactly prosperous, at least manages to get by with a stability it largely lacked in the past. The lighter hand of the Combine regarding cultural uniformity since the days of Theodore Kurita has led to a flourishing of the local neo-Nikkei culture over the past century. Sushi ceviche is a staple of the Gandian diet, and the local dialect mixes Japanese with Peruvian Spanish to a degree comparable to Rasalhagian Swedenese. Perhaps the most notable aspect of the planet's culture is the curious attachment the populace has to the *cabraracha*, known to xenobiologists as the Gandian goat-roach. It is precisely what it sounds like: a roachoid the size of a mountain goat. The natives of Gandy's Luck have effectively domesticated these hardy and surprisingly useful creatures, using sprayable scent cues to direct their behavior. Gandians harvest *cabrarachas*' sweet flesh for food, dry their organs for spices and simple medicines, and don garments hewn from their carapaces to protect against the elements. The *cabraracha* also played a critical role in the cleanup efforts: its unique gastronomy and cell structure allow it to ingest radioactive material and excrete a harmless byproduct. Unfortunately, these cellular requirements also prevent the *cabraracha*'s export, as it can only survive in the high-oxygen environment of its homeworld.

TERRAIN NOTES

The high-oxygen atmosphere of Gandy's Luck causes fires to start easily and spread rapidly. To represent this, take a -3 penalty to all rolls on both the Starting Fires and Spreading Fires Tables (see p. 40, *Tactical Operations: Advanced Rules*). In addition, all woods hexes on a map should be treated as jungle hexes (see p. 29, *TO:AR*).

TERRAIN TABLES

To randomly determine the mapsheets for a battle set on this planet, choose the region, then roll a D6 and select the map matching the result. The maps in this list can be found in the noted map set (MS), map-compilation set (MC), or map pack (MP).

The Mines
Note: All water hexes should be treated as hazardous liquid pools (see p. 47, *TO:AR*).

1: Oasis (MP: Deserts)
2: Caustic Valley (MP: Alien Worlds)
3: Mines #1 (MP: Deserts)
4: Mines #2 (MP: Deserts)
5: Lunar Base (MP: Alien Worlds)
6: Badlands #2 (MP: Deserts)

The Jungles
Note: When fighting in the thick jungles of La Selva, all jungle hexes should be treated as one level heavier than denoted in the hex: light jungle becomes heavy jungle, heavy jungle becomes ultra-heavy jungle (see p. 29, *TO: AR*).

1: Scattered Woods (MC 1)
2: Heavy Forest #1 (MC 1)
3: Holth Forest (MP: Tukayyid)
4: Heavy Forest #2 (MC 1)
5: Holth Forest (MP: Tukayyid)
6: River Delta/Drainage Basin #2 (MC 1)

SHRAPNEL

ALPHA STRIKE SCENARIO: STRIKE AND FADE

ED STEPHENS

RENFREW CITY
CORISCANA
WOLF EMPIRE
10 APRIL 3151

Stannik grunted and licked his cracked lips under his trim, graying beard as the pillar of fire descended on the horizon. Behind him, the rest of his solahma constable Point flipped tables and shattered windows as they prepared their firing positions. His radio crackled as the inexperienced artillery crews chattered about firing solutions. Soon, he would get his chance at a taste of glory. Too many moons had he spent rounding up inebriated, disaffected factory workers.

A pattering crash of falling rubble interrupted his musing. He peered through the window to his side to see a primer-gray Atlas, *tugging its shoulder free from the abandoned apartment building it had stumbled into. Grunting again, he hefted his SRM launcher, checked the arming light, and turned back toward the smoke trail.*

Soon...

The following scenario makes use of the *Alpha Strike* box set contents and can be played as a stand-alone scenario or to start an ongoing campaign. One player assumes the role of gamemaster (GM), controlling the Wolf Empire garrison, while the player undertakes the mission with their own mercenary force. Players can alternate the role of GM if they wish to each start a campaign force. Force card lists for the suggested forces below can be found at **masterunitlist.info** (MUL), but all other components can be found in the box set.

PLAYER'S SITUATION

Hired by parties unknown, the player takes their mercenary company on a strike mission to knock out two garrison headquarter buildings of the local Wolf Empire constabulary on Coriscana. Reconnaissance indicates the buildings are lightly defended by infantry, though the garrison has managed to ready nearby artillery batteries for the city's defense. A rapid assault and retreat should finish the job before the artillery can pinpoint the attacking forces.

As the DropShip descends towards the planet, however, five 'Mech reactor powerups are detected...

GM'S SITUATION

As described in *Empire Alone* (p. 27), the Wolf Empire finds itself besieged by probing attacks from mysterious mercenaries. The planet of Coriscana is garrisoned only by constabulary *solahma* units. After learning of attacks on Midkiff, the Wolves have pressed into service anyone with military experience, regardless of skill or background. With recently rebuilt 'Mechs and readied artillery batteries, the garrison scrambles to defensive positions and begins calling for artillery support the moment a DropShip begins descending on the outskirts of Renfrew, where the garrison headquarters lie.

GAME SETUP

Suggested Forces

Defender (GM)
Wolf Empire Garrison: 200 PV, all units are Skill 5:
- Mad Cat (Timber Wolf) Prime
- Warhammer C 3
- Phoenix Hawk C 2
- Atlas C 2
- Wasp C

Attacker (Player)
Mercenaries: 200 PV, all units are Skill 4:
- Pouncer D
- Dasher (Fire Moth) H
- Archer ARC-8M
- Blackjack BJ-5
- Wraith TR1

ALPHA STRIKE SCENARIO: STRIKE AND FADE

- Black Hawk (Nova) C

OR

200 PV selected from ilClan-era Mercenary units available on **masterunitlist.info**

PLAY AREA: 36" X 36"

Buildings from the *Alpha Strike* box set should be arranged into a scattered urban layout, with a central forested park using 7 trees, and a small wood on one edge using 3 trees. Two small 1"-high buildings should be reserved by the GM as objective buildings.

The GM chooses one edge of the play area as their home edge. They place the two objective buildings within 12" of their home edge, designating them with blue objective tokens. These hardened buildings are immobile (-4 Target Number) and can sustain 10 points of damage (CF 10) before collapsing. Dice can be used to track damage to the objective buildings, which collapse into an area of Rubble once destroyed.

The remaining buildings from the boxed set are either Small (7 buildings, CF 3) or Large (6 buildings, CF 5) and can also be collapsed into Rubble. The buildings can be disassembled and laid flat to represent areas of rubble.

Deployment

The GM deploys their force on the ground within 12" of their home edge, giving each unit their Ground movement TMM at the start of the game.

For the first turn, the player is considered to have won initiative, and moves their entire force on from the opposite edge. The Combat Phase then proceeds with the GM firing first, if they have any targets.

Optional: Use of the Multiple Attack Rolls optional rule (see p. 175, *Alpha Strike: Commander's Edition*) is recommended due to the low skill but high-grade equipment of the garrison.

OBJECTIVES

Destroy the Buildings: The player earns 30 VP for each objective building destroyed.

Make Them Pay: The player earns 10 VP for each building destroyed containing a *solahma* infantry unit.

SPECIAL RULES

Forced Withdrawal
The player's units operate under Forced Withdrawal rules. If any units are reduced to half Structure, or zero Armor and 1 Structure, they must move at best possible speed to escape via their home edge. The player may choose to retreat any unit off the board if it reaches their edge during the Movement Phase.

Nasty Surprise
Beginning on Turn 2, at the start of any Combat Phase, the GM may reveal that buildings contain inferno-equipped *solahma* infantry platoons waiting in ambush.

Use red objective tokens to designate two of these buildings. The designated buildings have the attack statistics of Skill 4 Heavy Urban Response Platoons (2/2/0 with the HT2/2/0 Special Ability), and use CF based on the size of the buildings as above (CF 3 or CF 5).

If a token forgoes firing, it may move to an adjacent building during the Combat Phase, as the *solahma* sprint for better firing positions; the GM must declare this movement at the start of the Combat Phase. If a building containing *solahma* units is collapsed during a Combat Phase when the *solahma* are not moving, the *solahma* unit is destroyed.

Zeroing In
Beginning on Turn 3, the GM gains one Thumper Cannon Artillery Support card per turn, which may be fired on any target point visible to defending 'Mechs or designated *solahma* buildings.

Beginning on Turn 5, the GM gains one Sniper Cannon Artillery Support card as well, which may be targeted the same way.

AFTERMATH
"GAH!" Phillip leaped back in surprise as the rubble of the building shifted to reveal a battered corpse, a Wolf constable, the rictus of an immense grin spread across his face. Phillip gathered himself, leaned heavily on his shovel, and cried out, "Bossman!"

"Ya, Phillip?" came a reply from behind a dusty mound of broken building.

"I tink der may be un'sploded ordnance in 'ere."

Phillip gazed at the grin on the corpse's face. He idly batted some dust from the chest of his overalls and frowned. He had never heard of a body smiling before.

He looked up across the road from the constable's resting place. There, collapsed against the side of a building, lay the remains of a

BattleMech, in a tangle of broken limbs. A Fire Moth, *if he remembered correctly. The hull was scorched and blackened, like a log from a doused cooking fire.*

He nudged some debris beside the corpse, revealing the business end of a short-range missile launcher. "Bossman?"

The player may continue to use any surviving units as a campaign force. Damage to units persists, but may be repaired at a price of 1 PV per Armor point, 2 PV per Structure point, and 3 PV per critical hit. If the player destroyed at least one objective building, they hold the field and may retrieve their destroyed units, paying full repair cost for all damage. Any excess PV earned from destroyed buildings may be used to purchase new units from the MUL (ilClan Mercenary faction), to add to their force.

THE WRECKONING

RUSSELL ZIMMERMAN

**STEINER STADIUM
SOLARIS CITY
SOLARIS VII
LYRAN COMMONWEALTH
15 AUGUST 3021**

Do-Hyun "Dangerous Danny" Adeoye hated this borrowed 'Mech with a passion that could melt armor.

"'Oh, Danny,' they said," he mimicked in a high-pitched, aristocratically accented voice, currently drowned out by the alarms blaring inside his 'Mech cockpit and neurohelmet. "'Just think of all the Pitbans,' they said."

Another hailstorm of long-range missiles blasted craters across the chest of his *Merlin*, sending the 60-ton titan staggering backward.

"'Solid Pitban 240 engines, Danny, we'll be rolling in 'em! Jenkins' *Rifleman*'ll be set for years!'" The taste of blood threw him off momentarily as the jostling and crashing made him bite his lip. "'And good LFT-50 jump jets! All the "lifty fifties" our *Shadow Hawk*'ll ever need!'"

He wrenched at the stupid *Merlin*'s control yoke and snarled savagely, almost desperately, fighting to keep the heavy 'Mech under control. With its feet back under it and the danger of falling past—for the moment—he turned his attention back to the 'Mech's targeting systems.

Pip after pip after pip danced before his eyes, a bevy of torso-mounted weapons, all with identical targeting displays. They flared red, each and every one of them, even as his expert hands aligned them with the broad, broad target of the enemy *Archer*'s chest.

Because every one of the weapon displays was tied to a Sperry Browning machine gun, and the Lion City Stables *Archer*-jock wasn't a goddamned moron, try as he might, Danny couldn't get his opponent to let him close to spitball range and tear him to shreds.

Eleven of 'em. Eleven damned machine guns. Dumbest thing he'd ever...

He stomped his *Merlin* forward angrily, stubbornly.

"'Oh, and the Magestrix Gammas, Danny,'" he singsonged to himself as he thumbed at a few of his firing controls, sending all the machine-gun barrels in the *Merlin*'s torso barking and chattering. He was out to keep morale up and put on a show for the viewers, but he also had other reasons for the reckless, feckless shooting.

"'Just think of the Gammas we'll get! Why, they're good enough for all the autocannons on a Pike, aren't they? And Pikes are good enough for ComStar, didn't you hear? Well, if the Gamma's target-tracking system is good enough for ComStar and all their money, isn't it good enough for yo—'"

His not entirely unbiased version of this most recent conversation with Oonthrax Stables' Senior Tech Alexander St. Croix was interrupted by another swarm of long-range missiles.

Despite Adeoye's best efforts, this latest waterfall of explosions blasted away the last of the armor on the *Merlin*'s torso. Despite the onslaught, even as his 'Mech staggered and stumbled, and a fresh wave of warning klaxons warned him of damage to the heat shielding of his Pitban 240 fusion engine, Danny leaned hard on the firing studs, keeping up a never-ending stream of lead as his torso-mounted machine guns fired merrily away at a target backpedaling from triple their effective range.

"'Oh, and Dangerous, don't forget those Holly LRM-5s! You know how Janet loves that long-range punch for her *Shadow Hawk*, so we'll really save some money getting those at this price!'"

The Lion City *Archer* had taken a pair of particle projection cannon hits early in their scrap. Danny had grouped them wonderfully, one searing blast of energy atop another, cratering the *Archer*'s chest just over the ammunition stores in the right side of the heavy 'Mech's chest. But a lucky—or unlucky, if you were Adeoye—volley of missile fire had taken out the *Merlin*'s PPC before he could fire it a third time, and then Danny'd found himself in his current predicament: outgunned thoroughly, chasing after an *Archer* in a *Merlin*, throttling forward hard as his enemy backed away and simply fired, fired, fired. The *Archer* staggered its launches enough to keep heat under control, and the *Merlin* just...staggered under the onslaught.

Finally, the incessant chattering of almost a dozen machine guns stopped, replaced by the whirring and clicking of hungry guns being fed nothing. Adeoye eased off his triggers with a soft smile. With the *Merlin*'s belly finally cleared of machine gun ammo, the odds of him *dying* from an ammunition explosion in this idiotic stunt went down significantly. Now just his *record* would get a little taste of murder.

"'Oh, Danny,'" he squealed as eleven machine guns chirped complaints and his targeting reticule flashed a no-ammo warning. "'A real champion takes one for the team. Think of the Pitbans, Danny! The Pitbans!'"

His singsong voice was banished as he triggered his communications system. There was no one to talk to—he was in a duel, a simple, brutal, one-on-one fight, and Adeoye hadn't been broadcasting at his opponent because he wasn't *winning* enough to gloat—but cockpit comms were the easiest way to log a recording. He most certainly *hadn't* been recording while he mocked his boss earlier in the fight.

"Adeoye to Stable, Adeoye to Stable. Weapons dry." Now Danny was all business, the clipped, matter-of-fact speech used in emergencies. Let the nerds chew on an official report. "PPC's busted, ammo's gone, opponent's evaded meaningful damage. Armor's in tatters, Pitban shielding's already damaged. Punching out to protect stables' investment."

And then he did, easy as that. Every MechWarrior worth their salt learned the ejection routine first thing upon riding a new 'Mech, and Adeoye had to give it to these Mountain Wolf assholes: they at least knew how to make the *Merlin* user friendly when it came to leaving the damned thing behind after a series of explosions tore the roof off and launched you skyward.

"'It'll be a cinch, Dangerous,' they said." His voice went high and whiny again, mocking his chief technician as his chute floated down and his Lion City opponent celebrated. "'From what I hear, all we need is to get this guy one *Merlin* win, and it's all ours. Easy money.'"

He sailed downward and bit the other side of his lip to bloody shreds as his ejection seat landed.

Unstrapping himself from his harness and watching his rival's *Archer* still lifting unscathed arms skyward to pose for the cameras, Dangerous Danny Adeoye spat blood. When next he spoke, it was a low-down growl, his words entirely his own:

"Easy money, my ass."

While his tone changed, the general sentiment of his complaints certainly didn't, not during the whole trip back to the Oonthrax Mall on the very fringes of Solaris City proper. While his stablemates trained with their personal rides and 'Mech techs and other staffers scurried here and there, Adeoye stood in what had once been a parking garage—now a 'Mech bay—and picked up his complaining anew as a horde of astechs worked on the savaged *Merlin*. He had a new loss to record in his logbook, his personal journal, his beloved, leatherbound handbook that was *supposed* to be documenting his rise to fame, later to be immortalized in an autobiography. If he had to journal about a loss in his quarters later, he was, damn it all, going to be taking it out on everyone between him and there.

"None of the damned walls were where I needed 'em to be," he said sourly, waving in the general direction of the Lyran arena where the disastrous bout had taken place. "Hell, none of the damned walls were *anywhere*. I'm telling you, Steiner Stadium's latest arena master is a *sadist*, man! He barely ever hits the hydraulics, just leaves the walls down, or *maybe* raises 'em to half height. He just loves seeing MechWarriors stranded out there with nothing to hide behind, letting us get picked apart!"

"Uh-huh." Astrid Poulsen, a square-shouldered refugee from Kirchbach and Danny's personal 'Mech tech, let his griping slide off her back. She wasn't sure what higher powers she'd angered enough to deserve Danny Adeoye becoming her personal burden, but there was no denying that soothing his ego and repairing his 'Mechs had become her life's work—often the former more than the latter. "At least it was a prelim match. Unranked, hardly anybody watching."

"Yeah, well, it's still on my record. And Oonthrax is still gonna be on my ass if we don't do something." Danny scowled. "How am I supposed to be a champion, to win, to do my job, when you give me a piece of crap like this?"

"What the hell do you want from me?" Astrid said resignedly. "You heard the bosses."

One boss was the fairly reasonable Senior Tech St. Croix. The other, though, the one even St. Croix answered to, was the owner of Oonthrax Stables, the thoroughly *un*reasonable Irvxx Oonthrax himself. A baron, ruler of not only their stable but the world of Laurent, Irvxx cared about two things: himself and his wealth.

"Some other blueblood nobleman has the baron's ear right now," Astrid said. "There's a free 'Mech in it for us, and you know he loves anything he doesn't have to pay for." She shrugged, making a face. "And then a steady stream of straight-from-the-source repair and replacement parts. The baron's licking his chops. We have to follow through."

"Pitbans and Majestrix Gammas and blah blah blah." Adeoye waved a disgusted hand. "I know, I know. Just…figure out how to make a *Merlin* good at fighting, okay? You and your people almost got me killed. The thing's a train wreck."

Mountain Wolf BattleMechs, the *Merlin*'s creators, preferred to call it a jack-of-all-trades.

When it had debuted in 3010, they'd called the MLN-1A a modern marvel, an act of wizardry, a yeoman's 'Mech for yeoman's work. It had been quite a departure from Mountain Wolf's reputation—inasmuch as they'd still *had* a reputation—for hyperspecialized machines, and instead was a well-rounded beast, built for reliability and ease of maintenance. The result was a heavy 'Mech beloved by technicians and quartermasters on backwater Periphery worlds more than by their MechWarriors, an easily jury-rigged machine made of some of the most common and rugged weapons in the Inner Sphere. There was nothing exceptional about it except its novelty, and as far as Adeoye was concerned, designing a new 'Mech wasn't some terrific accomplishment if the design wasn't to his liking. The *Merlin* was painfully mediocre. Neither slow nor fast, neither remarkably tough nor exceptionally fragile, not terribly well armed or particularly lethal at any specific range…just *mediocre.*

And Danny Adeoye knew mediocrity meant obsolescence here on Solaris VII, the Game World. Champions weren't made of "mediocre."

Solaris audiences wanted specialization, flair, something dramatic bordering on gimmickry. Adeoye had talked his tech into turning the *Merlin* into a close-combat "chainsaw" for this fight, only for the idea to backfire. It was time for other options.

Danny put his hands on his hips and glared down at the inventory logs. The *Merlin*'s Pitban 240 engine and LFT-50 jump jets were nonnegotiable: their client had insisted the core chassis and its movement profile not be altered. Along with its Magistracy of Canopus-supplied electronics—an Alpha communications setup and the Gamma target-tracking system—Astrid was not allowed to change the core conceit of the machine.

Its laundry list of weapons, though? That was the part Danny and Astrid had been given free rein over. The idea was to make a *Merlin* look good while showcasing its weaponry—the very same weaponry Oonthrax Stables would then have a steady supply of, straight from Mountain Wolf's own factory, wherever the hell *that* was—and the job had fallen to Danny and his tech to make it happen.

For this fight, they'd chosen to keep the sturdy Magna Hellstar PPC, giving him a wicked long-range punch. They'd pulled the other energy weapons, though, the Martell medium lasers mounted in each arm. That left the *Merlin* with a pair of piston-like club arms, simple and brutal. They'd opted for removing the Holly long-range missile rack, too, feeling it contributed far less than it consumed; like any LRM launcher, it was bulky, even before considering the ammunition required. They'd also pulled the Zippo flamer from its torso mount. The torso had then been turned into a veritable blender, a forest of machine guns, Sperry Brownings for days, a bristling field of chattering guns ready to spit close-range death.

The *idea* had been to reach out and touch an opponent with shots of opportunity from the hard-hitting PPC, use the Steiner Stadium's hydraulic-operated walls as cover, and then savage his hapless opponent up close with brutal clubbing attacks and a swarm of gnawing machine guns. The idea had not survived contact with the LRM-spewing enemy, though.

"Flamers?" Poulsen suggested, eyebrows raised.

Danny considered it. Flamers had been all the rage a few seasons ago, when a particularly flashy *Firestarter* jock, Antonio de Aguilar, had dominated the Class Two division. They were great ways to cripple an enemy 'Mech at close range, and it might be nice to not have ammunition to worry about…but they still required that closeness. Danny considered how helpless he'd felt after losing his PPC and finding himself stuck with just machine guns. Flamers wouldn't solve that issue. Danny *also* considered the very real possibility Poulsen might be suggesting it because extracting the machine guns from the half-wrecked torso and replacing them with a bevy of fusion-powered flamethrowers might be the easiest repair option.

"No," Adeoye eventually said, nodding as he shot down her idea and agreed with himself. "If that crackpot pulling the levers is gonna leave every damned wall and pylon down in Steiner Stadium, let's run with that. Let's be the *Archer* this time, not some overgrown *Vulcan* wannabe."

Astrid made a face. No flamers.

"Fix the PPC, or replace it, whatever," Dangerous Danny said carelessly. Figuring out whether to repair or replace was Poulsen's job, not his. "But then you get me every Holly five-pack we've got. Let's load this thing down with LRMs, see if you can…can…"

"See if we can make a SHD-2K slower?" Astrid piped up, name-dropping the most Lyran-mocked *Shadow Hawk* variant model in recent memory.

Adeoye gave her a dirty look. "See if you can 'showcase the firepower' or 'demonstrate the reliability of the Holly LRM-5' or whatever the hell you have to tell the bosses. See if you can give me a 'Mech I can malfing *fight* in! I'm not getting caught with my pants down *again*. I want you to give me as much long-range firepower as this damned thing can carry."

"And what if someone gets in close?" she said, lifting her eyebrows skeptically. Long-range missiles had trouble locking on to short-range targets, and their warheads didn't arm until the missiles had traveled a minimum safe distance from their launcher. PPCs had built-in field inhibitors that protected the firer from powerful feedback that could fry their electronics, and that made *those* weapons less effective at close range, too.

"I'm the MechWarrior," Adeoye said confidently. "I'll worry about that. Don't try to think so much, just do it, okay? Can you just do it? PPC, LRMs, load me up. It's my ass on the line out there, not yours. I work in the arena, you work in the garage."

Astrid started to open her mouth again, but he cut her off.

"So get to work in the garage," he hissed over his shoulder as he strode away.

**STEINER STADIUM
SOLARIS CITY
SOLARIS VII
LYRAN COMMONWEALTH
2 SEPTEMBER 3021**

"Well," Danny Adeoye said flatly.

His voice rang inside his neurohelmet as a Steiner Stadium hydraulic wall rose right in front of his opponent's *Crusader*, intercepting a fifteen-strong flight of LRMs and causing Adeoye's steady lock-on tone to fizzle out in a wave of disappointed beeping.

A heartbeat earlier, the scintillating blue-white beam of his PPC seared the air past his adversary, a miss he mentally chalked up to the Magestrix targeting system, or maybe to Astrid, or maybe just to bad luck; he had a ready stream of excuses for missing as broad a target as a *Crusader*, should anyone ever ask him about it.

"Ain't this some bullshit," he grunted as his *Merlin* was suddenly crashed into from below. A Steiner Stadium pylon rammed up from beneath him, 100 meters of steel and concrete spearing up from the ground and simply, effortlessly, inexorably battering his 60-ton 'Mech aside as it ascended.

Red lights blinked and flashed in the upended *Merlin*'s cockpit as the BattleMech hit the ground.

Adeoye cursed and worked the controls, utilizing the heavy 'Mech's internal gyroscope and his own sense of balance, transmitted by neurohelmet, to get the machine's legs back under it, to wedge its awkward piston-rod arms into the ground and push itself upright, to clamber back to its feet. He stood just in time for two dozen long-range missiles to splash against the *Merlin*'s torso in a rippling wave of explosions that staggered him back a step and nearly bowled him over again.

"Oh, right. You're after me, too, not just the damned arena master. I almost forgot." Danny shook his head as much as his neurohelmet would allow as he wrestled with his controls to line up his targeting reticule again. Another eye-searing beam of energy roared out from his PPC and scarred a savage line across the *Crusader*'s chest. Molten armor and sheared-off plating fell, and a second later Adeoye's own arcing flight of LRMs crashed home as well. A few dug up turf all around the Zelazni Stables 'Mech, but most of them cratered armor panels or blasted the off entirely, leaving a swath of damage all along the *Crusader*'s right arm and shoulder.

Just as his weapons cycled back to hot, but in the split-second before he could pull the trigger, another wall burst from the ground not ten meters in front of him. A dull-gray slab of concrete and steel cut off his line of sight and left him, cursing, to track the *Crusader* by indirect sensors alone. Adeoye kept one eye on the oncoming *Crusader*—"Man, he's really pushing that thing's top speed!"—and the other scanned his armor readouts. When the lunatic in the arena master's box finally lowered that section of wall again, Adeoye saw the Zelazni MechWarrior swiftly closing the gap.

"I'll give the *Merlin* one thing. It's got jump jets." Danny blasted off another alpha strike volley, ignoring the heat spike in his cockpit, and took grim satisfaction in scrapping another ton of armor off the battered *Crusader*. Then, as another wave of thirty missiles sailed his way, he jammed hard on his jump-jet controls and sent his *Merlin* soaring backward on jets of superheated plasma. He slammed into the ground just behind another 100-meter Steiner Stadium wall and flashed his teeth in a feral grin inside his neurohelmet.

"And you don't."

He panted as his heat levels slowly eased back down. Panted, and cursed Astrid for not being able to add more heat sinks to this junk heap he'd been forced to fight in.

"Now which way are you going?"

Danny shot a glance back to his sensors, watching to see if the *Crusader* had gone left or right around the nigh-unbreakable stadium wall. He backpedaled a few steps and swept the torso from one side to the other, ready to bring his weapons to bear regardless of which side his opponent circled.

The ground trembled, and the wall dropped more swiftly than it had appeared.

The Zelazni *Crusader* stood straight on, *just* on the other side of it, only a few dozen meters away. Basically point-blank. Squared up, ready to fire.

Danny pictured the Steiner Stadium arena master cackling and congratulating himself.

"Really?!" he had time to exclaim before the brawler closed in the paltry range that remained. At a distance, his *Merlin*'s PPC and fifteen total LRM tubes could fend off the *Crusader* and its twin fifteens. In close? He had nothing to meaningfully answer the heavier 'Mech's dozen short-range missiles, pair of medium lasers, or even—"Man, malf you!"—a pair of barking, gnawing machine guns.

The *Crusader* loosed the lot of it as it closed the gap, Danny's hastily fired PPC shot flying high. Warning lights flared red throughout his cockpit as blast after blast sawed away armor, and the *Merlin* reeled. His 'Mech's wireframe display went from green to yellow to red in several locations, and one leg almost buckled from a wave of SRMs that crashed against the knee.

"Oh yeah?" Adeoye licked his lips and tried to restore his confidence his usual way, through meanness. "Well, suck on this!"

He lashed out with both of the *Merlin*'s laser-less club-arms, brutal metal pistons, purposefully aimed high. There was no way some Zelazni jock was going to close the distance against *him*—against Dangerous Danny Adeoye—and not risk a cockpit full of steel. Danny didn't often purposefully try to attack an opposing MechWarrior instead of the 'Mech, but if this *Crusader* was going to force the issue, Adeoye was fine with rolling the dice on his opponent's life.

His *Merlin* lurched into the strike and leaned forward as both club-arms smashed down in powerful overhand blows, crashing down to shear off armor on either side of the *Crusader*'s cockpit. Adeoye bared his teeth in a snarl and leaned forward in his cockpit to match his 'Mech's stance, going head-to-head, posing like a stare down before a boxing match, almost smashing his cockpit into the enemy's.

Then, suddenly, he wasn't leaning at all. He was falling. Crashing. Tumbling, almost upended again. His *Merlin* slammed face-down in the Steiner Stadium turf, and Adeoye nearly blacked out from the impact of the hard fall. Standing over him, he saw the *Crusader* twisted at the hips, arms up for balance, still holding the follow-through of a powerful—no, devastating—soccer kick.

All of Danny's rage and frustration suddenly focused on a frantically blinking warning on his console display, helpfully informing him that his already-damaged leg had suffered critical damage, and could no longer safely support the *Merlin*'s weight.

"Say you're down?" a woman's voice crackled in his ear, coming across a half-dozen frequencies at once. The Zelazni jock.

Adeoye imagined she looked like that worthless lump, Astrid, and snarled back his reply. "Piss off!"

A pair of laser beams sawed surgically at his good leg, followed by a swarm of short-range missiles.

Adeoye flailed at the turf to try getting his *Merlin*'s arms under it again, to haul himself upright, to do *something* to fight back and turn this loss into a win. *A champion doesn't quit!* If he could just turn himself over, if this damned *Merlin* could just do what he told it to, if Poulsen could just tune the thing like he needed it to be tuned, he could shut up all the warning buzzers and shut up that smug MechWarrior and get the bosses off his ass and turn this streak arou—

Another arcing *Crusader* kick smashed into his *Merlin*'s side, almost rolling it over. Adeoye's eyes went wide as the fresh wave of alarms sounded, as his wireframe model updated itself in real time, and as he realized how many long-range missiles he was sitting on.

"Malfing *fine*. I give! I give, I give!" he shouted into his close-range comms, fists smashing against his cockpit console. To hell with the official recording this time, to hell with impartially telling the stable what had happened and why he'd conceded, to hell with all of it.

Adeoye just swallowed his pride to holler out his surrender, over and over, until the looming *Crusader* relented, and was proclaimed the winner.

He swallowed his pride and felt it turn to something else, deep in his belly. He thought of his journal. He imagined the crisp, clean, page he would have to mar with another loss.

I won't leave Solaris behind until I'm a champion, Danny had scrawled on the inside cover of that journal, years earlier. But how the hell was that going to happen until he left this damned *Merlin* behind?

THE OONTHRAX MALL
SOLARIS CITY
SOLARIS VII
LYRAN COMMONWEALTH
3 SEPTEMBER 3021

"What I want to know, Poulsen, is what the hell you're going to *do* about it?!" Danny Adeoye threw up his arms in frustration, almost making the seated Kirchbachian flinch over her dinner in the break room. Almost.

"And I'm telling you, Danny, my astechs and I will repair and refit it, but I need to know what weapons you want for the next bout." Astrid kept her voice level somehow, after he'd finally managed to corner her. "What do you want us to install as we fix it?"

"Something that'll *work*! The weapons I want are ones that will make this piece of crap *Merlin* work!" He got louder and louder, veritably pinning her in place with his presence. A handful of her fellow technicians sat at the table, similarly frozen there.

"All the weapons worked," she said flatly. There were no malfunctions. The *Merlin* worked fine."

"You and your people haven't made that *Merlin* 'work fine' for me even once! It's a piece of junk, and everything you do to it makes it even worse! Are you *trying* to get me killed out there? Is that it?"

"Look, sir, you put in the work order, we do the work. We'll tune it like you want. We just need you to tell us how to tune it."

"Make it *work*, Poulsen!"

"It works, sir. You just—"

"Just what?" Adeoye leaned over the table at her, loomed in fact. "I just *what*?"

He'd been looking for someone to take his frustration out on for not just hours, but days, weeks beforehand. Dangerous Danny's slide into mediocrity had been making him a worse person for a long time. This *Merlin* debacle, like magic, just might be the final straw.

"Lost," a newcomer said. Not just new to the conversation, but someone Danny didn't recognize. A man, maybe thirty, even-featured but unremarkable, Caucasian, and with just a hint of a smile on his face. "You just *lost*, MechWarrior Adeoye."

Adeoye and Poulsen glanced at each other, then to the other techs around the room, then to the newcomer. It seemed nobody knew who he was, and his sleek black-on-gray suit certainly wasn't a set of red Oonthrax coveralls. A tourist. Back here, somehow. Danny shuddered physically as he composed himself and tried to force on his plastic, good-for-interviews smile.

"Sorry, mister, I don't know who you are, but you can't be here." He pointed to the door. "The tours are supposed to keep you people out there, while we're in here, doing our wor—"

"'Doing our work?' Or were you about to say 'doing our *worst*'?" The stranger smiled affably, his light tone and friendly features at odds with what would otherwise be fighting words.

A woman hurried in behind him, eager to catch up and looking frustrated that she had to. She was as tall as he was, creamy-skinned, green-eyed, red-haired. She wore a brand-new, price-tag-still-on-it Oonthrax Stables T-shirt, but looked somehow *less* like a tourist than her companion.

If the man noticed her hurried arrival, it didn't interrupt him from finishing his appraisal of the situation. "Because buddy, if you *haven't* been doing your worst yet, we'd all just really hate to see it."

"What did you just sa—"

"I mean, especially Poulsen, here—you *are* Poulsen, aren't you? Can I call you Astrid? Heard a lot about you, great stuff!—and all the rest of your team. They're the ones who have to keep fixing your mistakes after all, right? So if there's somehow *even worse* to come, Danny boy, nobody here wants to see it."

Adeoye was simply gobsmacked. The burly MechWarrior wasn't used to anyone talking back to him much at all, but especially not... Who would dare to... How could someone...?

He stormed over to get all up in the newcomer's face. "Who the hell do you think you're talki—"

"I think—" The stranger slid sideways, slipping past Danny's bluster to lower himself into a break room chair as though he were part of the regular dinner crew of techs, his tone mild, faintly amused, not at all threatened. "—I'm talking to Do-Hyung 'Danny' Adeoye, MechWarrior, who's now riding a five-bout losing streak, the most recent two in an exotic 'Mech that's never been seen before in the Solaris Games, but that he's managed to botch anyway."

"My name's not just 'Danny.'" Adeoye stood over the smaller newcomer, bristling. "And if you don't watch your tone and get the hell out of this restricted area and back where you tourists belong, I'll remind you why they call me 'Dangerous.'"

"Well, golly." The newcomer looked up at him with a guileless face, eyes just a little wide but showing no fear. "I bet it's not because you're the eighteenth-best MechWarrior in a stable of eighteen MechWarriors, huh?"

Adeoye blinked slowly, as if he'd been slapped in the face. "What—what did you say to me?"

"You're the runt of the litter," the man said, somehow without malice; an observation, not quite an insult. "Your career is hanging by a thread, and frankly, if I were you, my 'Mech techs would be the *last* people I'd be talking to that way. I mean, your techs and food service workers, they've got a *lot* of ways to kill somebody, am I right?" The stranger glanced over at the dinner plate of the astech next to him, reached a hand toward a golden roll, and lifted his eyebrows questioningly, hopefully. "Well, *almost* the last," he amended, an afterthought.

"Who the hell do you think you are?!" Danny near-screamed, disbelieving what he was hearing.

The stranger held up one finger to Danny while looking pointedly at the astech next to him, down to the roll, and back to the astech, waiting. The stunned astech nodded, and the stranger reached out and plucked the yeasty roll from her plate. He began to pick it apart.

"I think *I'm* the last," he said, tossing a pinch of bread into his mouth.

"You... What?"

"I think I'm the *last* person you should be talking to like that." He chewed and swallowed. "I think I'm a graf of the Lyran Commonwealth. I think I'm the consort to the Duchess of Vendrell. I think I'm the president and CEO of Mountain Wolf BattleMechs. I think I'm here—*here* here, talking to you right now—on the personal invitation of Oonthrax Stables' owner, Baron Irvxx Oonthrax. He should be on the list, too."

Another pinch, another nibble of bread.

"That list I mentioned. Of people. Not to talk to that way."

He decided to treat himself after that little speech *and* give them all a moment to gather themselves, and tore off about half of the roll to stuff into his mouth.

Adeoye leaned against the table like his legs might go out from under him. The redhead who'd shown up with the stranger leaned against the doorframe, violently casual, arms crossed. Poulsen swallowed nervously. The astech seated next to the noble newcomer scooted her plate his way in case he wanted more than a buttery roll. It was his plate now if he wanted it, just as much as the cafeteria was now *his* room.

"Mmnf, fenk uu." Cheeks bulging, the noble gave her an appreciative nod. "Ish rlly gud breb."

"What are...what are you...sir, I mean..." Adeoye stood at the end of the table, hands on it, holding himself up. "What are you doing here?"

Brandon O'Leary wasn't much worried about table manners. Even stuffing his mouth with buttered rolls, even talking with that mouth stuffed, he knew he had everyone in the cafeteria outranked, outclassed, and outmaneuvered enough it wouldn't ever matter. It wasn't just the suit. It wasn't just the wealth. It was the...everything else.

Brandon had grown into his business. He had grown into his responsibility. He had grown into his confidence, his nobility, his station. Brandon had grown. MechWarrior Adeoye had a lot of growing to do, but he had potential.

The graf finished chewing and swallowing with one upheld finger to Danny's question. He gave the generous astech a friendly smile of thanks, grabbed her other roll to keep his hands busy, and turned his attention back to MechWarrior Adeoye.

"Right, sorry. I get distracted sometimes. It *is* good bread though, right? But, *ahem*, yes, back on track. The short answer? Winning. What I'm *supposed* to be doing here...is winning. Which is what I thought we were *all* here for. It's what Baron Oonthrax *told me* we were here for, which is what I thought my *Merlin* was here for, but we're not doing that. Why?"

We, he'd said. Brandon was already wedging himself into the group, taking part of the responsibility.

"Because your 'Mech is...is..." Adeoye started strong, blustering, with all the confidence of a man accustomed to bullying and complaining. Then he *visibly* remembered who he was talking to and trailed off.

Bran took the conversation by the reins again. "Before you continue that thought, please, a moment. I've been rude. I told you all who I 'thought' I was, but I didn't actually introduce myself, or my companion." He gallantly stood and sketched a little bow. "I am Brandon O'Leary. Mountain Wolf BattleMechs is mine. The *Merlin*—not just literally the *Merlin* you've wrecked twice, no; I mean even in the abstract, the idea of the *Merlin*, of every *Merlin*, not just this one—is mine. It is currently the sole BattleMech my company produces. It is an unassailable hit in the Periphery, but I'd like to interest good Lyrans like a good Lyran noble. Solaris is where I wanted to show off. *You* were how I wanted to show off."

He paused long enough to remind them all how the conversation had started.

"Before we all go around the circle and share our thoughts on the *Merlin* and why it has faltered here on the Game World, though, allow me to introduce my traveling companion."

He nodded at the redheaded woman, who stood up straighter at the gesture. It showcased her height and build, and she stood nearly at attention; this was someone accustomed to standing at attention, and she carried herself with a MechWarrior's grace.

"MechWarrior Adeoye, Technician Poulsen, assorted assistants, meet Cassandra Fox."

"'Captain' will do," she corrected, or perhaps insisted. "My friends call me Scarlet."

"Captain Fox was once Leutnant Fox in the Third Lyran Regulars, wherein she grew both comfortable and capable in the cockpit of heavy BattleMechs. She is now the most comfortable and capable person in the cockpit of a *Merlin*. Anywhere." Brandon stated this with the same certainty he had used to state his own name. "She helped design the *Merlin*. She refined the design of the *Merlin*. She test-piloted the *Merlin*. She currently pilots a *Merlin* as head of Mountain Wolf BattleMechs' security. She has seen combat in that *Merlin*, and to the best of my very literally expert knowledge, she has spent more time in a *Merlin* than anyone else alive."

Brandon took another sizeable bite of warm, soft roll to let Cassandra's combined qualifications sink in. Danny Adeoye didn't look any closer to *not* falling over.

"So."

Brandon let the word ring in the air.

"When I say the two of us know a thing or two about a thing or two, and when I say we're here to help, believe me." He clapped his hands together, making the whole cafeteria jump. "I'll ask again. Why aren't we winning?"

"Because the *Merlin* is…" Adeoye started, winding himself back up.

Brandon simply raised a curious eyebrow, all innocence and eagerness to see where the sentence was headed, and it entirely deflated the MechWarrior.

"Because the weapons configuration on the *Merlin* isn't…to my liking," Adeoye got out between gritted teeth.

"I see. That's too bad!" Brandon leaned forward, held eye contact, steepled his fingers and listened intently, eager to help. "And why is that?"

He gave no sign of having watched the fight footage, no sign of anger or impatience. His features, his body language, his tone, everything about him simply sounded sincerely interested.

Danny Adeoye *knew* he was walking into a trap, but couldn't see a way out.

"It's not…it's not good at…" he stumbled, out of steam when he was out of bravado. He couldn't yell at, talk over, condescend to, or threaten these two, so it took him time to gather his thoughts and present them a different way.

"The *Merlin* doesn't appeal to MechWarrior Adeoye's preference for overwhelming an enemy via specialization," Astrid Poulsen cut in to save him. "The stock *Merlin*, that is. So we, er, we customized them. Specialized them."

"Mm-hmm. He wanted specialization, right, yes, of course, I see," Brandon nodded along. "And remind me, how'd that go?"

Adeoye fell right into the trap, moving forward with volume alone.

"I mean, we had all these machine guns you sent, the Sperry Browning samples? And have you seen what a buzzsaw 'Mech can do? I figured I'd penetrate with the PPC, use the stadium walls for some cover, then get in close and chew 'em up!"

"Right. And how'd that go?" Brandon asked, all guileless repetition.

"If that damned *Archer* hadn't gotten lucky and blown my PPC so early, or I mean, if it had been something a little less tough than an *Archer*, like a, a *Rifleman* or a *JagerMech* or something, I would've…I mean, I could've…"

"Uh-huh. But listen, please. How'd that *go*?" Brandon's curiosity never wavered; he never raised his voice, just repeated himself.

Adeoye didn't respond. Anger flashed in his eyes, then helplessness. He looked from O'Leary to Poulsen—either to blame her or to plaintively beg her to take the blame—and then back, but never answered. Instead, his shoulders slumped.

"Right." Brandon nodded, holding Adeoye's gaze. "So, let's say that 'buzzsaw' build was the problem, or the luck of the Steiner Stadium walls. Sure. What if you'd used your next build? Hmm? Three Holly launchers, instead of all those Sperry Brownings? Designed for range?"

Adeoye started to nod along, back in it. "Right? Lean the *Merlin* into using range, y'know, and I could've—"

"You could have beaten, say, the *Archer*? At range? The *Archer*?" Brandon cut him off, but his tone still conveyed neither cruelty nor overt skepticism, just curiosity. He already knew the answer. Everyone in the room did except Danny. "Used the punch of the PPC to make up for the pair of Doombud twenty-tubers and the MechWarrior expert in using 'em, right? For sure, or maybe?"

"Mm—maybe." Adeoye nodded.

"Let's say that's *not* a coin flip, then. Let's say you're a better shot with LRMs than someone who's chosen to pilot a stock *Archer* on Solaris. Let's say the penetration of the PPC makes up for the fact they're chucking three times the missiles you are, or maybe they're just worried about heat enough to not shoot both launchers at once. Let's say they don't just ride it out and *stay* at range, because they forget they've got four times the ammo you do, since you had Poulsen just slap as many launchers on as possible, but no extra magazines. Let's say all that."

Brandon O'Leary spread his hands innocently and gave a little shrug.

"What if they remember they've got an engine, Dangerous? What if they just...walk forward, get in chose, and use those lasers?" *And their armor*, he didn't say. *And their raw tonnage. And their combat-designed battlefists. What if they do what that* Crusader *did?*

Danny withered again instead of responding. None of the techs in the room would hold his gaze, or Brandon's.

"Overspecialization is for bugs," Brandon said simply. "I know this is Solaris. I get it. I know the people want a show. I know every contender needs a hook, every pilot wants to be a champion, every crowd wants to be razzled and/or dazzled with something new every goddamned fight."

He sounded tired, not angry, despite the mild exclamation.

"But that's not what *Merlin*s do. That's not what *Merlin*s are for. That's not what Mountain Wolf is trying to sell."

Right now, at least, he thought, remembering his father's romanticization of the ancient, hyperspecialized *Sling* design, remembering his own hunger to bring back the all-energy-weapons *Night Hawk* as soon as he could.

One 'Mech at a time. We have Merlin*s right now. We sell* Merlin*s right now. Focus, Bran.*

"So, the bad news is, we've tried to make the *Merlin* something it isn't, twice, and it's crashed and burned, twice. So, let's stop trying that."

We, Brandon was kind enough to say again. Not *you*.

"The good news is, neither of those were formally ranked fights, nor title card affairs, nor particularly highly rated with viewers." It wasn't often a BattleMech manufacturer would be *glad* no one had watched their 'Mech showing off in a Solaris arena. "So, we're going to bounce back from that. We're going to erase our losses the only way anyone in history ever has: with a win."

Brandon nodded matter-of-factly, as though it were already decided and therefore accomplished.

"And we're going to do it at the Wreckoning."

The astech seated next to him choked on her food in surprise.

STEINER STADIUM
SOLARIS CITY
SOLARIS VII
LYRAN COMMONWEALTH
21 SEPTEMBER 3021

Cassandra Fox, grim faced and dour, jerked hard on the harness strapping her into her *Merlin*'s cockpit.

She wanted out; not of her cockpit, but of the situation. She wanted away. She wanted to be done. Cassandra Fox had wanted nothing in recent memory quite so badly as she wanted off Solaris VII.

Unlike her friend and employer, she didn't have extra nerves from being close to Marik space; Bran lied about it, maybe even to himself, but Cassandra had known him and the O'Leary family history long enough to understand that proximity to the Free Worlds League made him anxious. After he'd grown up on bogeyman stories about the Marik military razing the last Mountain Wolf BattleMechs facility to the ground almost a century ago, Bran had been more comfortable and at home in the wild Periphery than he was in "civilized" Lyran space (especially when that Lyran space was *this* close to the Free Worlds League). She'd seen it every time business had carried them to Hesperus II, and the Solaris system was even *closer* to Marik space. She understood his anxiety. She understood how badly he wanted this win, then to put the Game World in the *Ceridwen*'s metaphorical rearview mirror.

But no, interstellar geography wasn't why Fox wanted off this rock. She just hated *Solaris itself*. She hated what it did, what it meant.

War shouldn't be fun. 'Mechs shouldn't be treated like toys, fights like games, bloodshed like entertainment. BattleMechs were weapons, designed for killing and stopping others from being killed, not for sport. They were meant for battlefields, not arenas. Children should grow up aspiring to be MechWarriors because they want to protect and defend people, not because they want to be rich and famous. Families should grieve pilots blasted from their cockpits because those soldiers died fighting for something pure, not just piles of C-bills and flashes of media attention.

Corporate security wasn't the Sphere's most noble calling, but Cassandra still stood for something, every bit as much as when she'd been in the Lyran Regulars. Something more than glory. She protected people. She stood a post and kept another 'Mech factory from being turned to rubble. She did a job and held a line.

Damn it, Bran. Solaris was the last place she wanted to be, doing the last thing she wanted to be doing. She sighed. *I don't like your game here. And these stakes are too damned high.*

But the only way out is through, she told herself as she stalked her *Merlin* forward into the Steiner Stadium. *The only way to finish is to do the job.*

There was a cool blue icon on her radar, behind her and to her left: Adeoye's *Merlin*, pinging friendly after weeks of practice together. He was growing on her. A little.

Then the red blips began to appear, on the far end of the arena. A pair. Two more. Six. No, eight. Another sensor blink, a final tally: ten. She'd known to expect it, but still. Ten felt like a lot.

The headcount of enemies wasn't a surprise. But she knew the Wreckoning still had *some* monkey wrench to throw their way before the match would start.

"The Wreckoning," O'Leary had said weeks earlier, "is going to make everyone forget these losses. They're just warm-ups. It's the biggest unranked match on Solaris, with the biggest wagers, the highest ratings, and the hottest expectations. And we're going to nail it."

"I've reached out to the Green Griffins, a cooperative. They're hanging on by the skin of their teeth, barely making ends meet, and after a run of bad matchups, all they've got left are some of the lightest 'Mechs in town, but plenty of 'em. So, I challenged them. All of them, I mean. You two are taking on the whole co-op. Are you excited? 'Cause I'm excited!"

Fox shot a glance to an anomaly from her usual head-up display. She knew every centimeter of a *Merlin*'s cockpit, knew every light, every sensor, every reading, every nook and cranny inside and out. The oddball stood out. It was a temporary affair, an alert rigged just for this match, a Steiner Stadium text add-on that gave a live update about when the match started.

Ten.
Nine.
Eight.
Seven.
"Adeoye. Ready?"
"Roger that." He paused only slightly, the last few weeks having earned her, apparently, his grudging respect. "Captain."
Three.
Two.
One...
"So! Our two versus their ten. They'll have a few tons on us, but that's just going to get us better odds with the bookmakers! The real hard part's coming up, though." Brandon waved aside a total mass difference of eighty tons; the gap between the teams was more than the weight of a whole nother *Merlin*, and he called it "a few tons"!

"The Wreckoning, as some of you know, is a big hit because it always has a twist. An unknown handicap, levied against both teams, voted on real-time by fans. Whoo, that audience participation, huh? These Solaris citizens are ga-ga for it!"

And there it was: DUMP AMMUNITION appeared in flashing, unnecessarily red text on Fox's HUD. Obnoxiously. Demandingly. Incessantly. Cassandra knew she had five seconds to respond or be disqualified.

She didn't hesitate—it was about four and a half seconds more than she needed—and just responded with the smooth efficiency of a master MechWarrior and ejected all of her ammunition. Panels blew off the back of her *Merlin* after an "Are you really sure?" emergency-ejection confirmation command was given, and soon her long-range missiles and machine gun ammo cascaded out the rear of her 'Mech.

Cassandra was fine with it. Bran had warned this was one of the potential options, one of the curses the bloodthirsty crowd and the money-hungry arena master could levy on the combatants.

The Wreckoning was madness; Solaris at its dangerous worst. Every 'Mech on the field could lose the use of an arm or a leg; whole categories of weapons could be made illicit for a match; *all* ranged weapons could be branded off-limits; and so forth. In footage from last years' Wreckoning, which O'Leary had insisted Fox, Adeoye, Poulsen, and the whole team watch, jump jets had been mandatory for the duration of a bout, forcing both sides to leap around awkwardly, constantly, engines redlining and feet barely touching the ground, firing jets of superheated plasma as quickly as their cycling controls could manage. In another match, engines had to remain at full throttle for the entire duration of the event, 'Mechs careening at their fastest running speed the whole time, all while the Steiner Stadium walls still raised and lowered on a whim. Another Wreckoning's twist had required all combatants to only use reverse throttle, each 'Mech walking backward toward their opponents, then spinning, sidestepping, and shuffling awkwardly through a lunatic fight.

Compared to that nonsense, just losing the bulk of her ammunition, for just *those* two weapons? Fox could live with that. It just felt like a logistics malf-up, and every soldier had to deal with that from time to time.

Besides, Fox knew it wasn't the Holly five-tube or the machine gun that made her *Merlin* a danger. It was *her*.

Adeoye took longer to eject his ammo, but he did it. There was barely a split second left in their five-second window before his ammo waterfalled from the back of his 'Mech. She knew he didn't want to give up any firepower, lose any advantage. He'd spent the last few weeks drilling in a *Merlin* by the most-qualified person to drill someone in a *Merlin*—her—and the thought of losing any of his weapons had given "Dangerous" pause.

But he did it. Disqualification was on the line, and the MechWarrior did what he had to do.

Fox took that as a good sign.

"So, these Green Griffins, right? *They're a small outfit, recently made smaller by a few brutal matches. Former mercs, never really at home here, and Solaris has made that abundantly clear to them by leaving their commanding officer herself Dispossessed, her family's namesake* Griffin *down the tubes. She's hungry. They're all hungry. They're down to bug 'Mechs and anger, nothing left to their name but their skirmishers and recon machines.* Wasps, Stingers, Locusts, *and desperation. That's what they've got. That's who they are.*" Brandon's eyes had slid from technician to technician, then MechWarrior to MechWarrior, finally giving Fox a confident nod. "Sound like anyone you've fought before?"

Captain Fox's hands slid across her controls, and she designated incoming red blips by order of importance. Alpha through Juliet—she prioritized each one of them on the fly. She hadn't wanted to make the call until the Wreckoning had taken its pound of flesh; if every small or medium laser on the field had to be powered down, she would've ranked threats differently than if, say, every speedy little 'Mech was forced to run full throttle. The Wreckoning *could* have been crazier, she had to admit.

As it was, the oncoming horde—and ten sure felt like a horde—of enemy 'Mechs wasn't *too* terribly shaken up. They'd gotten off easy, just like the Mountain Wolf 'Mechs had. The ammo dump didn't reprioritize much from her initial gut check. She tagged them, updating her own readings and Danny's display screen, then got to work.

Wait. Fox scowled inside her neurohelmet and mentally corrected herself.

Opposing 'Mechs. Not enemy.

There was a difference, and a big one. She had to keep her head on straight, had to think about it the right way. She was here to do damage, not hurt anybody.

"The reason our *Merlins* haven't been winning is we haven't been treating them like *Merlins*. The reason our *Merlins* won't win here on Solaris is Solaris won't let them. *Merlins* aren't built for this. I should have realized it sooner, and that's on me. We set you up to fail, and I apologize." Brandon's gaze was mostly on Danny Adeoye for that part of his speech. Lots of nobles and CEOs didn't have it in them to apologize at all, especially to a "lesser," and most who did surely wouldn't look you in the eye while they tried it. But Fox followed Brandon for more reasons than just friendship. "We're done trying to slam a square peg into a round hole. We're going to use the Wreckoning and the Green Griffins to let our *Merlins* stretch their legs and do what they do. They're not duelists. They're not solo hotdog show-off machines. We designed the *Merlin* to be a workhorse, not a glory hound. They stand in militia units, they protect each other, and they stave off lean, hungry, desperate 'Mechs being run by lean, hungry, desperate MechWarriors. *Merlins* fight pirates. Let's show them that."

Target Designate Alpha, a *Locust* LCT-1E, was the first up, and first down. The Capellan Confederation's favorite *Locust* was—in this moment, in this match—the single most dangerous opposing 'Mech on the field. If she stopped to really think about that, Fox might have snorted, shook her head, or even smiled at the absurdity of that notion. As it was, she'd just calculated the firepower on the remaining opponents, automatically tagged them, and started leveling her long-range weapons.

Alpha started the fight with a quartet of lasers—a pair of mediums and a pair of smalls—carried by an LTV 160 engine that would launch those knife fighters' tools at Fox and Adeoye at nearly 130 kilometers an hour. But Adeoye's eye-searing PPC blast caught the *Locust* high and off-center in its sleek torso, blasting away the thin layer of armor over its chest and right hip and clawing away at internal components. His flight of LRMs—his *only* flight, the five missiles still loaded in the tubes when he'd dumped his ammo—scattered a handful of craters across the *Locust*, sending yet more armor flying.

Fox's own PPC shot, fired more methodically and purposefully, hit almost a full second later; low and mean, a manmade lightning bolt that savaged the light 'Mech's right leg and fused its knee and hip. Alpha fell, kicking, and skidded to a stop too far from the pair of *Merlins* to pose a threat any time soon.

Bravo was up next. A *Stinger*-3G, the heaviest hitter. Two medium lasers. The oncoming swarm of Green Griffins was just at the outside of their top range when that very *Stinger*, too, faced the focused fire of a pair of *Merlins*. Adeoye's PPC missed high, but Fox's burrowed into the humanoid 'Mech's stomach, a gut punch that blasted away armor and exposed oh-so-fragile internals. One of Cassandra's own red-white laser beams followed up, slicing away at the armor near the oncoming machine's left hip, but Adeoye scored hits with both of his arm-mounted weapons. One laser sliced a horizontal line high across the *Stinger*'s chest, but the other bored into the Green Griffin's naked belly and did terrible damage. The *Stinger* crumpled forward and shuddered on the turf of Steiner Stadium like a convulsing human before lying still.

Fox figured it was a gyro hit as she watched the light 'Mech awkwardly try to stand, then fall again. She tagged Bravo as down and shifted her attention to Charlie.

"Now, don't get me wrong, I'm not saying the Green Griffins are actual pirates!" O'Leary had said. "I mean they're a few bad days away from making the decisions mercs gotta make to not become *pirates*. Everyone knows the joke about the down-on-their-luck MechWarrior, right? That's them. These guys are an outfit called the Green Griffins without any damned Griffins left, or anything else that doesn't make a Valkyrie *look like an* Atlas. They're down to their dregs. They want this fight real bad. They want a change real bad. They're coming for your Merlins, and I mean literally. I bet them they couldn't take you. Those Merlins, their repair costs, and a cool million C-bills, that's what's on the table for them. They're licking their chops, boys, girls, and gentlethems. They're licking their chops and sharpening their knives."

The return flurry of attacks was just about the worst they could face. Over a half-dozen crimson beams reached out, clawing at the pair of *Merlins*. More hit than missed; this crew was running all-out, but knew how to handle their machines. Fox saw her cockpit wireframe light up with a damage update, and Adeoye's—since she was tagged internally as their lance commander—did the same in real time. Nothing critical though: their armor was doing its job. Their *Merlins* were acting their weight class. The swarm of *Locusts*, *Wasps*, and *Stingers* would have to try harder.

And try harder, they did.

There was barely time for their weapons to cycle again—Adeoye sent a hasty PPC shot into the dirt, but Cassandra didn't bother, saving her heat sinks—before the rush was on them. The Steiner Stadium walls wouldn't be deciding this match, not at the ranges the rest of it would be fought at. The lighter 'Mechs knew they'd have to get in close to overwhelm the *Merlins* and fight safely inside the comfortable range of their devastating PPCs.

The Green Griffins might be down a *Stinger* and half a *Locust*, but the clash was still 160 tons of 'Mech crashing into 120 tons. One of

them, an enterprising *Stinger* jockey, roared at Fox on pillars of flame, trying to drop-kick her clean out of her 'Mech.

Four per target, a full lance on each of them, they smashed the *Merlin*s, firing as they came. The smaller 'Mechs struck then rushed past, punching and kicking as they went, fishhook-turning to get behind their foes, swarming.

They wanted to make it a brawl, a bar fight. They wanted a back-alley mugging, eight on two, all chaos, fear, and threats from every direction. They wanted it to deteriorate so their numbers could carry them.

Hell with that.

Fox and Adeoye, together, right on cue, blasted their jump jets and leaped away. They rose side by side, arced gracefully, and landed together.

"I don't want to lose that bet," O'Leary had said. "I don't want to lose any of the bets I'm making here on Solaris. I don't want to lose this match." Fox wasn't sure if he could afford to. The way he said 'bets' sure made it sound like he was making a lot of them. Cassandra knew more than most people about the financials of Mountain Wolf BattleMechs, the O'Leary family, and Bran's wife, the Duchess of Vendrell. Cassandra worried. "But it's the bet I had to offer to make this match happen, the gauntlet I had to throw. All it means is we've got to do what we came here to do. Win. And to do that, we're going to fight together, like *Merlin*s are meant to. A team against a horde. Militia against pirates. Stock *Merlin*s. Stock enemies. We win this here, just like we win this on any planet that's bought *Merlin*s to defend it."

"Good!" Fox offered Adeoye her first word in the arena, and it was one of encouragement. She'd been worried the Solaris jock wouldn't stick with the plan and move with her. "We've got this! Remember, kicks of opportunity onl—"

"Firing on Charlie," Danny Adeoye said back, clipped, curt. Professional. Focused. He was all business, no bravado. It was nice.

Neither *Merlin* tried to brawl, to give the Green Griffins what they wanted. Every punch Adeoye or Fox threw meant one less medium laser firing, and they both wanted to fire those lasers. Their only capitulation to the fight's dogbite-close range was to occasionally send one blocky *Merlin* leg arcing out to slam into and trip a too-close opponent. Other than that, they kept cool heads and clear eyes; they focused their attention and focused their fire.

Adeoye didn't panic and try desperately to defend himself. He kept his cool and fired on the target tagged as Charlie, which was punching at Fox's cockpit as it ran past, lasers flashing—and the pair of them took it down. The *Wasp* -1A spat its anemic pair of short-range missiles at Fox before it fell, but it did fall. Riddled by a quartet of laser blasts and wrapped in the fire of two roaring Zippo flamers, it tumbled down, green paint charred and blackened where it hadn't been entirely blasted away.

"Roger," Fox said, fighting a satisfied smile at Adeoye's teamwork and the devastating results. "Delta's up."

"I believe in the Merlin*. I believe in our design, in what it can do, in what it's* doing*, what it's done for years for our clients. I believe in the MechWarriors who pilot them and in the job they do. I believe we can do that job here, in a few weeks, at the Wreckoning. Whatever the Stadium throws at us, whatever the Green Griffins try, I believe in our 'Mech and our MechWarriors and technicians. We're going to win this. If we do this right, if we trust each other, we're going to win this. Big."*

Delta was another *Wasp*, this one a -1L bristling with a single four-rack SRM launcher. Even with just those four loaded missiles left, it could pack a real punch, so better to take it down before it even had the chance to fire.

Plus, it was wailing away on Adeoye's *Merlin*, punching and kicking and tearing sheets of armor away, and Fox wanted to return the favor.

Lasers converged. Flamers roared. In the end, a kick from Adeoye sent the *Wasp*'s lower leg sailing one way and the rest of it sailing the other, and the SRM never did get a chance to fire. The 'Mech fell hard, twisting as it went, sliced open by crimson beams, spiraling into the dirt with its MechWarrior ejecting as it tumbled down.

"Echo, Echo, Echo," Fox called next, swinging her weapons to their new target quickly but not smoothly. Quickly, because she knew what she was doing, and the *Merlin* veritably danced under her commands. Not smoothly, though, because the Green Griffins' nagging, gnawing lasers had sliced into one hip, and her torso twist was a jagged, stuttering affair.

Their *Merlin*s' armor wireframes were more yellow and red than they were green now. Smaller and weaker or not, the Griffins knew their business. They were nasty. They were good. They were dangerous. Neither Oonthrax Stables 'Mech was entirely whole now.

A golden-white flash of light clawed across Fox's cockpit, a ragged swipe of Alpha's small lasers—limping Alpha, balancing precariously Alpha, stubborn, stupid Alpha—raking at her inside her *Merlin*.

Neither MechWarrior was entirely safe.

"I talked a lot about what we can lose, and why we've already lost the bouts we did. I talked about why I think we're going to win this one. I want to tell you what *we're going to win, when that happens."* O'Leary was good. He used "we" a lot. He included whomever he talked to, whenever he talked to them. Rival CEO, business partner, sneering nobleman, apprentice assistant technician, janitor. Everybody. Even the obnoxious Danny Adeoye, Bran had only excluded and browbeat long enough to jerk the leash and establish the situation. Now it was all us,

all we, all team. All family. "On top of some money from the bookies, if we win, Mountain Wolf is bringing on the Green Griffins, whatever you two leave of them. Whole cloth. We're absorbing their co-op. Win or lose, the GGs are changing their fortunes with this match, just like we are. Captain Fox will have a few more lances of security MechWarriors to boss around. Oonthrax Stables, as per my prior arrangement with Baron Irvxx, will have a steady supply of at-cost material from our facility. I'll win, the baron will win, even the Griffins will win, in the long run. But I haven't mentioned the rest of you yet. That doesn't seem fair."

Adeoye lost his left-arm laser to a twin burst of machine guns emptying into his *Merlin*'s shoulder. They took down Echo, but not in time; the LCT-1V gnawed away at him when it finally found the good angle it wanted, and the pair of *Merlin*s lost a goodly chunk of their close-in firepower.

"Alpha. Give 'em the business," Fox said.

Right on cue, the pair of them turned their ire on the limping, stubborn *Locust* that hadn't learned its earlier lesson. Both *Merlin*s loosed their machine-gun ammo at long last, coupled with their blasting flamers and pinpoint-accurate medium lasers. The put-upon *Locust* fell to pieces of rent metal and shattered skeleton.

Something exploded beneath Fox, and her cockpit filled with red lights just as a wave of heat took her breath away. Her rear armor had been breached, torn off across the board, and her engine shielding had just taken damage. Golf and Hotel, the remaining hostile *Stinger*s, had decided to empty their machine guns as well.

There was blood in the water, and the sharks were closing. Everyone could see how damaged the heavier 'Mechs were, how ragged their armor was, how close they were to failures across the board.

Every hit the *Merlin*s took dragged them closer and closer to a combat-loss grouping.

"On the table? I'd like to offer each of you a percentage. You've put in a lot of work on MechWarrior Adeoye's Merlin already, and you're going to put in even more. We'll need to restore it to a stock configuration, but then I want Captain Fox to oversee a top-to-bottom quality sweep with you, and I know that'll keep you all busy. You're in on that, Adeoye. You're going to see how it all goes together, from the inside out." O'Leary spoke with the confidence and certainty that came from being absolutely in charge. "In exchange for all that hard work, though, a bonus seems only fair. One percent of my winnings will go to MechWarrior Adeoye. Two percent of my winnings will be split between the rest of you. It doesn't sound like much, but I assure you, my wagers will be confident and bold, my winnings quite substantial. And under the table? Well, if any of you are tired of Solaris, the Mountain Wolf pack wouldn't mind getting a little larger. We're always looking for techs we can trust."

"Break, break, break!" Fox barked into her radio. It was time.

Adeoye's Pitban LFT-50 jump jets flared and howled, and Cassandra's did the same. He leaped away to their right, she bounded to their left. Reaching lasers converged on Adeoye's leg as he flew, and there was a flash of flame and shrapnel as he landed. Something in his leg buckled and gave way. His *Merlin* crashed to the stadium floor even as their remaining opponents—focusing their fire now, thinking they had their opening—swarmed away from Fox and toward him.

"I'm down." Adeoye's voice almost cracked as he reported in. He sounded pissed, and scared. He seemed under control, though.

Fox saw his damage updates. The fall had knocked his other arm laser offline.

"Stay low, MechWarrior," she replied calmly.

Fox planted her *Merlin*'s feet like the 'Mech was a gunslinger in a movie.

Their leaps in opposite directions had cleared the safe minimum ranges built into her biggest gun. Their jumps had put them at near-ideal ranges for everything a *Merlin* carried. Fox's PPC charged, fired, and began to recycle. Her sole volley of LRMs flew. Her lasers flashed and screamed, time and again. She didn't call out her targets or update their shared targeting protocols, didn't move a step, didn't twist or kick, didn't think, didn't pay any mind to her heat warnings.

She just aimed and fired, as quickly as her 'Mech could handle.

Fox knew her future, and the future of her company, depended on her now as much as they *ever* had while she'd faced off against actual pirates. Livelihoods and lives alike were hinging on her.

She fired, and bathed in the spiking heat of her screaming fusion engine.

Hotel went down, weakened armor speared through by her particle projection cannon. Foxtrot lost an arm, the limb spinning away from the shoulder after a secondary explosion, then had both legs cut from under it. Golf took a cockpit hit from one of Cassandra's lasers, then the MechWarrior ejected before a scattering of missile hits and her final PPC blast tore into the 'Mech's head. India took a PPC shot to its paper-thin rear armor. Juliet, its sensors finally picking up the wholesale carnage, stopped its bent-over slicing at Adeoye's armor and turned to fire a single crimson beam at Fox that she answered with an alpha strike that dropped it like a discarded toy.

"If—or should I say *when*—things go according to plan, this should mean six-figure bonuses for everyone in this room, whether you decide to leave with us or stay. Six figures for you, substantially more than that for Mountain Wolf BattleMechs." Brandon had a hint of a smile on his face.

Cassandra squinted suspiciously. If a single percentage point, split multiple ways, was going to result in...oh, damn it. He was betting a lot. *Too much.* It all fell into place. He wanted those damned JumpShips he'd been talking about, the pair Landgrave Wellby had for sale, and this must've been Bran's play to get them. Extra security MechWarriors, extra attention on the *Merlin*, extra eyes on the company—it was all excuse, all icing. That was his cake. This gamble was the future of the company against a pair of JumpShips TharHes Industries didn't want any more.

Everyone in the room gawked at how off-handedly O'Leary mentioned the potential bonus they'd all earn; most of them gaped at the prospect of such a sum, but Cassandra Fox glared at the enormous gamble her friend and employer was taking. What had he staked to wager so heavily?

"On your feet, Dangerous," Fox said, teeth gritted, slapping her overheat overrides one last time. It was the first time she'd acknowledged his Solaris nickname. It was also the first time she'd acknowledge that marketing and appearances mattered. "Stand up slow, and make it look good."

The heap moved. Its savaged torso rumbled. Splayed-out arms and legs shifted slightly. Smoking wreckage, twisted steel, glowing-hot stretches of armored plating and ravaged skeleton heaved.

Only one 'Mech arose from the junkyard-looking mountain of steel, the mass grave that had piled up around Adeoye. Only his. Only the *Merlin*.

You're welcome, Bran. Fox panted against the heat as she saw what would become the Wreckoning's money shot: a one-armed *Merlin*, battered, torn, and bloodied, standing defiantly from a pile of torn-apart enemies. Defiant. Victorious. Reliable. A survivor.

The camera drones swooped in low, and Fox's comms filled with the official announcements. She toggled her comm channel away from the Steiner Stadium arena master and channel-hopped from one frequency to another until she heard Green Griffins chatter.

"Everyone in one piece?" she cut in, with a tone that let her.

"Affirmative." The response was sullen, but came after only the barest of pauses.

"I'm glad to hear it," Fox said, and meant it. "Welcome to Mountain Wolf. We'll talk soon."

Then she toggled back to her shared comm channel with Adeoye, who was talking excitedly enough he hadn't noticed she'd left. He was a gladiator who'd never faced numerical odds like this. A duelist who'd never truly had anyone watch his back before. A peacock who managed to make his limping *Merlin* outright *strut* instead as the pair headed for the arena exit.

Cassandra let him talk.

"This was a longshot, Bran," she said off-comms to the dry, stale air of her cockpit.

But she smiled regardless. The future of Mountain Wolf BattleMechs, the future of the man and the company she'd hitched her wagon to, suddenly looked a whole lot brighter.

"So! Let's go out there and show Solaris what Mountain Wolf's all about, huh? I believe we can win this, and I think over the next few weeks you'll all come to believe that as well. We'll drill, we'll repair, we'll study, we'll prepare." O'Leary clapped his hands together with an air of enthused finality. Fox couldn't believe he was using his usual tone, making the wagers he must have been making. "But whatever happens at the Wreckoning, let's just, I dunno, have fun out there, huh? It's the Game World, so let's play the game!"

LEOPARD-CLASS DROPSHIP *CERIDWEN*
OUTBOUND
SOLARIS VII
LYRAN COMMONWEALTH
28 SEPTEMBER 3021

"'I'm not leaving Solaris until I'm a champion,'" Do-Hyun 'Dangerous Danny' Adeoye read aloud, looking down at his well-worn journal. He stood at a window and looked down at the orb of Solaris VII growing smaller in the distance. He'd only ever flown on one DropShip before this, the one that had taken him *to* the Game World.

Champion, he'd written in his journal the night before.

He shut the journal and tucked it into a leg-side pocket of his new coveralls—slate gray with orange flash, sporting the Mountain Wolf logo on a shoulder patch—then turned from the window to take in the bustling activity in the *Ceridwen*'s belly. Poulsen was there, talking to Captain Fox, astechs scurrying all around, making sure takeoff hadn't disturbed their 'Mechs too badly. Adeoye wasn't the only one in new coveralls.

A champion is someone who's surpassed all their rivals in a competition, who's defeated all their foes, who's left no question about their success. But there's another type of champion, too, he'd written, thoughtfully, pages and pages after his dramatic retelling of the Wreckoning.

A champion is someone who fights for a cause larger than themself.

Mountain Wolf BattleMechs was trying to do something, something *right*. Brandon O'Leary and Cassandra Fox had designed the *Merlin* to stand side by side with other *Merlin*s, to make a wall of armor that kept slavers, raiders, and pirates at bay. They'd made a 'Mech that put itself between danger and the Periphery planets that needed more help, more durable protectors, more than just *Wasp*s and *Stinger*s to keep them safe.

Danny had decided to join them. As part of Mountain Wolf Security, he'd man that post. He'd pilot a *Merlin*. He'd help protect the factory and the company that helped protect the Outworlds Alliance.

He'd be a champion.

SHRAPNEL

BATTLETECH ERAS

The *BattleTech* universe is a living, vibrant entity that grows each year as more sourcebooks and fiction are published. A dynamic universe, its setting and characters evolve over time within a highly detailed continuity framework, bringing everything to life in a way a static game universe cannot match.

To help quickly and easily convey the timeline of the universe—and to allow a player to easily "plug in" a given novel or sourcebook—we've divided *BattleTech* into eight major eras.

STAR LEAGUE
(Present–2780)

Ian Cameron, ruler of the Terran Hegemony, concludes decades of tireless effort with the creation of the Star League, a political and military alliance between all Great Houses and the Hegemony. Star League armed forces immediately launch the Reunification War, forcing the Periphery realms to join. For the next two centuries, humanity experiences a golden age across the thousand light-years of human-occupied space known as the Inner Sphere. It also sees the creation of the most powerful military in human history.

(This era also covers the centuries before the founding of the Star League in 2571, most notably the Age of War.)

SUCCESSION WARS
(2781–3049)

Every last member of First Lord Richard Cameron's family is killed during a coup launched by Stefan Amaris. Following the thirteen-year war to unseat him, the rulers of each of the five Great Houses disband the Star League. General Aleksandr Kerensky departs with eighty percent of the Star League Defense Force beyond known space and the Inner Sphere collapses into centuries of warfare known as the Succession Wars that will eventually result in a massive loss of technology across most worlds.

CLAN INVASION
(3050–3061)

A mysterious invading force strikes the coreward region of the Inner Sphere. The invaders, called the Clans, are descendants of Kerensky's SLDF troops, forged into a society dedicated to becoming the greatest fighting force in history. With vastly superior technology and warriors, the Clans conquer world after world. Eventually this outside threat will forge a new Star League, something hundreds of years of warfare failed to accomplish. In addition, the Clans will act as a catalyst for a technological renaissance.

CIVIL WAR
(3062–3067)

The Clan threat is eventually lessened with the complete destruction of a Clan. With that massive external threat apparently neutralized, internal conflicts explode around the Inner Sphere. House Liao conquers its former Commonality, the St. Ives Compact; a rebellion of military units belonging to House Kurita sparks a war with their powerful border enemy, Clan Ghost Bear; the fabulously powerful Federated Commonwealth of House Steiner and House Davion collapses into five long years of bitter civil war.

JIHAD
(3067–3080)

Following the Federated Commonwealth Civil War, the leaders of the Great Houses meet and disband the new Star League, declaring it a sham. The pseudo-religious Word of Blake—a splinter group of ComStar, the protectors and controllers of interstellar communication—launch the Jihad: an interstellar war that pits every faction against each other and even against themselves, as weapons of mass destruction are used for the first time in centuries while new and frightening technologies are also unleashed.

DARK AGE
(3081-3150)

Under the guidance of Devlin Stone, the Republic of the Sphere is born at the heart of the Inner Sphere following the Jihad. One of the more extensive periods of peace begins to break out as the 32nd century dawns. The factions, to one degree or another, embrace disarmament, and the massive armies of the Succession Wars begin to fade. However, in 3132 eighty percent of interstellar communications collapses, throwing the universe into chaos. Wars erupt almost immediately, and the factions begin rebuilding their armies.

ILCLAN
(3151-present)

The once-invulnerable Republic of the Sphere lies in ruins, torn apart by the Great Houses and the Clans as they wage war against each other on a scale not seen in nearly a century. Mercenaries flourish once more, selling their might to the highest bidder. As Fortress Republic collapses, the Clans race toward Terra to claim their long-denied birthright and create a supreme authority that will fulfill the dream of Aleksandr Kerensky and rule the Inner Sphere by any means necessary: The ilClan.

CLAN HOMEWORLDS
(2786-present)

In 2784, General Aleksandr Kerensky launched Operation Exodus, and led most of the Star League Defense Force out of the Inner Sphere in a search for a new world, far away from the strife of the Great Houses. After more than two years and thousands of light years, they arrived at the Pentagon Worlds. Over the next two-and-a-half centuries, internal dissent and civil war led to the creation of a brutal new society—the Clans. And in 3049, they returned to the Inner Sphere with one goal—the complete conquest of the Great Houses.

SUBMISSION GUIDELINES

Shrapnel is the market for official short fiction set in the *BattleTech* universe.

WHAT WE WANT

We are looking for stories of **3,000–5,000 words** that are character-oriented, meaning the characters, rather than the technology, provide the main focus of the action. Stories can be set in any established *BattleTech* era, and although we prefer stories where BattleMechs are featured, this is by no means a mandatory element.

WHAT WE DON'T WANT

The following items are generally grounds for immediate disqualification:

- Stories not set in the *BattleTech* universe. There are other markets for these stories.
- Stories centering solely on romance, supernatural, fantasy, or horror elements. If your story isn't primarily military sci-fi, then it's probably not for us.
- Stories containing gratuitous sex, gore, or profanity. Keep it PG-13, and you should be fine.
- Stories under 3,000 words or over 5,000 words. We don't publish flash fiction, and although we do publish works longer than 5,000 words, these are reserved for established *BattleTech* authors.
- Vanity stories, which include personal units, author-as-character inserts, or tabletop game sessions retold in narrative form.
- Publicly available *BattleTech* fan-fiction. If your story has been posted in a forum or other public venue, then we will not accept it.

MANUSCRIPT FORMAT

- .rtf, .doc, .docx formats ONLY
- 12-point Times New Roman, Cambria, or Palatino fonts ONLY
- 1" (2.54 cm) margins all around
- Double-spaced lines
- DO NOT put an extra space between each paragraph
- Filename: "Submission Title by Jane Q. Writer"

PAYMENT & RIGHTS

We pay $0.06 per word after publication. By submitting to *Shrapnel*, you acknowledge that your work is set in an owned universe and that you retain no rights to any of the characters, settings, or "ideas" detailed in your story. We purchase **all rights** to every published story; those rights are automatically transferred to The Topps Company, Inc.

SUBMISSIONS PORTAL

To send us a submission, visit our submissions portal here:
https://pulsepublishingsubmissions.moksha.io/publication/shrapnel-the-battletech-magazine-fiction

SHRAPNEL

DON'T LET YOUR MAGAZINE RUN DRY!
SUBSCRIBE TO *SHRAPNEL* TODAY!
store.catalystgamelabs.com/products/shrapnel-one-year-subscription

The march of technology across BattleTech's eras is relentless...

RECOGNITION GUIDE: ILCLAN VOL. 01

RECOGNITION GUIDE: ILCLAN VOL. 02

RECOGNITION GUIDE: ILCLAN VOL. 03

RECOGNITION GUIDE: ILCLAN VOL. 04

RECOGNITION GUIDE: ILCLAN VOL. 05

RECOGNITION GUIDE: ILCLAN VOL. 06

Some BattleMech designs never die. Each installment of *Recognition Guide: IlClan*, currently a PDF-only series, not only includes a brand new BattleMech or OmniMech, but also details Classic 'Mech designs from both the Inner Sphere and the Clans, now fully rebuilt with Dark Age technology (3085 and beyond).

©2020 The Topps Company, Inc. All Rights Reserved. Recognition Guide: IlClan, BattleTech, 'Mech, and BattleMech are registered trademarks and/or trademarks of The Topps Company, Inc. in the United States and/or other countries. Catalyst Game Labs and the Catalyst Game Labs logo are trademarks of InMediaRes Productions, LLC.

STORE.CATALYSTGAMELABS.COM

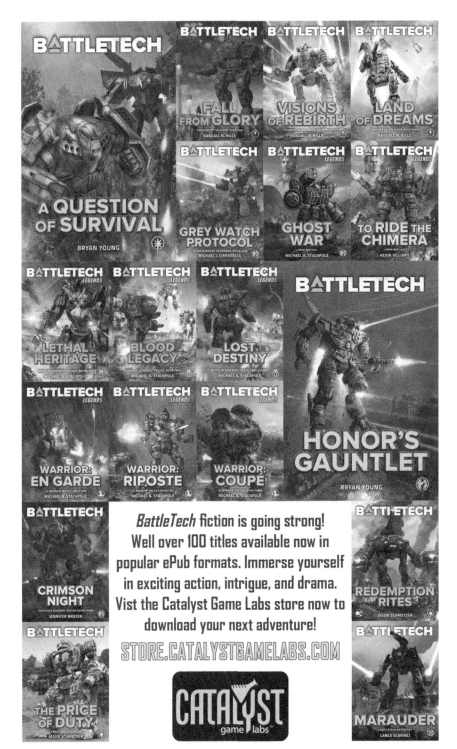

Made in the USA
Middletown, DE
30 June 2023